Long Sh

Whittington Edge

A Tale of Whittington Edge

by

Catherine Cliffe

COPYRIGHT

Long Shadows over Whittington Edge

purely coincidental. All of the incidents are pure invention.

For questions and comments about this book, please contact the author at Facebook – Catherine Cliffe loves cosy mysteries and strange happenings   Or   by   email catherinecliffe@yahoo.com

Published by Catherine Cliffe Publishing

LONG SHADOWS OVER WHITTINGTON EDGE

Welcome to Whittington Edge

Whittington Edge is a small town or a large village; no one is exactly sure which, in the Midlands. It enjoys a sense of being different, of having an atmosphere that draws in the right people; the people who will fit in.

I hope that you will enjoy this atmosphere and feel that you fit into Whittington Edge too.

Long Shadows over Whittington Edge is the first of a series of stories about this place and its unusual residents.

Catherine Cliffe

LONG SHADOWS OVER WHITTINGTON EDGE

DEDICATION

To D

With love

If you give me six lines written by the hand of the most honest of men, I will find something in them that will hang him.

Duc de Richelieu

1585-1642

French cardinal and statesman

Contents

Catherine Cliffe

Especially for you ©

CHAPTER ONE

Up until the moment that her rear offside wheel hit the pothole, talking on her mobile phone whilst driving was the only reason Lottie Colenso had to fear discovery.

She had left Jonas Milton laughing in the car park of the hotel where they had spent the weekend.

'You're never taking the hood off?'

'I am.' She had laughed too as he helped to peel back the canvas on her ancient sports car and stow it away.

'It's far too cold. You'll get a red nose.'

'Think yourself lucky you won't be there to see it.'

Her eyes smarted as she threw back her head and laughed a laugh that was caught on the wind and carried away to join the birdsong and the fluttering of leaves discarded by autumn trees.

She zipped away, waving to him as he shook his head and wiped his hands on his handkerchief. He was right; it was freezing, but, Jonas was laughing and that was all that mattered. She wanted Jonas Milton to think her wacky and fun to be with. She wanted to leave him with an indelible picture in his mind. And she didn't want that picture to be of a staid woman of a certain age.

Jonas was a professor – a sober enough career one might think – but he was surrounded all day with bright young things who could easily catch his eye and that would never do.

She could park further down the road and replace the hood.

This idea was attractive; the icy fingers of October explored her scalp with ferocious thoroughness. But Lottie was no quitter.

She was close to quitting half an hour later when the turn for Whittington Edge came up and her phone rang on the seat beside her. Jonas.

'Is your nose red?' he was still laughing.

Lottie tilted her head so that she could see in the mirror. 'Like Coco the clown,' she said laughing too. 'Hold on.'

She put the phone down and negotiated the bend before picking it up again. 'Where are you?'

'At the university. My lecture starts in fifteen.'

'I'd better not keep you then. Damn!'

'What's wrong?'

Lottie pulled to a stop and put on her hazard lights. 'I've lost a wheel trim. Got to get it back.' She was out of the car and running across the road.

'Where did it go?'

'I hit a pot hole. It bounced off and flew over the bushes on a traffic island.'

'Can't you get a new one?' 'Probably, but I'm there now.'

'You are one crazy lady, Coco, this could only happen to you.'

Lottie smiled. Wacky and fun to be with. Score one for Lottie.

***

The tangle of shrubbery pulled at her woollen dress and snagged her stockings. Tugging herself free, she realised that the cost of the wheel trims was a fraction of the cost of the dress and stockings that would now be ruined. But it was too late to worry about that and Jonas thought her amusing, so, with the perseverance of Stanley in hot pursuit of Dr Livingstone, she blundered through brittle branches letting out a small cry as her ankle almost turned on a stone. That gave her pause and she ensured that her footing was secure before moving on.

It was impossible to hear the traffic in the centre of the island. The trees formed a perfect sound barrier. Even the birds fell silent. She took a deep breath, regretting her impulse as she forced her way onward. Even her voice as she spoke to Jonas was hushed.

'The wheel trim can't be far away now.'

A clearing opened. In the centre was a pile of rags and on top of the rags was her wheel trim. 'It's landed on top of a pile of rags' she told Jonas.

'Serves you right,' Jonas laughed.

Fly tippers were a scourge.

Only a few steps now. Lottie carefully placed one foot in front of the other. The ground was uneven and soft. She giggled and Jonas laughed. She bent down, reached out, picked up her property, sighed with relief and straightened up. She gave Jonas a running commentary which she hoped was sparkling with wit. He was laughing anyway so that was something.

And that was when she saw the skull.

'Jonas, there's a skeleton here.' Her voice was a whisper.

'A skeleton?'

'A skull and a pile of rags.''

'I'll come to you. Where are you exactly?'

'No. Don't do that. I'm fine. Really. I'm nearly at home. I'll call the police from there.'

The shock rocked her back on heels that sank into soft earth. She staggered backwards a few steps until her free hand managed to grasp a sturdy branch and a thorn plunged deep into her palm. She winced. She blinked. A skull? On the bypass roundabout outside Whittington Edge? It couldn't be.

It was. And it had been wearing a red hat.

Thankfully, Lottie's brain closed down all her thought processes at this point and concentrated its efforts on removing her from the scene and back to the safety of her car. She pulled her hand free of the thorn and sucked at the drop of blood that welled up on her skin. Then, carefully, she made her way, step by sliding step, to the firmer ground near the trees. She hoped no one would see her bursting dishevelled and windswept, from the shrubbery. No one did. She could see her car now; a canary yellow haven waiting patiently, hazard lights flashing with their reliable rhythm.

Lottie was feeling better in a surreal sort of way. The rags, the red hat, even the skull were turning into some sort of hallucination. She couldn't really have discovered a body. Could she? Returning to her car, she tossed the wheel trim onto the small back seat and carefully drove away only to pull into a lay-by a hundred yards down the lane to regroup. She sat with her hands covering her face. This was impossible. This was not happening.

***

When she left Lyeminster and moved to Whittington Edge she had visions of herself as a countrywoman; a woman whose stack of mud-encrusted plant pots were photographed for glossy magazines. She had left her life as an investigator far behind. She had not expected to discover a body; no, a skeleton. Not here. Not in this new, secure life.

Part of her couldn't believe what she had seen. Part of her wished she had overcome her natural parsimony, waved the wheel trim goodbye and invested in a new set. The more honourable part of her was riddled by the guilt of this thought.

Checking that no one was near, she peeled off her ruined stockings and put them in her handbag. Any hope that this hadn't happened was dashed. Reality broke through again. A poor woman had died ages ago on that traffic island and no one had found her. How could that happen?

Someone must have reported her missing and sat by the phone day after day hoping for word that she was safe and well. The memory of the jaunty red hat faded in parts that had fallen from the skull made Lottie's lip quiver.

Hot tears replaced the icy ones brought on by the cold wind. Lottie bit into her lower lip. She had no cause to cry. She wasn't the body on the roundabout. She was a fortunate woman. She had to do the right thing. Even if it meant that her carefully constructed new life would suffer in the process.

But why should her new life be destroyed? The woman was dead. Nothing could help her now. Lottie was alive. Her life would be at risk if she spoke out. Possibly. These thoughts chased themselves around her head until she felt quite sick.

***

Lottie Colenso, the old Lottie Colenso, had found herself caught in the cross hairs of the nastiest villain in Lyeminster. She had given up her own, successful, rewarding life and career to reinvent herself in the village of Whittington Edge where she hoped this man would never discover her.

Now she'd found a body. That body must be reported. Life could be so unfair. She wondered if this was one of those karmic things people talked about and if trying to evade misfortune, made it come at you from a different angle.

Clear thinking was needed. Lottie prided herself on her clear thinking. She took a deep breath. The woman had obviously been there a long time. She could leave her and wait for someone else to come along and... No, she couldn't. Shame washed over her. Her family deserved and needed to know what had become of this woman. And, given the length of time she had lain undiscovered, the likelihood of someone else chancing upon her any time soon was remote.

But what about Lottie? No one knew where she was either. She supposed she would be required to attend the inquest and give evidence on how she found the body but, providing it wasn't a slow news week and no keen eyed reporter was standing outside the coroner's court with a photographer, and as long as a photograph of her didn't appear in the Lyeminster Echo she should be alright. Of course there was Marco to consider. And Jonas.

There was no going back. She had to do the right thing no matter what the cost might be to her.

She needed to think but her brain wouldn't cooperate.

Thoughts jumbled and jumped over one another. She had worked so hard to drop off everyone's radar. Now it would all be for nothing.

Lottie fired up the engine and continued on her way. She would do nothing hasty. The woman had been there long enough to reduce her to a skeleton; a skeleton wearing a red hat. Lottie gulped and bit down on trembling lips. Come along, Lottie, think rationally. A few more hours would make no difference. And, if anyone else should happen along in the meantime, the discovery would no longer be her responsibility.

This was unsatisfactory and made Lottie despise herself as a coward but it was the best she could do until she could think things through. Lottie prided herself on ice-cold logic. Once she had evaluated the information before her she would proceed in a logical direction. This had always been her way. But she had been working in her official capacity then; now this was capable of impacting on her own life. Her private life. And this could ruin everything.

***

Avril Major held the whip aloft. Before her quivered the body of Bob Rogers, her regular client for

Monday evenings who had asked for an additional appointment this morning. Fortunately he had also asked for a gag otherwise Avril would have been unable to accommodate him; Bob Rogers was a noisy customer and no mistake.

Despite the gag and the blindfold, Mr Monday, as Avril thought of him, was writhing and squeaking, moaning and groaning and she hadn't even made contact yet. Sometimes Avril wondered if these yokels were worth the bother. In London, where she had once run a similar establishment, the great and the bad paid a whole lot more than this for much worse treatment, and they didn't make such a fuss. She had really enjoyed her job when she lived in London.

A sharp rat-a-tat on her front door took her away from these wistful memories. A woman had to work hard to make a living what with wimpy men and constant interruptions. She hooked the whip in place on the wall, and pulled a fleecy pink housecoat that zipped from neck to hem over the black satin and scarlet lace confection she was wearing.

'Wait here and keep quiet.' She whispered to Mr Monday. Mr Monday wriggled. Avril went to the door, turned and looked at him before returning to administer a hefty thwack to his right buttock with a rubber paddle before hurrying downstairs. Mr Monday huffed deep moaning breaths through the gag.

Leonard the postman stood hopefully on the doorstep. 'I've got another parcel from your book club.' He said to the eye he could see through the crack in the door. 'I would have left it on the step but you said – '

'Yes, I did, Leonard.' Avril's hand snaked out and took the parcel from him.

She couldn't invite him in for coffee as she sometimes did because, although some inconvenience to Mr Monday lay within her remit, she didn't want him disturbing the neighbours if he tried to get free. And she certainly didn't want the postman telling all and sundry about a man imprisoned in Nook Cottage.

'I overslept this morning.' She yawned and watched as a canary yellow sports car swept around The Green, down the road outside her house and scythed into the car park of Horse and Trumpet Cottage the former Horse and Trumpet pub, home of Lottie Colenso.

'Mrs Colenso looks to be in a hurry.' Leonard was clearly distracted. 'I've got a parcel from her book club too.'

'I mustn't keep you.' Avril twittered, grateful for Lottie's excellent timing.

'Yeah...right.' All of the postman's attention was now on the yellow sports car and Avril, incongruously, was a little miffed.

Leonard was halfway down the path now and Avril was silently urging him to get a move on. He paused at the gate to sketch a brief salute before running, yes, running to intercept Lottie Colenso before she disappeared into her house. Avril closed the door with a sigh. She felt insulted by his haste.

'I hope you're behaving yourself, young man.' Sounds of muffled delight could be heard from the front bedroom in response to Avril's gravelly, smoke-damaged voice, and Avril returned to work, unzipping her housecoat and coughing with the effort.

***

Whittington Edge Main Street had been thronged with people when the little yellow car nosed through. Whittington Edge was the sort of place where women shopped with baskets. Every day.

Main Street was the heart of the place and news was gathered and disseminated there. If it was too cold, the Butterfly Bush, a coffee shop recently opened by Blanche Tallentire, was the next port of call. Only very good friends were invited into one another's homes in Whittington Edge.

Several people on hearing the throaty purr of Lottie's sports car turned to wave or call a greeting. Lottie reciprocated in kind. She had closed off all thoughts of the body she had found until later. This ability to compartmentalise had stood her in good stead in her former life and it would continue to do so now.

Today she drove the full length of Main Street before turning off and circling towards her home instead of her usual route; she needed to see normality to erase the pictures still whirling through her mind.

When The Green came into view she drove all the way around the large square with its duck pond and slid to a halt outside the door to the smoke room of the old Horse and Trumpet pub. She knew that some residents of The Green would think she was showing off; in fact, had she not had a straight run at her parking space, it was unlikely she would have made it unscathed. Lottie felt decidedly shaky.

When she swept to a halt she was glad that she had left so much of the old car park intact. The sports car was askew. Her little dark red runabout was neatly parked it its usual place. She switched off the engine and forced herself to take several deep calming breaths. Then, determined to behave in as natural a manner as possible, she looked in the rear view mirror and finger combed her newly blonded, newly curled hair.

That was when she saw Lenny, the postman, hurrying towards her. She opened the door, extended a long, slender leg, and rose effortlessly from the depths of the bucket seat; any twinges from her tortured joints being fiercely ignored.

'Morning, Mrs Colenso.' Lenny panted. 'I've got another parcel from your book club.

'Thank you, Lenny.' Lottie beamed at him. 'I don't suppose you have time to give me a hand with this hood, do you?'

Lenny puffed out his chest. He liked to offer small services to attractive ladies like Mrs Colenso.

'Leave it to me.' He said. 'We can't have you breaking your fingernails, now, can we?'

'You're so kind.' Lottie took the parcel from him. 'I'll just nip inside and put on some coffee. You will take coffee with me, won't you?' She hated wrangling with the hood.

'I noticed you'd lost a wheel trim.' Lenny said when Lottie saw him out forty minutes later. 'Get some cable ties from the hardware shop and I'll put it back on for you tomorrow.'

'Thank you, Lenny, I will.' Lottie's smile was forced; he had reminded her of the body when she had almost eradicated it from her memory. Temporarily.

She watched him walk to the gate and give her a small salute and then she closed the door and leaned against it. She was exhausted.

In the attempt to give the impression of continued industry since her retirement, Lottie had bought a desk and placed it in the old snug where a sideways glance would give her a view of the former beer garden. This was where she had toyed with the idea of planting a red tree like those on the roundabout. The thought caught her unawares, her heart plummeted again and bounced back to lodge painfully in her throat.

She had tossed ideas around ever since she saw the skull.

There was no way out of this. She had to report it.

The only person she trusted was Marco Romero. Marco was a detective sergeant at Woolstock. He had been the nearest she had to a friend in her former life. She had walked away from that life and Marco without a backward glance – almost – and now...

Her study also contained a sofa piled high with cushions and a lightly quilted throw. She sat on the sofa now. She needed to lose herself for just a few minutes then her brain would click back into gear and all would be well.

She pulled the throw over her and dropped into the deepest, darkest well of sleep. A hot tear of self pity trickled out of the corner of one eye and soaked into the cushions.

***

Jane Pendleton, wife of Charles Pendleton, the new rector of Whittington Edge, had also seen Lottie's arrival home. Now that Charles had been installed as the rector she felt able to undertake parish work. This she saw as a perk of her role.

Following the move to this delightful village from the parish of St Dismas in Lyeminster she had been waiting for the chance to do her part to help her beloved husband in his ministry.

Going from door to door she had met several of her new neighbours. She had been disappointed when there was no response to her knock at Hallelujah House. With a name like that she had hoped to find a warm welcome and a kindred spirit. Atlantis Warbeck next door, opened her front door and whispered, 'Cassie will be doing her meditation around about now.' She invited Jane into The Crow's Nest and closed the door.

Bill Warbeck, according to Atlantis was an artist of some note and had the temperament to match.

Atlantis had whispered and tiptoed until she and Jane were seated in a small sitting room far away from Bill's studio at the front of the house. Jane's artistic appreciation had never strayed beyond the Impressionists so, when Atlantis opened up a room decorated in blazing vermillion and filled with interesting oddments, she was pleased to be able to engage her hostess in conversation about her numerous hobbies rather than show her ignorance of Bill Warbeck's artistic achievements.

Jane was reasonably tall but Atlantis was taller. She flowed with diaphanous garments and had long frizzy ginger hair festooned with feathers and shiny green threads. Jane was fascinated and in the time she was there discovered that Susan Holland lived at Matchbox Cottage and was Lottie Colenso's best friend, Avril Major lived at Nook Cottage and told fortunes.

'Oh, I shouldn't have told you that, should I?' Atlantis covered her mouth with a hand encrusted with heavy rings. 'You wouldn't approve, would you? But I'm told she's very good. She does tarot cards and crystal gazing and stuff like that. Oh dear, there I go again.'

Jane smiled. She liked Atlantis Warbeck. She led the conversation back to Lottie Colenso whose name she didn't recognise from the parishioners she had met at Charles' induction. Jane was good with names and always remembered them; a valuable gift for anyone moving in diplomatic circles.

Lottie Colenso was a newcomer. She had pots of money and no one knew much about her but Atlantis would trust her with her secrets. Nice to know.

Jane Pendleton finished her cup of orange herbal tea and thanked Atlantis for her time. Atlantis seemed fey and in need of a friend. Jane wanted to make friends too. She had never really had friends since she left boarding school.

The list of parish activities didn't take long. Atlantis was not a mother so would not want to join the Mothers' Union, was hardly likely to want to join the Young Wives, and had an individual approach to flower arranging that would not fit into the format approved by the local Flower Guild.

The two women said their goodbyes on the doorstep of The Crow's Nest and Jane admired the flowers that still filled Atlantis' front garden when the rectory garden was a revolting gloopy mess of exposed soil and slimy green, decomposing, foliage.

She left The Crow's Nest and exchanged good mornings with the ever-disapproving Mrs Bettinson, the cleaner she had inherited with the rectory.

**

Jane nipped into The Priest at Prayer to drop off a handful of church magazines and Mrs Bettinson huffed from her front doorstep. Mrs Bettinson always made her disapproval audible and it took all Jane's resolve not to turn and acknowledge the reproof; Mrs Bettinson disapproved of pubs, probably because her husband was reputed to spend so much time there.

Jane Pendleton lifted her chin and made her way towards the western edge of The Green, the large square patch of grass which was surrounded by the best houses in Whittington Edge.

Hawthorn Cottage was the home of Mrs Bettinson and her husband. There were a few more cottages on the southern edge. Their occupants must be at work because no door was answered in response to her knock.

She crossed at the corner and began walking along the pavement down towards Horse and Trumpet Cottage, a property whose owner fascinated Jane. Earlier she had seen the yellow sports car whizzing around The Green and a middle aged woman at the wheel. This had caught her interest and she really wanted to meet this Lottie Colenso who, like Jane, was new to town. Glancing towards Horse and Trumpet Cottage and the yellow car parked at an angle, Jane suppressed a sigh and moved on.

Dunroamin belonged to a hardworking village family who would not be at home during the day,

Honeysuckle Cottage was a weekend retreat for some yuppies according to Mrs Bettinson. She knew nothing of the inhabitants of Lindisfarne or several of the other homes in the row but Matchbox Cottage was the home of Susan Holland.

Jane hadn't bothered with Hawthorn Cottage; Mrs Bettinson was daunting enough at the rectory without bearding her in her own lair. But Jane was not prepared to allow her cleaner to dictate her visits so she walked up the path to Dunroamin and rapped on the door. She could feel Mrs Bettinson's eyes boring into her back when she had to accept that no one was in and retrace her steps. She had no better luck at several more doors.

She missed out Matchbox Cottage and went straight to Nook Cottage. This had been her target ever since Atlantis had mentioned Avril Major.

***

Jane's mother's maiden name was Avril Major. Just the sound of the words dropped lightly into the conversation by Atlantis Warbeck was like a spear being thrust through Jane Pendleton's heart because Jane's mother had disappeared without a trace several years ago. They had been on holiday in London from her father's diplomatic posting in the Far East. Her mother had gone out shopping and never returned.

Jane assumed that measures were taken to find her but Jane was only a young girl at the time and was not included in any discussions that may have taken place. And, when she was older, her father refused to speak of the incident. Her persistence led to her being shipped off to England to become the ward of Charles Pendleton, her father's old school friend.

A large chestnut tree across the road shaded the door of Nook Cottage and lent it a spooky look, and Jane Pendleton, who had urged her husband to take the living in Whittington Edge mainly because she remembered her mother telling her that once she had spent time here, wondered if this Avril Major and her mother could be one and the same person.

She almost faltered. Her steps certainly slowed. It was foolish to say that she missed her mother but she did. Raised by a battalion of servants and only taken to meet her parents for a few minutes each day when a child, it was ludicrous that she should make any such claim. Jane knew that she couldn't miss something she had never really had but she didn't like loose ends.

Her mother had never been found and Jane wanted to know what had happened to her.

Taking a deep breath, she stiffened her spine and strode up to the door of Nook Cottage. If her mother had ended up here reading tarot cards and gazing into a crystal ball it could prove embarrassing for Charles. For the time being, it was best if she met this woman as the stranger she was and then she would have to decide what to do.

Charles had asked her over and over again why she wanted to move to Whittington Edge and she hadn't told him. She had let him think that she wanted to escape the Dismals as the St Dismas area was known in Lyeminster. Now, she may have to come clean. And how would Charles react to that? Could his career be damaged by the existence of a mother in law who told fortunes?

***

Avril Major had sent Mr Monday on his way. She was glad to be rid of him; the man was a liability. She was on the verge of telling him that he would have to go elsewhere, but he paid well and money had always been most important to her.

Although she regretted the passing of the prices she could command in London, Avril had been surprised at just how much these yokels were prepared to pay. She had no cause to feel hard done by.

She had just finished tidying everything away when Sonny rang. Sonny Gumbrill always had impeccable timing.

'I wanted to leave a message for Aunt Minnie.' Sonny said. 'I'll tell her you called.' Avril replied in her best cut glass accent. She replaced the receiver and went to the mobile that she thought of as her work phone. She rang Sonny's number.

'How you doin', Doll?' He asked.

'I'm fine.' She said. 'My book arrived this morning.'

'Just as well, otherwise I'd be clippin' somebody's fingers.' Sonny said with a warm, throaty laugh.

Avril laughed too even though she knew this was not a joke.

Sonny had a number of unpleasant punishments for those who crossed him.

'You have a job for Aunt Minnie?' she said, determined to keep this conversation on a professional basis.

'Yes. I've got a geezer called Arthur. White collar villain. You know the type. All big ideas and no brain. I need him rusticatin' for a bit. Things around him are a bit warm if you know what I mean and I want him out of here before warm turns to hot.'

Avril had just agreed to meet Arthur from the London train the next day when Jane Pendleton knocked on her door.

'Got to go, Sonny, there's someone at the door. I'll call you tomorrow to let you know everything's sorted.'

Sonny was displeased and she could feel his annoyance rushing down the phone wire like a tidal wave. He still thought that he should come first, that she should push anything and anyone aside to make way for him. And after the things he had done! It was the fault of Sonny's stupidity that she was stuck in this place instead of lounging by a swimming pool in Spain. She still loved her husband but she doubted she would ever forgive him.

With a sad little sigh, Avril cut the call.

Avril knew enough to find out who was on the other side of the door before she opened it. She ran upstairs swiftly and silently, and peered down from the room Mr Monday had recently vacated.

She saw a smart young woman with beautiful long straight blonde hair and the face of an angel. This beautiful face was tilted up to catch the sparse sunlight. She didn't recognise her but didn't see her as a threat either. She reminded herself that this was Whittington Edge and not the Elephant and Castle, and went to open the door.

Jane was on the point of admitting defeat when she heard the chain being removed from the door in front of her. It seemed as though the whole of The Green went out on Monday mornings. She wanted Avril Major to be in more than anyone else. She forced her face into a smile, not sure what she wanted to see when the door opened.

If it was her mother then a mystery of several years would be solved. But that also meant that she had to face the fact that her mother had walked out on her without a backward glance. But, no, her mother could have had a turn of some sort; lost her memory and gradually remembered that she was Avril Major and had, at one time, lived in Whittington Edge. Yes, that was possible. It also meant that the intervening period of her life was a blank and she wouldn't remember Jane at all.

The door opened.

The woman who stood before her bore no relation to anything Jane Pendleton could remember of her own dear mother. She felt all her muscles relax and her shoulders drop a couple of inches. She exhaled and forced herself to breathe again.

'Good morning,' she held out her hand, 'I'm Jane Pendleton, the rector's wife. I'm going round The Green this morning trying to get to know some of my new neighbours.'

'Come inside.' Avril Major said, her voice grating. She smiled a smile broad enough to show teeth flecked with scarlet lipstick. She had cherry red hair and wore severe black. Her feet were encased in black patent leather stiletto shoes. Wearing smart outdoor shoes inside seemed very sophisticated and Jane wondered if Avril had been about to go out but the welcome seemed genuine so she smiled and stepped over the threshold.

***

Lottie awoke and went into the downstairs cloakroom to rinse her face in cold water. The memory of the obligation awaiting her was daunting but she stood up straight and forced her head high and her shoulders back.

She would do this. Never let it be said that Lottie Colenso ducked out of a task because it was difficult.

She touched up her makeup and went through to the kitchen to make the call but she saw Susan Holland, her best friend in Whittington Edge pass by the Church Lane side of Horse and Trumpet Cottage and realised that a cup of coffee would strengthen her resolve and not affect the skeleton at all.

Susan waved and Lottie reached for the kettle. Lottie spent many years without friends. Now her innate caution ensured that she was making haste slowly.

She hurried to open the front door. Susan came into the hall.

She put her basket down on the floor and unwound her scarf.

'It looks so nice out there but it's really quite chilly.' She shivered and removed her coat. Lottie took both and hung them in the hall cupboard.

'The kettle should have boiled by now.' She said leading the way through to the kitchen.

'How was your weekend?' Susan smiled.

'Wonderful. And yours?'

Any hint that she was being pumped for information would make Lottie clam up. So Susan told her about the induction of the new rector; this being the only thing of note to have happened in Whittington Edge since Lottie and she last spoke.

'His wife is gorgeous.' Susan said. 'She can only be in her late twenties or early thirties at the most. She has glorious long blonde hair and alabaster skin.'

Lottie frowned. 'I must have the wrong man down as the rector.' She said. 'I've seen a little Mr Pickwick clone going around. I thought that was the rector.'

'It is!' Susan cradled her hands around her cup to warm them and sipped her coffee.

'Really?'

Susan was a very good source of gossip. She was a welcome visitor to any home in Whittington Edge. She was the go-to person for the care of treasured porcelain. Mrs Bettinson's clumsiness had made the repair of several breakages Susan Holland's new career since her divorce.

In this way Susan had her own hotline to all the rumours and gossip going around The Green and Whittington Edge.

The two .women dissected Whittington Edge life for a while and then Susan brought the conversation back to Lottie's weekend away.

'Jonas has a voice you could pour on pancakes.' Lottie said. Susan's eyes flew open.

'Wow!' Her surprise was twofold; firstly that Lottie had vouchsafed the information and secondly because of the information itself.

'He booked a suite at the Manor House hotel.' Lottie said. 'It's very swish there.'

'I know. Chris used to take me there in a former life.' The mention of Susan's former husband elicited scowls from both women before they continued.

They discussed the hotel and the theatre Jonas had taken Lottie to.

'He's very special.' Lottie said at last.

Susan thought she could detect a note of something interesting in her friend's voice. 'And?' she said.

'And...' Lottie paused to get her thoughts together, 'and I've not had a serious relationship since ... I don't remember, and I don't know if I dare have one now. And I don't even know if that's what he wants. Or if it's what I want for that matter.'

'Then there's no rush.' Susan said. 'Just think, if Jonas was pushing you to commit to a relationship you would have something to worry about. Maybe he feels the same way.'

Lottie wasn't sure how she felt about that. A perverse side to her nature wanted Jonas to be champing at the bit but she knew she would have felt pestered if he were.

'It's a shame you took your own car,' Susan said, 'he could have given you a lift home and extended the weekend.'

Susan was peering deep into her coffee mug as she said this and a good thing too because that was when Lottie remembered the body on the roundabout.

'I found a body on the roundabout.' She said quietly, half hoping that Susan wouldn't hear.

But Susan had heard and Lottie had to tell the whole story.

CHAPTER TWO

Jane had a problem and Charles was busy working on his sermon so she didn't want to arrive home too early. He liked to pace up and down in his study declaiming his words loudly to his imagined congregation to see how they sounded and she knew that her presence in the rectory cramped his style. So Jane left Nook Cottage and made her way past more cottages turning outside Lottie's home on the corner of The Green into Church Lane, through St Jude's Open and onto Main Street.

She glanced to the right as she stepped out of St Jude's Open on the corner of which stood the old rectory, a beautiful white Georgian house of perfect proportions that the diocese had sold years ago in favour of the ugly red brick monstrosity that she and Charles now occupied.

The old rectory was probably just as draughty as the new one but she would have suffered much to live in such gracious surroundings.

She liked The Green but Main Street was mostly Georgian and the street itself was wide. A collection of charming shops still managed to keep going despite current financial pressures, and family owned stores predominated. A few houses had been snapped up by firms of solicitors and estate agents and the board of a local estate agent was fixed to the front railings of the old rectory. Jane fought hard to prevent a sigh from escaping. Could she suggest to Charles that they rent this lovely home and abandon the draughty mausoleum of a place that they currently inhabited? Probably not, Charles was a humble man. Grandeur would not appeal to him.

Neither would comfort; Charles Pendleton was a hair-shirt clergyman. It could be difficult to get him to replace worn out shoes. It wasn't as if he couldn't afford to. Jane sighed.

Almost opposite St Jude's Open was the Butterfly Bush, a new tea room owned by Blanche Tallentire, a well known face in Whittington Edge according to people Jane had spoken to that morning. And this was where Jane Pendleton intended to go.

Her parochial rounds were finished for the day. Unsure whether she was pleased or disappointed that Avril Major had turned out not to be her mother. She was puzzling too over a letter she received that morning from a prisoner named Edna Derry. The letter had come out of the blue. She had taken it from the small bundle the postman handed to her and carried it into the front room; a place of icy splendour destined never to be used unless the bishop came to call.

Charles had found her there.

'That looks like a letter from prison.' He said.

Jane slit it open and withdrew the single sheet of notepaper. She read it and handed it to Charles along with another small slip that had fallen to the floor.

'Do you know...Edna Derry?' Charles asked.

'I've never heard of her.'

'What do you intend to do?'

'What do you think I should do?' She looked up into her husband's kindly face. Charles would know best. With him to guide her she would not go wrong.

'Prison visiting is seen as a very suitable vocation for clergy wives.' Charles said. 'But the decision must be your own, my dear. Think it over, ask our Lord for guidance. Then go where your heart leads you.'

This was all well and good. Jane knew that Charles was right; Charles held lengthy conversations with the Lord and these were a great comfort to him. Unfortunately, the Lord had never yet spoken clearly enough for Jane to be sure of his opinions.

She wanted advice. She really wanted to visit this Edna Derry because she was the first person ever to have asked her for anything and it felt good to be needed. But was that a good enough reason to meddle in this woman's life? What did one say to prisoners? What did one do on a prison visit?

***

The Butterfly Bush had an old fashioned bell and its chimes made her jump when Jane opened the door. She was the only customer and she looked around, surprised because the new tearoom was known to be very popular.

'Take a seat.' Blanche Tallentire called out. 'The menus are on the tables. I'll give you a minute then I'll come and take your order.

'You've chosen the right time to come in. The first rush has just gone and the next will be here in a little while.'

Blanche was polishing the counter and Jane was grateful because she really needed time to think.

First she had to think about Edna Derry. She said in her letter that she had seen a photograph of Jane's marriage to Charles and thought she looked so kind.

Jane sighed at the memory of her face framed in a cloud of gossamer tulle that lifted on a gentle breeze. Her husband had been caught throwing back his head in a rare laugh.

She had an enlargement of that photograph framed on their living room wall. Charles was afraid that it was too frivolous but on this Jane had taken a stand and she thought Charles was secretly flattered.

Flattery could be very seductive and Jane didn't want to succumb to the sin of pride by visiting this woman simply because she had said nice things about her. She wondered about asking to go on an official prison visitors' course but, if she visited Edna Derry it would be as a private citizen and Jane knew she had led a sheltered life and wasn't sure how she would cope with hardened criminals of the sort that she assumed would be in need of trained visitors.

She ordered a pot of tea and Blanche brought it. She also brought a small stack of magazines and Jane thanked her and opened one, staring unseeing at the colourful pictures of celebrities whilst she tussled with her thoughts.

Thoughts of Edna Derry swirled uselessly. No answer presented itself. She sent out a silent prayer and hoped that something concrete would return.

This freed her mind to consider the second of her puzzles; Avril Major. Could there be any link between the woman who disappeared seventeen years ago and the one she had met this morning?

Jane poured her tea and stirred it slowly.

She had never had a close relationship with either of her parents. Her father was a diplomat and her mother, though half English, had grown up on a tea plantation, the daughter of very wealthy parents, and had only visited her homeland once before she met Jane's father.

This visit took place when the young Avril Major was sent to Whittington Edge to stay for a year with – Jane had no idea who she stayed with – did she have family in the village? Why had she never asked so simple a question? It would have made her current situation so much easier.

Whatever the details, the visit to Whittington Edge had impressed itself upon her mind very clearly. As Jane grew older her mother would sometimes take her to the tea plantation where she had grown up. They would sit on the veranda looking out over the formal gardens to distant hills where the terraces were dotted with brightly clad workers. She would talk then of Whittington Edge and Adelaide Barrett, the friend she had made in those long ago days.

She had forgotten about Adelaide Barrett. It was beginning to come back to her now. Adelaide had been Avril's only friend when she was in England. It would surely be natural for her to remember her and gravitate towards Whittington Edge when she was in trouble.

Adelaide Barrett had towered over Avril. . At home, she was easily taller than any of the children except those at the European school she had attended. In Whittington Edge she was smaller than everyone. Her mother had laughed about this. Her mother's laugh was delicate; a tinkling sound that belonged with birdsong and wind chimes and the waft of spices on the breeze. Her voice too had a charming lilt. It was certainly nothing like the roughened tones of this Avril Major.

Jane's mother had been in awe of Adelaide Barrett. Adelaide had been fun, brave and a touch flighty. But, her mother explained, this could really have been the clash of cultures and no judgment of Adelaide should be made.

Their last conversation took place just before the fateful visit home. England was always referred to as 'home' and, to Jane's father, raised in the traditional way of aristocratic families it probably felt like home. It made her laugh to hear her mother speak of England as 'home'.

Her mother told her about Adelaide to demonstrate how English ways had moved on and relaxed. 'Don't be expecting everything in England to be like it is here.' She told Jane.

Jane had been so excited. She was going to see London. She would meet her father's family and had received a lot of tuition on the right things to say and do. She was going to stay in a hotel in Mayfair and her mother would take her shopping in stores she had only read about in the books that circulated amongst the tight, diplomatic and ex-pat community. These books, she recognised now, had been doing the rounds for so long that the London she anticipated had disappeared decades before she landed in the country.

She had met the Montrose family as promised. There was some frostiness that she put down to one of those cultural differences that her mother had told her to expect. Her mother had worn very pale makeup and Jane hadn't liked it; she liked the light tan of her mother's natural skin tones. The aristocratic relatives hadn't liked it either to judge from the way they looked down their noses at Avril and then slid their eyes to her daughter. Jane had not liked her father's family though it was obvious that they approved of her more than they did her mother. But soon they were gone.

Her father had taken her to a couple of museums and then her mother went shopping alone never to return.

***

The disappearance of Jane's mother had never really been mentioned in her hearing. She was there, and then she wasn't. A whole battalion of Montroses arrived at the hotel but she was excluded from their meetings. Jane never expected a close relationship with her parents but neither had she expected to be kept completely in the dark when her mother walked out of the hotel and into oblivion.

She was told that her mother had been taken ill and then Jane was returned home, alone, into the care of her ayah. Her heart had skipped guiltily when she heard of this illness because, somewhere deep inside lurked the yearning for a year of her own in Whittington Edge or somewhere similar away from her family home which was peopled only by servants whilst her father worked long hours and her mother used to be immersed entirely in her social obligations, which seemed to be enormous. Jane wanted to meet her own Adelaide Barrett and have some adventures. If her father felt unable to cope, as seemed to be the case, then what would be more natural than to send his only child to stay with some trusted family friend?

This was not to be. She was back in the Far East almost before her feet had touched the ground. Her mother was gone, never to return. Her father became more and more distant. Whenever she saw him, she asked questions. He made it clear that these questions were not welcome.

Then, out of the blue, she was summoned to her father's study to be told that another trip to England was on the horizon.

Jane's heart was tap-dancing, sure that her mother had recovered from the illness that afflicted her and they were travelling to England to collect her and bring her home.

But that wasn't it at all. She had packed a small suitcase to last her the four or five days her father had said they would be gone only to find a heap of trunks standing out on the steps. These were loaded into a van and sent to the docks. She saw her own name on the labels and ran back to her room to find her wardrobe doors ajar, and the room as empty as if she had never existed.

She didn't even ask. She knew she would not receive an answer. She climbed aboard the plane with her father knowing that her belongings were on a ship and steaming across the oceans. She still didn't ask.

It would have been pointless anyway. The whole time they were on the plane he worked at the papers he brought with him.

She was clearly a burden and she had been taught to keep quiet during these moods lest his volatile temper flare up.

Eventually they reached London where Charles Pendleton met them. He was unclear as to why his old school friend had asked him to be at the airport. Peregrine Montrose with the arrogance bred into him by centuries of entitlement, told Charles that he needed a guardian for his daughter and handed her over. There was no time for discussion as he was returning home on the next flight. And they had been together ever since.

**

'Would you like a refill?' Blanche Tallentire was standing beside her. The Butterfly Bush was now throbbing with life. Jane Pendleton, embarrassed to be occupying a table when business was brisk, hurried to gather together her belongings.

'There's no rush.' Blanche soothed. 'Stay where you are. We like to think that the Butterfly Bush is the place where people come to talk or to think. I'll bring more tea.' Jane subsided in her seat and ordered a slice of the Butterfly Bush's renowned fruit cake.

**

Marco Romero had been a colleague during her working life and Lottie felt bad just dropping off his radar. When she called his direct line at Woolstock CID, he had been stunned. She could hear the surprised silence. She could hear the surprise become disbelief, and then anger. Yes, Marco was angry alright, and she needed his help.

When she cut the call, Lottie spent several minutes pacing up and down, shaking with the shock of the discovery but more so with the fear of facing Marco who had always been her friend and now was...what?

He still drove the same aged blue car. She saw it pull into Church Lane. Lottie watched as he emerged lithe and graceful as always. He was a tall man with the Italian good looks he had inherited. He had always made women turn and stare and had given her a skipping heartbeat on more than one occasion. Now he ran his gaze over the exterior of Horse and Trumpet Cottage and gave the front window a narrowed look as if he could see her. He couldn't. She knew he couldn't see in. But it made her uncomfortable.

Catching herself behaving oddly, Lottie ran to the Church Lane door and stepped outside, a welcoming smile ready for him.

'I'm sorry,' she said as soon as he stepped into the kitchen.

'You should be.' He didn't look at her; he was taking in his surroundings.

'Keith Kendal threatened me.' She said at last. She heard Marco expel a loud breath.

Lottie moistened her lips. She had coffee ready, dark and rich as Marco liked it. She took a breath and assembled the things she needed. He wasn't going to help her, and why should he? She was the one in the wrong.

'I've got the coffee ready.' She said. She was fluttering. There was no other word for it. She despised herself but couldn't seem to stop. Marco was standing looking at her. He was a tall man and he seemed to fill her large kitchen. His eyes were dark and assessing.

'Please sit down.' She said.

'Where's the body?' He glanced around. 'I'm assuming there is a body.'

'It's on the bypass roundabout and it's been there for years. Do please sit down Marco and let me explain.' Exasperation crossed her face and she was the person he remembered once more. 'Do you really think I'd bring you here on a wild goose chase?'

He pulled out a chair and sat down after placing his mobile phone, radio and notebook side by side on the table. She smiled. He always did that. It was as if they had never been apart. She passed a mug of coffee to him.

'Tell me about the body.' He spooned in sugar and stirred.

He didn't look at her. She wasn't sure whether or not that was a good thing but it gave her the opportunity to drink him in and realise that he hadn't changed at all.

'I lost a wheel trim.' She began.

When the tale was told he picked up his mobile and called it in. 'I'd better not send this out over the radio or every rubberneck in the county will get there before the circus arrives.' He sighed. 'You will have to make a statement, obviously,' he said when he had relayed his news to the control room,

'Now tell me about Keith Kendall threatening you. And why you didn't report it. And, especially, why you didn't even tell me.' His voice rose on the last word and he banged his fist on the table making the mugs and Lottie jump. 'Good grief, Lottie, you always were a weird one.'

He shook his head whilst Lottie bristled. Weird? How dare he call her weird? One thing was certain, she was in no position to argue so she would file that away for later and get on with things.

'He didn't actually come up to me and hold a knife to my throat.' She said in a futile attempt at levity. 'I interviewed one of his foot soldiers on a matter totally unrelated to him. The man – I can't imagine what got into him – he started telling me all sorts of things to do with Keith Kendal's operation; the drugs, the women, the contacts he had with various people. All sorts of stuff I didn't need to know and certainly didn't want to know.

'Anyway, he must have gone back to the mother ship and when he was quizzed about our interview, he must have repeated everything he'd told me. I kept seeing Keith Kendal all around town after that. Once he was standing outside the pub opposite the office. He stared at me long enough to make me uncomfortable and I waited for a colleague to come out of the building and made an excuse to walk past him with her.'

'Maybe it was a coincidence.'

'Once is a coincidence.' Lottie said. 'Twice is troubling. A middle of the night phone call is enough to start paranoia setting in and the fourth thing...'

'The fourth thing?'

'He was on the corner again and he made his hand into a gun and shot me. I know it's stupid to take any notice of such things –'

'It's not stupid.' Marco was on his feet now, pacing the room. 'We need to talk about this. Really, I mean it. We do need to talk about it. And we will. Soon. But I have to go now. I have to meet the uniforms down at the bypass. There will be door to door enquiries; I'll make sure that I come to you. In the meantime keep this to yourself.' He looked at her face. 'Will the person you told have already passed it on?'

'I never said I'd told anyone.'

'You didn't need to. I can read you like a book, sweetheart, just as you can probably read me.'

If only.

'She won't have said anything and I'll tell her not to. She can keep a secret.'

'I hope so. That may be the only way I can keep you out of this.' He walked to the side door and turned. 'You should have told me. I would have organised protection for you.'

'Not as much as I would have needed.'

'No,' he shook his head, 'not as much as you would have needed with the likes of Keith Kendal after you.' He paused for a moment looking at her troubled face. 'Don't worry, I'll be in touch.'

And he was gone. Off to meet the crime scene team. Off to try to solve the mystery of a death that took place long ago. Lottie hoped that it had been a death from natural causes or, at the very least, accidental. And she felt excluded. She had never been a part of police work but she had been on the periphery and was always treated as a colleague by the officers with whom she came into contact.

But Marco had called her sweetheart and she didn't think she'd ever get the smile off her face.

She rang Susan the moment Marco left.

'No I haven't told a soul.' Susan assured her.

'Good. Please make sure you don't. The police have been and they need to keep it all under wraps for a while.'

'Sure. No problem. Are you feeling better now?'

Lottie thought about it for a second or two. 'Yes,' she said, 'yes, I am. He was very kind and he hardly told me off at all.'

When Lottie ended the call to Susan, she decided that what she needed was some hard, physical work. She had sanded the skirting boards in her bedroom and ran upstairs to begin to apply the paint. The smell of paint filled the house already and she couldn't wait to feel as if this room was finished; at the moment she felt as if she were camping.

***

Jane Pendleton realised that the Lord wasn't coming through to her very clearly about the prison visit. This was probably because Charles always told her that she should send her prayer and then put the whole subject out of her mind and wait for a reply. This Jane was unable to do. Much as she tried, she kept going over and over it in her head.

Then, she had a spark of intuition. Atlantis had recommended Lottie Colenso as the person whom she would trust with her secrets. Horse and Trumpet Cottage was on her list of visits to make; she hadn't intended visiting today, that was all. Perhaps she could talk to Lottie Colenso and see if it felt appropriate to raise the matter.

***

Lottie was glad of the interruption. She had almost finished the architrave around the door when a tentative knock at the front door had her up on her feet and hurrying to answer it.

Introductions were soon accomplished and Lottie ushered her into the house. 'Would you prefer tea or coffee?' Should she excuse herself and go and put the lid back on the paint? No, that would show that she had been interrupted and might prove off-putting to her visitor.

'Nothing for me, thank you. What a lovely kitchen.'

The sun broke through just as Jane Pendleton reached the threshold. It filtered through the leaves of the trees in St Jude's' churchyard and scattered bright spots of light on the warm earth tones of Lottie's kitchen. She had invested in handmade Italian tiles that had been arranged in a diagonal design all around the walls. This was the first time she had really appreciated the effect. The kitchen had been completed by the kitchen fitter and she loved it.

'Come through to the living room.' Lottie invited; the rector's wife must be entertained formally.

'Charles and I are new to the parish and I'm trying to meet some of my neighbours.' Jane said. 'May I offer you a copy of the parish magazine?' She handed the magazine over and launched into her list of parish activities and, even as she reeled them off, she could hardly imagine Lottie Colenso joining any of the groups she was advertising. 'I suppose you've seen a lot of comings and goings at the church hall as it's only across Church Lane.'

'Yes,' Lottie lied, 'the church seems to be very active in Whittington Edge.'

Jane smiled at this. 'The Young Wives and Mothers' Union join together at this time of year, or so I'm told, to put on a big Halloween party for the village. That will be at the church hall too. Will you be attending?'

'I'd love to.' Lottie lied again. 'And I hope I shall be allowed to make a contribution.' The aunt who had care of Lottie and her brother during their teens had told them that the church could always be bought off with a donation.

'Lovely.' Jane beamed. She took out a notebook and jotted Lottie's name down. 'I don't know if you've met Gwennie Furlong yet but she's the organiser as regards who is doing what. I have to make sure that I approach the correct person for these things; ladies' groups can be very...territorial.'

Lottie burst out laughing. 'I can imagine.' She said with genuine warmth. 'And I don't envy you. I already know Gwennie; I'm surprised she hasn't already dragooned me in for something.'

Jane laughed too and both women felt the atmosphere change. Some line had been crossed here and Lottie Colenso and Jane Pendleton were now friends and Lottie asked her if she was sure she wouldn't like a cup of tea.

'Thank you, I think I will.'

Lottie went into the kitchen to put on the kettle and Jane followed her just as naturally as Gwennie or Susan would have done. Jane sat at the kitchen table. She could see what Atlantis Warbeck had meant about Lottie Colenso. She would trust her with her secrets too, if she dared.

'It must be very hard being the rector's wife and trying to fit into a new parish.' Lottie said. She kept her back to her visitor; she could see that Jane Pendleton was struggling with something. When she used to interview professionally, it was often useful to drop something into the conversation and then try almost to become invisible and allow the ripples to reach wherever they could. 'I imagine it's a difficult job altogether.'

Her visitor's sigh was Lottie's signal to become visible again. She brought the tea to the table and sat down quietly so as not to disturb Jane Pendleton's thoughts.

'It is. But,' Jane drew the proffered cup towards her, 'I'm very new to this role and I see other women in my situation and they do such good work. I want to help Charles as much as I can. He's a very good man. He has such a strong calling and so kind a heart, I obviously want to make his life easier but I also want to help other people.' She looked into Lottie's face. 'Does that sound silly, or worse, self indulgent?'

'Not at all,' Lottie said.

She had never imagined herself as any man's helpmeet but she could see sincerity glowing in Jane Pendleton's eyes; this was clearly what she wanted and good luck to her. This lack of interest in this area of wifely duty could be what had driven a wedge between herself and Eric. She would think about that later. 'So what's the problem?' she turned the spotlight of her smile onto Jane Pendleton.

'I'm sorry to ask this, Mrs Colenso, but could we keep this strictly between ourselves?'

'Of course. I've spent all my working life keeping people's secrets. Yours will be safe with me. And do, please, call me Lottie.'

Sensing Jane's scruples coming under tension, Lottie began stirring her tea and making herself invisible again.

'I received a letter from a prisoner this morning, Lottie. The woman was asking me to visit and she sent a visiting order so I can show up at the prison or not as I choose. I don't know what crime she committed. She doesn't really tell me anything about herself at all. I don't recognise her name.' Jane shook her head. 'And I don't know whether or not to go. Charles says I must make up my own mind and trust in the Lord to give me the proper guidance.'

'Do you want to visit her?'

Jane looked up sharply. 'I do.'

'Then go.'

Jane was transfixed for a moment. 'But what if I'm doing it for all the wrong reasons?'

'It doesn't matter.' Lottie said. 'As I understand it, prisoners never talk about the reason they are in prison; it's one of the unwritten rules that you never ask another inmate what they did. I doubt you will be asking her what she did because you wouldn't want to cause her any embarrassment.

'If you feel any concern, you could always put the name into your computer and find out what she's done before you decide. I can't see you arriving at the prison gates with a rope ladder or a cake with a hacksaw baked inside it so what other problems can you see?'

'What if I go to visit her because I want to...I don't know; boost my own self esteem or something?' There it was, out in the open, she had confessed the sin of pride to this new friend and, surprise, surprise, the new friend didn't fall to the floor in outrage and shock. In fact, she was still smiling. She was leaning forward and patting her hand.

'Jane, this woman wants you to be flattered by her request. She would say anything to flatter you into visiting her but – this is the important thing – she could have sent that letter to any one of a number of people but she sent it to you.'

'She said she had seen our wedding photo in the newspaper and she thought I looked kind.'

'You do look kind. You are kind. She's a good judge of character. If you want to visit, then visit. If you were sitting here telling me that you wanted to visit to fit into some image you had of what a rector's wife should do, then I'd be trying to dissuade you. But you want to go because you may be able to help. She doesn't want spiritual comfort; she will have a chaplain on hand if that were what she needed.

'She may want something from you like chocolate or tights or other luxuries not freely available within the prison, and if you felt that you wanted to provide those things you would have to check out the rules regarding gifts with the authorities before you visit.

You could perhaps take some small gift to break the ice. Or, she may have seen your picture, thought you looked kind, and just wants to have a pleasant conversation.'

'You make it sound so easy.' Jane said.

'Life is easy, if you allow it to be.' Lottie told her.

Later that night, Lottie was to dwell on that small piece of wisdom and wonder if she actually believed it herself.

***

Lottie watched fondly as Jane turned at the gate and blew her a kiss. It was heart-warming to feel that she had done the rector's wife a good turn. Jane Pendleton was a genuinely nice person and, if Charles Pendleton was as noble as she said, then Lottie felt they were well matched in character if nothing else.

She closed the door, leaned on it for a moment or two to enjoy the buzz and then sighed deeply and decided it was time to get on with her day. She had a bedroom to decorate and it wouldn't paint itself.

As she stepped forward her eyes alighted upon the parcel Lenny had brought that morning. The new novel from her book club. She could surely allow herself a tiny peek. She poured out another cup of tea and took it through to the living room. Having paused to open the parcel, a couple of pages wouldn't hurt.

The parcel was very well wrapped with large amounts of shiny brown tape holding it securely. She picked at a corner and carefully began to peel it away. But beneath the sticky tape was brown paper, not the manila carton she had been expecting. She tore a corner off the brown paper and found a bundle of banknotes. Dirty banknotes. Lottie jumped and the parcel fell to the floor. Who on earth would send her banknotes? She picked it up, holding it between two tissues she had taken from the box on the coffee table. The police must have this. They needed to investigate her book club.

Surely that was ridiculous. No reputable book club would have sent out this parcel. Gingerly she turned it over. The address label read 'Mrs A Major, Nook Cottage, Whittington Edge,' she only just stopped herself dropping it again. Carefully she replaced the paper and sticky tape and put it back on the hall table. Then she went to wash her hands.

Lottie forced herself to go upstairs and paint. She felt as if she were on a rollercoaster that rattled between happiness and doom, and, at the moment, it had stalled at 'panic'. When the panic subsided, Lottie knew that she wasn't going to report her book club to the police at all because this was nothing to do with the book club.

This was to do with Avril Major and Lottie had enough trouble on her plate at the moment without dabbling in Avril Major's affairs.

Her instincts meant that she would keep her eye on Nook Cottage in the future though.

Eager to be rid of the parcel, Lottie was up and about in plenty of time to see Lenny delivering his mail the next morning. She opened the door before he was through the gate.

'Did you get those cable ties, Mrs C?' He beamed at her and handed over her letters.

'I did.' She smiled and placed them in his hand, 'and I also have a little orphan for you.' She placed the suspect parcel on top of the cable ties. 'I think this belongs to Mrs Major.'

Lenny screwed up his eyes the better to read the label. 'It certainly does. I'll nip back there now and get yours from her. She was getting ready to go out.' He dropped his post sack on the doorstep and ran back to Nook Cottage.

Lottie closed the door. She had no desire to see the handover. He was soon back puffing and panting to deliver her parcel and tackle the wheel trim. Lottie made him a coffee and took it outside. He took a sip and pronounced it 'perfect'. Lottie had purposely made it cool.

Soon he was knocking on the side door. 'I put ties on all the wheels just in case' he said handing over the spare ties and the empty cup.

Lottie was generous with her thanks and gave him £20 for his trouble. Then, when she had eventually closed the door on him, she returned to the living room, slipped behind the old bar counter, lifted the lid to the cellar and took the cable ties down to place them neatly on the empty racking that had once held cartons of crisps and salted nuts.

She looked around guiltily. These racks had been destined to hold nature's bounty in the guise of bottled fruits and homemade jam. Oh well, the road to hell is paved with good intentions Lottie knew.

CHAPTER THREE

Avril reached Lyeminster station on Tuesday in time to watch the London train arrive on the down line.

Lyeminster only had two platforms so, from her vantage point at the top of the steps, it was easy to see everyone who alighted. She picked out Arthur the moment he set foot on the platform. He carried a brand new suitcase; this, to the casual observer, meant he was either intent on making a good impression or that he had never left London before. The third explanation, the true explanation, was that this wasn't Arthur's own suitcase. This was a suitcase owned by Sonny; a suitcase with very special qualities.

Firstly, the appearance of the suitcase had been altered just enough for Aunt Minnie to be able to pick it out, and secondly, it was fitted with a tracker device so that Sonny could keep tabs on his errant employee.

Soon Arthur would be even more secure but, as Aunt Minnie watched him, she could see his nervousness. He looked about him, checking out his fellow passengers.

He might have been wondering if one of them was going to dart towards him and push him into the path of an oncoming express. If so he would have a long wait; the next train wasn't due for half an hour.

It was probably that, having left the safety of home ground, he was alert to the risk of bandits. Avril had found that Londoners really did have this notion that, even if the world didn't actually end at Watford, it became a frightening and savage place.

Hurrying back up the steps, Avril positioned herself just inside the station bookshop and watched his progress.

He looked around, clearly he had never been to Lyeminster before; yes, this was a fish out of water if ever she'd seen one.

Arthur stood at the top of the steps whilst the other passengers manoeuvred around him. Avril shook her head. The standard of villains was falling.

Nobody need tell her otherwise. And this was the white collar variety? Well heaven help us. No wonder Sonny had to get rid of him for a few days; this fellow patently hadn't the gumption to survive alone once trouble reared its head.

Eventually Arthur made his way to the clock, beneath which he and Aunt Minnie were destined to meet. Avril was wearing a grey tweed coat that had seen better years and now had a rusty patina, topped by a plum coloured hat. Iron grey curls frizzed out from beneath the hat. These did not belong to Avril; these belonged solely to Aunt Minnie. A carpet bag containing her own things was safely in a left luggage locker to be retrieved when she was ready to go home.

Arthur looked at his watch and then up at the clock. Avril was pleased to see that he only had the one suitcase; the last thing she needed was someone who thought he was here for several weeks. She scooted through the bookshop, out of the door on the opposite side and, slowing to a more aged pace, stumped around the corner towards the clock in her broken down Aunt Minnie shoes, puffing as if she had run all the way.

'Arthur!' she said when she reached him. 'How lovely to see you. My how you've grown.' Had anyone passing by been interested enough to eavesdrop on their conversation, they would have thought nothing of it, which was Avril's intention.

'Hello, Aunt Minnie,' Arthur replied happily. 'You don't look a day older.'

'That's as may be.' Avril pulled up her gloves and rearranged her handbag over one wrist. 'But I am, so you can give me your arm like a good boy and we'll be on our way.'

Arthur obediently held out an arm and Avril took it preparatory to leading him away from the station and towards the Tuesday afternoon bustle of Lyeminster.

She chattered all the way down into the subway never once straying from her role as Aunt Minnie. A young man with a guitar strummed along to his own version of Streets of London. 'Makes me feel quite at home,' Arthur said.

'Just remember this isn't London. People here remember things. We don't all wander about in our own privacy bubble in Lyeminster. We snoop unashamedly and what we hear, we pass on. Some people will ask questions, so don't go talking to anyone. Some people pass things on to the police.'

She had leant towards him to deliver this advice in lowered tones but she moved away and increased the decibels to comment on the subway itself. 'Oh look at that graffiti.' She said. 'I hate to see that. It completely spoils the lovely tiles on the walls here. It makes you wonder what sort of homes these ruffians come from.'

Aunt Minnie led Arthur to the ramp exit rather than the steps and soon they were walking along London Road surrounded by the grand Victorian buildings that she declared had been vandalised by later occupants.

Plate glass windows disguised ornate architecture. Fluorescent notices declared cut prices, and the pavement was an obstacle course of sign boards advertising pub meals or jobs for people who were lorry drivers or IT literate; whatever that might mean.

Aunt Minnie clicked her tongue with disapproval and took evasive action to avoid the pesky things.

The White Hart was an old coaching inn that had managed to survive into the present century as a very smart hotel. It wasn't the best hotel in Lyeminster, that being the Granby on Market Street.

But Arthur wasn't best hotel material; no one sent by Sonny was.

The White Hart was plush, the rooms all en suite with adult movies included in the price. The food was good too and the staff sufficiently obsequious. Arthur should be happy here. And if he wasn't – tough.

She stopped and dug into her bag.

'And you'd better wear this.' She said, fiddling about with an enamel badge and fixing it firmly to his lapel.

'What's that?'

'It's the emblem of a very old Lyeminster organisation. It'll guarantee you good service. But, don't worry; it's a sort of secret society. You don't have to know any fancy handshakes or anything, but if you see anyone else wearing the badge, don't mention it. They won't mention it to you either.'

It would be a miracle if they did – there was no secret society.

'Right,' Arthur said, patting the badge to check it was secure. 'You're sure I won't have to have a story to go with the badge, Aunt Minnie?'

'Absolutely. Mind you, that's another reason to keep a low profile, isn't it?'

Arthur might have thought it was a good reason not to wear the darned thing in the first place but he was relieved not to be at the bottom of the landfill and wouldn't dream of questioning anything Aunt Minnie said. She might report back. But she seemed a nice old bird; a bit dotty but harmless enough. He would soon have her wrapped around his little finger. And if she wanted him to wear her crappy little badge it was a small price to pay to keep the old girl happy.

'You're to make sure that every time you leave your room, you're wearing your jacket. The White Hart is a smart hotel. We don't want any sloppy behaviour to draw attention to you now do we?'

'No, Aunt Minnie.'

'Now, there's a café here, Arthur.' She indicated an establishment whose red, white and blue striped awnings fluttered in the autumn breeze. 'I'm going to go in and have a nice cuppa whilst you book in at the White Hart. You'll find it has everything you need.'

She eyed the café longingly. 'You take your time. The room's all paid up for a week. If you're here longer, we'll see to that, so you don't have to worry. I think I might have a slice of their cherry cake too. It's very good, you know.'

Without another word, Aunt Minnie tramped into the Belle Parisienne and left Arthur and his suitcase standing on the pavement.

The Belle Parisienne did not live up to its name. There was wrought ironwork aplenty and tables and chairs set up, rather optimistically on the pavement beneath the striped awnings, but inside the décor hadn't changed since its Mother Hubbard's Cupboard days.

Avril had often wondered if the owners had thought about that name before affixing it to their premises. Surely it didn't give the impression they wanted for a café.

It had been Mother Hubbard's when Avril first came to Lyeminster and the name had rankled from the outset. She had thrilled to the advent of the awnings and wrought iron and waited hopefully for some similar transformation to take place inside. But this hope had been in vain. Perhaps the money had run out. The Belle Parisienne did boast a stainless steel counter but Avril thought this could be an improvement which was due more to health regulations than the aesthetic inclinations of the proprietor.

Whatever, the Belle Parisienne did offer the best iced cream buns Avril had ever tasted and she selected one of these to accompany her pot of tea, forgetting about the cherry cake altogether. Her gaze slid to the blackboard which offered lattes and cappuccinos but Aunt Minnie would order neither of those things so she couldn't either.

The Belle Parisienne was a long narrow establishment with small alcoves well away from both windows and counter where confidential conversations could take place.

Avril slipped into one of these, right at the rear of the café where no one could sit behind her. From here she could see all there was to see. The door leading to the toilets was near to the counter and there was no rear exit. No one was near her and the curtained division between her table and the next, masked any activity below shoulder height.

She gave a huge sigh of relief as she sat down, watching the counter to see if the acoustics carried the sound to the woman who was serving. If they did, she didn't turn around. Avril hadn't seen this particular woman before so she had to make sure.

She opened her bag and took out a device the size and shape of a mobile phone. The screen lit up when she tapped a button and a little symbol moved slowly across it. It stopped then started again and Avril watched until its movements were all within a tiny area.

Arthur was in his room. She fixed this location by pressing a few more buttons, and then she waited.

When the device began to vibrate, she picked it up, saw Arthur emerging from the White Hart, and put it back in her bag taking out a tattered magazine in its stead.

Thankfully, Arthur had taken her at her word and she had had time to deal with everything she needed to do before he strolled in, waved to her and ordered a drink at the counter.

She was happily reading a romantic short story in Aunt Minnie's magazine when he picked up his tray. He had showered by the look of things; his hair still glistened with moisture. Aunt Minnie would berate him for this, warning him of the certainty that he would catch his death, as he joined her at the table. He too had a cup of tea into which he stirred four sachets of sugar. Avril shuddered and folded up her magazine, stuffing it into the depths of Aunt Minnie's capacious handbag.

She glanced at the clock behind the counter. One thirty. She had to keep him amused for another four hours. During this time she would itemise his duties; not calling home, not using any phone that could be traced, and not leaving his hotel after she escorted him back there until she came to collect him again. She would advise him of her arrival by mobile phone and they would meet up in the Belle Parisienne ten minutes afterwards; that way, she knew he wouldn't dare to stray too far.

She handed him a phone. It had no credit and he wasn't told the number of it so he couldn't use that to contact anyone. These telephone calls would be one way traffic only. In fact, Arthur had to keep his head down. By now she had refined a method of transmitting this message without losing her credibility as Aunt Minnie. She had also found a place so bereft of visitors that she could indoctrinate him without any danger of being overheard.

'I thought we'd go and have a look at the castle this afternoon.' She said. 'It'll kill a few hours and I think you'll find it interesting.' She could also issue veiled threats within its thick stone walls. This she usually did in the area of the old cells.

The look on Arthur's face said it all. He wouldn't find it interesting. He would rather spend the afternoon at the dogs, or, failing that, watching the racing on television or, better still, putting a few quid on at the bookies.

Aunt Minnie fixed him with gimlet eyes. 'When I can trust you, you can go to the bookies.' She said.

Arthur's cheekbones reddened. 'I never said a word.' He protested.

'You didn't need to. I can read minds, my lad, and don't you forget it. And don't forget, either, that you don't speak to anyone. So maybe the bookies' is out. You will be able to watch racing in your room though. In the meantime, we'll go to the castle.'

Arthur rose to his feet as meekly as a lamb.

The castle stood on the highest hill in Lyeminster which wasn't saying much because Lyeminster was in a valley. However the city had been a well fortified walled town in the time that it may have needed defending so it had never been much of a problem.

Arthur obediently trailed around after Aunt Minnie becoming more and more fed up as he was called upon to admire the lumpy wall hanging children of the city had made to mark the millennium. He stared into the eyes of Henry VIII and Elizabeth I in the cavernous dining room. He climbed creaking staircases wheezing all the way and mentioning, more than once, his need to stop smoking.

Eventually, Aunt Minnie decided that her charge was beaten down far enough and marched him down the spiral stone steps to the cells.

There were tableaux in the cells, of prisoners in varied states of dilapidation. Some had cuts and bruises, and all were ragged and wretched with the kinds of faces Avril had only seen in Hogarth etchings

These tableaux were viewed through the little hatches set in the doors which the old jailers could open to check on the wellbeing of their charges. Nowadays, a button to the side of the door switched on a light so that the full horror could be exposed in a single bloodcurdling scene. The first one never failed to make visitors gasp. Subsequent cells, whilst equally grisly, didn't have the same shock value.

The last gibbet ever used in Lyeminster was exhibited there too, at the end of the row of cells. Aunt Minnie paused to tell the story of Tom Phelps who, following an unsuccessful attempt to become a highwayman, had rotted within its frame where the old London road met the road from Sturman Cross,. She told how the birds had pecked at his body and how rats ran in and out of his rib cage. Then she told him that she would be in constant contact with Sonny during Arthur's sojourn in Lyeminster and that every detail of his behaviour would be discussed in full.

Arthur's protestations that he would obey all her rules and never venture out of the hotel unescorted, or even out of his room except for meals, that he would discuss his life with no one, that he would keep to the script she had given him, all came very readily after that. Arthur had lively images of rats running around inside his ribcage on the landfill.

Aunt Minnie was pleased. It always worked and today, within the thick stone walls of Lyeminster castle, it had worked yet again

As regards Arthur, all thoughts of sneaking out to a local sports bar after the old girl had left him fled his mind.

He was scared of Sonny. Anyone with any sense was. Sonny didn't know people. Sonny was people. There were tales whispered in dark corners about Sonny. About what his people did to other people; people who didn't do as they were told.

***

He had been nervous about going to Sonny when questions had been asked regarding a small scheme he was running. Sonny had been fine. He had listened. He had pursed his lips and thought about things. He had picked up his pen and tapped it on the desk, turning it over and over between taps. Sonny was never hasty.

The atmosphere in the room had become tense and still. The men behind him, the men guarding the door, hadn't moved a muscle and Arthur could feel his insides turning to liquid. Sweat ran down his back and his chest was feeling tight.

He nearly had a heart attack when Sonny stopped tapping and slammed the pen down on the desk.

'Right,' he said. 'You'll have to lie low for a bit. Now I know a place you can go and I have someone who can look after you. She's an old lady, getting on in years, and I don't want you causing her any trouble. You understand?' Arthur said he understood. 'You go and pack enough stuff for a few days. The boys will come with you to make sure you don't run into any difficulties. I'll make the arrangements. All you have to do is what you're told.' He glared at Arthur, picked up the pen and pointed it at him. 'And you make sure you do.' He said.

Arthur was effusive in his thanks and in his assurances that he would follow whatever instructions he was given to the letter. He still wasn't too sure that he would have the opportunity to follow these instructions. The boys 'going along to make sure he didn't run into difficulties' could be code for a short trip to the landfill site where a few banknotes would change hands and a few heads would be averted and Arthur would be no more. Arthur had heard stories.

However, he had been allowed to pack the suitcase Sonny had provided, and once he had been settled on the train with a ticket to this Lyeminster place – where the hell was that? – And, once the train pulled out of the station, Arthur began to breathe again. Sonny wasn't a bad chap. He was a good pal. He had watched Arthur's back and shown him that he was important to the organisation. Yes, Arthur was almost Sonny's right hand man. He was valuable. He was safe.

At this thought Arthur started to puff himself up. He watched the grim marshalling yards slip by, saw the stacks of containers in a yard just outside the city, heard the dull clank of the wheels on the rails as they cut across the points, held his breath as the wheels squealed against the tracks and breathed again when the brakes were released. He looked down onto back gardens with sheds and greenhouses. He even waved at a couple of kiddies who were playing on a swing. Then he settled back in his seat and watched the suburbs turn into countryside as the conurbation which was London was left behind.

By the time the train reached Lyeminster, Arthur had decided that he was one hell of a guy and that Lyeminster would belong to him. He would soon give this old girl, whoever she was, the slip, and do whatever he wanted. Sonny would never know.

Now he had changed his mind. She might be old. She might be odd. But Aunt Minnie was not dotty. She had a mind like a steel trap. She knew what she wanted and she wanted it yesterday. She was an old lady albeit with the backup of Sonny's operation, but she still had a presence all her own. And she scared Arthur even more than Sonny had done because he knew that if he upset Aunt Minnie, Sonny's fury would be unconfined.

***

Avril was ready to put her feet up but today was Tuesday and the dreaded Arnold Pickard was due tonight. Why couldn't it be Wednesday when Monty would have been her reward for spending this gloomy afternoon with Arthur? A smile broke out all over her face at this thought. Monty was the best. He was like Sonny but he lacked Sonny's nastier traits. With Monty it was fun all the way.

She sat on the bus; her lips curved in a reminiscent smile and watched the passing scene as it trundled past the window from the stop outside the station.

Having divested herself of Aunt Minnie's drab clothes and horrid wig and dreadful shoes, she was beginning to feel more like herself again. The years had dropped from her shoulders as she had changed in the large room dedicated to disabled passengers. Her own cherry red curls bounced around her shoulders and she had carefully outlined her lips in scarlet.

The bus passed in front of the White Hart. Avril glanced up and saw Arthur standing at the window of a room on the first floor. He may have been looking longingly at the bustle of people on London Road hurrying to return to their homes but she was fairly certain that he wouldn't stray. And, if he did, the device that was now in her shoulder bag would vibrate. If she didn't click the correct button within a certain length of time it would automatically call her mobile. If she didn't answer her mobile, it would automatically call Sonny. And, if it called Sonny... well, let's not go there.

Sonny rang between her first gin and tonic and her second; Sonny always had had a wonderful sense of timing.

'Did you manage to sort Arthur out?' he asked.

'Course I did. Piece of cake.'

'Glad to hear it. Where did you take him?'

'To the castle. Where else?'

Sonny burst out laughing and started to cough. 'Lor, gal, I wish I could be a fly on the wall some day and listen in to your lecture.' He said at last.

'It'd make your blood run cold.' Avril laughed. 'You should've seen his face. It were a picture. I haven't had any messages from the tracker.'

'No, his case hasn't moved either. I think he's got the sense to be a good boy. Expect another book club delivery next week.'

'Thanks love.' Avril said. Then she cut the connection and fished around in the bowl of potpourri on the hall table to find the key to the drawer and open the last book club offering.

She slit the tape sealing the parcel with a stiletto letter opener that she kept in the hall table drawer. The bundles of small denomination notes were tightly packed and, as usual, crumpled and dirty. Sometimes they were in such a disgusting state that Avril washed and ironed the notes before folding them neatly and putting them in her purse. She wondered what people in London did with their money to get it in such a state. This was only a passing thought because she knew exactly where this money came from.

Selecting a handful of the cleaner offerings, she folded them up and tucked them into the various compartments of Aunt Minnie's purse. Like her handbag, Aunt Minnie's purse was huge. She also had two of them. Identical. So that she could ferry around quite large sums of money without anyone realising how much she had about her person.

Arnold Pickard would be here soon. Avril loathed him. She provided dinner and conversation for Arnold Pickard plus the usual.

Why he couldn't enjoy his poor wife's company on Tuesday evenings was beyond her.

His wife probably wanted rid of him once a week and had given up 'the usual' as soon as she possibly could. He also persisted in preaching to her all the time. And afterwards, she had to kneel down and beg for forgiveness. If anyone needed to beg forgiveness it was Arnold Pickard, not her.

When she was first visited by the churchwarden he pretended to be on some evangelical mission. She had invited him in as convention dictated and sat with him in prayer when he asked her to.

Then the prayers took a peculiar turn. 'Look upon this sinner.' He had bellowed. 'She follows the trade of Rahab.' Who on earth was Rahab? 'Rahab the prostitute.'

'Now look here –'Avril protested.

Arnold Pickard held up a hand and anointed her with a revolting smile. 'It is not a fault, my dear. It is your calling.'

He then had the nerve to try to negotiate a preferential rate for himself, and Avril, who was caught on the hop by his knowledge, agreed to it. She had hated him ever since. How she wished his foibles were the same as Bob Rogers' and she could beat him with a stick.

All in all, Avril thought her day had gone rather well. But, then again, Avril didn't know that she and Aunt Minnie had been under intense scrutiny from one of her neighbours during the visit to Lyeminster.

***

Lottie had intended spending most of her day in quiet contemplation. Susan had called around to check that she was alright but she had places to go and hadn't stayed. It had been one of those overcast October days. The temperature had dropped suddenly and most houses around The Green sported thin plumes of smoke as fires were lit for the first time since spring.

She had lit her own fire too. Hers was an imitation wood burning stove that actually ran on gas. There would be no mess or smelly firelighters for Lottie Colenso.

Marco would call on her sometime today but talking to him had reminded her of the person she used to be; the fearless person who righted wrongs and confronted overwhelming odds; the person who led where others followed. Now she was skulking in Horse and Trumpet Cottage like a coward and she didn't like the way that made her feel.

When she saw Avril Major stride by her front window carrying a large carpet bag, she picked up her car keys and pulled on a coat. She would go into Lyeminster. The devil could take Keith Kendal, and she hoped he would, but she was now nothing whatsoever to do with the person she used to be.

The little red car was the perfect vehicle for camouflage in Lyeminster and Lottie slid behind the wheel turning over the engine and switching the fan to full blow in the hope of dispelling the autumnal chill more quickly.

The Lyeminster bus was just pulling away from the stop when she turned into Main Street. She slowed and followed it at a distance. She was trying to think of some reason to visit the city, somewhere to go, where to park, how to appear inconspicuous in case Keith Kendal was about.

She pulled into a parking space across the road from the station when the bus halted at a stop. No inspiration had descended upon her and she didn't want to drive aimlessly. Then she saw Avril Major alight and run across the road. Interesting. Where was Avril going? She was certainly travelling light.

Lottie was back in hunting mode. She was interested in Avril Major's movements since she had seen the money in the parcel, and it felt good to have the blood circulating again and her brain clicking into gear. She locked the car and sauntered across the road. A travel agent had an office just inside the station entrance and she slipped inside to riffle through the pages of a brochure whilst looking out for Avril. What on earth was she doing? This was madness.

No, she decided. This was not madness, this was therapy.

Her interest piqued when Avril reappeared. She was still carrying the carpet bag she had with her when she passed Horse and Trumpet Cottage that morning.

'Do you need any help?'

Lottie, shocked by the sudden appearance of a sales assistant, just had time to see Avril disappear into the disabled toilet before she turned to assure the woman that she was fine just browsing by herself. The assistant offered another brochure and Lottie took it without looking to see what it was. Then a frumpy old woman emerged from the disabled toilet. She was carrying Avril's carpet bag plus another bag otherwise Lottie would never have recognised her. Automatically, Lottie glanced down at the woman's legs. Yes that was Avril alright. Avril had good legs.

Waiting until Avril had passed the travel agent's window; Lottie thanked the sales assistant and tucked the brochures under her arm. Then she left in hot pursuit of Avril. This was fun. Why on earth was Avril coming to Lyeminster, changing into a disguise – and an unflattering one at that – and, she blinked and recovered her wits. Avril was going down the stairs towards the platform and leaving a bag in a left luggage locker. Lottie was enthralled.

She changed her vantage point from the travel agent's shop to the bookstall across the way. It was nearer to the stairs that led to the trains and had two exits so she was less likely to be discovered.

Mindful of drawing attention to herself, she picked up a book and flipped pages over whilst looking out of the window.

When Avril came bustling into the shop Lottie thought she had been discovered and took the book she was holding to the counter. She paid for it all the time waiting for the expected accusation to be directed at her.

It didn't come and when Lottie tucked the package containing the book under her arm with the travel brochures she saw Avril approaching the large station clock beneath which stood a tall cadaverous man.

Lottie was pleased with her first visit to Lyeminster. She watched Avril and the man march out of the station arm in arm. Avril talked to him constantly. Lottie followed. She watched Avril chattering away to the man until she parted from him outside a cafe and Lottie watched the man cross the road to the White Hart Hotel. How odd. Lottie retraced her steps to her car and drove back to Whittington Edge. She could almost believe she had seen part of a mystery. This was obviously a stupid thought but it kept Lottie from feeling totally redundant.

Horse and Trumpet Cottage was warm and welcoming when she arrived home. She hung her coat neatly in the hall cupboard and put the bag containing the book on her desk and carried the travel brochures through to the living room dropping them onto the seat beside her as she sank onto the sofa and kicked off her shoes.

Her conversation with Jane Pendleton ran through her head. Lottie had never been troubled by self-doubt. She had a clear mind and ice-cold logic – or, at least, that was what she had been told.

It had never played her false. She didn't succumb to emotion and her life was clear of ex husbands and children. It wasn't until she retired that she wondered if she hadn't kept her life too uncluttered.

She didn't want to marry again; she knew that. Lottie needed her own space. But the situation with Keith Kendal had set her off wondering why she had reacted the way she had.

She loved her job and resented having to leave. However, having thought about it, she could have done many things differently and had not needed to leave at all.

She could have told her manager about the perceived threat and organised a move to an office far away at the other end of the country. The police wanted her as a witness and she could have stayed away until the trial was over and Keith Kendal safely incarcerated.

She had not done that, or any of the other things she could have done. Lottie was not given to soul-searching but, recently she had begun to wonder if she was intended to take a different route through the next phase of her life.

The parish magazine Jane left the day before was still on the coffee table. Lottie picked it up and flipped over the pages. Cassie Mellon at Hallelujah House had an advertisement in there. She offered meditation and holistic therapies. Lottie was impressed.

Charles Pendleton wasn't trying to hog the limelight; he was allowing other beams of illumination to shine too. Charles Pendleton went up in Lottie's estimations. A massage...now that was an idea, she could go for that.

The word was out now about the body on the roundabout.

Police cars had been circling The Green all day, or so it seemed. Occasionally the chatter and beeps of their radios could be heard and Lottie had been on tenterhooks since she returned from Lyeminster waiting for the knock to come at her own door; hoping that Marco Romero would be on the doorstep when it did.

Then, suddenly, the cars all moved off leaving The Green silent in the dusk. Lottie felt the tension leave her body and then the expected rap at the door came.

'Come in, Marco.' She said.

'I hope you checked through the spy hole before you unlocked the door.' He said.

'I did.'

He looked at her for a long moment and nodded. 'Make sure you keep doing that. Don't get lax when you know Keith Kendal is interested in you.'

'Don't worry, I won't. I don't feel relaxed at all.' She blinked to ease the burning in her eyes and led the way through to the kitchen.

'No coffee for me, thanks.' Marco said. He looked at the display on his mobile phone and placed it on the table next to his radio and notebook before sitting down. 'How well do you know the people around The Green?'

'I know Susan Holland very well.' She said. 'She's really my only friend in Whittington Edge. Except for Jane Pendleton, of course; she's the rector's wife and I only met her yesterday but she seems a very genuine woman. Why?

'There's someone – I don't want to say who at this stage – who isn't what they seem.'

'And you want me to find out who it is?'

'I hope I'm not going to regret asking this, but yes. I know you of old, Lottie, and I know that you will ferret around until you find things out Nothing will stop you. You're more relentless in your search for answers than most of the detectives I know. That is meant as a compliment in case you're wondering.'

Lottie grinned. 'You're not just trying to keep me occupied and away from the real investigation, are you? Because, I wasn't intending to interfere.'

'I know you won't interfere. You never have in the past but your insights border on the mystical and I would like to make use of them if you're willing. So, what I would like you to do is talk to your neighbours, all of them if you can and see if you can find the one who doesn't ring true to me. Then, if you do identify them, tune in and see what you pick up. If no one stands out to you then I shall know that I'm imagining things. Will you do that?'

'Of course,' happiness was zinging through Lottie like the effervescence of a new love. She was back working with Marco again. 'It is someone I have access to, I hope. Whittington Edge adheres to very firm lines of demarcation. For instance, the only way I could talk to Mrs Bettinson would be to enlist her services as a cleaner, and only the really brave do that.'

'It's not Mrs Bettinson and that's the last clue you're getting.' Marco grinned. Then he sobered again. 'Don't be drawn out by anyone. Don't try to question them. All I want you to do is talk to them about things they are interested in; you'll find out all you need to know that way.' He looked at Lottie's astonished face and blew out a sigh. 'I'm teaching you to suck eggs, aren't I?'

'Just a bit,' Lottie was grateful for the steel that this had injected into her spine because she had been feeling a bit weepy.

'Let's have a coffee after all.' Marco grinned.

CHAPTER FOUR

Lottie awoke on Wednesday with a real sense of purpose; she was going to investigate. But, where was she to start?

In less than an hour, Lottie had dug a new notebook out of her desk drawer and was writing down a list of the people who lived around The Green. She would find ways to talk to each and every one of them and discover who it was that struck a discordant note when Marco spoke to them.

Her list wasn't extensive. There was Charles Pendleton and Jane at the rectory, Cassie Mellon at Hallelujah House, Bill Warbeck and Atlantis Warbeck at The Crow's Nest; the landlord of The Priest at Prayer was only temporary so it was doubtful that it would be useful if it were him but Lottie was thorough so she would see what she could find out. Then, unless she had missed anyone, only Susan and Avril Major were left. Surely there must be more people living around The Green than that. Lottie went to her front window and looked out. There were several cottages, homes to neighbours whom she had neither met nor seen.

She rested her notebook on the wide window sill and tried to work out the names of the residents. Where she failed, she noted the addresses giving each house a page of its own.

When she had finished she was dismayed at the gaps in her knowledge. She decided that an early morning stroll was called for. She would note down the names of the houses and find ways of contacting their residents.

***

In Pennyman Cottage Beau Derek was in bits. He dragged his hands through his long blond hair and wept into the phone. 'It's her, I know it's her.' He sobbed. 'It's my Adelaide; my lovely Adelaide.

Someone has taken her away from me. She didn't leave after all. I knew she would wait for me, Edward. I knew she wouldn't run away from me.'

'I know old chap.' Edward, Earl Berringer, far away at Berringer Hall, was also on the point of tearing out his hair. Beau was his brother and his heir and Edward loved him even though he found him as easy to understand as a Chinese puzzle box. 'Come home, Beau. Let us look after you. Sylvia misses you too.'

'I can't leave now.' Beau's voice was little more than a whisper. 'I must stay and arrange her funeral. She'll have the best, Edward, the very best.'

'I know.' The earl soothed. 'I know you'll give her the best but bear in mind that this may not be Adelaide at all. Keep hoping that it isn't. We both want Adelaide to turn up safe and well.' The earl took a deep breath. 'Would you like me to come and stay with you for a while?'

'No I couldn't ask that.'

'How about if I sent one of the girls?' Earl Berringer had four daughters. They all adored Beau and he hoped that one would offer to go to her uncle and see him through this ordeal. But, even as he uttered the words, he knew that his countess, Sylvia, would veto the idea. A young girl was really not the best companion for a middle aged, grief stricken man; especially a man as nervy as Beau. He began to formulate another plan.

'No, Edward, really,' Beau said, 'I love the girls but Pennyman Cottage is not the place for any of them at the moment. I feel a bit of a mess. They would fuss around me and make me worse. Sorry.'

'You're right, of course.' He paused for a second or two but then inspiration struck. 'I know exactly the right person for the job.'

'Who?' Beau Derek asked, not stopping to think that being referred to as a 'job' may not be the most flattering thing.

'Atlas.'

'Atlas? By Jove, do you think he'd come?' suddenly, Beau's world seemed a brighter place.

***

Dexter Hardman, Atlas to his public school friends, was feeling at a loose end as luck would have it.

Dexter was the product of an affluent if not titled family. He was one of those men who seem to have been born with every advantage. He was tall and handsome. At school he had been a strong sportsman and at Cambridge he was a rowing blue.

Everything he did, he did well. But he lacked the desire to apply himself to one thing. His independent means gave him the freedom not to worry about making a living. Therefore he had never launched himself into a career.

His qualities were well known amongst his friends and small, lucrative commissions regularly came his way. He had great organisational skills, great physical strength – hence the name Atlas – and he was the kind of man you could call upon at a moment's notice to babysit your emotionally raw younger brother and hold him together until he regained his grip on life.

'Beau, you say?' Dexter said. 'And they think that this body is that of his lady friend? I heard about it on the news, naturally. I didn't know any identification had been made. Of course I'll go. I'll get onto the estate agents straight away.'

An adventure. Dexter Hardman loved adventure. The first job was to contact an estate agent in this Whittington Edge place and find a suitable house. Then he needed to put the covers on his own place and... Yes, there was a lot to do. Dexter rang directory enquiries.

*****

Gwennie Furlong was Whittington Edge's busiest citizen. Long before Lottie, Beau, Earl Berringer and Dexter Hardman were dealing with their own excitements and problems, Gwennie was up and about.

Gwennie lived at Camp Hill, the council estate half a mile or so from The Green along Welham lane. She lived in the house on Burns Hill where she had been born thirty three years before.

To say that Gwennie shared the house with the ghost of her mother would be to understate the case. The late Mrs. Furlong was constantly sitting on her daughter's shoulder upbraiding her for every perceived fault. Gwennie was never free of the nagging voice that had made her old before her years.

So Gwennie tried, very hard. She was the person every organiser of every event and charity came to first. She worked at the library every day, covering hours convenient to everyone but herself. This morning as every morning, Gwennie's first job was to attend to Bella Fleet of Templar House. Mrs Fleet was feeling the weight of her almost ninety years and needed help and encouragement to prepare for her day. Gwennie liked Mrs. Fleet. She was full of kindness and wisdom with occasional dashes of querulousness when she was in severe pain. Gwennie could cope with that; she had grown up with querulousness.

As her cycle brakes squeaked to a halt Gwennie could hear her mother tut-tutting in her ear. Gwennie wondered whether the problem for mother was the cycle brakes or the time she was devoting to Mrs Fleet. She was soon to find out. Gwennie pulled out her keys and let herself in. Mother's voice cut in before she was over the threshold, 'you never waited on me hand and foot. I could have done with a bit of help but you never helped me.' Gwennie shook her head to dispel the complaining voice and made her way upstairs.

***

Gwennie next stop was the church hall to ensure that it was ready for the meeting of the Flower Guild.

Satisfied that all was well there, Gwennie emerged onto the corner of The Green and Church Lane and caught sight of Lottie in her front window. She waved tentatively and was delighted when Lottie looked up, smiled and mimed the offer of a cup of tea.

Gwennie hastened to the side door of Horse and Trumpet Cottage and was soon in Lottie's gorgeous kitchen. 'She thinks she's better than you, my girl' mother said. Gwennie almost replied 'she is, and I've you to thank for that'.

'I wanted to see you, Lottie,' Gwennie began, 'to make sure you had heard that a body was found in the village on Monday.' Lottie pushed a cup of tea in a delicate bone china cup and saucer towards Gwennie and picked up her own favourite china mug. She traced the design of red poppies with a carefully polished fingernail.

'I found it, Gwennie,' she said at last. 'The police asked me to say nothing otherwise I would have told you.'

She had been afraid that this most timid of her friends would be hurt to have been denied this knowledge, but Gwennie Furlong was a better person than that. Shock registered on her gentle face and then she was reaching across, covering one of Lottie's hands with her own and squeezing gently.

Lottie gave Gwennie a potted account of what had happened before moving on to things she wanted to know.

'I was looking around The Green when I saw you. I've realised that I know very few people and I want to remedy that. You know everyone Gwennie. I wonder if you would give me a few names so that, when I'm walking around, I can address them correctly.'

Gwennie was only too happy to oblige.

***

Cassie Mellon began each day with three hallelujahs. Her house stood on the side of The Green opposite Horse and Trumpet Cottage; the back of the house facing over the fields towards Camp Hill. It was hemmed in by Rose Cottage on one side and The Crow's Nest, home of artist Bill Warbeck and his wife Atlantis, on the other.

Cassie had bought Bide-a-While ten years ago, on the occasion of her last divorce, and changed its name to Hallelujah House even though to call it a house was to give the two-up -two-down delusions of grandeur.

On the Camp Hill side of Hallelujah House there was a Juliet balcony leading off the larger bedroom. Here, every morning as soon as the sunlight woke her, Cassie opened the French windows that led to the balcony, threw back her head, lifted her hands high to the heavens and sang out three lusty hallelujahs.

'Hallelujah!' She boomed. Birds were catapulted from their roosts and a whole murder of crows erupted into the air and cascaded down to the ground like a whirlwind of burnt rags. A murder of crows, a parliament of owls, and, a convocation of eagles. Cassie had been inspired by the collective nouns belonging to birds and remembered them still; an exultation of larks, an unkindness of ravens a watch of nightingales.

She recalled herself to the important work at hand. 'Hallelujah!' She boomed again. A distant kitchen window slammed shut muffling the curses being uttered by her nearest neighbour.

'HALLELUJAH!' The crows, having settled, now swirled up again.

'For goodness sake,' a voice cried out. 'Put a sock in it, Cassie.'

Having filled her lungs with God's good air, Cassie Mellon ignored her neighbour, telling herself silently that he was a vexation to the spirit.

She lifted her thoughts above such mundane things as Bill Warbeck and retired to her sanctuary. She lit candles and incense sticks. She folded herself into the shape of a pretzel and took a deep breath.

She filled the room with pink light. Today she was going to bring love into Whittington Edge. The aura of the entire village had been slashed to ribbons by the grisly discovery of the body.

She had to restore the equilibrium of her village, send healing to the poor person who had found the remains and send healing to the soul of the victim herself. It was going to be a busy morning.

Resting her hands palms upwards on her knees she took two more deep breaths before beginning to chant the mantra her guru had bestowed on her in India.

Minutes passed, Cassie was chilled out. She was grounded, centred and ready to work. She sent out love to the entire area. Slowly she encompassed the whole earth, the universe and beyond.

Cassie had love to spare and share with everyone.

'Peace and light' she murmured, 'peace and light'. The doorbell rang disturbing her peace and light. 'Oh bugger,' said Cassie, 'who the hell can that be?'

She tried to unwind her legs and almost fell over in the attempt. Running downstairs was no mean feat either; her half numbed ankles didn't want to cooperate. And then, when she reached the front door there was no one there, just a new telephone directory propped against the door frame.

Cassie picked it up and dropped it on the sofa then dragged herself back upstairs again to continue her daily programme with her half hour of meditation.

***

Bill Warbeck was setting up his easel pretending that this was for a new study. Carefully he placed a canvas on the pegs and stepped back to admire its pristine whiteness soon to welcome the sensuous strokes of his brushes.

He it was who had shouted to Cassie. Honestly the woman had no thought for anyone else. As if he didn't have enough to cope with, Atlantis kept brewing up foul smelling potions all over the house. Well, she wasn't going to burn anything in here. He had noticed her gazing at his sink and knew she was wondering if she could use it to dye the revolting wool that she insisted on gleaning from the barbed wire fences and hedgerows of the surrounding fields.

Atlantis chose that precise moment to drift, as languidly as her six foot frame would allow, into his studio and, at exactly the same time, the canvas slipped against the pegs of the easel and crashed to the floor.

Bill cursed, found a dent on the corner of the canvas and cursed some more.

'The gallery's going to love that; a canvas damaged before even the first stroke of paint is applied.' He rubbed the corner with a grubby thumb.

'Use a new one, darling.' Atlantis glided behind him and rested her cheek against his shoulder; not easy to do when Bill was several inches shorter than she.

'I can't afford to waste materials.' He barked. He was feeling sulky. Other artists could sell heaps of bricks and pickled livestock. He found it hard to shift even the smallest of his pieces. And his stuff was good; damned good. Better than theirs at any rate.

'No, darling, I know.' She cooed at him as she would a child in a tantrum. 'But you use a nice new one and get out your best colours and paint a picture that will knock their socks off. That'll show them.'

He was about to complain that he wasn't a toddler to be cajoled into good temper with patronising words when he remembered that an argument would delay her because she would insist on staying to chivvy him back into a good mood. And the last thing he wanted was to delay her. Today was the day that Atlantis went to… where the dickens did she go? He couldn't remember and, to be honest, he didn't care, provided she did go.

She planted a kiss on his ear. 'It'll show those planners too.' She stroked his hair. 'Just wait until they see your exhibition. And when your photo is in the paper and the world asks why Bill Warbeck, darling of the art galleries in London and New York, is not allowed to have a north facing studio. Then everyone will see what philistines they are, won't they?'

'Yes, they will.' Bill rubbed his face against the softness of her cheek, somewhat mollified, and passed the damaged canvas to Atlantis so that she could be the one to discard it and find him a new spotless recipient for what was bound to be a masterpiece.

'Shall I turn on the lights?' Atlantis crooned in her gentlest voice, not at all sure that the crisis was over.

'You may as well.' He shrugged and puffed out a few mighty breaths.

'I have to go or I shall be late for college, darling. Will you be alright on your own for a while?'

'Of cour – 'his snapped reply was cut off short. 'I'm sorry,' he raked his hair with a hand still stippled with the cobalt blue he had been using the night before. He didn't want to upset her. The last thing he needed was her to change her mind and stay. Because then she would know what he was really planning – and that would never do. He glanced quickly at his wristwatch. Crikey, the girl would be here in less than half an hour.

'You go, darling. And don't hurry back on my account. I intend to work for at least five hours nonstop. So go and enjoy yourself and don't give me a moment's thought.'

Today was the day Atlantis taught handicrafts at Lyeminster College. She had to load up her car with all her equipment and Summer Saunders would soon be here.

With self-serving generosity, he offered to help and soon had the car loaded and Atlantis driving away with a happy smile on her face.

Right. She was gone. Now for Summer. Bill hurried back into The Crow's Nest rubbing his hands together.

Inside the studio he pulled out the chaise longue that Atlantis had bought for him to rest on whilst waiting for his muse to descend.

He glanced out of the window to the fields and the footpath that ran at the back of the houses on the southern edge of The Green. There was no sign of her yet. Good, because he didn't want Atlantis to see her and come back to investigate.

If he had his timings right, Cassie Mellon would be back in her ridiculous yoga pose now and wouldn't see Summer Saunders arrive. These pieces of subterfuge had to be carefully planned.

Cassie, deep in contemplation, heard the crash of the dolphin doorknocker when Bill slammed the door but, in her meditative state, the penetrating sound passed her by as swiftly and silently as the whisper of an angel's wing.

***

Bill removed the new canvas from the easel and carefully withdrew his current masterpiece. He had been working on it for weeks since he watched Jason Flint and Summer Saunders cavorting on The Green outside his window.

He had taken photographs to support his request for an antisocial behaviour order. These young hooligans should be stopped. Why couldn't they confine their activities to Camp Hill? Why should The Green have to watch them?

Later, when he had developed the pictures, he made enlargements of Summer Saunders' face. She was a beauty. One picture captured her with her head thrown back. Jason Flint had been tickling her but the expression on her face was ecstatic and Bill Warbeck's mind wound itself into coils. This common slut of a girl would be his new muse. Then he had approached her and she had agreed to model for him.

His picture, 'Summer' was complete. He had told the gallery that it would be with them early next week. The gallery owner was going through a dry spell and was therefore prepared to paint a wall in the complementary shade Bill suggested would show the picture to its best advantage. He was half-heartedly excited about it too. He would have been enraptured had Bill allowed him to see it but Bill was secretive and his work erratic so the gallery owner's enthusiasm was guarded.

He had tipped off the art critic of the Lyeminster Echo that there may a major event taking place in his gallery and the art critic, starved of anything really noteworthy, was waiting to bring his photographer along and provide much needed publicity.

Bill knew that this was his best work yet. He knew that he was playing with fire inviting Summer Saunders to his studio again. Using so young a girl as a model was reckless but Bill never thought before he acted. He could still recall the trouble the last girl had caused. They had had to move to Whittington Edge because of her. But he couldn't stop himself. He couldn't resist dancing close to the flames.

***

Lottie had seen Atlantis Warbeck leave The Crow's Nest so there was no point visiting her. Templar House was out because Mrs Fleet, the owner, was an old lady who was almost bedridden. She would have to ask Gwennie when a visit would be possible.

Who on earth could she speak to? She was desperate to get on with her task and no opportunities had presented themselves. She had noted all the information Gwennie had given her in her notebook and knew she needed this promised activity.

Lottie had been trying to work out a way of approaching Beau Derek. He didn't actually live on The Green, his home, Pennyman Cottage, was hidden away just around the corner off Welham Lane. Susan had pointed it out to her but its entrance from the lane was formed by overlapping privet hedges so the house itself was obscured from view. Only the barley sugar chimneystacks were visible from the road.

She was in the kitchen already clad in her coat and warm winter boots walking up and down, pondering her problem. If Beau Derek had been introduced to her things would be easier. No, they wouldn't. What possible reason could she have to visit his home?

A rotund little man in clerical garb chose that moment to scurry past the Church Lane door. She hadn't spoken to the new rector. Perhaps this really was Charles Pendleton. Perhaps he was 'the one'.

She gave him a few minutes to unlock the church and get inside then she slipped out of the side door and followed him.

It had been a long time since Lottie ventured into St Jude's. The church was cold and clammy and the breath-clouded air redolent with the unmistakeable scent of old hymn books. Of Charles Pendleton there was no sign. She bowed her head to the cross and walked part way up the aisle before sliding into a pew and kneeling in prayer.

A door opened just as she sat back on the pew and the rector appeared. He saw her immediately and came down the side aisle to greet her.

Lottie soon found herself being invited into the vestry where the rector told her he had just made tea.

Ever since Susan had told her that Charles Pendleton and Jane were married, Lottie had puzzled about it. Jane was young, rich and beautiful. Charles was small, rotund and an unlikely choice for such a woman. After talking to him for half an hour, Lottie could see exactly what it was that had attracted Jane, and what continued to hold her attention. Charles Pendleton was kind.

'I met your wife.' Lottie said.

'Yes, she said so.' Charles beamed. He picked up the teapot and filled the dainty cup he had found for her. 'She loves it here, as I do myself. Whittington Edge is such a charming place. Have you lived here long, Mrs Colenso?'

'I moved in about six months ago.' Lottie thanked him for the tea and placed the cup on the edge of his desk. 'I lived in Lyeminster prior to that. When I retired I was looking for something different.'

'Peace after the hustle and bustle of a busy career, perhaps?'

'Possibly. I wanted...I'm not sure.' She sipped her tea noticing that Charles Pendleton watched her, a gentle smile curving his lips. He was possibly the most peaceful man she had ever encountered. 'This is going to sound silly but I think I'm looking for something more. My parents are doing work of a missionary nature. They left my brother and me with a maiden aunt when we were barely in our teens and took off for a tiny pacific island where they opened a school.'

'Was that hard on you and your brother?'

'No, not really. We had the option of joining them but we had different ideas and I suppose we were at that age when the idea of 'losing' the parents is quite attractive.' Lottie laughed. 'Our aunt called herself a bluestocking. She had her work at the university and a confidence in the ability of the young to bring themselves up if only they were left alone to do so.'

'How unusual. And how did that work out for you?' Charles Pendleton was smiling broadly now.

'Surprisingly well. We were fed and watered as she called it and were expected to fill in little forms to say where we were, who we were with and how we could be contacted whenever we went out. But otherwise we were free agents. It made us both very independent and I suppose instilled a sense of responsibility in us. I haven't really thought about it before but I think she did a good job.'

She had never talked about this to anyone. Charles Pendleton certainly had the knack of getting people to open up.

'And now?'

'Now I find myself interested in this New Age philosophy.' She looked at the rector and grimaced. 'I hope you don't find this offensive. I don't want you to feel that I'm rejecting the church; nothing could be further from the truth.'

'The church teaches that there is only one God.' The rector said. 'Therefore, no matter what route is taken to reach Him, there is only one final destination. Others would disagree with me but I am interested in the New Age philosophies too. There is a lot to be gained from them. The world is waking up to that and the established church must take notice.'

Lottie was stunned. 'I'm impressed.' She said. 'An open mind is a very attractive thing.'

'A wise man once likened minds to parachutes; they only work when they are open.' Charles Pendleton smiled his Mr Pickwick smile. 'May I suggest that you talk to Cassie Mellon? She is interested in a variety of holistic therapies and different ways of looking at things. I find her fascinating company. You may too.'

'I saw that she was advertising in the church magazine.' Lottie said. 'I was intending to call her.'

'I have been told by the police that you found the poor woman on the roundabout.' Charles said into the ensuing silence. 'I must admit that I thought that may have been what brought you to St Jude's today.'

'I did say a few words for her.' Lottie bowed her head.

Tears burned at the back of her eyes again. 'Obviously I didn't know her; I didn't live here and it's unlikely that she ever crossed my path in life.'

'But, in death, she has crossed your path and Cassie Mellon will tell you, I'm sure, that we always meet people for some purpose.'

'Do you really think that?'

'I see a lot that attracts me to the theory.' Charles Pendleton nodded his head slowly. 'I have talked to Cassie at length. I flatter myself that I never discount anything out of hand and this idea makes a lot of sense. Since discussing this with Cassie, I have considered many encounters which have taken place in my own life and I have found my reasons. Perhaps you will someday work out why you had to be the person who discovered this lady.'

Charles watched her for a moment. Then, when she didn't say anything he began talking about St Jude's and its long history.

'You have certainly researched it thoroughly'. Lottie said at last.

'Not I,' Charles corrected, 'Lord Derek. He is very interested in Whittington Edge and has amassed quite an archive of the village, its history, the old families etc. I see you are looking puzzled. Lord Derek Nash; I believe he is known in the village as Beau Derek.'

'How intriguing. I wonder if he has any information about the old Horse and Trumpet pub. It would be lovely to have copies of any photographs. I could frame them and put them on my walls.'

'Would you like me to contact him on your behalf?'

'I couldn't ask you to do that.'

'Part of my calling is to foster good relationships amongst my flock.'

Lottie could see by the twinkle in the rector's eyes that this was not meant to be taken entirely seriously.

***

The prison in Lyeminster was a huge grey stone affair with turrets and huge door in the shape and style of a portcullis. It looked more like a castle than the castle did and it was about five hundred years younger than the castle. It had been built to intimidate back in Victorian times. By way of contrast the prison where Edna Derry was incarcerated was a modern red brick building and the visitors' centre where Jane

Pendleton was taken to for her meeting with Edna was more like a department store coffee bar than the grim surroundings she had been expecting.

Edna was already seated at a table when Jane walked into the room. She was so busy looking around at her surroundings that she hardly gave Edna a glance. When she realised how rude she must seem she smiled broadly and turned the smile on the woman sitting watching her.

She was halfway to the table, hand outstretched ready to shake hands with the prisoner who had taken the trouble to seek her out, when the truth hit her. Jane stopped dead in her tracks. Her breath caught in her throat. It couldn't be. It had to be. It was.

She hadn't changed. Her olive skin was sallow but she hadn't changed. Darkness rushed in on Jane Pendleton and surrounded her, crushing the breath from her body as she fainted clean away.

***

Atlantis left her classroom in the college and paused by the front door. Should she go to the refectory for lunch? It was a sunny day. It would be quite crisp outside but she needed the cobwebs of the morning's lesson blowing away and there was a good sandwich shop near the market. She would pick up a sandwich and take it to the town hall square to eat it.

It was in town hall square that Atlantis' eyes seemed to deceive her. She had just taken a large bite of her succulent chicken salad sandwich and closed her eyes the better to savour the mingled flavours when footsteps at a rhythm she recognised marched towards her.

Atlantis was hastily trying to swallow her bite of sandwich when she opened her eyes and was startled to see a frumpy old woman walking towards her bench rather than the ultra chic Avril Major that she expected.

She paused, blinked, and then took another bite of her sandwich. She surreptitiously looked again as the woman and the tall, bored stranger, with whom her arm was linked, walked by.

That was odd. The woman had looked straight through Atlantis as if she had never seen her before. But Atlantis was not fooled. That was definitely Avril Major.

***

Bill Warbeck could hardly contain his excitement. She was here. Summer Saunders; sixteen going on twenty four, she was beautiful, ripe and surrounded by a faint aura of sin. Bill knew that his cheeks were flushed and hoped that she would put his high colour down to overindulgence in alcohol.

He looked at Summer Saunders walking down the bridle path behind The Crow's Nest and looked at 'Summer' and realised that he didn't need her here at all. His masterpiece was complete. Any more paint would spoil a brilliant piece of work.

The Summer in the picture had skin that was luminous, the colours of the emerald satin swathed around her and the blue of her eyes were vibrant. The satin should really have been blue to echo her eyes but Bill was a tight-fisted man without the imagination to change the colour of either the eyes or the satin. The black hair that fell in a cascade over the arm of the chaise longue to pool on the floor shone glossily, the composition was inspired.

But he had engaged her as a model and he wasn't paying her for nothing so he removed 'Summer' from the easel and replaced it with a gaudy abstract concoction that would be criticised for being derivative if ever it went to the gallery. He had painted this during his Picasso period. He had not only put the eyes on the same side of the woman's face he had also given her three eyes. He had given her three of everything else too.

'This is it.' Bill said when Summer Saunders approached.

He had covered what he now thought of as 'the Picasso Summer' with a cloth and put it on the easel. He had wanted to flaunt the real thing in front of his young model. He wanted to show her the sort of work he could do but Summer Saunders was unlikely to appreciate fine art. Pearls before swine, Bill told himself. Besides, some kindly and caring spirit had tapped him on the shoulder when he saw her walking by and told him that this girl could cause him trouble.

It was a pity he hadn't thought of that earlier before coaxing her to pose for him but Bill only ever thought when it was too late. Now he wanted her gone before she could get any crazy ideas so he swept the sheet away and exposed the portrait that he had told her was inspired by her beauty.

'Christ! That's the most God-awful thing I've ever seen.' Summer Saunders said.

He had been proved right. Summer Saunders was a philistine. She should never be allowed to see the beautiful picture that was her namesake. He hugged this knowledge to himself like a comfort blanket. She was common and had drenched herself in some nose piercing perfume that made his sinuses prickle and run, and she talked incessantly about 'Jase'.

His Summer was a naiad. She skipped around rivers singing the sweet song of the rippling water. She was a wood nymph who dwelt deep in forests where man never trod. She drifted amongst the trees and played tunes on the sunlit leaves.

His Summer bore no relation to this... he really had no words to describe her. She repelled him. She made his artistic soul scream with horror and he wished he had never contacted her; his dream was so much better than the reality.

'When my Dad sees this he'll want to know why I had to take my top off.' She said. Reality hit Bill like a sandbag. Her Dad? He had to get rid of her. Now.

He decided that the wise man would tell his wife of this sudden departure from abstract studies. And he would do exactly that. There was no other way.

He hadn't thought through at what point he would tell Atlantis. He couldn't hide the picture away; given the amount of time he had taken over it. And it was his best work ever. And, having produced his best work, he needed to exhibit it. Besides, the gallery was waiting for it to be delivered. Bill's brain was in a turmoil of panic. He scratched rough depictions of Summer Saunders on the Picasso Summer canvas; it was already dreadful, nothing could make it worse.

He needed the world to see the sort of work he was capable of producing. He needed recognition for his art. He needed fame.

Then those feeble little pen-pushers at the council would be sure to allow him to knock a large window in the façade of his Grade II listed house so that he could catch the north light just as Atlantis had said. That would show them.

The jangle of an alarm startled him and Summer, who wasn't startled at all, said, 'wassat?'

'It's a reminder not to let this session overrun as I have an appointment.' He said.

'Ok.' Summer leapt up from the chaise longue and clambered back into her anorak. 'Twenty quid.' She held out her hand and watched as Bill dug out his wallet and extracted four five pound notes, careful not to let her see the fat wad of cash that resided there.

She stuffed the notes into her jeans pocket and struck a pose. Her eyes ran the length of his squat little body and back to his face. Bill kept his features still and waited. 'So, when do you want me next?' She said.

Bill didn't want her back ever again; she had revolted him so much that he no longer felt a flicker of lust when he looked at her.

'I'll give you a call.' He said. 'I'm not sure at the moment.'

She shrugged, 'lemme know'. She blew her chewing gum out in a bubble and he watched, transfixed with distaste, as it burst with a snap.

And she was gone.

Surreptitiously, he watched her progress down the footpath behind the houses, silently urging her to walk faster, until she passed from view out onto the Welham Lane that led to Camp Hill. Then he breathed again.

He had to see Atlantis and he had to see her now.

Somehow, Atlantis would know what to do. Atlantis loved him and would save him. He packed his paints away and changed into a sweater and jeans and, as quickly as his legs and the red and yellow bus could reach Lyeminster, he presented himself at

Lyeminster College. Luck was with him. Atlantis' class had only minutes to run.

***

The receptionist told him the way to the refectory and he sat with a rapidly cooling coffee that he didn't want and a chamomile tea for Atlantis. Chamomile was supposed to calm the nerves, or so he hoped. He hoped it would calm the temper too.

Atlantis was soon seated across the table from him. Bill looked around. The refectory was full of students. She couldn't shout at him here. Atlantis watched him.

'What have you done?' she said. He opened his mouth to lie.

'I said, what have you done? ' And out it all came.

***

As soon as the early bus from Whittington Edge dropped her in town, Avril made her way to the Belle Parisienne to meet Arthur. There had been no messages warning of his absconding from the White Hart so she knew that he had stayed within its walls. She had been in the café for over an hour eating a hearty full English breakfast and reading the Daily Mail that the café kindly supplied.

All the time she had watched the screen of her tracking device. Arthur was in his room.

The newspaper was full of a murdered woman discovered in the early morning by a paper boy on his rounds. That should at least push 'The Maples Murder', as they had named the grisly discovery on the roundabout, off the front pages.

The Maples Murder, honestly these reporters; they had to give everything, even this terrible tragedy, a catchy little buzzword. What would they call this new one, this – she searched the report for the victim's name – this Rosa Garnett? She shook the pages back into line and folded the paper up as neatly as she could in deference to the next customer and returned her attention to her coffee.

When her breakfast ritual was complete, she called Arthur demanding his attendance at the Belle Parisienne and went up to the counter to purchase a pot of tea. The waitress offered to bring it over and scooped up the used crockery at the same time.

Avril foraged in Aunt Minnie's bag and pulled out the tatty magazine. She was re-reading the same story as yesterday when Arthur breezed in eager for company.

'What have you got lined up for us today Aunt Minnie?' He grinned giving her the benefit of a row of long, yellowed teeth.

'I thought we'd go to the museum. We have a Sebastopol cannon in Lyeminster, you know.'

'Lovely.' Arthur said.

Avril smiled to herself because the poor man looked as if he actually meant it. Mind you, he should after last night's conversation with Sonny.

The day went reasonably well if she discounted seeing that ginger haired girl who was married to the artist. Still she hadn't recognised her; Avril was sure of it. Who would? No one whilst she was dressed as Aunt Minnie.

***

'Not causing you any trouble, is he, ducks?'

'No.' Avril chuckled. 'He'd like to. Thinks he's the big 'I am' up from London and I'm really somebody's Aunt Minnie.'

'I hope you put him right.' There was an edge to Sonny's voice that boded ill for Arthur should Avril say the word.

'You know better than that, Sonny. I could crush that little worm under my heel any time I wanted.'

In truth, Arthur was driving Avril crazy. She hated him when he came the big London hot shot and she despised him when he grovelled. There was something about Arthur that reminded her of all the East End wide boys that she had known in her youth; all the festering little sores who had thought they could get the better of her. And one of them had. One of them, she wasn't sure which, was responsible for her being sent to prison and, if she ever found out who it was, she would swing for him.

Much as she would like to talk to Sonny some more, today was Wednesday and Wednesday was Monty's day. She wanted a sit down with a quick gin and tonic. Then she had to shower and dress in her best so that she would be ready to welcome him with suitable enthusiasm.

Avril had Mr Friday picked out as her pension. A wealthy man, he was revolting with his odious habits, but Avril, priding herself on being a woman who could view circumstances dispassionately, pick out the best option and go for it regardless of personal preference. She knew that he was the one to keep her in luxury once she grew tired of her current lifestyle. But Monty was also her favourite. He was fun.

'I'm sorry, love, I have to go. I'm expecting a gentleman.'

Sonny rang off. He looked at the telephone as if by doing so he could make it start talking to him; as if it might tell him what she was keeping secret. Sonny wanted his wife back. What was she doing hiding away in this Whittington Edge place anyway? She should be at home. With him. He picked up his pen and tapped it on the desk. He frowned and slid his fingers down the stem of the pen, lifted it and let it turn over. Then he tapped it again and again and again.

Eventually he did pick up the phone. He rang through to one of his henchmen. 'Get hold of Ronnie.' He said. 'Tell him I've got a little job for him.'

***

'Not bad.' Atlantis gave her verdict a few minutes after they arrived home. 'Not bad at all. 'She moved from one side to the other taking in the angles and the light. 'She's a luscious little thing, isn't she? I can see why my Billy boy was all hot under the collar when he came to meet me.'

'So what do you think?' Bill asked carefully. 'I have to send it to the gallery; they're expecting it. And it is my best work. I have to show it.' He was begging now. He didn't want her to veto 'Summer's' exhibition.

'Ye..s…' Atlantis said at last. 'Yes. I think you should exhibit it but not necessarily in the way you initially planned. When is the gallery taking delivery.' He told her. She nodded not taking her eyes from 'Summer' She looked at the picture for a few more seconds and nodded again. 'Come along, Billy boy. Time for a cup of herbal tea, and then I shall tell you how you are going to do it.''

Bill loathed and detested herbal tea but he was on the back foot here and he knew it, so he would drink hogwash if it would get him off the hook.

'Herbal tea.' He said. 'Lovely. Can I have peppermint?' He hated herbal tea. He especially hated peppermint tea, but the fire and brimstone preachers of his youth had impressed upon him the conviction that all repentance must come with penance and therefore he was selecting the flavour which was most abhorrent. And if Atlantis could find a way out of his trouble, he would do anything.

Anything.

'Peppermint?' Atlantis paused to stare at him. 'No, you can't have peppermint. Peppermint tea makes facial hair fall out.' She grabbed his beard and pulled him closer. 'I don't want you to lose your strength, do I, Samson?'

'No.' Bill croaked, his eyes watering with pain. He wondered if Delilah had ever pulled Samson along by the beard and, if so, whether he was glad to see the back of it. Or did Samson only have long hair? He wasn't too sure about that.

Atlantis foraged through the box of herbal teas and pulled a sachet out holding it aloft like a trophy. 'You can have rosehip.' She decided. 'How about that?'

'Wonderful.' Bill was ready to agree to anything. 'I'm glad I chose that one.'

Soon the Warbeck's kitchen was filled with the fruity aromas that held so much promise yet always disappointed.

Bill had approached his first cup of herbal tea with the anticipation of delight but the first sip almost made his eyelids turn inside out. He had done his best to avoid any further contact with them since then.

Atlantis placed a steaming cup in front of him now and watched with narrowed eyes as he breathed in the fragrant steam and declared it heavenly.

Hmm, Billy boy, she said to herself, I wonder what you've really been up to. 'Drink up.' She urged sweetly. 'You've got work to do.' She narrowed her eyes over her own steaming cup and determined to get to the bottom of this. He thought she didn't know about the other girl. It was a long time ago and she thought he had learned his lesson. It seemed now that he hadn't. She wished he wouldn't be such a skinflint. If he wanted a bloody life model, why the hell didn't he pay for one properly and have done? She sighed. Bill always had had an eye for the very young, tarty, kind of girl.

***

Lottie lay in bed that night reviewing her day. She felt she had made some progress with her investigation. She had spoken to Charles Pendleton; there was nothing about that lovely man to spark Marco Romero's suspicions.

She had made notes in her notebook and whilst she was about it she had made her notes about Jane too. She had filled in all the gaps with information Gwennie had given her.

Tomorrow she would ring Cassie Mellon and make an appointment for a massage. The ladies would be coming for their regular meeting and she could start to look forward to hearing from the rector about his offer to introduce her to Beau Derek.

Avril Major had marched smartly past Horse and Trumpet Cottage in time to catch the early bus into Lyeminster.

Lottie had her money on Avril Major being the person Marco was interested in but it would be far too easy to pick on her and ignore all the other possibilities. Besides, had she not seen Avril in disguise, she wouldn't think anything of the sort. Having said that, there was the money, and the fact that Avril had a lot of male visitors. She wondered if the tall man was staying at Nook Cottage. She must be alert and take more notice.

Bill Warbeck, he of the artistic temperament, would be difficult to talk to. Susan had told her how grumpy he could be if disturbed and Lottie intended leaving him until the very last moment.

Also Jonas had been most attentive. He had called each night since the discovery and she liked the attention.

CHAPTER FIVE

I think the murder was committed in the conservatory with the... with the crucifix.' Biddy Myers said. She glanced around the group of friends who met every Thursday afternoon and saw that they were giving her their complete attention. She executed a small drum roll on the table beside her chair with her perfectly manicured fingernails. 'And the murderer is...wait for the drum roll.' She grinned the mischievous grin that always made the others laugh and drummed her fingernails again, 'Arnold Pickard '.

As a way to make friends, Lottie had begun the Murder Club, taking the idea from a novel she had read, and inviting a few of the women she often met in the crime section of the library to meet at Horse and Trumpet Cottage every Thursday afternoon. They played Cluedo and gossiped and tried their hands at solving real murders that were in the news.

The Murder Club, to a woman, paused, blinked, and then roared with laughter. Biddy leaned back, satisfied with her pronouncement. 'There.' She said. 'I knew you would agree.'

'Hmm...' Susan Holland bit her lip and narrowed her eyes, seeming to take this joke seriously. The friends leaned forward, smiling, eager for the next development. 'Arnold Pickard?' She tilted her head to one side to further consider the possibilities suggested by this slur on the character of the churchwarden. 'I can see that he would have access to the altar crucifix,' she said, 'who did he murder, Biddy?'

'The doctor.' Biddy's eyes were bright with mischief and the group erupted into laughter again. No one liked the doctor or his awful wife.

Lottie was trying not to allow her shock to show. She didn't know Arnold Pickard. She suspected that he was Avril Major's Tuesday night visitor but needed more evidence. The reactions of her friends told her that he was unpopular and possibly too pious for his own good. The rolling of the eyes also suggested that the piety was a facade and had no substance. A hushed voice put forward the theory that Arnold Pickard himself could be the victim and the perpetrator the father of one of the choirgirls.

Lottie filed that snippet away to note it in her book later.

Further theories were put forward each more outrageous than the last and Lottie was caught up with the ridiculous hilarity of it all.

'Why do you think Arnold Pickard murdered the good doctor, Lottie? Susan asked her at last.

Lottie considered for a moment or two. 'Arnold Pickard did the murder but I don't think he murdered the doctor.' She said at last.'

'But the doctor is dead.' Susan took up the challenge as she always did. 'Biddy said so.'

The other members of the Murder Club waited for the fun to start. Lottie and Susan were the undisputed leaders of the club and their battles of wits were what the group looked forward to most on a Thursday.

'Indeed he is.' Lottie gave them all a sideways look. 'He died from an overdose of morphine administered by his wife who, unknown to the rest of the village, was a nurse prior to her marriage. She had been having a lesbian affair with Arnold Pickard's wife.

'The two ladies were having coffee mornings laced with drugs which the doctor's wife purloined from her husband's surgery. The rapidly diminishing supplies of drugs eventually became apparent to the doctor who challenged his wife. She admitted what she had done expecting that he would cover up the losses somehow but instead, he said he was going to report her. So she killed him.

'She and Mrs Pickard had a pact that if ever they were found out they would tell their respective husbands and run away together. The doctor's wife rang Mrs P and told her the game was up. She told Arnold that she was leaving him and Arnold went berserk.'

'So…' Gwennie leaned forward, eyes goggling, mouth agape. 'What happened?'

'Arnold Pickard killed the doctor's wife, Gwennie. He had no idea that the doctor was already dead. He ran to the church all wrapped up in his cloak. He stole the crucifix, ran to the doctor's house and bludgeoned the doctor's wife with it.'

'Just to keep his wife.' Gwennie said on a romance-laden sigh.

'No.' Lottie grinned. 'He didn't care a fig about his wife. He wanted to ensure that news of the lesbian affair never became public. He could lose his job as churchwarden – or so he thought.

'But what did he do with the body?' Gwennie wanted to know, eyes huge circles of excitement. 'We haven't discovered the body yet.'

'That is because the body is in your potting shed.' Lottie finished, her eyes wide with dramatic intent.

'How did it get there?'

'He put it in the boot of his car.' Lottie looked around, inspiration suddenly striking her, 'he does have a car, doesn't he?'

'Oh yes, a little red thing with a dodgy tail light' someone confirmed.

That was the car she saw on Tuesday nights. Mr Tuesday was thus unmasked.

She paused for a couple of seconds before rising to her feet with enviable speed and a no-nonsense smile. 'Now can I interest anyone in more coffee?'

Gwennie was looking like a rabbit in headlights. She gaped for a few seconds then was snapped back into reality by the fact that everyone was laughing. She laughed too. It was only a game after all. No one was really dead. And it was naughty of Biddy to change their weekly murder game by sneaking into it people they knew; people from their own village.

'If ever he found out, the rector would be mortified.' She said softly.

'But he never will find out.' Susan assured her. She patted Gwennie's hand. She knew how much the most timid member of their group worried. 'It's only a bit of fun.'

'I suppose so.' Gwennie murmured.

Blanche laughed. 'We should do this again. I think next week we should think of another local worthy who could be the murderer.'

'And another worthy we can polish off.' Biddy agreed.

This set off another gale of laughter from everyone but Gwennie who pinched the edges of her Peter Pan collar together with her bony fingers and bit her lip.

'Don't worry, Gwennie.' Lottie placed a fresh cup of coffee before her troubled guest and handed out china mugs to the rest of the group.

Gwennie always had to have her coffee in a china cup with a saucer. And the two had to match. This was not because Gwennie was troublesome; it was because she had been raised with a very strong sense of what was 'proper'.

Biddy followed Lottie in with a plate of biscuits and another of fresh cream cakes.

'Right,' Lottie smiled her best Chairperson smile and looked around at the expectant faces of her friends. 'After all the fun stuff for which we have to thank Biddy,' she nodded to Biddy and grinned, 'perhaps we should get down to our current case.'

Murmurs of general assent went up. Notebooks were foraged out of handbags, covers flipped open and pages rustled. Pens were clicked into operational mode and soon all eyes, bright with intelligent attention, were on Lottie again.

'We have a new case this week. Michael Garnett is suspected of the murder of his wife, Rosa.' Lottie read out the clipping from the newspaper that the club were working on.

'Rosa Garnett, 48, was found in the alleyway beside her semi-detached home in Durrington on Friday morning...'

She read on giving all the details printed in the newspapers. 'Now this, as we know, all took place a fortnight ago. Since then Michael Garnett has met the press and put out a statement begging for help in the discovery of his wife's killer.'

'I saw a documentary last year.' Biddy said. 'And, apparently, these press conferences are set up especially so that the police can get a – what do you call it? – a forensic psychologist I think it is, - to watch the nearest and dearest for signs of guilt. They watch the film of the press conference over and over again and they can tell by the body language if the husband or wife actually committed the crime.'

Lottie was secretly grateful to Biddy for her input because she had wanted to tell the group exactly the same thing herself but didn't know how to do so without causing curiosity about how she knew such stuff. She realised now that she was too much on the defensive. There were documentaries about everything on television these days. Anything she came out with that raised questions could easily be attributed to something she had watched in the dim and distant past. That was another piece of valuable knowledge to be filed away in her mind.

'Did everyone see the interview on television?' Lottie asked 'Yes,' came the chorus.

'And a nasty piece of work he looked.' Gwennie shuddered.

Discussions went on until the bells of St Jude's tolled out nine o clock and all eyes went to the grandmother clock which had, unnoticed until now, been chopping the evening into tiny pieces all the while they had been discussing their case. Gwennie gasped.

Debate continued for a few minutes but Lottie could see that Gwennie was becoming more and more agitated as the seconds passed. The poor dear needed to be safely locked inside her home by nine thirty and who could blame her. Whittington Edge was nothing like the Bronx but a few noisy teenagers running down the dark alleyways of Camp Hill could send Gwennie into a tizzy.

'I think it's time we called it a night.' Lottie said. 'And as preparation for next week obviously we should keep our eyes on the news and watch for any developments in the case but also it would be a good idea if each of us could think ourselves into Michael Garnett's mind and come up with a reason why he would want Rosa out of the way. No conferring. It would be helpful if everyone thought of something different.'

'Oh what a good idea.' Gwennie's eyes glowed with delight. This was wonderful. This was what she had waited her whole life for. Nothing in Whittington Edge had ever been so much fun. Her only regret was that mother and dad were no longer around to enjoy it with her.

Mother had been much more light-hearted before Dad died. It had been fun then. How they would have looked forward to her coming home full of the news of her evening. How they would have laughed about Biddy's joke – though they may have disapproved of her bringing the churchwarden into it; men of the cloth were only one step away from being saints according to Gwennie's parents and the churchwarden would join that illustrious band by association. But then, they hadn't been around to see so many fall from grace.

Lottie brought Gwennie's brown and fawn tweed coat and helped her on with it.

'There is something I need to tell you, Lottie, could I phone you when I get home?'

'Of course,' Lottie said.

***

It was October, mid autumn, and the nights were drawing in; stray wisps of mist floated through the evening air and pooled around the legs of cattle in the early morning.

The streets of Whittington Edge were cold and the lights had been flickering on in the cottages across The Green and down Church Lane since seven o clock. The night air was full of the mingled scents of coal and wood smoke and Lottie breathed it in. Lyeminster was a smokeless zone and she had missed these smells that transported her to an earlier time.

From the large living room of Horse and Trumpet Cottage, which occupied the vast corner plot between Church Lane and The Green, Lottie could see in both directions. She could also, on a clear day, see across The Green and right down Welham Lane.

Retirement wasn't going to be so bad after all.

Lottie put on the kettle ready for another cup of coffee and went to the door to watch her friends disperse to the far corners of the village. If anyone had told her even a year ago what her life would be like now she wouldn't have believed them.

Having spent years in the civil service, she had expected to remain there until she was forced to retire. She had even toyed with the idea of asking for an extension of service to stay on longer. In the event she had grabbed early retirement with both hands and this little gem in the middle of nowhere had proved to be an inspired choice.

She'd had plans to make handicrafts and join the women's institute. She would throw herself into this new venture with vigour. She would be a stunning success at this, naturally. Lottie had never failed at anything once she put her mind to it.

She would take classes in languages and then she would travel. She would learn to paint and make watercolour studies of the local landscape which she could frame and sell in one of the village shops. Tourists passing through would buy these and carry them home, proud to have found a small piece of rural England that they could hang on their own walls and point out to visitors.

Lottie never allowed the fact that she didn't know how to do a thing to stand in her way. She didn't know if there was a branch of the Women's Institute in Whittington Edge. She couldn't recall if Jane

Pendleton had mentioned it. She didn't know if there were tourists either. Neither of these considerations was allowed to pose itself as a problem to Lottie.

She hadn't realised that small town life could be such fun.

CHAPTER SIX

The girls, as Lottie thought of them, had all left now. Their fragmented conversations wafted to her on the icy breeze as she stood in the doorway to Horse and Trumpet Cottage and watched until they were all out of sight. As usual Gwennie was the last to disappear from view. She turned and waved and blew a kiss as she always did and Lottie's heart swelled with affection for this simple soul.

No one could dislike Gwennie. She was one of those people who were…nice. And there were few genuinely nice people around.

Lottie knew that from experience. Besides, it was easy to like someone who was in such awe of one. Jane Pendleton was nice. But was she a simple soul?

Knowing the way village politics worked, she wondered what rumours circulated about herself.

She was sitting by the fire now, having found the room chilly once the club members had left for their homes. Her phone rang. It was Gwennie home safely thank goodness.

'I've been talking to Bella Fleet,' she said. 'Did you know she's a keen photographer?'

'No, I didn't,' Lottie wondered why this would interest her but she didn't wonder for long.

'She takes photos of every new face she sees,' Gwennie said. 'She saw a newcomer today. He's tall and blond and terribly handsome.'

'Oh,' Lottie said 'I wonder who he can be.'

'I wonder,' Gwennie giggled. 'I'll see you soon, my dear,' and she replaced the receiver.

It took Lottie some time to work out that Gwennie was matchmaking.

Horse and Trumpet Cottage was cosy and snug just as a cottage should be. In fact, everything in the cottage was as Lottie thought it should be.

She had stripped hideous wallpaper from the walls, thick with layers of paint and tarry nicotine, and replaced it with gentle colours of emulsion. She had brushed vile scented wood treatment mixtures into beams and overseen the replacement of all the pipe work, electrics, and windows but she had left the old pub doors in situ.

The snug, the smoke room, the lounge; all were identified by their names engraved into panels of obscure glass set within stained glass surrounds in the oak doors. The smoky, hop laden scent seeped out when the house was left unattended for more than a few hours. She gave a sigh of pleasure and burrowed deeper into the overstuffed chintz of her sofa.

Beside her sat a box of her favourite chocolates, cherries in brandy, and she popped one into her mouth as she turned the page of her book, reading quickly, eager to reach the next part of the story.

The private eye was cornered in the alley behind a deli and the packet shop, where he bought his daily pint of Wild Turkey in a neatly wrapped brown paper package. The hero was an alcoholic. It seemed one had to be an alcoholic to survive as a private eye in New York.

He had been caught, Wild Turkey in one hand, pastrami on rye sandwich in the other, between two dumpsters heaving with foul, glutinous garbage. The bad guys had arrived, armed to the eyeballs and now the shooting had started.

Lottie bit another chocolate and broke through the chocolate to the cherry centre. Gunfire and brandy exploded at the same moment and Lottie almost choked. Her eyes watered. Bullets ricocheted. The private eye, so cool in times of crisis, hunkered down between the dumpsters, took a bite of his sandwich, opened the bottle of Wild Turkey and drank a couple of fingers to wash the sandwich down. It wasn't the way he had planned to eat his supper but a guy had to do what a guy had to do. Lottie pulled her feet up onto the sofa and turned the page.

***

'Good evening, Princess?' Gerald Myers glanced over the top of his newspaper and then returned to perusing the financial pages.

Biddy threw her shoulder bag onto one chair and her coat onto another. 'Very good, thank you, Darling.'

'Good…Good…' he murmured. 'Would you like a coffee?'

'You stay there, I'll make it.' She wandered into the kitchen to put on the kettle. She thought of Arnold Pickard standing in the potting shed wielding a heavy crucifix. Where would he have got it from?

Biddy thought this over for a moment or two. The crucifix he wore around his neck wouldn't have the weight to make it a deadly weapon. It would have to be the one that stood on the altar of St Jude's. When she recalled that the doctor's wife always insisted on polishing the crucifix herself, Biddy burst out laughing.

'Is something wrong, Princess?' Gerald called through from his chair by the fire.

'Nothing at all.' Biddy called back. She must remember to tell Gerald about Arnold Pickard and the crucifix. And the body in Gwennie's potting shed.

***

Matchbox Cottage was also on The Green. It was small as its name suggested and it was home to Susan Holland.

Chris had accused her of trying to make him look tight-fisted by choosing this as her home when they divorced. No one would give up the old Georgian rectory with its seven bedrooms and high ceilings, he said. But Susan had fallen in love with the little place. She loved its nooks and crannies, its beams and inglenook fireplace, its uneven floors and little steps at each doorway.

She also wanted rid of the old rectory because, love it as she did, she knew that it would always belong partly to Chris and that he would feel comfortable drifting in and out when his new marriage caused him problems and he wanted a little TLC. As Susan had told him at the time – no way.

She had drawn the curtains before she left home. The swish of the heavy fabric brought cosiness. The thickness of the curtains cocooned the room in silence. It felt warm and womblike. It was her private place where she could wrap herself in comfort and know that no one else had any right to be there. In fact, had she known how good a solitary life would be, she would have insisted on Chris moving out years ago. He could have had his own place and she her own. They could have met up for meals or for a chat and then retreated to their own private spaces. Susan decided their marriage may have lasted longer had they been semi-detached.

That was an idea. She was a young woman; not ready to give up men and sex just yet. What she needed was a man she could meet up with, a friend and lover like Lottie's Jonas, but not a husband. No, never again would she marry, but, yes, a semi detached sort of arrangement could be pleasant. She thought Lottie had got it organised just about right.

Three table lamps were glowing their welcome when she stepped inside. She had left a flask of hot chocolate ready beside her chair. A padded ottoman was positioned to support her aching legs – they rarely ached nowadays. The television had already been tuned to the channel she wanted to watch so all she had to do was kick off her shoes, slide her feet into her slippers and flick the television off standby.

The chair wrapped itself around her as warm as a pair of arms and a more comforting pair of arms than Chris's had ever been. Soon she was relaxing, chocolate steaming in its mug, gruesome cop show on the television, book on the floor beside her chair should the television programme not live up to its advance publicity and to fill in the huge commercial breaks they had nowadays. No man to worry about. No shoes to shine or briefcase to place by the front door for the work-weary executive. No brow to mop or shirts to iron. No rehashed arguments to listen to. She wondered, not for the first time, why she hadn't divorced Chris before.

Then she noticed the light flashing on the telephone. It was unusual for her not to have seen this the moment she came in. She reached out a lazy hand to press the button but the programme was beginning so she retracted it. Whoever it was could wait until the adverts; it was probably only a salesman anyway.

'Susan, where are you?'

Susan had pressed the message button as soon as the break came in the programme and now glanced at the phone, one eyebrow raised in disbelief at the tone of her ex husband's voice. She could hardly credit his nerve, what did he expect her to do, sit around waiting for him to call?

Probably. Yes, almost certainly.

Realising that she had missed the whole message, picking up only the whining voice, she turned the tape back to the beginning and re-played it.

'Susan, where are you? Anthony's ill and Patsy really needs some help right now and…and… I need someone to talk to.' His voice had taken on the wheedling 'poor me' tone that made Susan want to spit. But it soon changed to outraged husband mode. 'I thought you would be in by this time. Do you realise it's past nine? Where you go to in the evenings I can't imagine.' He sounded annoyed and surprised that she wasn't there waiting for him to call. Anyone would think she was his mother…or worse, his wife.

Susan huffed and took another sip of chocolate, glad that the evening had gone on later than usual. It would have been awful had she been available when he rang. It might be an idea to allow the message machine to filter all her calls for a few days or so. He needn't think that she would be offering tea and sympathy to her successor. Or maybe he wanted her to baby-sit the sick child so that he and Patsy could take off for the night. Fat chance.

She had missed most of the message again. She really ought to be able to keep her mind on the task in hand. But the programme was coming back on so she didn't run the message through again until the next commercial break. And, she consoled herself, had the message held any importance for her, she would have listened to it.

When she did, she found that Chris wanted to have a whinge about the problems of being the middle aged father of a four year old and the hardships of being married to a woman half his age who expected him to be able to do all the things a contemporary of hers would be able to do.

'Do you have any suggestions, darling?' He concluded. 'Yes.' She said to the empty room. 'Pick a wife of your own age, you stupid man. Poor Patsy. What a rotten bargain she had got. And how dare he call her 'darling'? The toad.

She was tempted to wait until the programme and the one after it had finished and then call back. Susan wasn't usually spiteful but in Chris's case she was prepared to make an exception. She could ring and tell him what a wonderful evening she had had. She could say it had been a girls' night out. That wasn't too far from the truth and it would rile him up big time.

In the end self-interest prevailed. She would ignore his whining. He had no call on her now and telling him about her evening would convince him that she was seeking his permission in retrospect.

Well, blow that. She extended a carefully manicured finger and wiped the message, refilled her chocolate cup and settled back to enjoy the rest of her evening.

***

Blanche Tallentire was the next to arrive home. Her house was one of the new ones on the development of executive homes built ten years previously halfway between Whittington Edge and Sturman Cross

'Hi, honey, I'm home.' She called out as she opened the front door.

Clive was immediately at the living room door, smiling. He enveloped her in a huge hug. 'How's murder?' He asked.

'Great.' She said. 'Tonight, we killed the doctor's wife. Well, not us, exactly, Arnold Pickard did it… in Gwennie's potting shed…with a crucifix.'

'I'll bet Gwennie loved that.' Clive chuckled.

'I doubt she'll sleep tonight.' Blanche grimaced.

'I've made a tray of tea. Come and tell me all about it.

***

Camp Hill was supposedly erected on the site of an old Roman fort.

It wasn't a large estate. Six roads, that was all. Each of them named after a poet. Burns Hill where Gwennie lived was the only one of the six roads that wasn't actually on a hill. In fact, the steepest road was named Longfellow Hollow. Whoever was responsible for the naming of roads, had obviously never ventured into the bandit country that was to become Camp Hill.

However the houses in Camp Hill were large for their type and all boasted massive gardens. Even the keenest gardener wouldn't ask for an allotment in addition to the plot attached to their home; the land allocated to each house was sufficient to provide enough fruit and vegetables to feed a family for a year and still have some over.

In fact one of the original residents had opened up a market stall with his excess produce and was now the proud owner of his house and a holiday home in the West Country.

Gwennie was a keen gardener. Her father had spent hours on his plot raking and hoeing and planting and sprinkling lime on the soil. She remembered him folding the outside leaves over cauliflowers, snapping them into place to keep the flower white. As a child she would creep amongst the rows detaching caterpillars from the cabbages, and she picked blackcurrants with her father, then topped and tailed them for her mother to make the best blackcurrant jam she had ever tasted.

Now she still went around each year placing heads of strawberry blossoms into old jam jars and she still jumped up with a small yelp if on the next visit to the strawberry bed she found rain beetles in the jars.

Gwennie's home was almost exactly as her mother had left it when she died, and her mother had changed nothing from choice since 1950.

The leatherette settee had never been in contact with a single bottom; the uncut moquette seats having always been covered with neatly edged pieces of fabric her mother bought from the market in Lyeminster and carefully hemmed on the old Singer sewing machine that still stood in the back bedroom.

The dining room suite had been the most recent purchase of the Furlong family, having been chosen before Gwennie was a teenager. The polythene covering had remained on the seats for two years before it began to fall apart, aided and abetted by Gwennie who found this new material fascinating. It didn't split like Cellophane did, and she had found that she could surreptitiously dig her fingernails into its yielding surface and create little ladder marks by running them along.

Whenever her mother saw her doing this, she reprimanded her saying 'that's a nice bit of polythene. It'll last years if you give it a chance'. But Gwennie didn't give it a chance. When it looked leprous, hanging in shreds from Gwennie's chair, Mrs Furlong grudgingly consented to its removal. 'Nice bit of polythene.' She muttered as she snipped it away with her scissors. 'Would have lasted years, that would. Given the chance.' Ever afterwards, she eyed anyone with suspicion when they sat on the unprotected chairs.

It was typical of Mrs Furlong to cut the remaining polythene from the chairs. Anyone else, Gwennie was sure, would have grabbed at it and torn it from around the legs and backs of the chairs. But, not her mother. Mother even folded paper bags before putting them in the bin; if they ever reached the bin. Mrs

Furlong was a recycler long before it became fashionable. She said it was a result of having been raised in a home still remembering the last war when nothing could be wasted. Gwennie had felt contrite. She wondered what other use that scabrous polythene could have been put to, had it been given the chance.

Gwennie opened her door, called out to the kitten that her mother would never have allowed into the house, and scooped up the mewing little scrap when it came running to greet her and tell her about its lonely evening and complain of her neglect.

Like Susan, Gwennie also left her supper ready and her lights on – another thing mother would never have allowed. She went into the kitchen and switched on the electric kettle. This was an avant-garde addition to her home brought on by noticing how quickly everyone else's kettles boiled in comparison to the old blackened relic her mother had brought with her to her marriage and prided herself on never replacing.

Outside the kitchen window the world was dark and still. A huge orange, mottled, moon, rode low over the hedgerows in a sky full of stars. She took her china cup and saucer and opened the back door.

'Come along, Snowflake.' She called to the kitten. 'Let's have one last look at the garden.' They wandered out into the night. A few of the local boys could be heard a couple of streets away. They were hanging around as usual. There was nowhere on Camp Hill specifically for teenagers and few of them wanted to walk into Whittington Edge. Even if they did, there would be little there for them. Camp Hill may be small but it was big enough to support a fish and chip shop and the youth of the area congregated there.

Gwennie glanced warily at the potting shed halfway along the garden path. She was being a fool. It had only been a joke. There was nothing untoward in her potting shed. The very notion was ridiculous.

Her garden gate stood open. It had been closed when she went out. She closed it and slid the bolt across though that wouldn't deter anyone who really wanted to get in. Then she and Snowflake went back indoors and Gwennie closed and bolted the door.

***

Whittington Edge was a pretty village set around a green complete with duck pond. Lottie had often dreamed of life in such a place but she had thought they only existed within the pages of books.

Whittington Edge had all the necessary components; an ancient church stuffed to the belfry with odd parishioners, beautiful cottages both thatched and tiled and, at this time of night, a deceptive air of peaceful secrecy. It was late at night that things really started to hot up in Whittington Edge.

It was close on midnight now and a sleepy village should by rights be sleeping but in her months in Whittington Edge Lottie had learned that only cities closed down early.

Any noise after eleven on Carlyon Road would have had her holding her breath and waiting for the sound of breaking glass whilst one hand hovered above the telephone at her bedside. Frozen in apprehension, her heart would pound and her mind immediately home in on thoughts of Keith Kendal. This was especially true after he had made his midnight call.

Here in Whittington Edge she sat beside her window in the darkness most evenings and looked out across The Green. This was her time of the day, when she could be herself; no longer guarding her tongue against the stray remark that may alert a listener to her previous life

The Priest at Prayer – the local pub directly across The Green from Horse and Trumpet Cottage – was still serving. Light as orange as the low moon shone from every window and heat vapour, mingled with illegal smoke, escaped from the small top windows of the bar.

Lottie's bedroom window was also open and the scents of the autumn evening drifted in on a breeze that also carried the voices of those leaving the Priest at Prayer. It was nearing the end of October and a few fireworks had been blossoming in the night sky for the last week or more, although more often it was the sound of firecrackers that split the night.

Like her sitting room, Lottie's bedroom, occupied the corner of the house so she had a window that opened over Church Lane too, but nothing ever happened in Church Lane so she rarely looked out of that one.

However tonight it was the window over Church Lane that eventually drew her attention.

Bert Bettinson staggered out of the door of the Priest at Prayer. Two small boys stood like sentries guarding both the door and the guy that was slumped over in a broken down pushchair. It wasn't until she saw the effigy that Lottie realised how soon it would be Guy Fawkes' night.

As each drinker left the pub, the boys shoved the pushchair out so that their prey had to stop or fall over it. It hadn't failed to work so far and she had seen the boys wait expectantly as men rummaged in pockets and coins changed hands. Then the pushchair would be drawn back and their benefactor allowed to continue on his way, usually chuckling at the cheek of the youngsters.

Now the pushchair was blocking Bert Bettinson's path. He gurgled a laugh and coins chinked. Then his path was clear.

She had heard the rowdy goodbyes and ribald remarks that accompanied him. She was wondering whether he would make it to his home two doors away from the pub without mishap when, out of the corner of her eye, she spotted a figure slip out of Church Lane. It was the swiftness of the movement that caught her attention and its furtiveness that quickly held her transfixed.

The figure scurried, bent over. It appeared to be clutching something close to its chest. And it was clad in a hooded cloak that billowed in the cold air. The investigator in Lottie told her that a cloak such as that should be held closely to the body to enable the wearer to benefit from any warmth it could provide. As it was flapping about unrestricted, it must be being worn as a disguise.

Which was absurd because anyone who saw him would know that this was Charles Pendleton. She was being fanciful, of course.

Seeing Avril Major in disguise had led her to seek deception in every innocent act. Lottie gave herself a mental shake.

Even so, for a second or two she imagined that the thing clutched to his chest was the altar crucifix and that he was en-route to Gwennie's potting shed hell bent on murder most foul.

The bell of St Jude's pounded out twelve dull bongs, muffled by the heavy night air. Midnight; the witching hour.

The cloaked figure stopped, glanced back over his shoulder towards the church and then continued on his way, running the next few steps as if he had lost time on his schedule and had to make it up. His white face made her think more of the White Rabbit than Mr Pickwick.

She sighed as Charles Pendleton disappeared into Welham Lane.

It was catching Avril Major in Lyeminster in her frump outfit that had her seeing intrigue around every corner. If Charles Pendleton was abroad on a cold October night he must have a good reason for it. She had heard that Sidney Vernon, one of his elderly parishioners was ill. That would be the most likely explanation. He would have had to visit St Jude's to collect the host to perform a last communion.

She hoped she was wrong but sent up a silent prayer to help both Charles and Mr Vernon in case she was right.

The door to Avril Major's cottage opened across the road and to the right of The Green and Avril's head poked out. Lottie had heard the heavy latch being lifted otherwise she wouldn't have noticed because Avril showed no light. There was a pause whilst Avril looked around The Green, her cherry red hair and milk-white face showing up more than she could realise.

Then she took a step back and a tall, thin figure slipped out of the house. Could this be the man she had met from the train?

Lottie smiled as Avril flapped a hand at her departing guest, impatient to have him off her property and away in the car that was parked under the huge chestnut tree the better to shield it from view.

Lottie had heard no rumours that Avril Major had gentlemen callers but, if called upon to do so, she could testify to this. She could even identify some of these guilty men. On Monday it was Mr Rogers who arrived. The same Mr Rogers whose wife went to visit her invalid mother more often than the village thought necessary.

Needless to say all sympathies were with the abandoned Mr Rogers. Needless also to say that the sympathisers were unaware of the comfort Mr Rogers took elsewhere.

On Tuesday it was Mr Pickard, the churchwarden's, turn.

Lottie's lips curved into a happy smile. Presumably Mr Pickard was therefore safe from religious mania although, come to think of it, he did wear one of these hooded cloaks and carried a book under his arm; surely not a bible.

Wednesdays saw a florid man arrive bearing heavy bags. Lottie hadn't worked out who he was.

But today was Thursday and the tall thin man was one Lottie hadn't seen before. This meant that the regular Mr Thursday had either gone away on holiday and Avril had taken a replacement from the subs bench or, the regular Mr Thursday was no longer a member of Avril's team of lovers. This couldn't be the same man she was meeting in Lyeminster, because, if so, why the disguise?

Mr Friday, Lottie had still to identify and Mr Saturday had a look that Lottie recognised. She found this disturbing because she would have put money on Mr Saturday being a policeman.

Avril Major was no oil painting but she was, in Lottie's mind at any rate, no worse than the majority of women of a certain age. In fact Avril was probably more attractive now than she had been in her youth. She had retained her figure which most married women of Lottie's acquaintance had not, and she dressed well and never ventured beyond her front door unless she was wearing full make up. No scampering down to the shop with a head full of rollers topped with a scarf for Avril Major; and not for Lottie Colenso either, come to that.

Avril's door was closed now and Lottie switched her attention to a group of youths who came into view. They were wobbling on bicycles at a slow walking pace. Their whoops and laughter echoed against the buildings as they came to a halt outside the Priest at Prayer. As if on cue, the doors opened spilling light as the last stragglers emerged.

Voices called their goodnights and the late drinkers began to disperse.

One of the youths propped his cycle against the pub wall and ran up the street to collect a staggering man who had caroused a little too well. She was interested to see that the boys collecting pennies for the guy made no move to hinder their progress.

The youth guided the man back to the bicycle and his friends crowded around supporting the bike whilst its rider, who was now astride the crossbar, held the handlebars and the man, who was lolling about dangerously, was helped onto the saddle.

The cycle was balanced and pushed and the rider stood on the pedals and put all his weight onto the higher one and, urged on by his friends, propelled the machine into motion. The old man, clinging to the youth's jacket, was slumped over to one side making the boy's work even harder. The youth's friends ran alongside the cycle applying steadying hands to the wobbling machine until sufficient speed was built up to keep it upright.

Not unexpectedly, the pair turned towards Camp Hill. Lottie silently berated herself for making this observation. The fact that the man was drunk did not necessarily mean that he was a council house tenant.

She told herself that she had made the assumption because he had needed transport home; had he lived in Whittington Edge he would have been able to walk home – even though it may have taken some time.

Eventually, the streets surrounding The Green were empty. The boys with the guy decided to give up for the night. It was time for bed. The rhythmic squeak of the pushchair wheels was getting closer and Lottie looked out to see if she recognised any of the young entrepreneurs. As they walked, one of their number was sharing out the takings. Coins clinked and delighted exclamations proved that they had made more than expected.

Beneath the street light something glimmered in the darkness and Lottie leaned forward, frowning in concentration. Then she too laughed. The guy was wearing gold shoes. What a title for a detective story that would make; The Guy Wore Gold Shoes. She wondered if Americans knew about Guy Fawkes. As far as she knew they reserved firework displays for the fourth of July; the celebration of their more successful attempt to rout the British king.

The village was soon dark and no one else was to be seen. Lottie had many years of early mornings behind her and had promised herself that, when she retired, she would stay in bed until nine every morning. Early rising was proving a hard habit to break and this time spent watching her new neighbourhood was one of the ways she was employing to reset her body clock. Her new home was ideally situated for observing the village and she was finding that she learned more about her neighbours during her midnight vigil than she did during the day.

The clock at her bedside showed the time to be a quarter to one when she eventually closed the curtains and turned on the light. She had two more chapters to read and then her book could be put on the hall table with the others that were waiting to be returned to the library.

***

Avril Majors was also preparing for bed. Mr Thursday, the fishmonger, was an interesting companion but he always smelled of fish. Now Avril had no objection to a nice piece of cod baked in the oven with thinly sliced onion and grated cheese; there was nothing better, but the smell of fish on Mr Thursday was awful. And he had cold hands too; shaking hands with Mr Thursday was like shaking hands with a fish.

She had sprayed air freshener around her sitting room the moment he left, and showered long and hard. Now, alone in the attic bedroom of Nook Cottage, she anointed her skin with expensively perfumed lotions.

Avril's own bedroom paid homage to current fashion. She had a hardwood floor and magnolia walls. In this resided black and chrome furniture with no fripperies whatsoever. If a nun could be said to live in austere elegance, Avril Major lived like that nun.

After the day she had had, Avril wouldn't be averse to joining a convent.

Arthur, after only two days, was having withdrawal symptoms about his horseracing. She had had to accompany him to a bookie's to stop him whining. Really, much more of this and Arthur would be receiving a visit from Sonny's henchmen. She had taken him back to the castle cells in an attempt to reinforce her instructions but the atmosphere couldn't work its magic a second time and Arthur lit up a cigar and puffed smoke upwards, setting off an alarm.

She scolded him soundly but he didn't even pretend to be listening and stood by, totally uninterested, when the security guards found them and threw them out.

'You were lucky there, Arthur,' Aunt Minnie said when they found themselves standing on the pavement outside the castle walls, 'if they had called the police, questions would have been asked.'

Arthur had the grace to apologise but she could tell his sorrow didn't run deep. The trouble was that Arthur thought he was home and dry. He had made the mistake of thinking that Lyeminster was totally divorced from London. 'If they had picked you up, the Met would have found out. They have computers, you know. Everything on the police database is joined up nowadays. All over the country.' It was no use. The man stood there like a pudding. He wasn't listening. Or, if he was, he no longer cared.

***

Sonny, on hearing this during their daily catch-up call, was furious. 'You say the word, Doll, and I'll have the blighter back here so fast he'll get friction burns. I won't have him messin' you about, Doll, I really won't.'

Sonny's anger was sufficient to calm her down as it always was. Knowing Sonny was ready to step in and crush the little cockroach made Avril feel better.

As soon as she had cut the connection with Sonny, she rang Arthur and read him the Riot Act. She threatened him with a trip to the station the next day where she would buy him a ticket back to London and have Sonny's goons waiting for him.

For an anxious few minutes she watched the screen of her tracking device but Arthur didn't make a run for it. If he had, she had a contingency plan. If she ever had to put that contingency plan into operation...well, suffice it to say Arthur would be sorry...

CHAPTER SEVEN

G wennie and Snowflake had been tucked up in and on the bed respectively for a couple of hours before Lottie finally went to sleep. Gwennie's last thoughts had been of taking a trip into Lyeminster to buy a duvet. The shiny, rose-pink, satin eiderdown that had covered her bed for countless years was too slippery for Snowflake to complete the ascent onto the bed with any confidence and Gwennie was worried that it was too cold for the kitten to sleep on.

Duvets were big. She would have difficulty getting it home on the bus. Would the shop deliver? Should she consider mail order? Gwennie's mother hadn't trusted mail order. She said that they sent you things that were nothing like the pictures in the catalogues and they never lasted five minutes because they were all trash. Did Gwennie dare to try it?

Mrs Fleet would be bound to know. Although in her eighties, Mrs Fleet was very modern in her outlook. More modern than she, Gwennie often thought.

Gwennie was still mulling this over when she let herself into Templar House the next morning. Mrs Fleet was awake and sitting up in bed with a cup of tea courtesy of her tea making machine.

Gwennie carolled out a happy greeting and was glad to hear an equally happy response; on a bad day Mrs Fleet could be difficult in the extreme. She hurried up the stairs giving the huge portrait of her employer's worthiest ancestor a wide berth. The man had been a favourite of the Prince Regent and looked decidedly dodgy to Gwennie's innocent mind. His knowing eyes and rakish smile sent scary, excited quivers through to the depths of Gwennie's soul.

Besides the enjoyment of murder mysteries that she shared with the Murder Club, Gwennie also had a sneaky passion for historical romances of the daring kind. If she had to take these up to the issue desk in order to borrow them, she wouldn't read them at all. All that silver foil on the covers, and the pictures… well it made her blush just to think about them. But Gwennie could easily issue these books to herself whilst keeping a lonely vigil on the issue desk over lunchtime.

When she read the books, the hero always took on the features of Mrs Fleet's ancestor and, lying in her bed at night, Gwennie sometimes imagined herself to be an innocent young lady at court in this gentleman's heyday. The things that had happened during these daydreams had the power to make her blush so she gave him a coy smile as she scuttled beneath his handsome gaze and darted along to Mrs Fleet's bedroom.

'Good morning, Gwennie, come and talk to me.' The old lady said, patting the counterpane. 'I've been so looking forward to seeing you.'

Gwennie perched on the edge of the bed and launched into her plan for buying a duvet. She explained her reasons as she used to have to explain her reasons for any purchase when mother was alive.

'You must do what you think is right, Gwennie,' Mrs Fleet said firmly, 'and we don't want poor little Snowflake to be cold, now do we?'

Gwennie glowed in the warmth of Mrs Fleet's understanding.

Mother had always wanted chapter and verse on every thought Gwennie had, or so it seemed. In fact, sometimes, Gwennie thought that mother could look directly into her head and rummage around through her thoughts searching for ones that didn't meet with her approval. And, it had to be acknowledged that most of them didn't. Mrs Furlong made a lifelong commitment to disapproval.

'So you think I'm doing the right thing?' 'Absolutely.'

Gwennie's gratitude was such that she stood up and began tidying things on Mrs Fleet's dressing table. She knew the old lady hated to have disorder anywhere.

'Leave that alone, Gwennie,' Mrs Fleet said, 'that's Rachel's job. She's not much of a cleaner but she may as well do something for her money.'

'Do you want me to help you get up?' Gwennie offered.

'Yes, my dear, then perhaps we could go for a walk around the garden; I'm feeling quite good this morning. I would like to have some flowers on my table. There are so few around at this time of year and you are the most imaginative person I know when it comes to flower arranging.'

Gwennie basked in the warmth of the compliment. No one had ever paid her a compliment in mother's time. And she had never been held up as the best at anything. Mother thought that praise made children conceited. She wanted praise herself though, for every little thing.

***

Lottie woke to birdsong and a brilliantly sunny morning. It was such a luxury to wake when the sun was up. For so many years she had lived like a mole; never seeing daylight during the winter months.

Now she was keen to start her day with a brisk walk around The Green just to get the blood flowing in her veins and to utilise some of Gwennie's information.

She stretched, smoothing her limbs across the cool sheets. The duvet made crackling noises.

***

'You were late back last night, darling.' Jane Pendleton said when her husband entered the kitchen. He was walking slowly and looked as if he had the weight of the world on his shoulders. Jane knew that he had gone to visit an ailing old man last night. She didn't want to say the wrong thing so she put down the whisk she was using to scramble their breakfast eggs and put her arms around him.

Charles' arms came around her reflexively. He hugged her and she felt his body shudder. 'He's safe with our Lord now.' Charles said.

Jane's eyes filled with tears for the loss of the valiant soul who had lived a long and good life but she couldn't understand why Charles was so upset; Sidney Vernon had been a hundred years old.

'His last words were a prayer for you and me, my darling.' Charles said.

Jane's tears fell then and she suspected that calming her was the only thing that held her wonderful husband together.

'What do you have planned for today?' Charles said at last.

'I'm going to contact the prison about a return visit.'

'So soon? You got on with this lady well then?' Charles was worried that his wife may get too deeply into this but didn't want to say so.

'I disgraced myself.' Jane twisted her fingers together into a cat's cradle of embarrassment. 'I fainted. I think it must have been the heat in there. I didn't even get to shake hands with the poor woman. I must go back.'

'Of course you must. Though you shouldn't let it prey on your mind. It will have provided interesting conversation.' It was providing interesting thoughts for Charles too. Young women didn't usually faint. 'Are you sure you're feeling well? Do you need a check up?'

'I'm fine, darling. It was the heat. I'm sure of it.

Charles beamed. He must take even greater care of his lovely, young wife.

***

Lottie Colenso rarely visited Lyeminster these days. She had no desire to run into any of the people she used to work with but, when she did need to go to the city, she reminded herself very firmly that she was Lottie Colenso and no one else. And even though she had almost rubbed shoulders with former colleagues, no one, to date, had ever given her a second glance.

During her previous life she had discovered that middle aged women could become invisible. But not to those who were actively looking for them.

A better camouflage was to dress to be noticed, and this Friday morning, clad in a dress of peacock blue which was fringed with orange, and swathed all around with an emerald green pashmina, and wearing a jet beaded cap, Lottie Colenso knew that she would not be overlooked. She would attract little real interest though; people would see the clothes and the elaborate make up and not look at the person inside them. Another disguise. Lottie found that these days she was always in one disguise or another but she would never, never be tempted into the sort of disguise favoured by Avril Major.

Upon her retirement, she had packed up all her business suits and taken them to the charity shop before she left the city and no one in Whittington Edge had any knowledge of her former life. With the slight change of name and the change of her mode of dress, she thought she could remain undiscovered for years. She renamed her ex, Eric, and promptly allowed them to have split somewhere back in the mists of time. Lottie would be a brave, and merry widow; a divorcee, no matter how glad to be so, sounded so sad to her ears.

In the same charity shop that had received her largesse so gratefully, she had found a flapper outfit of dress and cap, both encrusted with jet bugle beads. The cap fitted her and so did the dress and Lottie Colenso could see what her new look was going to be; she was going to become an interesting eccentric. How could she be more different? Keith Kendal would never recognise Lottie Colenso if he fell over her in the street.

Lottie would deny that this had anything to do with her new look – had anyone known about Keith Kendal and thought to ask.

As she strolled around the market keeping her movements fluid, resisting the urge to march as her alter ego had been wont to do, all her hard won confidence was shattered as she caught a flicker of recognition in the eyes of a man she had hoped never to meet. Keith Kendal.

He paused and glared at her. It was him. She looked away and adjusted her pashmina, trying not to show by her actions that her heart was hammering fit to burst, but he reached out as if to touch her and Lottie's heart stopped in her chest. Nausea swept over her. She could feel perspiration breaking out all over her body. Was this it? Would he dare to attack her in a crowded market place on market day?

Yes, he would. And she knew from experience that no one would intervene. People were too afraid to get involved nowadays; there were so many incidents reported of members of the public who had tried to help when others were attacked or when property was being vandalised only to find themselves stabbed or murdered. No, no one would come to her aid. And who could blame them?

She pretended interest in the nearest shop window. She willed him to go away and her panic to subside. She needed her wits about her. She couldn't afford to fall apart. He could be pulling a knife out of his pocket as she stared at this display of army surplus items in the window. Please don't allow him to be doing that.

Please. Not now.

Not here.

Summoning all her self control she tilted her chin up. The beads on her cap clacked together.

He was the real reason she had retired. This was the one person who she knew meant her harm. Then just as she knew he was about to speak another voice cut in.

'Lottie! Fancy seeing you here.'

In the reflection from the glass she saw the man's brow pucker in a frown then saw him withdraw his hand slowly, as if he wasn't too sure. He grimaced, stared at her and the owner of the voice for a few seconds before giving a sort of shrug and turning away only to turn back and glare at her again.

She could see that he hadn't been entirely fooled. He knew who she was, or, at least, he thought he did. But today he wasn't prepared to act on his suspicions. He turned at last, hurrying away unembarrassed at the imminent mistake from which a stranger had saved him.

And the stranger was Gwennie.

Lottie drew in a deep breath and let it out again soundlessly. Suddenly her heart stilled and the dreadful pounding in her ears subsided sufficiently for her to hear the everyday noises of the market again.

'Gwennie! How lovely to see you.'

She was so pleased that Gwennie had not adhered to her mother's lesson that first names were not allowed in the street. Like eating sandwiches and laughing, first names were kept for private places according to the law laid down by Gwennie's mother. Lottie allowed a tinkling note of joy to enter her voice 'how lovely to see you. Do you have time for a cup of tea?'

'Oh!' Gwennie glanced around her as if she had committed some unpardonable solecism. 'I didn't mean to – I mean – '

'I was intending to have one myself and I've been putting it off because I didn't want to sit alone; it always makes one look so…friendless, I always think.' Lottie had lowered her voice to a conspiratorial tone. 'Please say you'll join me.' At this point Lottie linked her arm through Gwennie's and she saw Gwennie weaken.

The note of entreaty in her voice silenced all Gwennie's unspoken concerns. Here was a much loved friend who needed her help. Gwennie's heart swelled with pride.

'I would be honoured.' She said.

And Lottie's eyes almost fell out of her head.

***

The Rose Bowl café was up one flight of stairs on The Approach, the small paved area that joined the marketplace to Market Street. The doorway was almost hidden between a haberdashery shop and Mordred's Emporium.

The sign over the door was claret red with gold swirly lettering which read: 'purveyors of fine teas'. As Mordred's Emporium was practically opposite Montague Flaxton's butcher's shop with its swirly dark green and gold sign, Lottie thought some competition or collusion may have been involved when the sign writer was hired.

Once inside the doorway the staircase was narrow, allowing little opportunity for conversation although Gwennie twittered happily to Lottie's back as they trudged up the steep steps.

If it were possible to enter a time warp and see Lyeminster as it had been at the turn of the previous century then the Rose Bowl was one of the best places to enjoy the experience.

Lottie paused in the doorway, ostensibly to make an entrance, but actually to repay part of her oxygen debt; she was allowing herself to get out of shape. Something must be done about that. She could attribute some of her breathlessness to shock but not all.

A waitress whizzed past them carrying a large tray upon which was a matching teapot, milk jug and sugar bowl together with two china cups and saucers all in the Rose Bowl's signature design of red floribunda roses. The wide floorboards creaked with every footfall and Lottie's gaze dropped to see the wood, shiny with wear.

'There's a table by the window, ladies.' The waitress called over her shoulder. 'I'll be with you in a minute.'

Lottie obediently led the way to a table for two, circular and draped with a pink cloth topped with white lace, which stood in solitary splendour in the bay window overlooking the Approach.

'Will this do, Gwennie?' She belatedly asked her companion.

'Oh, it's lovely.' Gwennie, bright eyed, unbuttoned her coat and stacked bags containing her purchases in the gap between the window and the table. She looked around happily and Lottie knew that visits to tea shops were more of a treat to Gwennie than she had imagined possible.

Down in the market place she could see Keith Kendal. He was looking around and rubbing his chin. Lottie felt a shiver run down her spine. Was he looking for her? And, if so, how long was he prepared to loiter hoping that she would reappear unaccompanied by the guileless Gwennie?

Lottie toyed with the idea of asking the waitress if there was a back way that she could use to escape unnoticed. But then, she looked at Gwennie and knew that she wouldn't be able to explain such behaviour. And what would Gwennie tell the rest of the Murder Club? The last thing Lottie wanted was to encourage questions. That may lead to speculation about her past.

Had she been alone it would have been a different matter.

The waitress arrived, order pad in hand. She smoothed the already pristine lace cloth and smiled at her customers. She wore a black dress and lace edged pinafore but, happily, was not obliged to wear a cap.

Lottie had made great show of reading the menu and smiled at Gwennie who seemed genuinely interested in the limited range of fare.

'What would you like, Gwennie?' She ventured, hoping that first names were allowed within the walls of a tea shop. As tea shops were seen as primarily the preserve of females, it seemed they were.

'They have toasted tea cakes.' Gwennie gave her handbag a sidelong glance and Lottie knew that she was worrying about the cost. 'Although plain buttered toast is just as good.'

'As this is my treat,' Lottie said firmly, 'I think we should have both, and tea, please, a large pot.' She looked up at the smiling waitress. 'And could we have jam and marmalade too, please. Oh! And honey.'

When the waitress had scurried away Lottie looked at her companion and saw that she was quite pink with pleasure.

'I really can't expect you to pay for all this, Lottie.' Gwennie said at last.

'Rubbish. Of course I shall pay for it. You're doing me a favour, my dear. I always feel so self conscious sitting alone in a café.' She looked across the table and saw that her excuse was positively inspired. Lottie had never felt self conscious in her life; hardly understood the concept, in fact. But Gwennie could empathise; for Gwennie, feeling out of place was a lifelong experience and Lottie had picked up on this fact.

The waitress arrived a few minutes later with their order and Gwennie hastily offered to pour. Lottie glanced out of the window and saw that Keith Kendal had gone. Maybe he hadn't recognised her at all. Maybe he was going to ask her for directions or something similarly innocent.

Maybe nothing. She had seen that look of hatred in his eyes. He had known who she was alright. Lottie tried to ignore the sick feeling in her stomach. She knew that, had Gwennie not intervened, she would have given herself away. Really, she must be more careful. She was Lottie Colenso now. No one else. Lottie Colenso. She took a few steadying breaths to reinforce the message.

'Here you are, dear.' Gwennie handed over a cup of tea and Lottie thanked her. 'This really is a treat.' Gwennie continued. 'I've often wondered what it's like in here. It's very nice isn't it? Very select.'

'Yes, it is nice.' Lottie agreed, looking around and trying to work out what 'very select' really meant. It was a phrase she had heard used by elderly ladies –

never men, and never anyone of Gwennie's age – and she again realised how Gwennie's mother had aged her daughter before her time.

'My mother used to come here with Mrs Harrison.' Gwennie continued in hushed tones.

'So this is one of your regular haunts then.'

'Oh no, dear, I never came. Not when mother was with Mrs Harrison.' Gwennie's face was pinched with shock at the suggestion and her hand went to her chest.

'Oh.' Lottie said, not knowing what other response was expected. She didn't like to ask who Mrs Harrison was. From Gwennie's manner, she assumed that anyone with any local knowledge whatsoever not only knew who Mrs Harrison was, but revered her as wholeheartedly as Gwennie's mother obviously had. Lottie didn't really 'do' reverence so she steered the conversation away from the sainted Mrs Harrison and towards the toasted teacakes each crowned with melting butter.

'These are delicious.' She closed her eyes the better to appreciate the mingled flavours of yeast, spice and candied peel. When she opened them again Gwennie was still cutting her teacake into tiny sections small enough to pop into her mouth without having to bite them. Didn't the woman have any teeth?

No, that wasn't it, she stifled a sigh, Gwennie was being genteel. This woman really needed to get out more. But who was strong enough to take Gwennie by the hand and force her to update her image by half a century?

Maybe she could do it. Ok so the jam and Jerusalem bit had come to naught but people were a different kettle of fish. She could turn Gwennie into a project. She could lure her into more fashionable clothes. There was no hope of her going for the overtly outrageous such as Lottie herself had recently embraced, but surely she didn't need to look such a frump.

The word 'frump' leaping into her mind as it did brought back memories of Avril Major and her disguise. Lottie forced it to the back of her mind and concentrated on Gwennie.

Gwennie eventually popped a triangle of teacake into her mouth. It must have been stone cold but she gave every appearance of enjoying it.

'Delicious.' She said wiping her fingers on a linen napkin. Lottie reached out and took another teacake.

Whilst Gwennie was busy with the teacake Lottie kept watch over the unfolding scene in The Approach. It would be lunchtime at her previous place of employment and various faces that she recognised passed by.

She saw the prissy woman from the finance department. Lottie couldn't recall her name. Then a very familiar face came into view. Pete Cunningham. Well, well, well. She hadn't seen him in months, obviously. But, thinking about it, it could actually be more like a couple of years. She felt a warm glow at the sight of one of her old lovers.

Work had once been her life in more than one way; it had been her love life as well as her reason to exist. She had taken lovers from all grades above and below her own during her many years in the job. She had felt no awkwardness about this and moved on easily once the current affair was over.

She had been careful to remain friends with her exes. She had never broken up with one man to take up with another; this was where trouble lay, and, if the break up was really so that another affair could be allowed to flourish, she always kept the new man on the back burner for a couple of months before beginning a new intrigue.

This had worked well for her. She had retained her old friends. But, and this was a big 'but', she wasn't sure that she could call on them all to join forces and help her.

Where did that thought come from? Did she really believe that she was in danger?

...Maybe... Mm... and maybe she should stay away from Lyeminster for a little longer. And maybe she should stick to Gwennie whilst they were here.

Across the pavement Montague Flaxton emerged from his doorway wiping his hands on his blue and white striped apron. He looked this way and that. Looked up to the sky and squinted into the weak sunlight. He closed his eyes and Lottie could see him take a few deep breaths before returning to his shop.

A dowdy woman wearing a coat of indeterminate colour was walking past Montague Flaxton's shop. She was holding the arm of a tall man in a smart blue blazer. It was Avril Major and the man she had collected from the station the other day. They looked an odd couple obviously but there was more to it than that. Lottie eventually put her finger on what was wrong. She would never have expected a man so dapper in his appearance to have such a woman on his arm.

He wouldn't have looked out of place with Avril in her usual garb so why was she dressing like this? But that wasn't it. Yes, something about them made her feel that Avril was calling the shots and her companion was unhappy about something.

'More tea?' Gwennie held the teapot aloft and Lottie gave her the benefit of her thousand watt smile, immediately forgetting about the couple who were now turning into Market Street and heading off towards what the council liked to call the cultural quarter.

'Yes please.' She said, eagerly lifting her cup to welcome a refill. The tea twisted from the china spout like old fashioned barley sugar and Lottie's mind was off on another of its ramblings.

'The tea looks just like barley sugar.' She said out loud. Do they still make barley sugar sticks, do you think? They used to cost three pence when I was a child. My father used to bring one home for me on Friday nights.' She smiled to herself.

'I used to love those.' Gwennie enthused. 'And Cherry Lips and...' she was off on a catalogue of all the sweets she could remember from her childhood.

Lottie joined in with Flying Saucers and Sherbet Fountains.

Soon they were laughing and well into the toast and jam.

'Have you had any further thoughts about Michael Garnett?' Gwennie poured another cup of tea, replaced the teapot on its brass trivet and tweezed a cube of sugar from the china bowl with silver plated tongs. 'Everything is so nice here, isn't it?' She added.

'Lovely.' Lottie agreed, deriving more pleasure from this tea party than she would have ever have expected. Then she remembered that, only moments ago, she was considering turning Gwennie into a project. It felt patronising now. Lottie suspected that Gwennie could teach her just as much as she could teach Gwennie. Gwennie knew how to enjoy herself; Lottie feared that she had never mastered that skill.

Her first instinct had been to crush Gwennie's question about Michael Garnett by telling her that this was for the meeting, not for discussion otherwise. Now, humbled by the other woman's ability to find so much enjoyment in mundane things like a cup of tea with a friend, she changed her mind and decided that she should behave like a friend not as if she were some superior officer putting an underling in their place.

Discussion of the Rosa Garnett murder kept them occupied throughout the rest of the tea and toast.

'Have you finished your shopping?' Lottie began to gather her draperies around her. 'May I offer you a lift home?'

'I was going to buy a new duvet from Pennyfeather's.' Gwennie bit her lip. She was footsore and weary and, although the rest and the tea had restored her a little, the prospect of trudging right up Market street to Pennyfeather's reminded her how exhausted she was and made her resolve falter.

'May I come with you?' Lottie beamed at her. 'It's so long since I went to Pennyfeather's. I may see something I like. Then we could go home together. My car is parked in The Exchange. If I wouldn't be in the way, that is.'

Gwennie gushed her enthusiasm for the plan and soon Lottie had settled their bill, taken possession of more than half of Gwennie's packages and they were heading towards the departmental store in Market Street discussing the finer points of duvet buying.

Lottie forced her steps to remain easy and her gait languid.

When Gwennie said something amusing, Lottie threw back her head and laughed. At first Gwennie was startled, but the second time it happened she joined in, her laugh ringing out like a young girl's. It sounded wonderfully liberated and Lottie silently thumbed her nose at 'mother' whom she was sure, was turning in her grave.

***

Pennyfeather's had changed little since the war. Its escalators were rattling old wooden affairs and counters were clustered together all over the place. Staff milled around offering help and well groomed smiles. And that wasn't the only surprise awaiting Lottie.

She had never spent the best part of an hour deliberating over the purchase of anything, let alone a duvet. When she entered a shop it was because she was driven by necessity. She knew what she wanted and headed directly to the place where the desired object could be found. She then found the one that fitted her, or the one that was the right colour and she carted it to the checkout and queued to pay for it. This usually took a maximum of ten minutes, often much less.

Today she followed Gwennie around the bedding department, debating the merits of down and feather or polyester filling. At Gwennie's bidding she asked for guidance and then dismissed the sales assistant so that she and Gwennie could discuss the purchase in greater detail. And, amazingly, she found that she was enjoying herself.

When the purchase had been made and three duvet covers had added a frightening number of pounds to the bill, Pennyfeather's provided a burly escort to carry the burden to The Exchange car park. Both women were grateful and walked alongside him briskly.

'If you like, you can give me your keys and I'll fetch your car for you'. The man offered.

Lottie was sorely tempted but her little runabout was temperamental as only a small car could be. 'Nothing would be more welcome.' She told him. 'But if you don't hit the accelerator at precisely the right time, it floods and nothing will induce it to start.'

Lottie had owned two cars for years now. One was the yellow sports car, the love of her life. The other was a dull red hatchback. You would see at least thirty of them driving around Lyeminster any time you visited.

The hatchback was not an expensive car. It was reliable – very important in Lottie's former line of work – but it wouldn't stand out like the sports car would. Lottie had paid to change its number plate on her retirement so that no one would recognise it were they interested enough to give it a second glance.

'Very well, Ma'am.' The man hefted his load higher. 'I was hoping to save you a walk.'

'Thank you, that was very kind of you.' Lottie smiled at him. He didn't believe her; she could tell that. But she shrugged it off.

He stowed the dark blue Pennyfeather's bags in the boot of Lottie's car and then took all the other bags and packages too, carefully fitting them all together, slamming the boot lid down and checking it was securely latched.

They thanked him and he clicked his heels and strode back to the shop.

Lottie paused when Gwennie made a strange moaning noise. 'What's wrong?' She looked up to see

Gwennie frowning in concentration. Her gaze followed Gwennie's but she could see nothing.

'It was that man again.' Gwennie said, shaking her head and stepping briskly into the car. 'I'm sure it was.'

'What man?' Lottie was feeling shaky. Determinedly, she forced herself into 'Lottie' mode and threw her bag over into the back seat.

'I must have been mistaken. Ignore me.'

Lottie turned the key, kicked hard on the accelerator at the optimum moment and jammed the gear lever into first. Luckily she had found a space where she could drive straight out and this was what she did now, making the tyres squeal on the concrete floor.

Following the arrows, she negotiated the route to the exit, but, on the next floor down, she had to slow for a pedestrian. He heard her coming and waited. She eased around him in the confined space and raised her hand in thanks. That was when she realised it was him; Keith Kendal. Her foot automatically stamped on the accelerator making Gwennie lurch in her seat.

He knew. She could see in his eyes that he knew it was her. And he knew she should be alarmed. Well, blow that. Lottie Colenso was not intimidated by any man. She, Lottie Colenso, had never met him before so why should she be afraid of him.

His lips parted over large, jagged, teeth, showing a gap where one was missing, and he saluted her with one finger. This salute was sinister; a threat because, from the salute, he lowered his hand and mined throwing a knife. Keith Kendall's accuracy with a knife was legendary. Lottie gulped, her eyes wide.

With what she later realised was remarkable presence of mind, she forced a smile to her lips and blew him a theatrical kiss as if she were thanking him for waiting for the car to pass. She shouted 'thank you, darling' to him through the closed window, hit the accelerator again and the car, protesting at the unaccustomed ill-treatment, careered around the corner.

'Sorry about that, Gwennie,' she said when she was on the final approach to the Market Street, 'I caught the pedal with the toe of my shoe.'

'Oh...I...I thought it must be something like that.' Gwennie's voice quavered.

Lottie tossed back her head and laughed until Gwennie joined in.

'Did you see that man's face when you called him 'darling'?' Gwennie bit her lip. 'I do envy you, Lottie. You're so…so confident.'

If only you knew, Gwennie, if only you knew.

CHAPTER EIGHT

Gwennie invited Lottie in for coffee when they finally reached her home in Camp Hill. Lottie accepted, thereby surprising herself; she was not the sort of person who made small talk and called around for coffee and a chat. All Lottie's conversations were held to a particular purpose, and were conducted for just as long as was required to fulfil that purpose.

The instant the thought hit her, Lottie corrected it. That was the way she used to think in her former life. The new Lottie, on the other hand, always had time for everyone. Lottie was nothing like the woman she had once been; nothing at all. Weird men didn't pretend to shoot or throw knives at Lottie. Lottie had no enemies. She hadn't had time to make any yet. So, as the car rolled to a halt and Gwennie issued the invitation, Lottie leapt out of the car full of eager acceptance.

'I can help you carry your things in.'

The boot once opened, Lottie handed the smaller packages to Gwennie, hauling the larger and more cumbersome ones out herself.

'I should take those.' Gwennie protested.

'Not at all; you have to unlock the door.' Lottie beamed as she nodded towards the front door and the window beside it where sat Snowflake, mewing frantically at her mistress and pawing the window pane. 'You've been missed.' She said pulling down the boot lid whilst propping the bundle containing the duvet against her chest with her chin. The operation was completed with her elbow and soon she was hurrying up the path after Gwennie.

Once she was inside Gwennie's neat little house, Lottie realised that she didn't want any more to drink.

'You must want to organise your duvet.' She said. 'On second thoughts, unless you need any help with it, I think I'd better push on.'

Gwennie looked at her and Lottie could see that she was torn. 'I promised you coffee.' Gwennie protested.

'I know but, to be honest, all that tea we drank at The Rose Bowl...' she allowed her words to trail off and was rewarded with a relieved smile from her friend. Soon she was on her way back down from Camp Hill to Whittington Edge

Horse and Trumpet cottage was her refuge. She opened the front door and it reached out its warm, beer-laden breath to enfold her and welcome her home. She latched the door and sank against it, closing her eyes as soon as she knew she was securely within the thick stone walls again. Her breath escaped in a long low sigh. Then, pulling herself together, she inhaled deeply and told herself that it was ridiculous to be so afraid. She was going soft. Besides, the man's quarrel was with a person who no longer existed. She was Lottie Colenso; a totally different person. No one had any argument with Lottie Colenso. If she told herself that often enough she may even come to believe it.

The entrance hall used to be the private entrance to the living quarters of the Horse and Trumpet public house. She had painted the hall in softest lemon which contrasted well with the black chest and corner unit which were the only pieces of furniture it held.

Lottie slipped the emerald green pashmina from her shoulders and folded it neatly before placing it in the chest on top of several similar garments all in the brightest of jewel colours. Her beaded shoulder bag and cap she stowed in the otherwise empty corner cupboard, the top of which held a large brass bowl full of silk flowers.

It had been her intention to keep this full of real flowers in season but the disadvantages of removing dead heads, changing the water and picking up wizened pieces of foliage or berries from the hall carpet outweighed the joy of fresh flowers and a heavy investment in the silk alternatives soon ensued.

Having refused coffee at Gwennie's house, Lottie found herself wandering through to the kitchen to put on the kettle. She needed to think this thing with Keith Kendal through. She really ought to tell Marco that she had seen him just in case he had taken her registration number and decided to trace her. And something else had struck an off-key note but she couldn't remember what it was.

She took the church magazine with her because diverting her mind often brought it back to where she needed it to be.

She was sitting at her kitchen table an hour later, a mug of coffee in her hands when the phone rang.

Having given herself a good talking to, Lottie was feeling much better; relaxed and back on an even keel. Cassie Mellon's advertisement in the church magazine had tempted her to call at Hallelujah House across The Green and enjoy a 'relaxing aromatherapy massage'.

She had just taken the cordless phone from its holder, thinking to ring ahead rather than visit unannounced, when the phone in her hand rang.

'Horse and Trumpet Cottage.' Lottie said following the Whittington Edge convention. When in Rome...

'Lottie? Is that you, Lottie? It's Gwennie here. And I've found...I've found a body in my potting shed.'

Vivid images raced across the screen of Lottie's imagination. The doctor poisoned with morphine by his wife who had once been a nurse and who had been having a lesbian affair with Arnold Pickard's wife.

Arnold Pickard and the crucifix. Or was it one of the wives poisoned by the doctor? She couldn't remember. Rubbish, of course. All of it. But then she remembered the cloaked and hooded figure of Charles Pendleton hunched over and hurrying from St Jude's at midnight and forgot all about Sidney Vernon.

'Don't touch anything.' She yelled down the phone. 'I'll be right there.' She slammed the phone down on the kitchen table and collected what she needed. Soon she was in her little car chugging back up to Camp Hill. She ought to have rung the police or told Gwennie to ring the police but Lottie wanted to be sure first. She didn't want Gwennie to be intimidated by a whole scene of crime unit descending on her. Having taken Gwennie on as a project, Lottie was taking her responsibilities seriously.

***

Cassie Mellon was playing soft music and burning invigorating oils as she gave Avril Major an aromatherapy massage. She heard an almighty crash from next door and wondered if Bill Warbeck realised that he too made noises. If he did maybe he shouldn't be so quick to yell at her and slam his kitchen window.

Avril heard it too because Cassie felt her start. 'Quietly now.' Cassie intoned. 'Ignoring all outside noises...' she felt Avril's tense muscles relax beneath her fingers. 'That's better.' She said. 'And relax...'

Cassie liked Avril Major. Avril was one of those quiet ladies living a quiet life in this small town. She kept herself to herself and, Cassie was sure, lived a spiritual life, as she did herself.

Yes, all in all, Cassie felt she and Avril were soul mates. There was a Mind, Body and Spirit fair coming to Lyeminster soon and Cassie was seriously considering asking Avril if she would like to come along.

Avril had enjoyed her massage but she didn't have time for that whale music that Cassie insisted on, and the incense or whatever it was, was playing havoc with her sinuses. Still, it was something to do to pass an afternoon and Mr Slippitt was due that evening.

Such an unfortunate name for a man, Avril thought, especially a man like Mr Slippitt who was unlikely to have slipped anything... oh really, she shouldn't be thinking such things.

Mr Slippitt – she never had found out his first name – missed his mother. The couple had lived amiably together since Mr Slippitt senior had slipped away to his celestial reward. Avril almost laughed at the words her mind had chosen and she schooled her features into something more becoming. More decorous.

Mr Slippitt liked things to be decorous. He liked doilies and Royal Doulton china and fairy cakes. And he liked his sandwiches with the crusts cut off.

When he had first outlined his requirements she had been worried lest she be forced to drink weak tea with lemon but all was well; he liked a strong cup of tea just as she did herself.

Every Friday he arrived carrying a small nosegay of flowers which he presented to Avril with a courtly bow. Having gained access to her home he smoothed his overcoat onto its hanger. He stood before the hall stand and smoothed his hands over his hair.

Then he smoothed his tie and the front of his cardigan before flourishing a crisp and smooth handkerchief of the most sparkling white and polishing his spectacles.

During this ritual, Avril praised him for his thoughtfulness in bringing her flowers, gushing with gratitude for such an unexpected gift. She made tea, being careful to set it out daintily on a tray before carrying it through to the sitting room. There he would hasten to relieve her of her burden and wait for her to seat herself on the settee before taking possession of the big armchair by the fire.

Avril took care to unplug the phone when Mr Slippitt was due. He disliked interruptions, especially those made by telephones.

She also switched on the chimes on her wall clock. At all other times these were switched off because they reminded her of her grandmother's parlour and the bongs which punctuated silent Sundays all those years ago when reading a book was the most exciting thing she was allowed to do.

Now, lying face down on Cassie's couch listening to Cassie's hypnotic voice, she realised that she only came for these massages on Fridays. And, on the Fridays that she didn't come to Cassie, she spent a leisurely afternoon in the bath in her black and gold bathroom before anointing herself with fragrant oils.

The notion came to her that this was an odd carry-on since Mr Slippitt had no interest in sex; at least, she had never seen any sign of it. She wondered if he was gay and, if so, why was he wasting time drinking tea and eating fairy cakes with her when he could be doing something more to his taste.

Another laugh had to be bitten back. No, there was nothing more to his taste. Mr Slippitt always looked as if he had just been polished; he wouldn't want to sully himself with sex.

This time Avril did laugh. She felt Cassie's fingers hesitate and her cooing pause for as long as it took for her client to disguise the laugh as a cough and restore herself to spiritual mode, concentrating on the matter in hand.

Avril was wondering how much longer this was going to take. She wanted to sneak a look at her wristwatch but there was no way she could do that surreptitiously. Cassie had a clock counting out its heartbeat of minutes and Avril hoped that less than sixty of them had passed because she had antimacassars to arrange on chair backs and lavender polish to spray on the radiators so that Mr Slippitt thought that she had polished to his late mother's exacting standard. In actual fact Avril employed the services of Mrs Bettinson once a week. Mrs Bettinson was old enough not to know what the various gadgets were that Avril sometimes forgot to lock away in her toy cupboard.

Mr Slippitt was the least demanding of Avril's clientele yet he was the one she worried about pleasing the most. When she was ready to retire, she already had

Mr Slippitt's enormous wealth marked down as her pension. She sighed and wished it were Wednesday.

Monty came on Wednesday. He arrived promptly at seven still carrying with him the odour of the meat he had been cutting up all day. He had a red face and bright piggy eyes. He laughed a lot and could barely keep his hands off her whilst he crossed the threshold. Their Wednesdays were fast and furious full of jokes, rude stories, and slap and tickle.

Monty was a laugh alright. He was the sort of man she might have married, had she not married Sonny. But it was as well that she hadn't because she liked other things too; things that Monty wouldn't understand at all. Monty wouldn't understand that sometimes she liked the playacting of a proper tea party. Monty, as a husband, would be a slob. But the sex would be fun.

'Just rest there and come back into the room in your own time.' Cassie instructed in the irritating sing-song voice that drove Avril crazy.

Avril pretended to be returning from the astral travels that Cassie insisted she take.

'And how was that?' Cassie persisted, her voice still ethereal. 'Nice?'

'Wonderful.' Avril stretched her arms and kept up the pretence. Avril was good at pretence; after all it was her stock in trade.

'Where did you go?' Cassie asked, sending Avril into a panic.

Where did she go? She hadn't been anywhere. She had been here, for goodness' sake.

'The Taj Mahal.' Avril said, inspiration suddenly rescuing her.

'The Taj Mahal?' Cassie repeated. 'Now that's very interesting.'

Avril didn't think it was interesting at all. It was the picture on the calendar on Cassie's wall and thus was the first thing Avril had seen when she was casting about for a sensible reply to Cassie's ridiculous question. However, Cassie seemed happy so, once again, Avril had pleased her companion.

'The Taj Mahal is a universal symbol of love.' Cassie beamed. 'You might not have noticed but I have a picture of it here.' She swept an arm in the direction of the calendar.

'Well I never.' Avril said, her eyes round with wonder, 'who would have thought it?' She was rapidly pulling on her clothes realising just how little time she had before Mr Slippitt arrived. 'How much do I owe you? I have to dash.'

'Slow down, Avril'. Cassie made soothing motions with her hands. 'Don't ruin all our good work.'

Avril forced a dreamy look to her face. She suspected, heaven forbid, that if she didn't slow down, Cassie would have her back on the couch again.

She made her escape and was soon tripping lightly down the path from Hallelujah House and back to her own cottage. She paused beneath the vast branches of the chestnut tree that sheltered the vehicles of her many visitors from prying eyes and inhaled the wonderful perfumes of autumn. Anything to rid her nostrils of the cloying scent of the oil burner.

A quick glance at her watch told her that she had ample time to perform the tasks that would make Mr Slippitt happy.

***

Avril may not have been the world's best housekeeper, but she was organised. She had converted her box room into an office. Here she kept her computer so that she could surf the web. She also had a filing cabinet that she had picked up at a car boot sale. In the filing cabinet a box was labelled with each of the days of the week and in each box resided the special things that made that particular day special to that particular client.

Nothing in the boxes identified the men, of course. Nowhere on her premises was there any hint of names or addresses. She had a mobile phone for them to call and each month, as regular as clockwork, she changed the SIM card so that their calls could not be traced. Avril was a professional after all. She never called any of her clients on her land line or on her personal mobile which was on a contract and therefore traceable to her.

Avril felt that she would have made a good secret agent and conducted her business as if the men in her life were high ranking civil servants, or members of parliament or minor royalty as the newspapers always described them when a scandal broke.

Avril happily imagined herself into the role of courtesan to the rich and famous as she hauled out the Friday box and set to with the lavender polish and the lace edged fripperies.

***

With Lottie's mind occupied, it took one of those quantum leaps and she knew what had seemed off when she and Gwennie were looking out of the window of the Rose Bowl.

Montague Flaxton had come out of his shop for a breather. She had once been to his shop when she was looking for something to fill her freezer and whilst she was deciding between her options he greeted another customer who was obviously flattered by the fact that the butcher remembered her name.

'Good morning, Mr Flaxton.' She gushed. 'What a lovely day it is for the time of year.'

Mr Flaxton agreed that it was indeed a lovely day and returned his attention to Lottie after a short exchange.

Lottie noticed when she left the shop that the name Montague Flaxton was emblazoned in green and gold over the door. Lottie squinted. She was sure she had seen him somewhere else, but it wouldn't come.

CHAPTER NINE

Lottie if she should call the rest of the Murder Club before she went to Gwennie's. Then she pictured the expression on the face of the senior investigating officer if he arrived to take charge and found five women of a certain age ranged around his crime scene.

Having decided that she couldn't in all conscience send for them, Lottie had to find a way to excuse herself for not having done so. She thought. Hard.

Friday. It was one of Susan's days for The Butterfly Bush and Biddy had said something about going away for the weekend to a health spa.

Friday, yes. So, that left Blanche who would also be busy at The Butterfly Bush.

Lottie smiled to herself. She could go and help Gwennie without feeling guilty. She found that she had paused at the entrance to Longfellow Hollow and whilst it was generous to think of the other members of the group and be concerned about their feelings, Gwennie needed her. Now.

The little house on Burns Hill looked just as it had when she left it less than two hours ago. She parked, glanced around, stepped out of the car and locked it and glanced around again. No sign of trouble. She pretended to be searching for something in her pocket whilst she listened and sniffed the air. Nothing untoward presented itself. She had no sense of twitching net curtains either. Another good sign.

In close knit communities, people tended to tune in to whatever was going on around them instinctively. Lottie was sure that a person going missing would have transmitted itself all around the six streets by now. Groups of women should be gathering on corners to talk about the missing person. That meant that the body was someone from outside Camp Hill.

She bit down on her lower lip and wondered whether protocol could be abandoned in the face of murder. In other words, dare she enter by the back gate? As there was still no sign of Gwennie, she decided she probably dared.

Gwennie was in the garden when Lottie's black stiletto heels announced her progress between Gwennie's house and the one next door. She called out 'Lottie, is that you?' in a tremulous voice. Her back was turned to the door of the shed and she stood, ramrod stiff, ready to repel any invaders. She visibly relaxed as Lottie turned the corner and she could see her at last.

'Oh Lottie, thank goodness it's you.' She took a step forward and glanced behind her lest some opportunist should take that split second to leap into the shed and mess up the evidence.

'Are you alright, Gwennie?' Lottie placed an arm carefully around Gwennie's shoulders and gave her a quick squeeze. She felt Gwennie relax and then stiffen her spine.

Lottie was pleased. Yes. That had been the right thing to do; the 'Lottie' thing to do. She was getting the hang of this. The quick hug had given Gwennie strength. It had also spurred Lottie on to greater things.

Did other people monitor their behaviour as closely as she was doing? Unlikely. She reminded herself that other people didn't have the complicated life that she was forced to live.

'I'm fine now you're here.' Gwennie said, confirming Lottie's own thoughts. 'Are you ready? I'd already opened the shed door before I knew about the body, of course, so I haven't bothered to put on gloves or anything.'

'Good thinking.' Lottie nodded and prepared herself for the sight of blood and gore and whatever else was lurking behind the plain wooden door. She hoped that she lived up to Gwennie's faith in her. Ok, so she had discovered the body on the roundabout but that had been a skeleton; this was likely to be...ugh it didn't bear thinking about. She took a deep breath. She had to be strong for Gwennie and not show herself up.

Gwennie took a step back and grimaced as she reached past Lottie to open the door once more. The door hinges creaked and Lottie closed her eyes for a second to centre herself. She smelled the 'shed' smell of Hessian sacks and sun-warmed creosote.

What she couldn't smell was blood or...or any of the other things that she knew she should be able to smell. Her long association with crime novels told her that there should be a rare concoction of revolting odours assaulting her nostrils before the door was even fully opened.

This discovery had led her to keep her eyes closed. She sniffed some more, keeping one hand on Gwennie's arm to prevent her bursting into the shed.

She knew that Gwennie hadn't moved a muscle and was unlikely to so perhaps she was holding onto Gwennie as much as she was holding her back.

Slowly she opened her eyes and looked around. The shed was as neat as a new pin. Shelves had coffee jars suspended from their undersides. Each jar held nails or screws. More large nails had been hammered into the framework of the shed and garden tools were hanging between them. There was a lawnmower and a Strimmer and a bicycle that looked as if it had been a birthday or Christmas present to Gwennie back in the days before the stylish cycles came out. It was shiny and well-oiled and it was still Gwennie's usual mode of transport.

And there was a sack and, protruding from it was a misshapen leg clad in a thick nylon stocking of the sort Lottie's grandmother used to wear. At the end of the leg was a swollen foot wearing a gold shoe.

'There's something wrong here.' Lottie took a step forward into the shed. Gwennie twittered her alarm. The heat of the day, little though it might have been, was concentrated into the musty smell of the shed and made her catch her breath, but she still couldn't detect the odours that should have been there.

'I'm so sorry, dear.' Gwennie bustled in behind her. 'I should have called the police. I should never have involved you. But, you see, I knew you were good at this sort of thing.'

'No.' Lottie said. 'That's not what I mean.' She took another step forward and reached out a finger as if to touch the swollen leg. Gwennie gasped. 'It's alright.' Lottie assured her. 'Listen.' She waited whilst Gwennie settled down then she allowed her finger to make contact. She gripped Gwennie's arm a little tighter to ensure that she knew silence was important. Then she jabbed. Hard. The unmistakable sound of scrunching newspaper came from the leg and Lottie breathed a silent sigh of relief.

'What was that?' Gwennie's voice trembled and she began to wring her hands.

'That,' Lottie said, 'is the sound of a guy. Brace yourself, Gwennie.' Lottie took a grip on the edge of the sacking and jerked it away revealing the bent and twisted form of the guy complete with pushchair that she had seen the night before outside the Priest at Prayer.

Gwennie uttered a little squeak of horror before the truth registered. Then she was laughing and clutching her bony chest and dabbing at her eyes with her handkerchief. Lottie could see the scrap of lace edged muslin fluttering and realised that Gwennie and Jane had the same taste in handkerchiefs.

'Come along, Gwennie,' she said, 'let me make you a cup of tea. You've had a terrible shock.'

***

Mr Slippitt arrived promptly. He always did.

Avril usually liked punctuality in a client but, in Mr Slippitt's case, she would have liked it if, just once, he was late. Or early; anything that could be interpreted as spontaneity, she would have enjoyed. She wanted him to become just a little unbuttoned.

The word 'unbuttoned' almost made her laugh out loud and a good hostess never laughed at her guests.

'For me?' Avril took the bunch of flowers that he pushed at her and clutched her bosom with her other hand. 'What a surprise.' She said. 'How kind of you.'

This ritual made his cheekbones turn pink. He turned away, removing his jacket whilst holding his face averted from her and muttering something under his breath that she knew was intended to stem the flow of her gratitude.

Yet she knew that he liked fulsome praise; men of his type always did. So Avril continued her twittering and watched out of the corner of her eye as her descent from competent businesswoman to dithering nincompoop pumped up Mr Slippitt's self esteem and caused him to straighten his normally stooped shoulders and lift his chin.

Job done, Avril thought. She smiled, making sure that her smile was tentative and nervous. Mr Slippitt turned to the hall mirror to adjust his tie and smooth both hair and cardigan. Avril excused herself meanwhile and scurried into the kitchen to put the flowers into the vase she had already prepared for them and to switch on the kettle ready to complete the tea making ritual.

She had set out the Scrabble board in the expectation that Mr Slippitt felt inclined to play; he usually did. She would have preferred him to choose Draughts, she could more easily lose at Draughts, and her losing was an important ingredient in their Friday evenings.

Mr Slippitt was hopeless at Scrabble yet, surprisingly, he adored the game. Avril had learned early on to 'lose' the dictionary. Otherwise he consulted it at every turn. and, when it became clear that his spelling was at fault or the word he had chosen didn't actually exist, Mr Slippitt visibly crumpled and Avril was put to the extra trouble of having to pump him up all over again.

Nowadays, she consigned the dictionary to the Saturday drawer of her filing cabinet and retrieved it later.

'Oh, wonderful!' Mr Slippitt rubbed his hands together when he saw the game already laid out on a table adjacent to the sofa. 'Scrabble.' He lifted up a face wreathed in smiles. 'Oh, sorry, let me assist.' And so saying, he negotiated his way through the obstacle course of fripperies Avril had placed around to dress her home the way he liked it, and reached out for the tray complete with dainty tray cloth and a crystal vase containing a single rose.

'This is delightful, my dear,' Mr Slippitt ran an eye over the tray, approving of all he saw, 'and did you embroider this tray cloth with your own fair hands?'

'Of course.' Avril lied. 'It took an age to get the colours absolutely right but I think I triumphed in the end.'

Triumphed was the right word. She had had to tug the darned thing out of the hands of Fanny Barstock at St Jude's last sale of work. It almost ended up as a fight.

'You must keep up the good work.' Mr Slippitt said. 'You were obviously meant for such delicate pursuits; so few ladies these days realise the importance of making a good home. My mother always said...'

And he was off.

Avril poured the tea and sat back in her seat, allowing his patronising balderdash to slide uncensored past that part of her brain that cried out to remind him that this was the twenty first century and women today did not see their lives revolving around a man and making sure that his home was up to scratch.

The clock chimed out the half hour and Avril proffered cake. Without pausing in his diatribe, Mr Slippitt selected one and bit deeply into it showering crumbs and words with equal enthusiasm. Noticing this, he brushed the particles from his cardigan and onto the floor. Avril said nothing. He was a good payer and she could push the vacuum cleaner around afterwards.

***

Bill Warbeck's day had ended on a much happier note. The gallery owner had phoned in raptures over 'Summer'.

'She's wonderful.' He said. 'She's perfect. I've got the photographer from the Echo coming to take pictures tomorrow and the art critic wants to interview you and your model. I expect you'll be free for an interview?'

Bill bridled slightly at the implication that he had nothing to do that couldn't be put aside at the whim of this jumped up twerp in a pink bow tie but he crushed the thought almost immediately and agreed. When fame came he would have his revenge.

'You see,' Atlantis purred as she draped herself over him, 'Lanty was right. You only had to change one tiny detail and now that trollop from Camp Hill has no power over you at all.'

The 'one tiny detail' that Bill had to change was to paint over Summer Saunders's face and hair replacing it with a glowing representation of Atlantis. Now Atlantis's tangled titian locks tumbled over the scroll of the chaise longue.

The face had changed hardly at all but Bill had painted over Summer Saunders's blue eyes with Atlantis's green. He had covered the swathe of black hair that had pooled on the floor of the original composition with bells and seashells and feathers – all the things that Atlantis usually wore twisted and twined through her Medusa-like tresses.

Bill, conscious of the rapidly approaching deadline, had pulled out all the stops. He had painted day and night. What had begun as a chore to be undertaken merely to preserve his reputation had turned into a labour of love. Curls formed themselves easily and effectively beneath his brush. Bill had always been able to paint hair. This was an important skill for a portrait painter but he had never put it fully to use before.

Atlantis' eyes glowed liquid green with only a few well placed dabs of emerald to match the satin of the main composition.

Bill was enthralled and enchanted. Atlantis would be his muse. No one could criticise him for using her as a model and, if occasionally, he changed the shape of a certain feature to emulate some other woman who interested him, no one would say a thing. In fact, it could become a signature idiosyncrasy of his work. People would take time to examine the features of his portraits and try to figure out whose nose or lips he had incorporated into his latest masterpiece.

Yes, the world was spreading itself out for Bill Warbeck to take his place. All he had to do was step forward and take it by storm. And to do that, he had to get rid of the bags under his eyes before the photographer demanded his picture.

***

Lottie hadn't been aware that Avril had a visitor early on Fridays. She never noticed anyone leaving before. She had seen a man arrive much later but this was not him. Today, she was upstairs hanging a few dresses onto padded satin hangers when Mr Slippitt slipped out into the evening. He left a lot earlier than Avril's usual callers and Avril didn't bother checking out the street before allowing him to leave. So, maybe this wasn't a 'gentleman caller' at all. Maybe this man was a relative.

Whatever he was, Lottie was drawn to the window to watch his departure. She made minor adjustments to the drape of her curtains, in order to disguise her true interest, and noted that he had not parked beneath the chestnut tree but had actually left his small grey car outside Horse and Trumpet cottage.

Lottie leaned forward to supervise his leaving. The nerve of the man. How dare he park outside Horse and Trumpet cottage and thereby give any casual observer the idea that he was visiting her.

She almost laughed out loud as this thought struck her; village life with its parochial social mores must be getting to her.

Lottie reminded herself that her alter ego no longer existed and that she had to devise totally new standards for the totally new person who was Lottie Colenso. This reaction may indicate that Lottie

Colenso was inventing some standards of her own. Whilst this was all well and good, it would be noticeable if the local eccentric began to be touchy about who parked outside her house.

Avril had long since closed her front door. Not a brother or a nephew then. Surely she would have stayed at the door and waved to a close relative as he drove away. Maybe he was her insurance man. Now that was a possibility; he looked like an insurance man, or a rent collector or a brush salesman. The lack of a suitcase full of samples spoke against the last option.

The car started on the first turn of the key and Lottie watched as it puttered off around the green and down Welham Lane. She was still watching the point in the distance where the grey car had disappeared when a cheery 'cooee' drew her attention back to the street below.

'Lottie come on down.'

Lottie blinked a couple of times then called back, 'I'm coming.' She abandoned the dresses on the bed and rushed down the stairs. Susan Holland stood on the doorstep. She was bursting with some news and

Lottie stood aside to allow her in before Susan knocked her over in her haste.

'Have you heard the news?' Susan asked.

'What news? You're never going back to Chris.'

'Chris? This has nothing to do with Chris. No, it's the new man.' Her smile darkened for a second and she frowned. 'Chris? Whatever made you think I'd take him back?' Shaking her head, she smiled again. 'Never mind. There's a new man in the village. A man with a mint of money and, according to form, he's drop-dead gorgeous.'

'Sounds promising.' Lottie said, wondering as she did so if the man was intended for Susan or herself; Susan fancied herself as a matchmaker, but, as far as Lottie could see, Susan's need was greater than her own. This must be the man Gwennie mentioned.

'Kitchen or living room? Coffee or tea? '

'Kitchen and wine.' Susan decided. 'I think this may take two glasses of your best merlot. Each.'

'I haven't seen him myself yet, but I'm told he's gorgeous.' Susan said as she swirled the merlot around the large glass. 'I love these glasses; they give the wine room to breathe.'

'Who told you he was gorgeous?' Lottie ignored the remark about the glasses; she could get back to that later if she wanted to, and she wasn't sure that she would want to.

'Avril.' Susan continued to swirl.

'Avril? Avril Major?' Lottie took a sip of her wine so that her expression would not be so easy to read.

'The very same. Our happy medium.'

Lottie choked on her wine. Susan leaned forward to slap her on the back. 'Didn't you know?' She shook her head. 'I thought everyone knew.' She peered into her glass as Lottie dug through her voluminous skirts to find the pocket containing her packet of tissues. 'But no, I don't suppose everyone does. I only know because my cottage is attached to hers. She does psychic readings, crystal ball and all that sort of stuff.'

Lottie had found a tissue and wiped her eyes when a terrible thought struck her. 'You can't hear anything, can you?'

Susan dutifully cocked an ear to listen. 'No..oo.' She said at last.

'Not here.' Lottie's impatience showed for a split second. 'When you're at home. From Avril's cottage.'

'Of course not. They were built to last, these cottages.

Just imagine if they were built like today's flimsy houses. You'd be able to hear everything that went on next door.'

Lottie was stunned. She must have got it wrong.

'Oh, no.' She pulled a face. 'That would be awful. Just imagine if you could hear old Avril communing with the spirits.' Susan started to laugh and soon Lottie joined in. 'What made you think I'd have Chris back?' Susan said.

'I think I was in need of a drink. Put it down to finding a body in Gwennie's potting shed.'

'What!'

Lottie wished she hadn't said anything. This was taking her further and further away from the drop-dead gorgeous man who had fallen into their midst. So she told the tale of the body in the potting shed as quickly as she could.

'And it was wearing a gold shoe.' She finished. 'Have you ever seen a female guy before?'

'Can't say that I have.' Susan said. 'Funny, that.'

'What's funny?'

'The doctor's wife wears gold shoes.'

'She does?'

'Yes. She's at that funny age where older women start wearing gold shoes and carrying gold handbags and sometimes, heaven help us, they wear gold headbands and things too.'

'Oh.' Lottie said, making a mental note not to buy the gold trimmed shoulder bag that had caught her eye only a day or two ago in the window of the shoe shop on Main Street.

'And you said that the body of the doctor's wife would be found in Gwennie's potting shed.'

'Did I?' Lottie wanted to get away from this subject. It was making her feel a bit queasy. 'Are you intending to make me work for it, Susan?'

'For what?'

'Info on the new man. For goodness' sake, try to keep up.'

'Oh yes, sorry.' Susan held out her glass for a refill and watched the wine rise satisfactorily to a higher level than it had the first time. She took a sip. 'Mm... Lovely. Yes, well, his name is Dexter Hardman and he's tall and broad and has a thatch of blond hair. No receding hairline has been discerned; neither does he have a bald patch.

'No one is tall enough to inspect the relevant area of his scalp but Fanny Barstock was on the top deck of the Lyeminster bus and she had a bird's eye view and is sure that he doesn't have one. Fanny says she would have been able to see more clearly had he been dark haired but she is sure that all is as it should be. Or, that he wears a wig.'

'How is it that everyone has seen him but me?' Lottie wanted to know.

'Because he has taken the old rectory. Therefore he is on Main Street in full view of anyone passing by.'

'The old rectory. Your old home.'

'Exactly. Which means that I am first to hear any gossip about its inhabitants. I tell you, Lottie, they fairly beat a path to my door whenever anything happens to the old place. Usually it's a bit of a pain; after all it's nothing to do with me anymore. But, on this occasion, I'm quite enthralled.'

I see.' Lottie said, struggling to think of something more intelligent to say. 'Why ever did they sell the place?'

'The church commissioners?' Susan shrugged. 'I've no idea. It was in the perfect position I would have thought, being across St Jude's Open from St Jude's; far more convenient for the rector than trekking from The Green.

Mind you, it did need some money spending on it when we bought it. Actually it needed gutting and a complete refit. I suppose that's why they sold it; too stingy to pay out to bring the place out of the dark ages. But the house they bought for poor old Charlie instead of it isn't much better. It's as draughty as I don't know what.

We viewed it before the old rectory was put on the market and every time you opened a door another slammed shut in the gale that constantly blow through the place even in summer. It must be hell in winter.'

'When did this Dexter Hardman move in?' Lottie asked, eager to haul Susan back on course.

'Aha! I knew you'd be interested. And I think he moved in last weekend. Do you fancy an early evening walk? I thought we could cut down Church Lane and through St Jude's Open to Main Street. Then, perhaps, we could find something to interest us.' She gave an arch smile.

'Good idea.' Lottie grinned and leapt to her feet. It was time she did something silly.

'Are you going to wear one of those pashminas?' Susan asked.

'Of course. Do you want to wear one too?'

'With jeans?'

'Why not?'

Lottie swathed Susan in flame orange and herself in sizzling scarlet. If, by any chance Dexter doodah saw them he wasn't going to have the satisfaction of thinking that they were skulking around. They sallied forth, leaving Horse and Trumpet cottage by the side door which led straight onto Church Lane.

St Jude's Open, the narrow cobbled walkway next to the church was bounded on one side by the silvery grey stones of St Jude's and on the other side by the back garden of the old rectory. Lottie and Susan slowed their steps as they negotiated the uneven surface. A pleasing tenor voice rose on the evening air.

'Beautiful dreamer, wake unto me,' he sang.

Lottie and Susan paused, locked eyes and started to hurry, only just managing to reach Main Street before they started laughing. They turned left so that they didn't pass the front of the old rectory. Then they slowed their steps to a seemly dawdle.

Susan glanced back as if she expected Dexter Hardman to materialise on his front doorstep and challenge them.

'If he's as good looking as you've been told,' Lottie said, 'and he can sing like that, it seems likely that Whittington Edge is in for a bit of a shake up.'

'Keep walking.' Susan whispered. 'He's following us.'

'How do you know?'

'I recognised the sound of the front door closing.'

Experience made Lottie keep walking. But it wouldn't allow her to be followed for many steps. 'Let's cross over the road.' She said, 'I want to look in Tidyman's window.'

'Good evening, ladies.' A voice said; a deep, rich voice full of promise and mystery. 'Out for a stroll? May a humble newcomer join you?'

Uh-oh.

The 'humble newcomer' had positioned himself next to Susan and seemed to be giving her his complete attention. Lottie refused to bridle at this. She had never been short of male attention and her friend could certainly do with some because, at the moment, Lottie was sure that Susan was feeling lonely and may be reckless enough to accept Chris back if he said the right things and Chris, from all she had heard, was a rotter.

Lottie inspected Dexter Hardman with as much thoroughness as good manners would allow. He stood close enough to Susan to make her look up and be aware of his height, but he didn't loom over her. Lottie liked that. His eyes twinkled – that would please the ladies. And he appeared to have a full set of teeth which spoke of care and money being lavished on them through the years. His clothes weren't bad either. He was wearing a suit and the Main Street of Whittington Edge was not really the place to parade a suit. Whittington Edge was more used to country tweeds, but it was a very nice suit; expensive and well cut. This was not off the peg. And neither were his shoes – if shoes could be said to be off the peg.

The thing about Dexter Hardman that had really irritated her was the way he stood in the middle of the road and ushered them across.

Whittington Edge was not the swinging metropolis of the midlands. The bulk of the traffic went around the village via the bypass. Lottie looked up and down the road and saw no vehicles at all apart from Miss Flewitt on her ancient tricycle. Anyone would think Dexter Hardman was a lollipop man and she and Susan his infant charges.

'It's a joy to meet new neighbours.' Dexter said as he waited for both his companions to step up to the safety of the opposite pavement before doing likewise and protecting himself from the onrushing danger of Miss Flewitt's tricycle.

'It is.' Susan gushed.

Lottie rolled her eyes before recalling that she was in full support of any new romantic interests her friend might develop.

'I know where you live, of course,' he trained the spotlight of his gaze on Lottie who almost took a step back. She hoped he hadn't seen the eye roll. 'You live in that delightful cottage next to the church.'

'That's right.' Lottie tried to compete with him on the smiling stakes but realised in time that she didn't have the equipment; her teeth, though good were not the huge sparkling tombstones that he sported. He must have spent an absolute fortune on them.

'But I don't know where you live.' His gaze returned to Susan, softening and becoming intimate despite his surroundings. He seemed to shrink several inches and was soon eye to eye with Susan, making Lottie feel decidedly de trop.

'I have Matchbox Cottage.' She said. 'On The Green. Near to Lottie.'

'Lottie?'

'Lottie Colenso.' Lottie said holding out her hand.

'Dexter Hardman.' He countered, engulfing her hand with his and shaking it firmly. Lottie could have sworn that he had forgotten she was there. She suppressed a smile. He had a nice handshake too; not too firm and not clammy at all.

'Susan Holland.' Susan said allowing her hand to be taken and held for just a moment or two too long.

'Mrs Holland.' Dexter Hardman's tone as he repeated the name was much as the spider's must have been when he invited the fly into his parlour. 'You, if I'm not mistaken, are the previous owner of my house.'

'Really?'

Lottie couldn't see but she was almost sure that Susan was batting her eyelashes at Dexter Hardman.

'Yes, I'm at the old rectory.'

'Of course. You must be.' Susan said.

'I know this is a terrible cheek.' He said. 'But could you show me how to light the central heating boiler. I've been having terrible trouble with it.'

'There's a knack to it.'

'Well, if you could possibly spare the time to show me how to master it. Not now, of course.' He added hastily. 'I don't want to spoil your evening walk.'

Susan gave Lottie a quick look and Lottie smiled. 'It's no trouble at all.' Susan said, suddenly losing her

dopey look and reverting to her usual efficient self. 'Come along. I'll soon have you working the thing as if you'd lived there forever.'

Dexter Hardman looked put out when Susan and Lottie darted back across Main Street without waiting for him to clear their path. Lottie could see that here was a man who liked to be in control. Perhaps she should mention this character trait to Susan later. Surely one control freak was more than enough for any lifetime. After Chris…well.

Susan had her hand on the big brass doorknob before she realised that the old rectory was no longer her home.

'Oops.' She said. 'Sorry.' She stood back and had to dash down the steps again to allow Dexter to precede them into his house.

Once inside she paused and looked about her. She hoped he wouldn't offer to let them see over the old place. It held too many memories and she didn't want to encounter any of her ghosts.

'I suppose it's much changed.' He said when he noticed her interest.

'I would expect it to be.' She kept her tone businesslike. 'Let's have a look at that boiler. It's freezing in here.'

'I apologise for that.' He said. 'But, given your expertise, doubtless it will be almost tropical in no time. Please, come this way.'

He led the way down the passage and through the kitchen eventually reaching the utility room where most of the machinery supporting the household was located.

Lottie glanced around. It was a lovely house. She hadn't known Susan when she lived here and, like Chris, she found it hard to imagine anyone wanting to leave. The house itself was gorgeous, its ceilings high. She imagined that the rooms would be airy and calm. And the outlook onto Main Street would make it another perfect vantage point for midnight musings such as she herself indulged in.

The boiler burst merrily into life. Lottie jumped.

Susan allowed it to heat up a little and then turned it off again. 'Now you try.' She said. 'Hold this lever and push it to the left. Then hold the match – no, you have to strike the match before you press the lever. That's right. Strike the match, now hold the lever. And push it to the left. No, the left. That's right. Now apply the match. See. It's easy.'

The pilot light promptly went out.

'You have to hold the lever for a few seconds until it settles down. Try again.'

He tried again and the flame lit and stayed lit.

'I see.' He said. 'How clever you are. I'm not sure I'll ever find it as easy as you seem to do.'

Lottie didn't think he would either, especially if the man couldn't differentiate left from right.

'You can call on me any time.' Susan said. 'For anything you need to know about the house. I lived here for a long time.'

'You're too kind. Now,' he rubbed his hands together and looked around as if he wasn't sure where he was, 'let's see what I can offer you. Tea, coffee, wine? Something stronger?'

'Wine would be very acceptable.' Susan assured him.

'Wine. Ok. Red or white?'

'We both like merlot. If you have any.'

'I do. That is one of my favourites too.'

Lottie suspected that hemlock would be one of Dexter Hardman's favourites if the woman he was trying to chat up professed a liking for it. Dexter Hardman may prove to be too smooth for his own good.

He led the way back towards the front door and Lottie wondered if he was intending to kick them out onto the street. But, of course he wasn't. He opened the door to one of the rooms that overlooked the street and pushed it wide.

'Take a seat, ladies, and I shall return.'

'This is a gorgeous house, Susan.' Lottie whispered as soon as he was out of earshot. 'It must have been a hell of a wrench to leave it.'

'In some ways,' Susan conceded, sitting on one of the brown leather chesterfields that faced each other across the Adam fireplace. 'In others, I couldn't wait to get out. Look, he has a grand piano.'

Lottie sat beside her. The sofas were so big that a gap large enough for two more people was left between them. Lottie hoped that Dexter Hardman wouldn't choose to interpose himself.

'And I can play it too. Sorry, did I startle you? Would you like to hear the piano? It shows off the acoustics of the room rather wonderfully, I think.'

Without waiting for them to accept his offer, Dexter Hardman put down the bottle of wine and the glasses that he held suspended by their stems between his fingers and stepped over to the piano. He slid into the seat and rattled off a few arpeggios before running seamlessly into some complicated piece full of grace notes and hands crossing over one another.

Lottie saw a guitar propped up in the corner and hoped that, if she saw it, Susan would keep quiet about it.

Soon, but not quite soon enough for Lottie, the piece was finished. It swelled up to a rousing crescendo and crashed down into a mass of chords. Susan, bless her, applauded. Lottie joined in when Dexter's modest smile was turned on them.

'I could play something with lyrics if one of you would like to sing.' He offered.

'Not me.' Susan laughed. 'I have a voice like a cracked pot.'

'Never. I'm sure.' He said.

'Beautiful dreamer?' Lottie said before she could stop herself.

'Ah, you heard me. I was singing to my garden. I'm told that it helps the plants to grow. I suppose that you ladies are expert gardeners; so many of the fair sex are.'

'Gwennie's the gardener.' Susan said.

He noticed the wine bottle and glasses on the table. 'My apologies, ladies, I should have poured the wine before inflicting my humble musical talents upon you.'

Lottie frowned. That was the second time he had referred to himself as 'humble' and she decided there was nothing humble about Dexter Hardman at all.

The cork came out of the merlot bottle with a satisfying pop and, Lottie noted, there was no crumbling around the edges as there usually was if she used a corkscrew. Dexter was relating a tale about a sommelier at one of the top London hotels all the while he was uncorking and pouring, sniffing, swirling and handing out glasses.

He hitched up his trouser legs and sat down on the sofa facing them.

'So, tell me about Gwennie the gardener.' He invited. 'I take it she is a friend of yours. Have you ladies been friends ever since schooldays? Not so long ago I know.' He beamed.

Lottie wanted to curl up and die. Not long ago, indeed. She wondered if her Lottie persona should giggle and become all girly at this sort of heavy-handed compliment. Before she became Lottie, she certainly wouldn't have done. She would have sliced through his smarmy charm with her sharp tongue and cut him down to size.

She must stop thinking about the past; she must live in the present. Lottie smiled graciously, showing that she appreciated the compliment but was in no way convinced that his words bore any relation to the truth. She was a middle aged woman and was happy to be so. Not for Lottie Colenso the coy attempts to convince anyone she was ten years younger than she actually was.

Susan, not given to such soul-searching, was already telling him about their little get-togethers on a Thursday afternoon. Luckily Lottie managed to head her off before she mentioned the Murder Club.

'We all met at the library.' Lottie said, taking over the conversation so that Susan could think before she put her foot in it any further. 'Now we go straight from the library to one of our houses.'

'And how many are there of you?' He asked.

'Five.' Susan took a large sip of wine.

'So that's you, Susan, and you, Lottie, and Gwennie the gardener and who else?'

'There's Blanche.' Susan said. 'She owns The Butterfly Bush.'

'Oh? The charming tea room across the way. I'd noticed it.' Dexter said.

'I help out there sometimes,' Susan smiled.

'Then I shall definitely put a visit to The Butterfly Bush on my itinerary,' Dexter said.

Smooth, Lottie thought, very smooth. He would need watching.

'And your fifth member?' he asked.

'Biddy.' Susan said.

'And what is special about Biddy?'

Susan and Lottie exchanged glances and shrugged in unison.

'Biddy's beautiful.' They both said, also in unison. 'I look forward to meeting Biddy.' He said. 'I don't suppose I could join your book club, could I?'

Susan looked at Lottie with panic in her eyes. She hadn't expected him to try to angle an invitation and she knew that she had gone too far. She had made their meetings seem too inviting. Now she had no idea how to back-track. What if he thought she had been trying to lure him into their fold?

'Sorry, ladies only.' Lottie smiled to soften her words. 'But you could come round to tea one day. I'll get the girls together and arrange something. I'll let you know. If that's what you would like.'

'You're too kind. I'd love it, if it's not too much of an imposition. It's difficult. Being a stranger, you know. Getting to know people.' His head began to droop at this point. He peered deep into his wine as if the colour of the wine could infuse a rosier glow to his life.

'Indeed'. Lottie said before he could produce a violin and start playing Hearts and Flowers.

'Lottie is a new arrival so you two will have a lot in common.' Susan said.

Lottie shot her a warning glance and Susan abruptly turned her attention to her wine glass.

'Really?' Dexter Hardman bestowed all his attention on Lottie. Lottie found his regard quite uncomfortable.

'Yes. But I lived nearby for years. Where did you come from?'

Dexter Hardman paused for a second or two, he fixed her with a calculating gaze, and then his lips curved in a small smile. He hadn't wanted to turn the conversation towards himself, that much was apparent. But he allowed her to steer him away. The look he gave her said that he intended to return to Lottie's past at some more propitious time.

Lottie dismissed this thought. She was being fanciful again; or paranoid. Dexter Hardman wasn't even interested in her. His attention was centred on Susan; either he was attracted to her or he wanted to make friends with the one person who could light his boiler. But he never answered her question.

He smiled and looked at Lottie holding her gaze for too long before shifting his attention to Susan once more.

'I wonder, Susan, if I could trouble you for your telephone number?'

'Of course.' Susan waited for him to find his diary and rattled off the number quite happily. It would make a change to have a man other than Chris call her.

She was attracted to Dexter Hardman in a shallow sort of way. She had no illusions about him, or so she told herself. But he was tall and handsome and it would be pleasant to be the envy of the town instead of 'poor Susan whose husband has taken up with a younger woman'. What would be better, absolutely better, would be for Chris to see them together.

Dexter was younger than Chris. And he was more handsome. And he didn't look flattened by life as the unwilling father to a small child.

He never wanted a child when he was with her.

Whereas, for a fleeting five years sometime early in their marriage, she had desperately yearned for a baby, Chris would have none of it. He had countless reasons why a child would ruin everything they held dear, and he enumerated them at length until she shut up and kept her anguish to herself.

Funny, she hadn't thought about this for some time, yet, now she had awakened the memory, the pain was every bit as sharp as it had been then. She should now be looking forward to holding a grandchild in her arms. Chris had prevented her doing this. All sympathy for her ex-husband evaporated.

Lottie, the more earthbound of the two, watched Dexter carefully enter Susan's name and telephone in his diary and thought 'a little black book'. Oh p-lease.

When they left the Old Rectory, Lottie noticed that Dexter detained Susan for a second or two. She pretended not to notice and stood at the top of the steps breathing in the sweet autumn air and enjoying the sight of the centre of Whittington Edge from this elevated vantage point. From here she could better admire the architecture, so different from that of the old village ranked around The Green.

She and Susan eventually said their goodbyes and strode back to St Jude's Open and Horse and Trumpet Cottage where they finished the bottle of Merlot they had left open on the kitchen table.

'I think he's going to ring you.' Lottie grinned, eager to show that she harboured no thoughts of Dexter Hardman.

'Do you think so? Would you mind if he did?'

'I'm almost sure he will and I won't mind a bit. Why on earth should I?'

'What do you think of him, Lottie? Really?'

'I think he would be perfect for a fling and disastrous for anything else.' Lottie said, deciding that honesty was the best policy, especially with a friend. Especially whilst they were talking about first impressions and only before things became complicated.

'My thoughts exactly.' Susan agreed.

Lottie breathed a sigh of relief.

When Susan left, Lottie went up to her bedroom to continue hanging up the dresses that she had left on the bed. Thus she was in an advantageous position to see when a black jaguar car swept slowly around The Green and came to a gentle halt outside Matchbox Cottage less than an hour later.

Ten seconds must have elapsed and Susan came into view attired in a very expensive silk dress that shouted its designer origins even from that distance. Dexter Hardman leapt out of the driver's seat and hurried round to open the door for her and, once he was sure she was comfortably settled, he drove off. As they passed Horse and Trumpet Cottage, Susan looked up at Lottie and waved. Lottie gave her a thumbs-up.

It wasn't that Lottie envied Susan. She had no yearnings for Dexter Hardman. He was too smooth for her taste. And his constant assertions that he was 'humble' put her off. But Lottie's weekend stretched ahead unblemished by plans. She wanted a date too.

Jonas's timely telephone call was just what she needed. 'After your rotten week, you deserve a treat,' he said and Lottie agreed to join him for the weekend at a park complex which, he said, was enclosed and full of goodies like 'swimming pools and bicycle trails and a fantastic gym'. Lottie wasn't too sure if this was her thing but the thought of the promised cabin in the woods and no obligation to get fit swung it in his favour.

A twinge of guilt struck when she realised that she had done nothing to further her investigations. Perhaps a weekend away may fire her thoughts in interesting directions.

At least she had Dexter Hardman to enter in her notebook. She went to do this before it slipped her mind.

CHAPTER TEN

Gwennie covered lunchtimes for the other library staff every day, but Thursday was early closing day so she started earlier and stayed a little later to enable her colleagues to leave. When the full time library staff had gone, Gwennie would shelve the books that were on the trolley and take the time to select the bodice rippers that were her clandestine reading matter.

At one o clock, Susan came in, dumping a heap of books on the counter and dashing over to the crime section to choose more.

She was seated in one of the comfortable armchairs already halfway through chapter one when Blanche arrived. Blanche shrugged off her winter coat and draped it on an adjacent chair before perusing the shelves herself.

Blanche Tallentire looked forward to Thursday afternoons; not only was it Murder Club day but it was half day closing at the Butterfly Bush. She loved the Butterfly Bush beyond anything but there was no disputing it was very hard work.

Lottie had appeared just after half past one and selected her books with swift efficiency. Biddy was the last, darting into the library, pink cheeked and sparkling with life and prettiness. Lottie eyed her surreptitiously. She looked different. Seemingly the weekend at the spa had done her good. Lottie didn't wonder at it, she and Jonas had had a fantastic time. She doubted that she glowed as Biddy was glowing but...on the inside...

Just as she was thinking this, the most gorgeous man Lottie had ever seen pushed through the glass doors. Heads turned, noted who it was and returned to their books. He looked around and spotted Biddy. Biddy beamed and hurried to meet him.

'Wow.' Lottie murmured. She was interested because this man had been at the park that she and Jonas had been to at the weekend and she had wondered who he was and why he was alone.

'Gerald, Lord Whittington.' Susan enlightened her, watching as Gerald and Biddy's heads drew closer.

'Lord Whittington?' Lottie's brows almost disappeared into her hairline.

'Oh, I see you didn't know that Biddy was the lady of the manor.'

'I wonder if Gerald went to the health spa too.' Lottie mused. 'Because both of them look absolutely splendid.'

'I imagine he would.' Susan glanced over at the couple again. 'They are practically inseparable. Isn't that amazing?'

'Ye…s.' Lottie agreed. 'It is, isn't it?' She cast a sideways glance at Susan. 'Did he just pass Biddy a note? She's blushing.'

'Biddy said he still asks her out on dates and invites her to clandestine meetings.'

'It's certainly one way to keep the romance alive,' Lottie laughed.

'I think we could all do with a long weekend at a spa.' Lottie said when Biddy joined the others. 'Whatever did you get up to?'

Biddy held out her hands. 'I got my manicure done and my nail fixed.' She said fluttering ten perfect pink ovals before their faces. 'And I have a date tonight.'

Lottie was glad she could join in the ensuing laughter.

Gwennie hurried over carrying an ecru canvas tote bag of the sort that the library had recently been selling to their readers. She had packed this carefully with the more lurid covers face down at the very bottom of the bag then her headscarf tucked in all around them and the books that she thought were more acceptable visible at the top. She had a dread that one day she would trip or the handles of the bag would burst and her shameful double life would be revealed to the world.

'Everyone ready?' Lottie looked around at the group. She frowned at Gwennie who held her bag clutched to her. 'Do you need any help carrying your bag, Gwennie?'

'No. No, thank you. I'm fine.' Gwennie gave a wary smile.

'Come along, then, I have cream cakes.'

Expressions of delight greeted this and the Murder Club trooped out into the bright, cold afternoon. It would soon be time to put the clocks back and then they would be making this journey in the gathering gloom.

'Now then,' Lottie said when all were seated with either tea or coffee. Cakes and biscuits were ranged out on the long table before them. 'Michael Garnett. I haven't heard any more about our case. Has anyone else?'

Dexter Hardman strolled past Horse and Trumpet cottage shortly after the meeting of the Murder Club commenced. Lottie saw him but didn't draw anyone else's attention to his presence. She suspected; he was angling for an invitation to join them.

Lottie was fascinated to watch him walking around the Green. Perhaps he was taking a constitutional and the timing of this was coincidental. Perhaps, nothing. Something told Lottie that everything that man did was with a purpose. Look at the way he had intercepted Susan and herself when they were out walking. That was no accident.

She had seen Susan earlier in the week and she told of the wonderful meal Dexter had taken her for. At the Manor House Hotel, no less. Where a different wine had arrived with each of the six courses. The food was beautifully prepared and impeccably presented as it had been when Jonas took Lottie there.

At this point Lottie had wondered what this meal was going to cost Susan and wondered also if Susan was agreeable to the price. After all, it was a long time since she and Chris had split up and, recalling her own weekend, she couldn't begrudge any pleasure to her best friend.

She had fixed Susan with a questioning glance but Susan laughed.

'No there was nothing like that.' She said. 'He delivered me back to my door and didn't make any suggestions about coming in for coffee. And, the next day he sent me flowers.'

'He's moving in for the kill.' Lottie had said with a grin.

Now she looked around the group. Susan and Biddy were both looking pleased with themselves. Perhaps Dexter was lurking about waiting for Susan to leave Horse and Trumpet Cottage so that he could whisk her away somewhere.

'Michael Garnet has been on the news only once as far as I know.' Susan was saying now.

Lottie, thus reminded of her role as doyen of the murder club, concentrated her mind on the matter in hand.

***

When Dexter Hardman made his third sweep of the footpath outside Horse and Trumpet cottage, Lottie could stand it no longer. He paused right outside but he wasn't attempting to look in. Rather, he was looking around as if checking the source of some sound.

Then a man ran up to him. The newcomer's hair lifted and wafted about in the breeze. He was easily the same age as Dexter Hardman, possibly even older, or younger; he had one of those faces that defied categorisation. He had the look of a dilettante about him.

Birds of a feather, Lottie thought, he and Dexter Hardman. Beau Derek, She had seen him around, of course, and seeing him now reminded her that the rector had promised to arrange a meeting between them.

'I see Dexter Hardman has found a friend.' She said. Four heads turned to see who had commandeered the attention of the latest attraction in town.

'Oh, that's Beau.' Susan said. 'I wouldn't bother if I were you. He's an odd one. No one knows what he does for a living. He's been around Whittington Edge for years. He lives at Pennyman Cottage, you know, that house I showed you just round the corner on Welham Lane.'

'He's a remittance man.' Gwennie said. She took a sip of tea unaware of the interested gazes now fixed upon her.

'A what?' Biddy asked.

'A remittance man.' Gwennie repeated. 'He comes from a really wealthy family but he did something to blot his copybook and they send him money to stay away. He comes into the library most days. I think they call him 'Beau' because his name is Nash.'

'I thought it was because his name's Derek.' Blanche said. 'Yes, that's right; Derek Nash.' Gwennie nodded enthusiastically. 'But we all call him Beau.'

'Whittington Edge is certainly full of interesting characters.' Lottie said not letting on that she already knew who Beau Derek was and that he was supposedly a lord of the realm.

'He seems to have pots of money.' Gwennie said. 'He has his own house and everything. He isn't a tramp or anything like that.' Lottie knew he wasn't a tramp; Lottie Colenso could spot a handmade suit from more than twenty paces.

'I wonder what he wants with Dexter.' Susan said.

Lottie hadn't been at all surprised that he had collared Dexter; she already had them marked out as kindred spirits. She watched them cross the road together and sit on a bench opposite Horse and Trumpet cottage. Happily this bench faced towards the Green and not towards her home. A peal of laughter rang out from both men.

Much discussion of the Rosa Garnett case ensued. The game of Cluedo seemed to be lost somewhere between this and the cakes but no one complained.

As the weeks had progressed, kindly gossip became one of the staples of the Murder Club.

Previously, Lottie had discouraged this. She had never been a fan of gossip professing to find it damaging. But she was a new person now; she really must keep reminding herself of this. She was the opposite of the person she had once been.

Besides, nothing malicious was ever part of their meetings. Gossip was now therefore not only allowed, it was to be encouraged. Especially now that Lottie had a reason to glean whatever she could about her neighbours.

Allowing the discussion to continue without her, Lottie kept an eye on Dexter Hardman and Beau Derek – which was the name she considered most appropriate due to his flowing locks.

They sat on the bench for a good half hour. At intervals they laughed. Beau gestured towards the vast horse chestnut tree beneath which Avril's callers parked their cars.

Lottie wondered about Avril's gentleman callers. Lottie had never seen a woman approach the door. Susan said that Avril was a medium and that she held séances and did private readings for people. Lottie wasn't so sure. But Susan had been Avril's next door neighbour for a while now and presumably she would have been quick to work out what Avril was up to.

Another point was that women were more likely to be investing in psychic readings or trying to make contact with the dead.

This, to Lottie's mind, was not a masculine pursuit.

A chance word drew Lottie's interest back to the group in her own living room and she only glanced out of the window again when the couple on the bench fell to quiet discussion. She narrowed her eyes. They behaved like old friends. She noted that their heads were now closer together and Lottie, not a believer in universal feminine intuition but a great believer in her own, was sure she was seeing a friendship being rekindled.

Dexter and Beau were both men of means. Both were tall and blond, wore handmade shoes and beautifully tailored suits. Beau had been ostracised by his family. Dexter was a mystery. But were they a mystery to one another?

Appearances would indicate that they weren't. Beau leaned back, slapped Dexter on the shoulder and both men laughed loudly. Then they carried on their conversation once more.

Lottie's glance alighted on Biddy. Lady Whittington. Who would have thought it? But having thought about it, who would be surprised? Biddy was princess material; anyone could see that. And her husband was a looker, no dispute there.

Lottie had seen Gerald at the weekend. She hadn't seen Biddy at all but Gerald was around buying things in shops and ordering food to be delivered to his cabin. Lottie didn't know which cabin Gerald was using because she hadn't really taken much notice of him. If Biddy had been there, he must have kept her prisoner the whole time.

Biddy's happiness refuted any accusation of ill treatment at the hands of her husband. She must have been tied to the bed. This thought struck Lottie as so funny that she had to make an excuse to go into the kitchen until the threatened laughter was under control.

The truth was more likely that Biddy spent the whole of her weekend having sumptuously luxurious spa treatments and enjoying the attentions of her gorgeous husband.

Biddy kept giving the clock a surreptitious peek. Lottie could tell that she couldn't wait to get away.

Soon it was time to leave. The coats were collected and put on. Goodbyes were said and the women all trooped out into the brisk evening air.

As usual, Lottie watched Blanche drive away and the rest cross the Green and scatter to their respective homes. She couldn't help noticing that Biddy seemed to be in more of a hurry than usual and, once the last straggler had been lost to view, she darted upstairs to look out of the window of her bedroom.

This time she sat by the window overlooking Church Lane because this had a view of the Glimpse, a tiny roadway barely noticeable from the road, that led to the Manor House. Lottie's instincts were on red alert.

Soon a small car emerged. The headlights were switched on only as the car joined the road. It zipped under a streetlight. It was definitely Biddy's car. Dates and clandestine meetings; she wondered what was planned for the remainder of Biddy's evening.

Maybe Lord and Lady Whittington were the people who had alerted Marco's interest. Dutifully, Lottie retrieved her notebook from the locked drawer of her desk and made the relevant entry. She felt guilty doing so because this was obviously just innocent fun. She hoped that her action didn't translate to envy of the Whittingtons.

She wanted to be a merry widow, not a jealous harpy.

***

Earlier that day, Jane approached the prison gates determined that she would not disgrace herself again. She had telephoned the prison to try to talk herself back inside but it had taken Charles' gentle intervention to secure her a second visit so soon after the last. She didn't know what he had said and didn't ask; just facing her mother again after all these years would be enough of an ordeal.

Her only memories of the last visit were the stricken look on her face, the joy burning in her eyes, the tears overflowing, the outstretched hands that Jane was told not to touch. And then the flash of recognition, and the blackness descending.

Not again. Never again. And certainly not today.

In preparation for the visit she had eaten lunch at a pub far enough away not to be full of other visitors to the prison. For Dutch courage she had drunk a couple of vodkas, which would hopefully not be discernible on her breath.

She had a notebook and pens in case she needed to make notes should they be needed. And she was dressed in her favourite outfit. She had dressed casually last time but her mother had always liked to see her dressed to the nines so this was what she had done.

The same gates. The same queue. The same depressed women with pushchairs. The same men keeping their eyes downcast. The same pall of shame overhanging the entire scene as if the visitors were the ones serving sentences, not the women they were visiting. But of course, they were serving sentences – and they were innocent of all guilt.

Then, inside, the queue moving slowly. Passes being checked. Security procedures endured. Gates were sliding open, unlocking, sliding closed and locking again in a constant clamour. Voices echoed as staff passed their groups of visitors on to colleagues further inside. Through more doors.

And then, at last. She was there, face to face with her mother who stood to welcome her and rapidly subsided into her chair when ordered to remain seated.

'I'm sorry,' her mother said.

'What happened?' Jane countered.

That was all it needed. The floodgates opened and Avril Montrose, known in this place as Edna Derry, told her tale.

By the time she left, Jane was shell-shocked. This was wrong. It was barbaric. There should be something she could do. But there wasn't. Her mother had been tried and found guilty by due process of the law. There was nothing anyone could do. And, much as she wanted to shout her mother's innocence from the rooftops, much as she wanted to publicise her mother's plight, start petitions, put up posters and man barricades, she had promised she would do none of these things.

'But I want to help,' she had said

'You cannot. No one can. I should not have contacted you but I wanted to see my own dear child one more time. I am satisfied now. You are a married lady with a wonderful husband. Go back to him my darling and forget about me.'

She had risen to her feet when the bell rang. She tried to smile. She said goodbye. She said she would visit again.

'No, you must not try to contact me again, Jane.'

So Jane had walked away. Just a few steps. Then she turned and looked back at little Edna Derry in her shapeless uniform. Edna must have felt her daughter's eyes on her for she turned.

'Forget about me, Jane,' she said as an officer stepped up to lead her away.

Jane was in plenty of time for the Lyeminster train but she didn't catch it. She didn't catch the next one either. She roamed around the station pretending interest in the destination boards with their ever changing displays. When tears threatened to overwhelm her, she watched a train pull out and joined the people waving goodbye from the platform. A few tears were allowed in these circumstances and they relieved the pressure in her throat.

Then she found her own platform and waited in stunned misery for the train to take her home.

***

Lottie, troubled by the note she had made in her investigation notebook, sat in her bedroom window later that night, looking down on Whittington Edge as it slept. But not all of it was sleeping. A wisp of smoke rose from beneath the chestnut tree opposite Nook Cottage. Had she not been so troubled she may not even have noticed it.

She leaned forward and concentrated her gaze on the spot below the smoke but she could see nothing moving in the darkness. Then a red dot glowed. Yes, there was someone smoking beneath the tree. Who on earth would want to stand under the chestnut tree at this time of night smoking a cigarette?

The muffled chimes of St Jude's told her it was midnight. Through the narrow ventilation gap in the window Lottie heard the unmistakeable sound of Avril opening her front door. The creak, the milk white face peering around The Green, then the emergence of Mr Thursday and the quiet closing of the door once more. It was all as it had been last week except that, as Mr Thursday drove away, a man stepped out from beneath the chestnut tree, watched the departure of the car, and then walked briskly towards Horse and Trumpet Cottage.

Lottie watched him. He was a short man. She couldn't really see his face well but she was sure he would have a horrible face. This she told herself was pure imagination. She couldn't see the man properly. He was certainly no one she knew. She leaned further back as his footsteps clicked briskly beneath her window, round the corner into Church Lane, past the cottages and into St Jude's Open and thence out of sight.

Imagination it may be but he made Lottie shudder and she knew that she would recognise his distinctive walk anywhere.

***

At the rectory Jane Pendleton didn't know what to do. She hadn't been able to tell Charles; she hadn't dared. This could ruin his career. Whatever would the bishop say if he knew that her mother was a convict? She had thought it bad enough that she may be a fortune teller. But this? Jane gave a bitter laugh. This would be the last straw. It would break up her marriage or get Charles thrown out of his living. But she couldn't leave her mother to rot in jail for an offence she had not committed. Perhaps she should phone her father. No, she couldn't go behind Charles's back. What could she do?

The bishop had so far treated Jane as if she were a great asset to Charles and the diocese. He wouldn't feel the same way if he knew the truth.

Atlantis Warbeck's words came back to her: Lottie Colenso was the only person with whom she would share her secrets. Did Jane Pendleton dare to talk to Lottie Colenso about a secret as dreadful as this?

CHAPTER ELEVEN

Morning, Doll.' Sonny said when Avril answered her phone. 'I've got some good news for you. I want you to put Arthur on the train back to the smoke.

'I can't say I'll be sorry to see him go.' Avril said.

Once Arthur had got used to the rules he had settled into his life in Lyeminster reasonably happily. He had even stopped dropping hints about going to the bookies. If he was gambling by phone Sonny would soon find out and deal with him. Unfortunately, Arthur saw himself as a ladies' man.

He started showering the dowdy Aunt Minnie with extravagant compliments. He would not only stand aside for her to precede him through doors, he would bow, sweeping out one arm as if she were Queen Elizabeth and he Sir Walter Raleigh. Aunt Minnie twittered obligingly at his flamboyant gallantries and laughed at him and gave him playful slaps. Inside, Avril was seething. This sort of stupid behaviour would get him noticed.

'I reckon he's suffered long enough, don't you?'

'I think I've suffered long enough.' Avril replied with a rattling chuckle. 'What are you going to do with him now?'

'I'll need to test him out but, if he's learned his lesson, I'll find another little job for him.'

Avril didn't really care what Sonny did with Arthur. Arthur was a pain in the neck. He didn't necessarily deserve to be snuffed out but a good kicking would have been in order and she would have like to be there when it was administered; she might even be tempted to help dish some of it out.

No, a sigh escaped her, since her arrival in Whittington Edge she had done everything possible to present herself to the world as a lady; she must keep up appearances.

She checked the time. If she was to have Arthur on the late morning train she would have to get moving. She phoned him on the mobile she had given him and told him to get packed.

***

Jason Flint, Summer Saunders' boyfriend so loathed by Bill Warbeck, was in the garden of Nook Cottage tidying up the shrubs for the winter and clearing away the dead leaves. Avril opened the back door and called to him.

'Have you finished your cup of tea, Jason? I have to go out and I want to lock up. Put it on the counter in the kitchen when you're done. I'm going upstairs to change.'

'Will do,' Mrs Major.' Jason called back.

***

Arthur was almost jumping for joy. No more visits to that bloody gloomy castle. No more traipsing around Lyeminster squiring Aunt Minnie through the market. Why couldn't Sonny have a stylish aunt instead of this old bag? Still, what did it matter? He would soon be back in the Smoke with his own people. What tales he would be able to tell them.

***

Ronnie was good at his job. He was one of the few people Sonny employed who was capable of thinking for himself. This was why he had been tasked with finding out about Avril's activities in Whittington Edge; Avril was the most important person in Sonny's life. He wouldn't entrust anything to do with her to the sort of lame-brain he usually kept around.

Another reason was that Ronnie had never met Sonny's wife and therefore was in no danger of being recognised. The third reason was that Ronnie had no compunction about doing what needed to be done should it be called for.

He had taken a room in a Travelodge on the fringes of Lyeminster nearest to Whittington Edge having borrowed a car from another associate who was ready to report it stolen should the need arise. He had relayed his findings to Sonny regularly every night since his arrival. Now his mobile burst into life with a cheery tune.

'Ok, Ronnie, you're on. She'll be in Lyeminster taking Arthur to the station for the 11 o'clock train.'

'I'll let you know.' Ronnie said before snapping his mobile shut and packing everything into his case and carrying it down to his car. He locked the car and crossed the car park to wait for the Whittington Edge bus. He wouldn't risk the car being seen in Whittington Edge.

***

Jason Flint was halfway to Camp Hill when he remembered the mug he had left in Avril Major's garden. As soon as she said she had to go out he had finished the dregs of his tea and begun putting all the tools back into the shed. He heard the key turn in the back door and thought nothing of it. He locked the shed, put the key under the plant pot outside the door and made his way along the path that ran behind all the houses down that side of The Green.

His footsteps slowed. There was no point going back. Avril had already left. He couldn't get in. All he could do if he did go back was put the mug on the kitchen window sill and hope she saw it and took it in when she returned. No, it was just as safe on the bench by the shed. Jason picked up the pace again. It was Friday. So what if he had taken a day off school, he had money in his pocket and the weekend stretched ahead.

***

The Green was as quiet as the grave when Ronnie approached from Welham Lane. His nocturnal meanderings around Whittington Edge had shown him every alleyway that could prove useful. His daytime wanderings told him which residents were observant and which were not and whose living rooms overlooked The Green.

He knew who was at work during the day and who was at home. He knew what time the women went shopping. And he knew that approaching Nook Cottage via Church Lane would not be a good idea. That would take him along two sides of Horse and Trumpet Cottage and Horse and Trumpet Cottage had a long frontage on both sides, and a very alert occupant.

So he had left the bus further down Main Street and walked through a warren of streets and these little back lanes that seemed to be peculiar to Whittington Edge until he reached Welham Lane.

From there he could walk along the far side of The Green and cut down the alley behind Nook Cottage. He kept his head down as he walked and he carried a violin case.

The violin case appealed to Ronnie's sense of the dramatic.

It held the tools of his trade and carried with it the image of gangsters. Also, in a place like Whittington Edge there was bound to be some old geezer ekeing out his pension by giving music lessons.

Ronnie knew that the last thing he looked like was a musician so he wore a beret and a long scarf thrown over his shoulder in order to create that image.

Luckily for Ronnie, Nook Cottage boasted a conservatory that obscured the view of the back door from the place next door on one side. On the other side was a brick wall with no windows at all. He had seen the mug that Jason Flint had left outside and picked it up with a gloved hand. It was this sort of detail that made neighbours think you had a perfect right to be entering a house. It was the work of a moment to jemmy open the door and then he was inside.

He left the mug on the kitchen table and did a quick walk through first to make sure no one was inside and then he went through again more slowly.

It took less than fifteen minutes. He had found the filing cabinet with all the props that Avril used. There was no sign of her having a man living with her – Sonny would be pleased about that. There was no trace of a diary, no framed photographs showing a happy couple or anything else at all to cause Sonny concern. No photographs at all, come to that.

Ronnie left Nook Cottage as silently as he had arrived. It was a shame about the back door but the old girl could claim that on her insurance. Besides, if she didn't feel totally safe in this dead and alive hole, she may be encouraged to go back to Sonny. Now that could net him a bonus.

He took a quick backward glance at the house before he let himself out onto the back lane. The door didn't look damaged; Ronnie was an artist. It wouldn't look damaged from the inside either. He knew how to jemmy a door so that no one would know until they tried to lock it again.

***

Avril had exchanged a few words with Jane Pendleton as she passed her outside Horse and Trumpet Cottage. Jane's responses were polite but the woman was obviously distracted. Avril would have liked to ask if she were quite well but she didn't have time to bother this morning so the question was better not asked. Besides, the rector's wife was turning into the gate of Lottie Colenso's place now. She must be doing more of her 'parish visiting'. It was to be hoped that she had sorted herself out; she had behaved most peculiarly when she called at Nook Cottage. Avril had wondered if she was quite the ticket.

Lottie, keeping a weather eye on Whittington Edge as usual, noted that Avril Major was carrying her carpet bag again. So she was off to Lyeminster to visit the railway station and don a disguise.

What was it with that? She was up to something and Lottie was irritated that she had no idea what it was.

Her concentration on Avril and her odd behaviour was such that she failed to notice Jane turning into her gate. She heard the latch click and was in time to catch sight of her before Jane reached the large porch. Lottie hurried to open the door.

'Come in,' she said standing back, smiling broadly, eager for company. 'I'll put the kettle on – or would you prefer coffee. We can have the real stuff. It's hardly worth setting the machine up just for one.'

'I have a message for you from Charles.' Jane smiled gratefully as Lottie helped her off with her coat. 'You wanted to talk to Beau about his local history project?'

'Yes, I did. Has your husband managed to arrange something for me?'

'He has indeed. Beau has invited you for lunch tomorrow.

'He says that if you can get to Pennyman Cottage for about half ten to eleven he will show you things that he thinks will interest you and then you can have lunch and talk about anything you would like to know. He is very excited at the idea of a kindred spirit in Whittington Edge, Charles says.'

'That's so kind of him, and kind of Charles too to set things up so speedily.'

More of this small talk carried the women through to the kitchen and accompanied the coffee preparations. Lottie's antennae were vibrating. Jane Pendleton hadn't only come to see her to pass on the message about Beau; Jane had something on her mind.

'Did you reach any decision about your prison visit?' Lottie asked when the silence had stretched too long.

'I wanted to talk to you about that.'

Jane's distress was palpable. This promised to be important and Lottie wanted to give it her full attention. She sat at the table 'Take your time, there's no hurry.' She said.

Jane quickly filled her in on her childhood out in the colonies, her upbringing surrounded by servants and little contact with her parents, the visit to London and her mother walking out of the hotel never to be seen again.

'How dreadful,' Lottie said when some words were needed to oil the works and get the conversation going again. 'What did you do?'

Jane shrugged. 'We went back home.' She said. 'But that's not the important thing.' Lottie was careful not to allow her to see her shock. 'My mother's maiden name was Avril Major.' She said. 'She spent all her life abroad apart from one year when she was sent to Whittington Edge because her mother was terribly ill. She used to tell me about Whittington Edge, Lottie. She made it sound wonderful. Like, you know, like the sort of England that only exists in Sunday night television drama.'

'So, are you telling me that Avril Major, our Avril Major at Nook Cottage is your mother?' Lottie tried to keep the horror out of her expression and her tone of voice. Avril Major, Jane Pendleton's mother? She supposed it may make sense of the disguise. Sort of.

But it would need some thinking about.

'No.' Jane shook her head. 'I wondered, I must admit. But I went to see her when I started my parish visits and I couldn't see anything I recognised in her at all. To be honest I was glad.' Jane grimaced and Lottie smiled her understanding.

'Then, on Thursday, I went to the prison to see this Edna Derry person. Except she isn't Edna Derry at all; she's my mother. My mother is a criminal. But she isn't really. Not in the way they think. I can't tell Charles; he would be so shocked. He wouldn't say so, of course. He's such a darling and such a kind man and I know he would stand by me and he would also accept my mother.'

Even as she said this, Jane had doubts. Would he really accept it? How could he? 'But he's an honourable man too and he would insist on telling the bishop and he could lose his job and his job means so much to him. He has a real calling, Lottie.'

Her voice had risen and raced on a crescendo of despair. Lottie put a hand over those that were threatening to shred Jane's pretty lace handkerchief into tatters.

'Take a breath, Jane. This isn't the end of the world.'

'But it is.' Jane wailed.

'No, it isn't. Sit quietly for a moment. I'll finish off the coffee and then we'll go through it step by step and see what is to be done.'

Lottie's calm manner worked its magic on Jane and she took a few deep breaths whilst casting grateful glances Lottie's way.

Maybe Lottie could work miracles. Maybe she could find a way through this. If anyone could, Jane thought that Lottie could well be that person. Atlantis had been right. Lottie was trustworthy. She would help her.

Lottie kept her back turned. She told herself that this was to give Jane time; it actually was to give Lottie time to think of a way to make good on her promise.

When the coffee was steaming its deep, dark fragrance into the air Lottie sat opposite her visitor as quietly as she could. She didn't want any sudden move to scare Jane Pendleton away.

'So,' she said at last, reaching out to take one of Jane's hands in her own, 'what did your mother do to end up in jail?' Even as she said the words Lottie was worried that her approach may prove too abrupt. She tightened her grip on Jane's hand.

'She was caught shoplifting at Derry and Toms in London.' Jane whispered. Lottie waited. 'It was on that first day when she went out shopping. My father took me to a museum or an art gallery; I can't really remember which it was. My mother went shopping.'

Tears began to flow. 'She only went shopping, Lottie, nothing bad should have happened to her.'

'And this was how long ago?'

'Seventeen years.'

Lottie's brows rose. Seventeen years? What on earth had Derry and Toms sold that was valuable enough to condemn anyone to seventeen years for its theft?

'I didn't know that Derry and Toms was still in existence.' Lottie silently cursed herself for saying something so inane.

'It isn't and it wasn't then. Derry and Toms was a store she went to when she visited England as a girl. She wanted to go back to it, to see it again, you know how it is. It's changed hands. But to my mother it was

Derry and Toms so she told the police that her name was Edna Derry. She didn't want to embarrass my father – he was a diplomat – and his family were in town at the time so she couldn't be taken back to the hotel by the police because his family would see and they already thought he had married beneath him.'

'I see.' Lottie wanted to get back to the theft that had cost seventeen years of Edna Derry's life. 'So that was why she wrote to you.' Lottie pasted a bright smile on her face. 'She must have been so thrilled to see you again all grown up and radiantly happy.'

'I don't know. I recognised her immediately and I fainted. Then I went back on Thursday and saw her again.'

'I'm not surprised you fainted. It must have been a terrible shock.'

Jane smiled for the first time since she arrived on Lottie's doorstep. 'You can see why I can't tell Charles, can't you?' She pleaded.

'Yes, I can. But surely there's something you can do to help your mother. Shoplifting doesn't usually carry a seventeen year sentence.'

'No, it doesn't, does it? And that's where Avril Major comes in, Lottie,' Jane stared straight into Lottie's eyes and something Lottie saw there made her recoil, 'I want to kill her, Lottie, I really do.'

Lottie didn't doubt it for a moment. Jane's face had changed and taken on a frightening cast; Lottie could believe anything of her. She was half relieved when Jane leapt to her feet and decided to leave, but she couldn't let her go in this state. Lottie calmed her down again, reassured her and eventually managed to persuade her to sit down and drink her coffee. And thus it was that Lottie, who was usually so keen an observer of The Green and all its visitors, failed to see the man who was to start a train of havoc in Whittington Edge.

'Tell me how Avril Major figures in your mother's situation.' Lottie said after a while.

'When she was first sentenced, she was put in a cell with another woman called Dolly. Dolly was in for running a brothel. She was nearly at the end of her sentence and I suppose the prison authorities thought she would keep mother company and keep her own nose clean at the same time because she wouldn't want to do anything to lose her remission.'

'Makes sense.'

'Yes, I thought so too. Dolly befriended my mother and mother was eager to befriend her. She told her all about her life. Dolly was most attentive. Especially so when she spoke of Whittington Edge. My mother was a total innocent. She had lived a protected life.

'She had never met anyone who would be nasty or two faced. So she told her about Whittington Edge and Dolly asked lots of questions which mother answered.

'Then one of the really vicious women on the wing attacked mother and blacked her eye. Apparently the injuries she received were nothing really, not in terms of what can happen, but mother is a very small lady and wasn't used to violence in any form and she went to pieces. Dolly promised to help her.'

'And did she?'

'For a start off she did. She stuck to mother's side like glue.

But this showed the other inmates that she was scared and they jeered at her more and more. Mother was an absolute wreck. Dolly was due to be discharged in a matter of days and the threats began to escalate. Mother told Dolly that she was frightened of what would happen once Dolly was discharged. Dolly said she could fix it so that mother would get a cell all to herself. Mother, knowing no better, jumped at the offer.' Jane looked at Lottie and her eyes filled with tears.

'What happened next?'

Common sense came to Jane's aid. 'I can't tell you what happened next. It's too terrible to talk about. I'm sorry but I really can't. Please keep this to yourself, Lottie, like you promised.'

'Of course I shall,' Lottie reassured her whilst wanting to take hold of this wisp of a thread and pull until the entire story was unravelled.

'And you believe that Avril Major, our Avril Major, is this Dolly person?'

'I don't really know. I'm clutching at straws. I didn't like her when I met her. She does have an accent that isn't local. I'm not good enough at recognising English accents to tell if it's a London accent. But how could it be anyone else? She listened to mother and... and stole her life.'

Lottie schooled her features into a serene mask. 'We don't know that Avril Major from Nook Cottage is this Dolly, now do we? She could be an innocent woman who just happens to share the same name.' But Lottie knew that Avril Major did have a London accent. She didn't share this with Jane; she was worried that Jane may do something to avenge her mother.

'How likely is that, Lottie? Really? Avril Major surely isn't so common a name. I haven't lived in England for long but I've never met another Avril at all. Have you?'

'No,' Lottie sighed, 'no I haven't.' She took a deep breath. 'But we still don't know that she is Dolly.' Lottie was fighting here. She didn't want Jane Pendleton to do anything drastic and land up in the next cell to her mother. She almost laughed out loud when that thought presented itself. Jane Pendleton murder anyone? Never.

It gave Lottie no pleasure when she wrote up the account of her meeting with Jane later that night and, if she were honest with herself, only her innate attention to detail made her do it. She had run too many successful investigations to be tempted to omit any details from her case file. The notebook was, in Lottie's mind, her case file and she would keep it faithfully.

She couldn't do it as soon as Jane left which was what she would normally do; she was too upset to do that. She had paced around the house finding small tasks to occupy her hands whilst her brain struggled with the story she had been told and ways that she could discover the truth without revealing Jane's secret to anyone else.

She couldn't call upon Marco to enquire about Edna Derry's cellmate without telling him as much of the tale as she knew. If he were to ask questions about a prisoner, he needed a specific reason for doing so; a reason he could note down in his records. So, no, Marco had to be kept out of this unless and until it showed itself to be linked in some way to the body she had found on the roundabout, and that was hardly likely. The picture of that poor woman's remains burst into her mind's eye again and Lottie felt like weeping.

In the end she decided that she would visit Avril Major. She could at least check out her accent and be sure her assumption was correct. She was supposed to do tarot readings, wasn't she? Lottie decided that she would make an appointment for one of those. She could also see if she could get Avril Major to open up about her past. Maybe that way she would discover that Avril Major was a local woman who just happened to have the same name.

Yes, a local woman who had a habit of meeting the London train in Lyeminster whilst wearing a disguise...

CHAPTER TWELVE

Pennyman Cottage was amazing. Lottie stepped out from between the neatly clipped privet hedges that shielded Beau Derek's house from Welham Lane and was transported to a different world. Whittington Edge was a pretty place; that was one of the reasons she had chosen to live there. Whittington Edge felt frozen in time. The shopping baskets, the formality of only using first names when invited to do so, the necessity of receiving an invitation before calling even on friends; all these things reminded Lottie of a former age.

Her own home life had not been like that. Her parents had been free spirits. The aunt who had taken her and her brother in had been a university lecturer with all the bohemian attitudes that accompanied the role. People were dropping into their home all the time, shedding piles of books, heavy sweaters and scarves in heaps and sitting cross-legged on any available piece of floor to talk and talk, often for hours at a time. Lottie and her brother were welcome to join in their discussions and the intelligent visitors who peopled her life imparted new and exciting ideas to her by osmosis. It had been a wonderful time.

And now before her stood Pennyman Cottage. It had been built of a rose coloured brick many years ago and must be one of the oldest dwellings in the town. Barley sugar chimneys twisted high above the roofs releasing gentle swirls of white smoke into the cloudless blue sky. They reminded Lottie of the stream of tea Gwennie had poured into delicate china that day in Lyeminster. She smiled. The windows twinkled. The sun was almost at its zenith and caught the diamonds of leaded glass and reflected off the uneven surfaces as if the house had been glazed with mirrors. A pink dovecote stood off to the right and a pink dove cooed and took flight when she crunched up the gravelled drive.

Beau Derek must have been looking out for her or else he had some sophisticated early warning system because he opened the heavy, studded door before she had time to knock.

'Welcome, dear lady,' he stepped back and swept out an arm as if he would sweep her into the house with the gesture.

Lottie was reminded of Dexter but Beau didn't make her feel creepy. She stepped over the threshold into the oak panelled hallway. Good manners prevented her looking round whilst her host watched as she would have liked to do.

'It's so good of you to agree to see me, Lord Derek,' she said, shaking the hand that he held out to her. 'The rector said you were studying the history of the village and I wondered if you had any interesting material on the old Horse and Trumpet public house.'

'Indeed I do, Mrs Colenso. But first, shall we have a cup of tea or coffee? I know you haven't come far but it's a chilly day.' He rubbed his hands together as if he were the one to have braved the cold morning. 'Do please come this way and take a seat by the fire.'

He led the way across to another room and Lottie quickly checked out the hall.

Fine linen fold carving embellished the panelling. Bunches of carved fruit clustered in corners. On either side of the door to what Beau called the parlour, carved heads leaned in as if trying to eavesdrop on conversations taking place within. Lottie smiled.

'Make yourself comfortable, Mrs Colenso, and I'll fetch hot beverages. Would you prefer tea or coffee?'

'Coffee, if it isn't too much trouble.' Lottie said.

Beau hurried away leaving her standing marooned on a beautiful Aubusson carpet. She turned slowly. The room was exquisite. An ormolu clock stood slightly off centre on the mantelpiece so as not to detract from the intricately carved overmantel. Delicate china ornaments abounded; Beau Derek, she decided, must like dusting.

The sound of light footsteps made her hurry to seat herself by the fire as he had suggested. A large supper table stood between the chairs that flanked the fire and Beau rested the tray there and sat down to pour coffee from a huge silver pot.

'You have pink doves.' Lottie said unable to hold back the words.

'Yes,' Beau said on a sigh, 'the lady liked pink.' He held out a cup of coffee which Lottie took with a carefully disguised grimace. She could tell she had stepped on a sensitive area but Beau quickly recovered and led her away from dangerous ground.

'How are you enjoying Whittington Edge and your lovely home? I've taken a keen interest in the renovations you've made. The old Horse and Trumpet stood empty for many years. It has an interesting history and I thought it a shame that no one cared for it any more.

'I was delighted when you bought it though I must admit I was worried that you had taken on too large a task.

'I love it.' Lottie said taking an appreciative sip of her coffee. 'This coffee is wonderful.' Beau nodded acknowledgement.

'I love Whittington Edge. I've made some good friends here. I never had many friends before. I was a dedicated career girl and,' Lottie realised that she was heading into dangerous territory again, 'and, after my husband died I threw myself into my work.' She looked down at her lap hoping that mention of a dead husband would be enough to prevent Beau from probing too deeply.

'What line of work were you in?'

'Insurance.' Lottie said. This had been the stock answer when she worked for the Department, it wasn't exactly a lie but it was not a subject to excite the interest of most people and it was usually an effective conversation stopper.

'Did you enjoy it?'

'I enjoyed the attention to detail.' Lottie wondered how she was going to get him off the subject before he strayed too close to the truth.

He treated her to a long, assessing appraisal and eventually nodded. 'Yes,' he said, 'I can see that you would be very good at that sort of thing; details interest you. It wouldn't have been just a job, it would have been meat and drink to you.'

Lottie didn't know what to say to that so she said nothing.

'I'm hoping that Horse and Trumpet Cottage has a long and interesting history.' Lottie said when Beau Derek asked her what she wanted to know about the village. 'I used to read the Dr Syn books as a child so I suppose I'm hoping for highwaymen, smugglers, and a secret tunnel connecting my house to the manor house or old rectory, or, best of all, the crypt of St Jude's – that sort of thing.' She laughed when she saw his face and he joined in. 'I'm going to be disappointed, aren't I?'

They were in Beau's study. It was a large panelled room on the first floor overlooking the back of the building.

'Maybe just a little though I can understand your devotion to Dr Syn; he was one of my favourites too.' Beau pulled a folio of plans towards them. 'The story of Whittington Edge and Horse and Trumpet Cottage is a story of one man's ambition being thwarted, but it's an interesting story nonetheless.'

Lottie tried not to let her own disappointment show.

'Great things were planned for the village.' Beau said. 'The then Lord Whittington had visited the famous spa towns of his day. He particularly liked Bath and Harrogate and he had the notion that he could turn Whittington Edge into a similar place. He had visions of high society converging on his town and of himself being the Beau Brummel of the assembly rooms.'

'Were there assembly rooms here?'

'Good Lord, no. There was no spring that he could turn into a spa either but I think there was a touch of the Mad King Ludwig about this particular Lord Whittington. He didn't see that as an obstacle at all.'

Beau ran a beautifully manicured finger over the map tracing a blue line that enclosed The Green and very little else. 'You see this? This is the extent of Whittington Edge at the time. As you can see, here is The Green. This is the manor house. This is Pennyman Cottage where we are now.' He straightened up and looked her in the eye. 'That was all he had to work with but from that he intended to create something marvellous. And,' Beau turned to another plan 'to some extent he succeeded. Look. He built Main Street.

'If you've ever wondered why the road and pavements are so wide, this is your answer. He decided that he needed a street that would impress people used to the grand architecture of Bath and Harrogate. He built Main Street and lined it with the Georgian buildings we have today. 'A lot of people were infected with his enthusiasm. The old Horse and Trumpet was set to be the largest coaching inn in the district.'

He pulled out another plan that showed the front elevation of Horse and Trumpet Cottage. It was a lot larger than Lottie's current home and she frowned.

'Where did the rest of it go?' She leaned closer to take in the details.

'It never existed.' He told her. 'By the time he was ready to build the stables and the yard, the locomotive had been around for a little while. It had progressed from being the novelty it started out as when no one died from travelling at more than four miles an hour. The writing was on the wall for coaching inns so the Horse and Trumpet became a public house instead.'

'What a shame.'

'He was destined for more disappointment. He urged the railway company to bring the line to the village. That would have made us more important than Lyeminster and would have brought people and industry to the area. But Lord Whittington died before he could pull sufficient strings and the line went to Lyeminster instead.'

'I feel quite sorry for him.' Lottie said. 'But I'm glad he didn't turn Whittington Edge into an industrial city.'

'Me too, but let me get to one of my reasons for wanting to talk to you.' Beau said. 'I can't offer you highwaymen or smugglers but I may be able to offer you land.'

'Land?'

He directed her attention back to the plans on the table. 'This land at the side of Horse and Trumpet Cottage belonged to the proposed coaching inn. I suspect that it still does. I think you should look into it.'

'Why would I want more land?' Even as the words left her lips, Lottie knew she had said something way beyond stupid. The look on Beau's face reflected that thought straight back at her.

'Because. It. Is. Land.' Beau said patiently. 'They're not making any more of it you know.' He smiled and Lottie smiled too. 'The reason that you want this land is: you could extend your own house to more than three times its present size, you could sell the land and make enough money to make the remainder of your life extremely comfortable, you could build a couple of large houses on the plot and sell them and make megabucks, you could turn it all into a rose garden. Whatever you decide to do, you need to do it quickly.'

'Why?'

'Because I suspect that the brewery that owned the pub are waiting for you to fail to notice. They will then be able to claim the land for themselves. Then they could build... who knows what. There are many odd little quirks to do with these things.'

'I'm very grateful to you, Lord Derek, but I have no idea how I would go about this.'

'I used to keep an eye on my father's interests in this regard.' Beau said. 'I still do the same for my brother – at a distance of course. I would be honoured if you would allow me to act for you. It would give me something to occupy myself with in these troubling times.'

'I would have to pay you.'

'No. No, you wouldn't need to pay me. I have more than enough money for my purposes. If you gave me more, that snivelling little weasel of a chancellor would get his greedy hands on the lot, and that we must avoid at all costs.'

'Then, if you're sure, thank you.' Lottie said.

Beau held out his hand and Lottie shook it. 'I shall need authority from you to deal on your behalf. I have prepared a document for you to sign to give me that authority. It is restricted to dealings concerning that piece of land only; I'm quite happy for you to show it to your solicitor before signing it. Only speed is of the essence. These things take their own sweet time and we don't want to be close to the wire on this. We need to act quickly.'

'What are the troubling times you mentioned, Lord Derek?'

'Please call me Beau. It was my soubriquet at school and I understand it has become so around the village and I rather like it. And I shall call you Lottie, if I may.'

Lottie had read the paper he had given her and decided that its simplicity rendered it unnecessary to take it to her solicitor.

Besides, she trusted Beau implicitly even on so short an acquaintance. She signed it and gave it to him.

'The troubling times. Yes.' Beau took the signed paper and set it down on his desk. 'Let me tell you about those over lunch.' He shepherded her down the stairs and into the dining room of Pennyman Cottage. It was vast – and cold. 'I thought we could use the breakfast room,' he said, 'it's just through this way.'

The breakfast room was a cosy little room. Central heating kept it warm even though the sun had long ago slipped away from its windows.

Beau seated her carefully and left the room only to return with a heated trolley. From this he produced an array of delicious dishes.

'Do you like to cook, Beau, or do you have one of the village ladies chained to the Aga?'

Beau threw back his head and laughed. 'One of the village ladies did help to organise this but she left long ago.' He leaned forward to speak conspiratorially, 'but she didn't cook this, it comes ready made from a shop in London. All she had to do was defrost it and heat it through.'

'Everything is wonderful.' Lottie sank her fork into a tender piece of lobster and conveyed it to her mouth where it almost melted. 'This is amazing.' She said. 'Amazing' was the word that had been skittering around her brain ever since she saw the pink doves. 'Tell me about the troubling times.' She said.

Beau poured wine into a large stemmed glass. He didn't ask Lottie what kind she wanted but she saw that he had noted what she was eating and had chosen for her with that in mind. She tasted it. It too was delicious. And to think that people in Whittington Edge thought this man only a step up from a tramp.

'I came to Whittington Edge in pursuit of my fiancée.' He said. 'Adelaide wasn't considered suitable as a wife for me. If my sister in law had produced a male heir it wouldn't have mattered but she had four daughters and was beyond the age of wanting to keep having children until a boy turned up.

'My father and my brother argued about this a lot but my brother loves his wife and refused point blank to keep expecting Sylvia to have a child every year just for a title.

'Father gave up on him then and turned his attention to me as I am my brother's heir.' Beau smiled. 'I should tell you that my brother is an earl and needs a son, or so my father believed. Unfortunately for him, he had been so intent on bullying Sylvia into having a son that he hadn't noticed me falling in love with Adelaide, one of the housemaids. Of course he wanted me to find someone more suitable. I refused. My brother, God bless him, resisted the temptation to join forces with father and thus make his own life easier. Instead he supported my choice and said that Adelaide was entirely right for me.'

'Was your father very angry?'

'Incandescent. He...he threw Adelaide out of the house. I didn't know she had gone. She left a note with Sylvia saying that she was coming home to Whittington Edge and that, if I still wanted her, I should follow.'

'And you did.' Lottie smiled at him.

'Yes I did but I was too late. My father worked himself up so much that he was dead before morning. My brother told me to follow Adelaide but my mother pleaded with me to stay for the funeral. I did as she wished and when I reached Whittington Edge, Adelaide wasn't here. I didn't know where to look. I went to the address she gave me and she had obviously been there; her clothes were in the wardrobe. But she wasn't here. I don't know where she went.

'I couldn't leave. I waited. I bought this house. I bought the pink doves. She had always liked pink.'

Lottie looked away as Beau found a handkerchief and dabbed at his eyes.

'And she never returned? She never wrote to you, or...or to Sylvia?'

'No.'

'I'm so sorry.'

'She wouldn't have left me, Lottie, even though she may have thought that I had abandoned her. There would only have been two or three days at most, or so I thought, before my letter telling her what had happened and explaining that it would be a week or two before I could join her would have reached Whittington Edge.'

'As you thought?'

Beau smiled at her. 'I knew you were attentive to details.' He said. 'Yes, I found my letter still sitting on the silver salver in the hall the day after my father's funeral. The butler was very loyal to my father and he had 'held it back in case I came to my senses'. That was the way he put it. So poor Adelaide was here, all alone and sure that I had forsaken her.'

'I'm so sorry.'

'Thank you.' Beau took a deep breath. 'But now I suspect that the lady you found on the traffic island may be my Adelaide.'

'Oh no!'

'Can you tell me anything about her?'

Lottie was in a quandary now. She knew that the police kept some specific piece of information secret so that only the murderer would know about it and she didn't want to foil their efforts in any way.

'I didn't really notice anything.' She said. She went on to explain how she came to make the discovery and overemphasised her shock and instant recoil. Thankfully, Beau understood this and accepted it without question.

'In a way, I'm hoping it was her.' His voice was soft. 'At least, if she's been there for all those years, perhaps she didn't give up hope of my keeping my word.'

'I'm sure she didn't. She knew you, Beau. I've only known you for a couple of hours and I can see that you're a man of integrity. You would never have left Adelaide just because someone else told you to. You would and did fight for her. You loved her, Beau.'

'I'm a weak man, Lottie. Anyone who knows me will tell you so.

'I wouldn't believe them if they did.' Lottie lifted her chin and smiled at him. 'I couldn't see you going into the boxing ring against a heavyweight boxer, but I do see you standing your ground on a matter of principle. You are the sort of man who works quietly in the background to try to make life better for other people. That's a wonderful quality and I, for one, admire it.'

'Thank you, Lottie, my dear.'

'Have you told the police of your suspicions? They must be eager to identify the poor woman and a name would give them a valuable lead to follow.'

'I'm ashamed to say that I haven't. I suppose I'm in what it is popularly called 'denial'. I was holding out a faint hope that if I didn't mention its name then it couldn't come true.'

'Would you like me to tell them?'

'Would you? Please? You could tell that handsome detective who sneaks into Church Lane. He would know what to do.'

Lottie stared at him in horror. He knew that Marco was a detective. And he had noticed him calling at the side door. If he had seen him, who else knew?

'Don't worry,' Beau said, 'I'm sure no one else has seen him and they wouldn't recognise him as a police officer if they did. They would think you had a follower, Lottie.' He gave a little laugh and Lottie did her best to join in. 'I shall not breathe a word to anyone about him.' He assured her.

'Thank you.' Lottie smiled. 'And I shall tell him about your suspicions. Can you give me a few more details?'

Lottie made notes in the back of her diary. They returned to Beau's wonderful study and he showed her photographs, copies of the Whittington Edge census and newspaper clippings from over a hundred years ago.

'Would you tell me about Adelaide, Beau?' Lottie tilted her head to look into his kindly face. She hoped that talking about his fiancée would give him a measure of peace.

'She was lovely,' Beau sighed. 'She was a tall girl; almost as tall as me. But she always felt she should hide it. That it was unfeminine to be tall. Or for a tall girl to wear pink for that matter. I told her to wear pink, and high heels and to hold up her head and be proud of who she was.' He sighed again. 'I think she was happier when she was being true to herself.'

'I think we all are,' Lottie said. But all the time she was doing a sort of inventory of the woman she had found. She remembered that the shoes beside the body were large; she hadn't thought of that before. And the dress the skeleton wore could have originally been pink. She wouldn't tell Beau but she was almost sure that it was his Adelaide who had lain undiscovered on the roundabout for so many years.

***

The shadows were lengthening when Lottie left Pennyman Cottage. She accepted Beau's offer to escort her part of the way because she was reluctant to end their pleasant day. He walked her around past Hallelujah House and The Crow's Nest so that she would approach Horse and Trumpet Cottage from the side where the land that Beau wanted to claim for her lay.

Lottie's interest had been awakened by his revelation and she had intended to walk this way. It was more pleasant to have Beau's company whilst she did so.

'You see,' Beau said, his arm describing a wide sweep that encompassed all before him, 'that whole tract of land should belong to your property. If the brewery is trying to pull a fast one, we need to get in ahead of them and make the claim in your name. But don't you worry; I shall be onto it first thing Monday morning. I am not without contacts.'

Lottie stared at the land. She had never noticed that the land was enclosed with fencing identical to that surrounding Horse and Trumpet Cottage. There was easily enough land for a whole row of small houses to be built next door to her. What if the brewery were waiting for a decent interval to pass before they stole the land out from under her?

'Thank you, Beau, and thank you too for a wonderful day. I've really enjoyed our talk and the delicious lunch. And Pennyman Cottage is an absolute gem. You must be so proud of it.'

'I hope I can look forward to many more occasions when I can entertain you there.'

'That is very kind. I shall look forward to welcoming you to my home too. I shall contact my friend as you requested and report back.'

'And I shall look out the photographs I have of the old Horse and Trumpet public house and we can get copies of them made up for you. I believe the printer in Main Street is also a keen amateur photographer; he should be able to reproduce them and clean up any faults that time may have wrought. Unless,' he added quickly, 'you know someone who can work wonders with a computer.'

'No one that comes to mind.' Lottie laughed. 'I think we're a generation out of step with such things, Beau.'

The last rays of the sun slanted across the front of Lottie's home slashing red patches of colour over her windows. 'Red sky at night,' she said looking up at the sky.'

'Yes, another fine day tomorrow but it doesn't bode well for next week; we shall have rain then for sure.' Beau sighed. 'I'll leave you here, my dear. Be in touch.'

'I shall,' Lottie said. Then she startled herself by reaching up and giving his cheek a quick kiss. 'Goodnight, and thank you again.'

Beau returned her kiss and buttoned up his thick camel coat as he walked away.

**

Bill Warbeck was at the gallery early on Saturday morning. 'Summer' had been hung on the specially painted wall and he had called in to check that its presentation was pleasing to his eye. The gallery owner always went through this little charade but he made it clear that this was a formality and that Bill's daubs were not important enough for him to change anything regardless of what he said. Or that was usually the case.

Today, the dapper little man was dancing attendance on Bill as if he were Sir Joshua Reynolds and Thomas Gainsborough rolled into one.

'Step this way, Bill,' the man simpered, 'Summer is adorning the main gallery. She is a sheer delight,

Bill, my dear. And your choice of colour for the wall was inspired. I have trained some discreet lighting so that it picks up the vibrancy of her hair. I'm so excited about this. The art critic of the Lyeminster Echo is bringing his photographer to take a carefully lit shot. In colour. They are talking about issuing high quality prints to all their readers; there would be royalties for you right there, Bill. There could be a great deal of kudos in it for both of us.'

Bill Warbeck began to swell with pride. His chin with its grizzly, bushy, dirty, beard lifted a fraction. He ran a paint bespattered hand over it and thought he may nip into Dubarry on Main Street when he returned to Whittington Edge.

That hairdresser woman should be able to tidy things up a bit and she should be cheaper than going to a real barber.

He had to look the part because it was more than likely that the Lyeminster Echo would want a picture of him too.

He was busily working out the remainder of his day when the gallery owner threw open the double doors leading to the main gallery and stood aside.

On the wall opposite a composite of Atlantis and Summer Saunders swathed in shimmering emerald satin looked out coquettishly at the viewer. The breath caught in Bill's throat. After seeing the picture day after day in his messy studio, he had no idea how good it would look.

He had chosen the framing himself but had accepted the finished article already wrapped in tar paper and delivered it to the gallery without looking at it in its finished state.

Reminding himself to breathe, Bill took a step forward. The gallery owner was twittering away beside him but Bill was oblivious. The lighting made the flesh glow, the eyes sparkle with mischief, and the hair – Atlantis's hair – catch fire.

It was sensational. Bill could hardly believe that this piece of perfection had been wrung out, stroke by stroke, from the bristles of his brushes.

When he arrived back at his studio, that study of vines weighed down with rashers of bacon and bunches of blackberries was going straight into the stack and he would begin another study of Atlantis. This one he would call 'Autumn'. Atlantis's colouring was autumnal and anyone making the link between Summer Saunders and 'Summer' would be thwarted.

He wished now that 'Summer' had depicted Atlantis, arms reaching up to the sky, head thrown back as if she were a blossom in full bloom showing off her beauty to her maker. 'Autumn' he was thinking, should be of Atlantis crumpled on the floor like a fallen leaf. He could heap copper leaves around her and pine cones and he was sure Atlantis could suggest other items from the piles of detritus she collected.

But, if 'Autumn' was a withered heap on the floor, what would 'Winter' look like? Bill frowned. It seemed as if his own brilliance had brought yet another burden.

***

Gwennie always offered to do the Saturday afternoon shift at the library. All the married women needed to do their weekend shopping but were happy to return to relieve her so that she could get home early.

Few people had time to collect library books during the afternoon but for those who needed it, the library must remain open.

The women of Whittington Edge were shopping or talking with friends in the Butterfly Bush. The men were at home watching football on television after a lunchtime drink in The Priest at Prayer. So, it was only the occasional child who ventured in although most of them were at the park running around and letting off steam.

The library at Whittington Edge could easily close for Saturday afternoon but the county council insisted that it remain open until seven o clock to keep in line with the libraries in Lyeminster and Gwennie quite enjoyed the solitude and the chance it gave her to dust the shelves and line up the books so they looked welcoming.

Mrs Bettinson pushed the vacuum cleaner around twice a week and the tracks it left on the carpet showed just how inefficiently she did it. Gwennie shook her head at such slovenliness. If a job's worth doing it's worth doing well. At least that was what mother used to say.

Endlessly.

Usually as a criticism of Gwennie's youthful efforts to help.

The realisation that she was silently quoting mother's oft repeated words made Gwennie sigh. Her secret dread was turning into mother.

This mournful thought was interrupted when the door opened.

The arrival of Fanny Barstock, the self-appointed leader of the Women's Institute, the Young Wives and the flower arranging club soon put paid to Gwennie's happy mood.

The sight of Fanny Barstock barging her way through the library doors like an icebreaker cutting a new route through the Northwest Passage made Gwennie's shoulders droop.

'Ah, Gwennie, just the person I wanted to see.'

Even Gwennie couldn't be taken in by this. Everyone in Whittington Edge knew that she worked the Saturday afternoon shift at the library. The unwelcome thought that followed was that Fanny

Barstock had come to the library specifically to see her.

'May I help you choose a book?' Gwennie offered, still hoping to glean a good deed from such unpromising beginnings.

'Good Lord, no.' Fanny shuddered. 'No, Gwennie my dear, I'm far too busy to squander time by reading.' She made it sound the most frivolous occupation in the world which was a bit rich considering that Fanny instituted bingo at the church hall and Gwennie knew she was the first person to take her seat at every session.

Gwennie's shoulders drooped even further. 'Sorry, Fanny, books are all we do here. Although we have a few films on DVD and music on CD if that was what you required.'

This was a valiant effort on Gwennie's part and she knew that the Murder Club would be highly amused. And, to be honest, it was the thought of recounting this to her friends, and this thought alone, that was keeping her from becoming a quivering wreck under Fanny Barstock's gimlet eye.

'You profess to be friends with this Lottie Colenso woman,' Fanny said as if denouncing a traitor, 'I need you to talk to her. This is for the good of the whole village, Gwennie.'

Fanny Barstock bridled in the way that Mrs Bettinson bridled when she was spreading slander and Gwennie prepared herself to defend her beloved Lottie from whatever malicious rumour was coming her way.

'I'm sure Mrs Colenso would be amenable to doing something that would benefit the 'whole village'.' Gwennie countered in her most caustic tone.

'Oh, well, good,' Fanny Barstock deflated like a punctured balloon. 'What I want her to do is help out with the Halloween Party.'

'In what capacity?' Gwennie had an instant image of Fanny Barstock trying to boss Lottie around and a smile curved her lips.

'She couldn't be co-opted to the committee that goes without saying.' Fanny said. 'But it wouldn't hurt her to contribute something towards the refreshments.'

'I'll ask her.' Gwennie shrugged and turned back to the shelves. 'Though I don't see why you're afraid to ask her yourself.' She dusted diligently and watched Fanny Barstock, marooned in her peripheral vision, floundering for something else to say, and outraged by the suggestion that she needed to hide behind Gwennie Furlong of all people.

In the nick of time, the first of Gwennie's colleagues returned to the library and called out a greeting. Gwennie, not daring to glance around lest she be turned to stone by Fanny Barstock's gorgon gaze, called back and Fanny Barstock, worsted for possibly the first time in her life, faded into the background and slunk out into the cold afternoon.

Gwennie resolved not to leave for at least another half hour lest Fanny Barstock be waiting to buttonhole her again.

***

Bill Warbeck was being unbearable. He was so full of himself because 'Summer' was such a success. Atlantis was grinding her teeth. He marched up and down the hall of The Crow's Nest waving his arms around like some old actor spouting Hamlet. Badly.

She took herself off to the kitchen to throw a couple of fish portions into a pan of water. She could boil up a small pack of frozen peas. That would have to do him because the thought of sitting opposite Bill whilst he bragged on interminably was more than anyone should have to listen to.

***

Lottie had her key in the front door when she heard rapid footsteps. Avril Major emerged from Church Lane carrying her carpet bag. What better time to do anything than the present?

'Mrs Major,' she called out. Avril approached and Lottie leaving the keys dangling from the lock, hurried down the path. 'I understand you are well known for you tarot readings. I wondered if you would be willing to read my cards.'

Avril's eyes travelled over Lottie before she forced a smile that couldn't reach her eyes.

'I'll look at my diary and call you, if that suits you.' She said.

'That would be wonderful.' Lottie managed to produce the sort of smile that she was sure the Cheshire Cat left behind. 'I'll await your call. I have an answering machine if I'm out when you ring.' And without prolonging their conversation any further, Lottie retraced her steps.

***

Avril was in a hurry too. The new superintendent of police assigned to Woolstock police station was expected.

After the unfortunate experiences that led to her departure from the East End, from Sonny and ultimately from London, she had vowed that she would never have anything to do with coppers ever again.

This guy had been a lowly sergeant when she was running her former business. Something must have happened. He must know where the bodies were buried or something because he wasn't a patch on the higher ranks that had attended her soirees. And now he was a superintendent! Mind you, they had to move him to this stultifying backwater so that he could cope. How he had got onto her was a worry but he had recognised her and there was nothing she could do about it.

He had called her as soon as he had his feet under his desk. He didn't exactly blackmail her into resuming their 'friendship' but she hadn't allowed things to reach the sort of territory where threats belonged.

No, Avril had heard the voice, made the connection and invited him round. Giving a friendly copper a freebie was par for the course. The payback was that he would protect her from any police interest – and look how well that had worked in the Smoke. Coppers, she could spit at the very thought of them.

The moment she entered the hall of Nook Cottage, Avril knew something was wrong. Her sixth sense alerted her to danger and kicked in with a vengeance. She ran upstairs and checked around. Nothing was out of place. Nothing was missing as far as she could tell. There was no visible damage; no sign of disturbance.

The living room looked exactly as she had left it. The conservatory was fine. The kitchen was fine too. No...No, something was wrong. Then she saw it. Jason Flint's mug was sitting on the kitchen table. It hadn't been there when she left. Jason had been in the garden tidying up the leaves.

In her mind's eye she could see the mug on the bench by the shed. She had asked him to bring it inside but he hadn't, and she hadn't wanted to wait for him to do so because she was in a hurry so she had locked up and gone to Lyeminster.

Had she locked up?

Yes. Absolutely. Avril didn't make mistakes of that magnitude.

It was the work of a moment to discover that the door had been jemmied. Jason? Surely not. He was a bit of a fly character and liked to think he was the local hard man. Avril almost laughed out loud. Jason Flint, hard? He should cocoa. Jason Flint didn't know he was born.

The alarm on Avril's mobile phone told her it was time to ready herself to welcome Mr Saturday. She hurried to do so but the fact of the break-in wormed around and around inside her head until she was uncharacteristically in a stew. So much so that the first thing she did when Mr Saturday arrived was to blurt out the whole thing to him.

His only concern, naturally enough for a bleedin' copper, was whether or not his visits to Nook Cottage were documented anywhere.

Avril regretted her impulsive words immediately. Why hadn't she kept quiet? Now he was sniffing around like a perishing bloodhound and she had unwittingly given him an 'access all areas' pass.

When would she learn that you never, ever, tell a copper anything?

***

Marco Romero was still working away in Woolstock CID office when Lottie called.

'Lottie, great to hear from you. Do you have anything for me?'

'I do, but not what you're expecting. Have you identified the body yet?'

'No. Do you have a lead?'

'I may have.'

She told him about Adelaide Barrett and Beau Derek. 'Don't be hard on him for not coming forward sooner, Marco, the poor man's in pieces about her.'

'Are you going soft in your old age, Lottie?'

'I think I may be. Just be patient and don't let him see how angry you are.'

Marco sighed. 'I'll handle him with kid gloves. I'll go to see him when I leave off in about,' there was a short pause, 'about ten minutes. Will you be in later if I call round to see you?'

'Yes, I've nothing planned for this evening. If you're free too, I could cook dinner.'

'That would be great. I'll see you later then.'

Lottie dug around in the deep freeze and found something to put in the oven for dinner. She had often wanted to invite Marco to share a meal with her but the thought of issuing the invitation had put her off. Now she had done it quite spontaneously and he had accepted. Whilst the oven worked its magic Lottie retired to her study to write up her notes and look forward to seeing Marco.

CHAPTER THIRTEEN

Susan paused in the process of putting her key in her front door to take a look around The Green before going inside.

Sunday was, or could be, the loneliest day of the week. She was wise enough not to allow this to happen. She had joined the gym to keep fit and ward off osteoporosis, and also to meet hunky men, or so she told everyone. In actual fact she had joined to have somewhere to go on Sundays.

The church was not for Susan. She loved churches and often visited them out of hours; she felt uplifted by the atmosphere, the architecture and the art, but the service had held no attraction for her since they changed the old prayers for new, user-unfriendly versions intended to dumb down the act of prayer as far as she could see, whilst removing all the poetry and grandeur of the old form of words.

The final straw came when the congregation was urged to shake hands with people all around them and, in one church, heaven forbid, they were asked to hug the person next to them. That was it. No more church services.

She was also wary of being inadvertently roped into the merry band of widows and maiden ladies who twittered around the vicar after the service competing to perform small favours for him or giving him slippers they had knitted, offering to embroider hassocks and vestments and altar cloths.

Really, Susan did not see herself in this role at all. So, she went to the gym and punched the air and tied her almost middle-aged body into knots ignoring the creaks and stifling the groans, relentlessly keeping a smile on her face even as she brushed the sweat out of her eyes and averted her gaze from the red-faced woman in the mirror.

After the exertion, she had a sauna and a shower and told herself she felt all the better for it. And sometimes she did.

She was ready now for a coffee and a rest. But she wanted company. The house always seemed quieter on a Sunday than at any other time.

That was when she saw Lottie taking her customary walk around The Green. She was a lot later than usual, Susan noted. She coo-ee-ed and waved when Lottie turned around. Lottie heard and waved back, crossing The Green speedily, with no thought of the effect of wet grass on her smart boots.

'Been to the gym?' she asked unnecessarily as she took in Susan's attire. 'How was it?'

'Exhausting. I tell you, Lottie, keeping up with these twentysomethings is no joke. They are indestructible.'

'So were we at their age'. Lottie laughed. 'I hope you were going to invite me in. My day stretches ahead devoid of plans or diversions.'

'Mine too. Come in. Could you drink another coffee?'

'I can always drink another coffee, especially when you make it.' Lottie followed Susan inside and took off her wet boots giving the leather a quick wipe with a tissue she found in her pocket. Hanging her coat and hat on the hall stand, she followed Susan through to her bright little kitchen.

She was always amazed at what Susan had done with so small a space. There wasn't room for a table, of course, but Susan had a couple of high stools beneath the bar. She pulled one out and sat on it whilst Susan busied herself with coffee and cafetiere.

Lottie had been talking to the neighbours. Today she had encountered an old gentleman snipping dead foliage in the garden of Norton House near to Templar House. He and his wife were intending to sell up and move into a new, sheltered community that was under construction in Woolstock. Nothing about him could interest Marco but she had another note to make in her book.

Gradually her pages were filling up and Lottie felt a fine sense of achievement.

**

Avril Major, next door in Nook Cottage, was having another of her conversations with Sonny.

"How are you doing, ducks?'

'I had a break-in, Sonny.' The moment the words were out Avril regretted them. It didn't do to show weakness to Sonny. And it was an indication of how much this trivial thing had upset her that she had now twice blurted it out and to the two most unsuitable people she knew.

'What did they take?' Sonny's jokey manner abruptly changed to serious business; he couldn't afford to let her know that this was no surprise to him whatsoever.

'I can't see that they took anything. Someone had been through my filing cabinet, though.'

'What was in it?'

'Nothing to identify any of my clients. No one had found my book club parcel.' She could hear a sigh of relief from Sonny, but, suddenly she wasn't too sure about there being nothing to cause her trouble. There was just one little thing... but it wasn't a loss she could put down on her insurance claim.

Sonny, happy that she hadn't tried to hold out on him, soon reverted to his own interests.

They talked about Sonny's club and mutual friends from the old days. Sonny teased her with little snippets of information that he hoped would make her miss him and London and tempt her into coming home before he returned to the subject of the invasion of Nook Cottage.

'Keep me posted, Doll,' Sonny said. There was a pause before he spoke again. 'And, I'm sorry to do this to you when you already have enough on your plate, but could you collect another of my men off the eleven o'clock on Monday? His name's Ronnie. Ron's an easy one. All I want is for you to collect him and show him the way to the Granby. I'll take care of everything else from this end. You won't need to babysit this one.'

'Are you sure? It's really no trouble.'

'Positive, Doll. Ronnie'll be doing a little job for me. That's why he'll be staying at the Granby.'

'I could easily give him the tour Sonny.'

'Not likely. I don't want the poor fella back on the next train.' Sonny's chesty laugh turned into a cough. Avril laughed too. She didn't ask about Arthur; she didn't care a fig about Arthur; he was enough trouble when he was in Lyeminster.

Talking about the break in with Sonny hadn't made Avril feel any better as she had hoped it would. The superintendent's performance last night had driven her crazy.

He had poked his way all through her house, snooping into all her drawers and cupboards, even the filing cabinet; she had almost blushed until she noticed that sight of her 'toys' had him in a sweat.

Then the stupid old git had demanded a sandwich bag so that he could take Jason's mug back for fingerprinting. What did he think he would find on it? Jason Flint's fingerprints? It didn't take a superintendent of police to work that one out. And did he think sandwich bags grew on trees?

***

Sunday was Avril's only day off and she decided to try to enjoy it despite the disquiet that was fomenting inside her. She was worrying about the missing item.

The last thing she needed was that turning up in some pawn shop and one of her neighbours laying claim to it. When it was traced back to her she could find herself inside again. It was an impulse that was all. The damned woman had been bragging to her, flaunting the ring, telling her how valuable it was, saying how her man had thought her worth more than just a single diamond and had had this array of precious stones specially made just for her. She had turned her hand from side to side so that the light caught the facets of the stones. She had invited Avril to admire the ring and Avril had.

Avril had pronounced it the most beautiful ring she had ever seen. And, when the time came, Avril had removed the ring from the infuriating woman's finger and kept it for herself.

Avril shuddered, wishing, not for the first time that she had resisted the temptation to purloin the ring. Back to the present day, she told herself. The ring was missing and she would deny all knowledge of it if it ever surfaced. After all, if someone was dishonest enough to break into Nook Cottage and steal, they were also dishonest enough to lie about what they had stolen. Maybe that would work. Yes, that was the angle she would take if she were ever questioned about the ring. Ring?I didn't lose a ring. I didn't think I had lost anything. I thought it was some kids daring one another.

Yes, that's what she would tell them if they asked about the ring. Avril heaved a huge sigh and decided to get on with her day.

She had agreed to read Lottie Colenso's tarot.

She found her diary and ran her finger down her appointments for the coming week. Reluctantly she wrote 'Ronnie 11 o clock' in the space allotted to Monday and worked out that she could fit Lottie Colenso in for an afternoon reading before Mr Monday arrived for his 'special' as he liked to call it.

***

Back in London, Sonny Gumbrill turned the ring that Ronnie had liberated from Nook Cottage over and over in his hand. He had it valued by a trusted associate the minute he received it. He knew a pricey piece of tom foolery when he saw it.

The actual value had almost made his eyebrows fly off the top of his head. He would put money on it coming from that butcher.

Yeah, that was who was after his Doll. Well, Sonny Gumbrill would see about that. Or, Ronnie would. The only thing in Doll's favour was that she hadn't tried to hide the break in from him. But she hadn't mentioned the ring, now had she? No, she bloody hadn't. She was planning to leave him and no one, no one left Sonny Gumbrill until he called time. So, over to Ronnie. He'd better do a good job.

**

For Jason Flint, the knock on the door was no surprise.

Woolstock CID adhered to the tried and tested method of investigation which involved the rounding up of all the usual suspects and squeezing them all until one of them, hopefully, squeaked. And Jason Flint was one of these; their main man, actually.

It gave him a frisson of delight to know that he had at least this claim to fame. Jason had visions of himself as a real geezer. A player. One of the all time greats.

He was also the guilty party for many minor misdemeanours, but not for this one and he saw that as no reason for them to haul him out of his bed on a Sunday afternoon and drag him down to the cop shop.

To tell the truth – and he wasn't likely to do that on a Sunday afternoon – he had been inside Nook Cottage once and he had taken the opportunity; well, you have to, don't you?

It wasn't as if he had gained anything on his walk through from old Avril's house. Except a shock.

Boy that was sooooo funny. All that stuff in the filing cabinet! Who would have thought she would even know what it was for?

Everyone knew that Avril was a fossilised virgin. But his walk through was done one day whilst she nipped out to the shop and forgot to lock the back door, it wasn't done recently at all. So he needed to keep his wits about him and not divulge anything beyond the kitchen which is the only room he ever legitimately had access to.

Jason Flint did get a shock when he was hauled up before the Super, however. Because, having been told that that worthy officer was going to have the files trawled for every unsolved crime that he could put down to Jason Flint, he was bailed and told to come back the following day at noon.

He wasn't even asked if he had committed the crime. The Super did all the talking. Jason's job was just to listen. The nasty old git even said that to him: 'I don't want to hear from you, Flint, you are here to listen. Make sure you do.'

Jason sometimes did a bit of work for old Avril and, if she made him a cup of tea, he would put the empty cup inside, on the kitchen counter except for yesterday when he forgot. It was only good manners, wasn't it? And Jason's mum was very hot on good manners. 'Manners maketh man, Jason', she said. And though Jason knew this was a load of old claptrap, he still found himself doing these little things, unless he was clever.

So he knew that they could have lifted his fingerprints from inside Avril's house. Even off the back door handle, if they bothered to look, that is. He had been in the kitchen the day he did the garden. He often was.

She would ask him to reach something down from a high shelf or lift anything too heavy. He didn't mind doing that stuff for the old girl and she always added a little something to his wages.

Avril was not a bad old stick. He didn't think they would have identified them yet though. As far as he knew, fingerprints took a long time to do. And he didn't see what use they would be anyway. No court would accept fingerprint evidence about someone who had every right to be in the house, would they? Naturally, he did not offer this great insight.

Jason Flint had been doodling on his notebook through one of his lessons when the teacher said something that caught his attention. He was on about some French geezer called Rich Lowe. Jason thought that was a funny old name for a French bloke but the French were a peculiar lot; you couldn't trust them not to take an English name just to fool you. But anyway, this Rich Lowe bloke said something about if you had a handful of lines written by anyone, he reckoned he could find a reason to hang them.

These words struck a chord with Jason and since then his rule with coppers was never to tell them anything. Nothing. Nada. Diddly squat. If they told you something, you shrugged. If you knew they had proof; you still didn't say anything. If they threw you a curved ball, you called for your brief.

Easy.

Jason Flint had never been interviewed by the Super before and he felt as if he had been promoted. Usually all he got was some little woodentop; Jason could easily run rings around them.

It was sometimes a laugh to build up this great story and watch the woodentop's greedy little eyes working out how close to a promotion this collar would get them, only to tell them it was all a joke and pull the carpet from under their feet.

You had to be careful doing this, of course, because some of them couldn't actually take a joke and might try to fit you up. Just like the Super was going to fit him up now.

Jason didn't necessarily mind going down for a few months; it would add to his CV, make him look harder. But he didn't want to go down for a piddling little break-in that he didn't do.

Jason Flint knew what these coppers were like; something upset them at home and they'd fit the next poor geezer up like a kipper. Well, not him, they wouldn't. Not Jason Flint. Just let them try.

But for now, Jason Flint was going home. They even gave him a lift back in a police car which was a change. And they offered to collect him the next day, cheeky buggers. Jason shrugged and told them they could if they wanted.

Now he knew that they were only having a laugh at his expense. They had no intention of giving him a free ride to Woolstock. Coppers always make it as difficult for you as they can, don't they? Then they try to stitch you up for failing to answer bail. Another few days to add onto the sentence if they're lucky; if they get one of them magistrates who want to bring back hanging.

Still, Jason was going to be fitted up and he was going to get something out of it. For a start he was going to get under that superintendent's skin and rattle him a bit.

So, when he didn't turn up at Woolstock nick at noon and they did send a car round, he could tell them quite honestly that he had been expecting to be collected, hadn't he?

Jason did a nice line in wide-eyed innocence. Not that he'd fool any of them, of course, but he'd have the laugh on them. 'You ask your officers,' he'd say, all polite, 'they'll tell you. They offered me a lift in. And I was waiting for them.'

And there wouldn't be a thing the Super could say. Now, would there?

***

'You're late taking your walk today.' Susan said as she and Lottie took appreciative sips of coffee.

'I had a late night. My friend Marco came round for dinner last night.' As soon as the words were out Lottie wondered if it sounded like a boast.

'He came to see me this morning.' Susan said. 'He's such a nice man.'

Susan was the closest and therefore the bravest of Lottie's friends. She had seen Marco's car parked in Church Lane a few times and had asked Lottie about it. Lottie admitted that Marco was her friend but that she kept quiet about it.

'Was this about the murder?'

'No, it was about Avril Major.' Susan knew from Lottie's face that she had yet to hear about the break in at Nook Cottage. It was gratifying to be first with a piece of news. 'Avril had a break in. Honestly, here in Whittington Edge, it's unthinkable. He seemed particularly interested in Jason Flint so maybe we should keep an eye out for him.'

'Isn't he the young lad who does your gardening for you?' 'Yes, and he's a good worker – or at least as good as anyone these days. And I think they've got the wrong person. He was here earlier in the morning. He only did an hour, picking up leaves and generally tidying round. Then he went on to work at Nook Cottage. He was still there when Avril went out.'

'And that's why they're looking at him?'

'Yes, I know but... I don't know, it seemed as if they had made up their minds that Jason Flint was the culprit and I could almost swear he had left before I went out shopping.'

'Did you tell Marco that?'

'I told him I was almost sure because I couldn't really swear to it; not in a court of law, I mean.'

This interesting dilemma was thrust from their minds by a frantic hammering at the front door of Matchbox Cottage. Susan and Lottie exchanged glances then they heard Gwennie's voice calling to Susan.

'Oh dear, what can be wrong?' Susan got up and hurried to the door. As she passed the front window she frowned. 'There's a crowd gathering next to your house.' She said to Lottie.

Gwennie dashed into the room wild eyed and breathless. 'Oh Lottie, dear, thank goodness you're here. I was looking for you both and here you are together. What luck.'

'What's going on in Church Lane?' Susan wanted to know.

'It's the rector. They say he's been attacked.'

'You go, Lottie, I'll ring for an ambulance.' She looked at Gwennie, 'I don't suppose anyone has already called, have they?'

'I doubt it.' Gwennie said. 'Everyone's panicking. That's why I thought you two were needed.'

***

Lottie and Gwennie arrived at Horse and Trumpet Cottage, and ran through to the side door. There spread out before them was a tableau that looked to Lottie like an oil painting she had once seen of the death of Nelson.

The rector lay unconscious on the flagstones of Church Lane with a whole clutch of women twittering around him and the doctor scowling because his Sunday had been disturbed.

Jane Pendleton knelt beside her husband and several of the hangers- on looked as if they would like to tear his hand from Jane's if only they dared.

'The poor man must be frozen.' Lottie said. She hastened back inside and returned with several blankets which she heaped onto Charles without asking permission of the doctor. Lottie and the doctor's wife had clashed swords shortly after her arrival in Whittington Edge and the look he gave her showed that he would like to protest. He didn't, of course.

In the distance, the sirens of an approaching ambulance could be heard and Lottie saw that Jane and her unconscious husband needed rescuing.

'Anyone who would like a cup of tea or to sit down is more than welcome to take refuge in Horse and Trumpet cottage. I shall go now and make copious amounts of tea. The doctor will doubtless wish to stay with his patient.

'I suggest that Mrs Pendleton is the only person the rector really needs at the moment unless there are any witnesses to what happened.' She ran a glance over the group and eyes refused to make contact. 'Although perhaps you should stay with her, Gwennie. We don't want her being bullied at a time like this.' She glared pointedly at the doctor who had a bit of a reputation for such tactics.

Gwennie, in the meantime was growing in confidence and stature. She could do this. She could be Lottie's right hand woman and the rock to which dear Jane could cling at this dreadful time.

Lottie marched away totally convinced that everyone apart from Jane and Gwennie would follow her.

She was right.

There had been great speculation about what had been done to Horse and Trumpet cottage since her arrival and no one would throw up the chance to see for themselves. Her dislike of inviting all and sundry into her home was pushed aside in the need to deprive the doctor of his audience.

As Lottie headed back into Horse and Trumpet cottage she could hear Jane telling Gwennie that there was a wedding that afternoon and her poor Charles would now be unable to officiate.

Lottie regretted her impulse almost immediately. It was all very well to put one over on the doctor by inviting everyone into Horse and Trumpet cottage for tea thus depriving him of his moment of glory but it was something else entirely when about twenty twittering women trooped after her into her home.

A woman in a strange woolly hat teamed with an orange kaftan dotted with purple sequins introduced herself as Atlantis Warbeck. Lottie blinked when she saw that the purple sequins were also affixed to her face, encircling her eyes and swirling over her cheeks in a complicated pattern. There was a tribe somewhere that adorned their faces with tattoos in a similar style; Lottie had seen a programme about them once. Maoris, maybe. Or was it the Aztecs? She wasn't too sure.

She pulled herself together. Given the outlandish mode of dress Lottie had assumed of late, Atlantis probably saw in her a kindred spirit. Lottie dutifully beamed her approval. She had seen Atlantis about, of course, but they had never actually spoken and niceties such as introductions were essential in Whittington Edge.

Whatever Atlantis thought, she was soon given charge of the teapot and assigned a small team of helpers. Lottie was good at delegation. Lottie Colenso didn't consider herself to be a lazy person; or a religious person, come to that. It was merely that, in her opinion, the good Lord had intended her for certain things. And making tea for the masses was not one of them.

Besides which, she was a newcomer – probably would remain so for the next quarter century if village life was what it was reputed to be – so, she had a duty to talk to her neighbours. Get to know them. Learn what made them tick. Find out all their secrets whilst preserving her own.

Lottie allotted herself the job of keeping up the spirits of the troops and taking the opportunity this tragedy had provided to grill as many villagers as possible. She must remember names so that she could enter them in her notebook. .

She collected a small stool and carried it around in order to sit next to anyone she chose, and dispense sympathy whilst, at the same time, pumping them for information. Lottie was back on the scent and her blood raced through her veins. She had always been an adrenaline junkie and the chase of the investigation was the way she indulged herself; abseiling from a multi storey car park or bungee jumping off a bridge was not her type of thing at all.

The first person to enjoy the spotlight of Lottie's gaze was Mrs Bettinson. Lottie knew her to be the cleaner at the rectory and therefore one of the most knowledgeable people in the room. After all, she cleaned at several other places too though Lottie had no idea where. Also, Mrs Bettinson looked like a fish out of water. Given half a chance she would turn tail and run, and a golden opportunity would be lost.

Having said that, Mrs Bettinson must also be pretty fleet of foot; she had been at the front of the crowd watching Charles Pendleton lying on the ground and yet now was ensconced in Lottie's own favourite armchair.

'We haven't met before.' Lottie said, sweeping her stool close to the arm of Mrs Bettinson's chair and making it impossible for her to escape. 'I'm Lottie Colenso and I'm new to the village. I hope you will help me to fit in.' She moderated her voice so that her innate self-confidence was disguised.

'You're not all that new.' Mrs Bettinson retorted more sharply than Lottie thought necessary. Perhaps the woman had an unfortunate manner.

However, whatever was called for, Mrs Bettinson made it clear that nothing would be forthcoming. She responded to all Lottie's overtures with the same noncommittal answers, keeping to monosyllables wherever possible.

Lottie, uncharacteristically, gave up, rose to her feet, patted Mrs Bettinson's arm as if she had bestowed a gift of wisdom beyond price on the woman and looked around for her next victim.

Mrs Bettinson pulled her arm away pointedly and growled her disapproval so loudly that the two women sharing the adjacent sofa turned around to look and then exchange meaningful glances.

Lottie couldn't help noticing that the whole of her guest list comprised of women and all they were interested in was the recent break in at Nook Cottage.

Lottie listened carefully but no one mentioned Avril's gentlemen callers. The opinions on Jason Flint as the culprit seemed evenly divided.

The Church Lane door opened and a waft of autumnal air heralded the arrival of a newcomer. Lottie was involved in deep discussion with Fanny Barstock at the time and would have had to screw her neck all the way round to see who it was. In her mind she had already decided it must be Gwennie or Susan or both. Or even Jane.

Then the initial pause in conversation became a whisper and a rustle as ladies sat up straight and patted their hair and rearranged their outspread knees into more comely postures. Lottie knew that this could only mean that her visitor was a man.

She couldn't believe that any of the men of Whittington Edge that she knew would invade a ladies impromptu get together and therefore it must be…Dexter Hardman.

Slowly she excused herself from her current companion and rose elegantly to her feet. Every muscle in her thighs and calves was screaming and she hoped that her knees wouldn't crack like gunfire – it had been known to happen – but, pride bore no pain and Lottie was rising and turning like Venus from the seashell amongst the waves. She knew that she had everyone's attention, and the envy of those who had allowed their own physical grace and flexibility to slip.

Quick thinking had long been Lottie's thing. Dexter Hardman was a prize. He had obviously taken the town by storm and she would place herself on the same level of acquaintance as everyone else if she retained the formal mode of address.

'Dexter!' she carolled as she stepped daintily between chairs and occasional tables, hands outstretched. She intentionally gave the impression of speed whilst taking care not to catch anything and send it tumbling to the floor. 'How lovely of you to call.' That should give everyone the impression that Dexter Hardman was a constant visitor. 'As you can see we have had a spot of unpleasantness and all the ladies have congregated here for tea.' Coded message to Dexter Hardman: Horse and Trumpet Cottage is the focal point of the whole town and I am the person to whom everyone turns in times of trouble.

She forbore to add 'as usual' lest some unimaginative creature like Mrs Bettinson decide to take issue with her.

Dexter Hardman, not a whit surprised by this strange behaviour, took a step forward, took her hands in his and raised them to his lips. Lottie quivered with delight; not because Dexter Hardman had kissed her hand but because of the ripple of envy that reverberated off the walls of what had once been the old Lounge bar.

There was probably only one person whom Lottie would not wish to witness this piece of gallantry and that person chose that precise moment to follow Dexter Hardman into Horse and Trumpet Cottage.

'Susan!' Lottie snatched her hands away, leaving Dexter bent double over thin air. 'How lovely to see you.' She swept Susan into an engulfing embrace and managed to whisper something about not knowing what had come over Dexter.

Luckily Dexter recovered quickly and bestowed the same kiss upon Susan making Lottie wish she hadn't said anything because Susan was pink with pleasure.

'Someone has clocked Charlie –' she stopped when she saw Fanny Barstock's eyes, round with shock. '- Mr Pendleton over the head.' She said.

'Yes, that's what I came round about.' Dexter interrupted. 'I thought I might get in touch with the rural dean. Old friends you know. Apparently there's supposed to be a wedding this afternoon. It would be a shame to spoil it.'

'Yerse,' Mrs Bettinson said, 'It's that Marlene Stokes and er fancy man.' All eyes turned to Mrs Bettinson and brows were raised begging for more information. ''Er's marryin' some old bloke she met at work. Widower 'e's supposed ter be. Course, St Andrew's ain't posh enough for Miss high and mighty Marlene, oh no, 'er don't like the church. Want's summat prettier than St Andrews.' She shrugged and bridled showing what she thought of such a shallow outlook on faith, religion and a bride who wanted a pretty backdrop for her wedding because there was no church anywhere prettier than St Jude's.

Knowing glances were exchanged all around. No one liked St Andrew's church. It was a newish church, built sometime during the late sixties and it suffered from all the architectural foibles of its time.

When it was completed people waited for the builder to come and remove the scaffolding from the tower only to find that this was an integral part of the design.

It was possible that some of the faithful had grown to love the white concrete structure which had turned grey and was now striped with streaks of black and rust. But it was unlikely that anyone could love the building.

Congregations there were poorer than at churches in adjoining parishes and no amount of veiled scolding from the pulpit could change things. The church was an eyesore and there was no convincing people otherwise.

'It's so big and cold.' Some brave soul offered. She shivered despite the heat. 'St Jude's is warm and cosy. It wraps itself around you. You can feel your ancestors watching you down the centuries, joining in the service with you. I think the very stones - '

'Let's not get fanciful.' Someone broke in. 'That horrible bit of netting is what I don't understand. Netting! Dangling from the tower. Now, what's that all about, I'd like to know.' This was accompanied by another self-righteous hoisting of matronly bosoms.

'I believe the net is one of St Andrew's emblems.' Lottie offered recklessly. 'Wasn't he one of the original 'fishers of men'?'

All eyes swivelled towards her as if she had said something outrageous.

'Well,' Mrs Bettinson said when the ensuing silence became too brittle to tolerate, 'e'll be catchin' no fish with 'is net stuck up there, and I knows that for a fact.'

'Um... so what do you think about the rural dean?' Dexter Hardman put in quietly. He leaned forward and somehow managed to direct his question to each of the ladies individually. Lottie wondered what he did for a living because he had some unusual talents.

'You should probably consult Mrs Pendleton.' She said, hoping that he wouldn't dash off immediately to carry out this suggestion.

The disapproving glares that had been fixed upon Lottie suddenly faded away as Dexter Hardman's presence was remembered and none of the assembled number wanted to be thought of as argumentative or shrewish by this handsome and personable newcomer.

'He has a lovely singing voice.' Lottie heard someone whisper. Obviously she and Susan weren't the only ones to wander down St Jude's Open when Dexter was communing with his flowers.

Dexter Hardman was beaming all around. Lottie couldn't help wondering if he had come to Whittington Edge simply because it was a village and would have an ever available supply of widows and maiden ladies who would be only too willing to fawn upon him.

At that very moment a plan presented itself and Lottie's mind began to sift through all the people she had met since arriving in Whittington Edge to work out who would best serve the purposes of her little scheme.

'The ambulance arrived just as I came in.'

Lottie looked around and saw a mousy woman with one finger held aloft like a schoolgirl seeking permission to speak.

'Were they loading Mr Pendleton into the ambulance?' She asked.

'They hadn't got that far.' The woman's voice faltered as if she were in some way to blame for this and may be accused of deserting her post. 'Sorry.'

Lottie made her way to the side door with its view out to Church Lane. Gwennie was standing there alone, wringing her hands and watching Charles being ferried away to the hospital. She opened the door a crack and called to her.

'Is everything alright, Gwennie?'

Gwennie turned, smiled and heaved a great sigh. 'Oh Lottie, dear, thank goodness you were here. They've taken him to hospital to be checked over and dear Jane has gone with him, obviously.'

'Then, if you're free now, Gwennie dear, I wonder if you would have time to help me.' Lottie kept her voice low and conspiratorial. Gwennie hastened up the path, her head held high, eyes bright as a robin's, eager to be of some service to this woman, no, this lady, mother never liked the term 'woman', who had rapidly become a goddess in her eyes.

'What do you want me to do?' She asked.

'There's a woman inside. I don't know who she is but she looks terrified. Do you think you could go and sit with her and put her at her ease? She's wearing a navy blue coat and hat.'

'Oh I know who you mean.' Gwennie beamed and straighten up. 'She is a nervous little thing.'

Lottie saw this, as progress coming from Gwennie,

She parted company with her latest guest and went to make her a cup of tea. It was important that Gwennie's special place in Horse and Trumpet Cottage be demonstrated.

She had heard about Fanny Barstock's attempt to unsettle her protégé and she intended to put paid to that immediately.

Returning from the kitchen with the cup and saucer which she bestowed on Gwennie with great ceremony, she was pleased to see Susan and Dexter Hardman huddled together and deep in conversation.

Dexter was not the man she would have chosen for any of her friends as a husband or anything halfway as serious as that. But he was the catch of

Whittington Edge and an affair with him would do Susan's morale no end of good. Therefore this friendship was to be encouraged and when Lottie saw Atlantis Warbeck edging towards them, bent on insinuating herself into their conversation, Lottie stepped in front of her, effectively cutting Atlantis out.

She proceeded to question Atlantis about her life and interests. Across The Green she could see The Crow's Nest, as beautiful a cottage as could ever be imagined.

By this time Lottie had heard about the intransigent town planners who refused to allow Bill Warbeck to remodel the front of his house to incorporate a large window. She had been told how artistic he was and how his work hadn't achieved greater recognition because Bill was ahead of his time.

Between the lines, Lottie discerned that Bill was a bore and a bully. Every time his name was mentioned she could feel Atlantis shudder slightly. Her eyes became haunted and, without ever even meeting the man, Lottie took against Bill Warbeck.

The thought crossed her mind that she should turn Atlantis into a project and show her how to manage her man better. But she already had an ongoing project in Gwennie so Atlantis would have to wait.

'Bill has a new picture in the gallery in Lyeminster,' Atlantis said.

'I shall have to go and take a look,' Lottie beamed.

'Oh, perhaps I wasn't supposed to say anything yet,' Atlantis covered her mouth with a shaky hand.

'I shall say nothing,' Lottie patted her arm and felt Atlantis relax.

Marlene Stokes' name was mentioned again and Lottie wondered if any decision had been reached on contacting the rural dean.

Now, Lottie had no idea who the rural dean was nor what his function within the church was, but she knew that poor Marlene Stokes, who was too proud to be married in a church reminiscent of a fire station, should be allowed to have her perfect wedding. And, whilst she knew little about Dexter Hardman and wasn't too impressed by the little that she did know, she was willing to accept that he knew sufficient about ecclesiastical matters to be entrusted with doing the right thing.

Looking around, she saw that Dexter Hardman was now alone. Susan was busy talking to someone Lottie didn't recognise so Dexter could be approached without upsetting her dearest friend.

'What did you decide in the end?' She said as an opening gambit.

'Sorry? Dexter blinked and his gaze darted away from Susan as he looked for clarification.

'About the rural dean. We don't want the poor bride to turn up and have no vicar, do we?'

'No, no indeed. So, do you think I should call him?'

'Certainly. The phone is in the hall, or there is another in the kitchen if you prefer. Feel free to use either. I don't think you'll hear much if you try to use the one in here.'

As he uttered his thanks and scooted off to use the phone in the kitchen, Lottie was amused by his sudden lack of confidence.

She would have thought Dexter Hardman equal to almost anything.

People began to make their excuses and leave once it became apparent that no further tea and coffee were to be offered, and the empty biscuit plates were not going to be replenished. And now that the doctor had left the scene, Lottie was quite relaxed about letting them go. Prior to his departure, no one would have been allowed to leave. The doctor was an unpleasant man and Lottie disliked bullies.

Dexter Hardman returned to the living room to find it empty apart from Lottie, Susan and Gwennie.

'Have the ladies all gone?' he looked around as if expecting them to reappear.

'Yes, as soon as the biscuits ran out, they followed them.' Susan quipped.

Dexter smiled and Gwennie could be heard to sigh. 'You have a message on your machine, Lottie,' he said, 'the light is flashing.'

Lottie ignored the flashing light until her friends had left. It had been an interesting interlude and she had learned a few things that may prove useful to her investigation.

***

'Mrs Colenso? It's Avril Major here. I've looked at my diary and I could read your tarot for you tomorrow afternoon. If you would like to call back and confirm any time between one o clock and five thirty if that is convenient. I look forward to hearing from you.

Lottie replaced the receiver after returning the call and went through to her study to update her notebook.

She spent a lot of time editing and amending her notes to ensure that her reflections were entered accurately and sometime during the afternoon the merry pealing of bells broke into her thoughts. She paused for a moment.

Marlene's wedding must have gone ahead. That was good. She wondered how Charles Pendleton was. Was he still in hospital? And who would have attacked their gentle rector and left him unconscious and bleeding in Church Lane?

***

Marco Romero tapped on the door of the Bettinson's cottage early that afternoon. Mrs Bettinson would have been one of his first calls but he had to wait for her to return from one of her many cleaning jobs.

He had watched her laboured progress along the side of The Green and given her time to take off her coat and outdoor shoes and make a cup of tea before he followed her to her door. Mrs Bettinson had used the back door but Marco, his business being official, had knocked at the front.

'Yerse'll ave to push it.' Mrs Bettinson wheezed from the other side of the door.

Marco pushed and thought for a moment that she hadn't unlocked it. But the door groaned a little, squeaked a little and finally burst open almost knocking little Mrs. Bettinson off her feet.

'I were expectin' you.' She said, shuffling away from the door and allowing him into a small living room the temperature of a blast furnace. 'Sit down. I'll get yer a cuppa tea. I'm 'avin' one meself so yer'll 'ave ter join me.'

Marco sat down gratefully. The heat was making him feel dizzy. He shucked off his coat and loosened his shoulders.

The spotlessly clean living room had been polished to within an inch of its life. Marco counted four layers of carpet and rugs placed on top of one another and wondered if the floors were really so cold as to make this necessary.

Soon Mrs. Bettinson was back with a thick white mug full of thick brown tea.

'I put yer four sugars.' She said as she handed it to him. 'That's what me 'usband 'as.' I reckons as most men's the same.'

Marco Romero had heard about Mr Bettinson and was not pleased to be lumped together with him. But nonetheless he smiled and sipped the tea and found that the extra sugar counteracted the tannin in the tea and made it almost palatable.

'I'm here about the break in at Nook Cottage, Miss Major's house.'

'It's alright, I knows all about it. Nice lady, Miss Major.'

She stirred her tea.

Marco Romero let a silence develop. It didn't do to pummel these simple old dears with questions. It was better to let them proceed at their own speed. Unfortunately, Mrs. Bettinson seemed happy to sit in silence, and the heat was threatening to put him to sleep before she spoke again.

'It 'appened yesterday.' She nodded still staring into the depths of tea the colour of tar. 'I cleans for 'er so I should know.'

'And did you see anything that I should know about?' Marco Romero asked sipping the tea again and finding it really not that bad after all.

Mrs. Bettinson gave him a sly look. He needn't think that she would be telling tales about one of her ladies. Mrs. Bettinson subscribed to the unwritten law that she felt should dictate the behaviour of cleaning ladies everywhere; she told nothing of what she saw in any of her ladies' houses. Cleaning was like the confessional; a sacred trust between lady of the house and daily lady.

'I saw that young Jason Flint.' She said. 'But he's always around. 'E does gardens for some of the folks around The Green. I often comes across 'im. I gives 'im a cuppa now and then.'

'And you saw him yesterday?'

'Like I said.' Mrs. Bettinson nodded. ''e was at that Matchbox cottage next door. Ever so nice lady that Mrs. 'olland, yer know. 'er used to 'ave that big old rec'try on the Main Street, 'er did.' She stirred her tea again. 'That were afore 'er 'usband went off with some floozy as worked with 'im. Got a kiddie now or so they says.'

Marco made notes. This was all grist to the mill. Mrs. Bettinson wasn't going to tell him anything detrimental about Avril Major but she could fill in a few gaps about other villagers. Marco, always had time for this type of person. Even if they were determined to keep secrets about their chosen subject, they could still give invaluable insights into other people; insights that could prove useful in subsequent interviews, even subsequent cases.

'Did Jason do any gardening at Miss Major's house yesterday?'

'No. Not so far as I know. He might o done' she added brightly, 'only 'e didn't come round when I was there. I cleans early.' Mrs. Bettinson was a wily old bird and knew that her visitor wasn't satisfied. If she didn't come up with something, he would know she was holding out and would dig deeper. Mrs. Bettinson didn't want him digging too deep. For one thing, he might talk to the Social and they didn't know about all these cleaning jobs she had. 'I'll tell you one strange thing about Miss Avril,' she said.

'Yes?' Marco Romero prompted when his interviewee seemed to have slipped into a brown study.

'Yer see that sideboard over there?'

Marco glanced at the biggest sideboard he had ever seen. It had huge bulbous legs and bow fronted cupboards. On its top was a vast lace runner which in turn was covered with lace doilies each of which held a framed photograph of, presumably, a family member.

'Yes.' He said warily.

'That sideboard 'asn't been moved for nigh on fifty years.' She said. Marco could hear the note of pride in her voice and wondered where this was going. 'Miss Avril now, she moves 'er furniture about all the time. I goes in there an' almost measures me length. Every time. I tells yer, it's a death trap. Now then.' With this the lady flopped back in her chair and waited for the true significance of her words to sink in.

'Really?' Marco raised his eyebrows and returned her knowing look. He wondered if he could ask a question without diminishing his authority. Then he reminded himself that people like Mrs. Bettinson didn't recognise authority in anyone younger than themselves. She was the type to deliver a clip round the ear to the superintendent, should she think he deserved it. This thought cheered Marco up no end

'It's not nat'ral.' Mrs. Bettinson continued. I never move my furniture about. Yet Miss Avril, yer goes round there and everythin's in one place. Go the next day and it's all somewhere else. I tell yer, it's not nat'ral.'

'I see what you mean.' Marco said, not seeing at all.

'And on Sat'days,' Mrs. Bettinson added, 'I sometimes goes in there and there's tables everywhere. And them fancy chairback things. All over the place. They's never there any other day. Odd I calls it.'

'Only on Saturdays?' Marco queried gently.

'Yerse. Like I told yer. Only on Sat'days.'

She sipped her tea. 'And I'll tell you summat else,' Marco's brows rose in query, 'You needn't go trying to blame that break in on young Jason Flint. He didn't do it. I know he's a scallywag but 'e didn't do that. Now you listen to me.'

Marco did listen.

Marco stayed a while longer pumping Mrs. Bettinson ever so gently to see if any more revelations seeped out. None did. But what he had got from her fascinated him. What strange behaviour. So strange, in fact, that he wondered if she had made it up to tease him. He discounted this idea almost immediately. He doubted that Mrs. Bettinson had enough imagination.

He rose to his feet with thanks for the tea and the sit down. Old ladies appreciated a sit down and this was one of his ways of currying favour with them.

'I'll leave you my card.' He said, handing the white card bearing the police crest to her. 'If you think of anything, anything at all, please give me a call.'

The look on Mrs. Bettinson's face told him that, if she had to put money in the box, there was no way she would call him. He dug around in his pocket and came up with a coin.

'If you do have to call, I don't see why you should be out of pocket.' He said.

He put the coin down on the sideboard, carefully making sure that it landed on a couple of layers of lace and not on the highly polished wood.

'You're a gent.' Mrs. Bettinson said, treating him to a fiendish grin. He half expected her to pick up the coin and bite it. She didn't but she watched it as if he might snatch it back and tried to stand between him and the coin until he was safely out of the door.

***

If Marco Romero had been surprised at the speed with which the Super sent a couple of colleagues to arrest Jason Flint, Jason wasn't.

As far as Marco Romero could see they really didn't have sufficient evidence to arrest. To pick him up for questioning, yes. Arrest? Definitely not. But that was what the Super said, so that was what happened.

Now Mrs. Bettinson was saying they'd made a mistake and Marco Romero agreed with her.

CHAPTER FOURTEEN

Avril was in a good mood when she started out for Lyeminster to collect Ronnie. The sun was shining and the sky was blue. The maples on the bypass roundabout were perfect in their glorious crimson.

Seeing the maples ruined her mood. A secret had been hidden by those maples for many years. Now it had been revealed and police in their droves were descending on Whittington Edge and shaking her security.

She averted her eyes from the roundabout and the lone police car that sat on the grass verge probably waiting for the murderer to return to the scene.

She tried to recapture her former mood by remembering the fiasco that surrounded the return of Arthur to London.

She had been running it a bit fine that day. She summoned Arthur from his hotel room to make sure he had packed everything; the number of times Sonny's employees, exiled by their own stupidity in Lyeminster, left stuff behind in their rooms was unbelievable.

She supposed it was to do with them being men. They had probably had some poor woman fetching and carrying and picking up after them since they were born.

Avril had no great opinion of men. Except Sonny, of course, Sonny was different. And Monty.

If Sonny wasn't always in the back of her mind, Monty would take centre stage.

Avril had a mental checklist: had he got all his belongings with him being top of the list. Then she had to get him onto the train. That was unlikely to be as simple as it sounded.

Luckily, Avril made it to the Belle Parisienne at the pre-arranged time and found Arthur sipping coffee seated in what was now their regular booth.

He leapt to his feet when she puffed into the cafe. 'Sit down, Aunt Minnie,' he said, 'I'll get you a nice cuppa.'

Aunt Minnie sat down and puffed some more. She thanked Arthur for the tea and forced herself to slow down and pour it at an Aunt Minnie speed; she even managed to make the stream quiver as she poured. Old ladies always trembled when they poured tea.

'Have you got all your things?' She said at last.

'Course I have.'

'You've not left any clothes in any of the drawers?'

'Course not.'

'Nothing in the bedside table?'

'No..o'. Arthur's reply stretched with impatience. Aunt Minnie ignored this. She had no time for his finer feelings.

'You've not left your razor behind? Or your shaving foam?'

The look on his face said it all.

'Hang on a mo, Aunt Minnie, I'll be back in a tick.' It was more like fifteen minutes before he came back. Aunt Minnie had by then finished her tea and she met him outside the Belle Parisienne, making a quick dash for the door as soon as her tracker told her he was on his way out of the hotel.

After that it was plain sailing and Arthur was installed on the train.

'You needn't wait to see me off.' He said when it became apparent that that was precisely what she intended doing.

'Oh, but I must, Arthur. My little Sonny would never forgive me, else.'

The mention of Sonny made Arthur fairly snap to attention and no further mention was made of him being left unattended on the platform.

***

The moment she saw Ronnie, she knew she was collecting a different calibre of villain. And it made her blood run cold. Avril liked the station. To her it was a link to her old life. If she wanted to, she could climb down onto the shiny silver rails and follow the up line all the way to St Pancras.

She sighed. London was in her past now. She knew that about a quarter of the people in the country lived within the M25 but that wasn't London, not in her eyes. London was the area around the Elephant and Castle, where she grew up. Where they knew her as someone else entirely. It was also the place where the real Avril Major was languishing in prison but she didn't need to think about that.

In her pocket her fingers found the little badge that she had given Arthur to wear. He hadn't wanted to part with it. Said he had grown attached to it. But Aunt Minnie had insisted on having it back. It had united Arthur and her little tracker device as it would connect many others in the future.

She wasn't to give the badge to Ronnie. Avril was puzzled. What could Ronnie be doing up here for Sonny? And why was he to be allowed free rein and a room at the Granby?

It was almost time. Aunt Minnie made her way to the bend in the steps halfway between the station concourse and the platform; her vantage point, where she always watched the passengers as they alighted from the London train.

The eleven o'clock pulled in noisily. The loudspeaker crackled and an announcement was made.

About two dozen people piled off the train. The frequent travellers were standing ready in front of the doors before the train stopped. When it did they sprinted for the steps leaving the strangers behind to climb down carefully, minding the gap as instructed, looking around, unable to follow the flow of pedestrian traffic because the rush was out of sight before they even put one foot on the platform.

Aunt Minnie recognised him at once. Not that she had ever seen him before.

She ambled up the steps until she was out of sight of the platform. Glancing around, she couldn't see Ronnie. She burst into a run. Up the steps, into the station and into the bookstall.

She stood behind a rack of paperbacks willing her heart to stop pounding and sending silent thanks to Sonny for not wanting her to babysit this man whilst cursing him for sending him at all.

Her racing heart was not all the result of her exertions. She could see the man's mad eyes even at a distance. All of Sonny's men came to Lyeminster incognito and she knew why Sonny had given this one the alias of Ronnie.

Taking all her courage in her hands and telling herself that Aunt Minnie was an old lady and therefore puffing to get her breath really was just part of the role, she walked to the back of the bookstall, out the alternate door and hurried round the outside of it to approach the clock and the man standing beneath it as if she had just come from the street.

'Hello, Ronnie.' She said with an enthusiasm she didn't feel. I can't remember the last time I saw you. My, you 'ave grown.'

'I saw you on the steps, Aunt Minnie.' Ronnie said, his voice as flat as his eyes.

'Had to nip to the ladies. Now, come along. I have to get you to the Granby, and then I'm going to do my shopping. I've no time to lose so step lively.'

No linking of arms this time. No superfluous words. No 'getting to know you'. Aunt Minnie wanted rid of this man.

As a girl, living in the Elephant and Castle, she had heard stories of the twins. They were treated almost like celebrities. They were remembered with respect and gratitude because they kept the East End safe for ordinary people.

But there were other stories too. Stories told by people who actually knew them. Stories told in whispers and only to people who could be trusted. Yes, she could see why Sonny sent this man to Lyeminster under the pseudonym of Ronnie.

***

Woolstock police station was a mellow brick building composed of arched windows and numerous gables. Its woodwork was painted blue and it had a blue police lamp but otherwise it could easily have been mistaken for a village school.

Jason Flint knew that if he annoyed the Superintendent too much, he might be late for his date with Summer Saunders and, as he had plans for that evening after he left Summer, he didn't want to be late. That way he could see Summer and walk her home like a gentleman as his mother insisted. Then he could get on with business.

Surprisingly the Superintendent didn't keep him waiting. Usually they did. They left you cooling your heels just because they could. Jason reckoned that they saw you walk in – they were probably watching through that CCTV camera that was trained on the front door – then they went and made a cup of tea whilst you sat there like an idiot.

But not this time. This time, when Jason went to the front desk, the woman hardly had time to slide the window open before the man himself was there saying he would take Mr Flint through to the interview room. Mr Flint, mark you. Not bad eh?

The Superintendent went out of the office and the woman buzzed Jason through to be met on the other side. The room he was shown into must have been cleaned up. It had the same orange hessian on the walls and the window was four rows of glass blocks rather than a proper window pane and there was the old recording machine on the table ready to take down his every word and convert it into a guilty statement, but it smelled a lot fresher than they usually did.

Jason Flint, who had been questioned on numerous occasions but had never yet been charged with anything, knew the drill. The officer had the seat nearest the door. Acknowledging this, he walked past the Superintendent and went to sit down.

As he passed him, he felt a friendly hand on his shoulder and wondered what the hell was going on. Stranger still, the man smiled at him and sent a woodentop to fetch them both coffee. Then, when they had their coffee, he sent the other copper away entirely. And it was real coffee, not canteen muck.

'How are you doing then, Jason?'

'Alright.' Jason Flint was more daunted by the smile than anything. He glanced at the tape machine. It wasn't switched on.

'Glad to hear it, mate.'

Another smile accompanied these words and Jason began to feel scared. Coppers never smiled at you unless they had you bang to rights. He had come here expecting to be fitted up for the burglary. And, truth to tell, he had no real argument with that seeing as he'd done several burglaries, even if he didn't do this particular one and he needed something to give him some kudos; the gang had been a bit difficult to handle recently. Surely old Avril wouldn't put in a huge list of stuff to the insurance company, would she? Nah... not with what she had to hide. Besides, she couldn't put much down because Jason had been on his Jack Jones so he couldn't have carried a lot. He had no transport. But the way this geezer kept grinning, he knew he was probably going down for murder.

Murder? They weren't going to fit him up for that murder, were they? Jason's cockiness deserted him. An ice cold sweat broke out all over his body.

In his mind he was working out his alibi. If the body had lain there for nearly ten years, he would have been less than ten years old at the time. Below the age of criminal responsibility. He was safe. It was a long time later that he worked out that he hadn't actually murdered anyone and therefore shouldn't have been afraid.

A tap at the door heralded the return of the woodentop who now held a bundle of files in his arms. There must be at least twenty cases there and Jason Flint knew that they were all going down on his account. The superintendent must have been bloody busy. He must have had the whole nick up all night to find this many.

The woodentop left again. The files were left stacked on the table. They weren't even mentioned and Jason knew he was in big trouble.

Remember Rich Lowe he told himself. Don't say a bloody word.

***

As it happened he didn't need to because the big man started talking. Jason flicked a glance to the tape machine again, it still wasn't switched on.

'Don't worry about that, Jason.' The copper said. 'That's not switched on and you'll notice I haven't cautioned you. That's because we're having a friendly chat.'

He paused to allow Jason to acknowledge this kindly remark. Jason said nothing. Friendly chat? Fat chance. You didn't have friendly chats with coppers; you had verbal fencing matches and the odds were well stacked on their side.

'You've been lucky so far, Jason, and I want you to stay lucky.' He said when no response was forthcoming. Now he tapped the pile of files. 'These are all little jobs. You were probably responsible for this one.'

He eased out a thin folder from the heap. It was little more than a file cover really and the reason for that became apparent when he opened it. Only a few sheets of paper were attached to it.

'This is a record of the break in at...3 Westminster Gardens, Sturman Cross.' He glanced up at Jason who remained unmoved. 'On the same day, numbers 5, 7 and 9 were also robbed.'

'I weren't there.' Jason said.

'How do you know? I haven't even told you when it happened yet.' The Superintendent said. His voice was calm and slightly amused.

Damn, damn, damn. Remember Rich Lowe. Jason felt foolish.

'The thing that makes these robberies almost forgivable is that they were all perpetrated on big houses with good insurance. I really don't like it when little scrotes like yourself prey on your own kind, Jason. Believe me, if you had broken into a handful of houses in Camp Hill, I would be down on you like a ton of bricks.'

The Superintendent paused to sip of his coffee. He riffled through the heap to find a couple more files and placed them on top of the one he had just shown him.

Presumably these were the files for the other houses in Sturman Cross that he had just talked about.

Jason Flint licked his lips and took a sip of his own coffee.

If push came to shove, he could admit to those and have them taken into consideration. He'd made a mint out of some of the stuff from those jobs.

'You can trust me, Jason, I'm your friend.'

Friend! Who did he think he was kidding? Trust a copper?

Never in a million years.

'You're my friend, are you?' Jason's lip curled. 'And what's so friendly about hauling me in here two days running? You tell me that.'

He turned away in disgust both at himself for failing to keep schtum and this fat old copper for trying to pull the wool over his eyes.

'It's friendly,' the Superintendent leaned forward as if he was afraid of being overheard, 'because I'm going to give you a break.'

'Oh yeah. Is that what all these are for?' Jason indicated the heap of files. 'To give me a break? I don't think so.' He folded his arms and buried his chin in his chest, leaning back and slumping further down on his chair.

'Wait and see, Jason, wait and see.'

The Superintendent was still talking quietly. He should be shouting by now. Either that or he should have the tape running.

Jason Flint was puzzled.

The next file came off the pile. It was a report of a fight in Lyeminster one Saturday night. It happened round the clock tower. It had been a stupid thing to do really because there were cameras dangling from every lamp post round there. And one by one the photos were pushed across towards him.

One was enough. Jason didn't understand why he had to be shown every bleedin' one. Yes, that was him. He could recognise his own face, couldn't he? He didn't need to see it from sixty different angles.

Jason hadn't realised the detail that these cameras could pick up. Even the badges on his leather jacket could be identified from that. He wondered why this had even been reported. It was only a scuffle over some lager being spilt.

It wasn't as if he'd injured the bloke. They were both too drunk to fight anyway. A couple of swings at one another and they both went home, honour satisfied.

'Did he report this?' Jason said, unable to keep silent in the face of such weaselly behaviour.

'No, lad, it was picked up on routine surveillance.' The Superintendent said soothingly.

Jason, annoyed with himself again, slumped further into his chair and looked at the ceiling. If he couldn't keep his trap shut he would make it easy for this old copper.

He still didn't know what he wanted. So far he'd come up with nothing. What was he playing at?

If it had been any of the other CID blokes, Jason would have known what he was up against. They were old friends, sort of thing. But this bloke...well, Jason knew he had come to Woolstock on promotion and word had it that he intended getting another promotion whilst he was here. They said he came from the Met, and everyone knows what they're like, don't they? Jason had watched re-runs of the Sweeney on television.

'This break-in was very near my own home.' The Superintendent was saying now.

Too right it was. They thought it was the Superintendent's house, didn't they? Still, it had been a stupid thing to do. But you know how it is, they were all fired up on turbo lager and it seemed a good idea at the time; hit the new boss's house and all that. Trouble was, they were too fired up to find the right place.

They knew as soon as they went in. You could always tell a copper's house; they had pictures of themselves in uniform with all the silver pips and shiny buttons and that. Arrogant bunch really when you come to think of it. Probably only went into the job for the silver buttons.

A glimmer of a smile flicked the corners of Jason Flint's mouth at this thought.

'Do you find this funny, Jason? Breaking into people's homes? Do you, Jason?'

He was still being too bloody calm for Jason's liking. And no, Jason didn't find it funny. Not anymore. Not after that house he was talking about. They knew straight away they'd hit the wrong place and that sobered them. Jason had insisted that the gang all club together to send the woman some flowers and he posted an envelope of money through the letterbox to pay for the busted lock.

'No.' Jason said at last. 'No I don't.' And he hadn't broken into a house after that. Not until he broke into Avril Major's that is. And he didn't really break in there. There was just this overwhelming urge to find out what her secret was. He knew she must have one because everyone had a secret.

'This lady received flowers and compensation following your visit, Jason.' The Superintendent said. 'Nice touch. I like that Jason. I think I like you. That is why I think you're worth a second chance.'

Here it comes. Jason thought. This is where he tells me what he's stitching me up for. He took a long slow breath. He didn't want to faint and really show himself up. And he didn't want this bastard knowing just how scared he was. He took another breath and another and slowly began to relax.

The superintendent pulled the next few files off the stack. 'I won't bore you with these.' He said. 'You didn't do them anyway.' He dumped the files on the smaller heap and selected another small stack. 'These now, you did do. But I still won't bother you with them because we both know the score.'

In this way he went through the whole pile. Jason was beginning to feel sick. Some the Superintendent showed to him, some he didn't. Approximately half related to crimes Jason Flint actually had committed. The other half consisted of the ones the Superintendent thought he could pin on him. Jason was seriously worried now. Never mind about getting away early so that he could see Summer Saunders before he got on with the main work of the evening. He would be lucky if he went home at all. Ever. Well, at least for eighteen months. He could get two or three years for all this lot. The really scary thing was that this old geezer knew exactly which jobs Jason had done. He never put a foot wrong.

'Now, Jason, here's the thing.' He was leaning forward in confidential mode again. Jason didn't trust this one little bit. 'Miss Major is...well let's say she's a friend of the family. I'm not happy about her being upset and I don't want her persecuted anymore. Get it?'

Persecuted? What sort of rubbish was that? He took a stroll through when she was out shopping. That was all. Jason Flint wouldn't call that 'persecution'. He liked old Avril. He did her garden. Surely she hadn't put him forward for this.

'So? What do you want me to do about it?' That was alright. Rich Lowe couldn't hang him for that.

'I want your word that you'll leave her alone. No more breaking in. No more rifling through her knickers drawer.'

Rifling through her knickers drawer! As if. Yuk. Jason's face said it all. The Superintendent smiled in acknowledgement.

'Also, if you hear of anything about Miss Major, you know the sort of thing; I shall expect you to call me immediately. And in consideration of this – and I shall want your word on this, mind – in consideration of this, I shall take all these files and close them.

A couple of them will be put down to your account but they will be insignificant crimes that wouldn't warrant you doing time. And I shall let you off with a caution. How does that sound?'

It sounded unbelievable to Jason. A quick glance at the tape machine proved that its little cogs were still stationary.

This couldn't be happening. It was too good to be true.

'Of course, if you take the deal and later renege on it, I shall find a big juicy case that will get you ten years and I'll fit you up so tight that not even the Lord Chief Justice could get you off. Understand?'

'Yes.' Jason said; some response was necessary.

'And do you want to take me up on my very generous offer?'

Jason thought for a moment or two. Was this for real or was it a trick of some kind.

'No tricks, Jason.' The Superintendent said. 'But I do need to have your answer now. Do you want the deal?'

'I s'pose.'

The Superintendent sat up straight in his chair. He rang a bell and the woodentop came back to collect the files. 'We won't be needing these anymore, Jones,' he said, 'send them to be archived, would you?'

'Sir.' Jones took the files and marched out of the door closing it quietly behind him.

'Now then I shall need a statement from you on these two cases.' The Superintendent pulled a statement form from beneath the files and began to write. 'Don't worry about this Jason old mate. I'll do it for you. All you'll have to do is sign it.'

Now that everything seemed to be coming right for him, Jason could breathe again. He didn't feel entirely comfortable yet and wouldn't do so until he had been cautioned and released. But he was beginning to get his old sparkiness back.

'Right.' The Superintendent put down his pen and read out the statement.

When he handed it to Jason he read it too.

Twice.

Carefully.

It all looked okay. Apparently he had kicked over a litter bin and given some old girl a mouthful when she complained. This was a thing Jason would never do.

He had never seen the point of petty vandalism; what was in it for him? You couldn't sell it, could you? You couldn't actually make a profit. So where was the point? And his innate good manners wouldn't allow him to mouth off at an old dear. He liked old ladies and they usually liked him.

However, that was the case the Superintendent had chosen and the break in at Avril's place was added as a matter to be taken into consideration making it much the minor offence. Anyone looking at this later would think that he had confessed to the break in to clear his conscience.

'Is this on the level?' Jason asked in a last ditch attempt to clear up the mystery.

'Absolutely.' The Superintendent held his palms up in a gesture of good faith. 'You sign on the dotted line and I'll have you out of here in...' he glanced at the clock on the wall, 'twenty minutes tops.'

Jason signed.

Fifteen minutes later he was waiting for the bus to take him home to Camp Hill and he was feeling cocky again. Jason Flint, the untouchable. In his pocket was a card with the Superintendent's direct line number in case he heard of anyone else persecuting Avril. As if!

He was tempted to put the card in the nearest bin but decided not to. He had a direct line to the head honcho. He may be able to use that to his advantage later.

He could hide it inside the folder of football cards he had collected when he was a kid. The only reason he hadn't got rid of it was because it had cost so much to complete the collection. Now, at last, it was going to be useful.

Besides, Jason Flint was savvy enough to know that a Superintendent of police, the chief of Woolstock station, the man who had only come to this backwater to make a name for himself that would carry him into an even bigger job in the Met., would not be off-loading a bunch of cases to the archives when he could easily have added them to the charge sheet.

The thing with Jason Flint was that people thought he was thick. They saw the leather jacket and the haircut and pierced eyebrow and looked no further. The uniform said 'layabout' or even 'dim layabout' but he wasn't.

It suited him for people to think it because they weren't so careful what they said in front of him as they would be if they knew he was up for six starred A levels.

Today had been an epiphany to Jason Flint; he liked that word. Epiphany, yes, good word that. Yes, today had been an epiphany. Sitting in that interview room and seeing how easy it would have been for the coppers to stitch him up and send him down for a handful of years had made him stop and think.

His mother was always telling him that he had a fine brain and shouldn't allow himself to be led astray by his less academically gifted friends. Poor old duck didn't know that Jason himself was the leader of the gang and that they all followed him. Still, what she didn't know wouldn't hurt her, now would it?

Anyway, after today she never would know. Jason had sat in the interview room with its burnt orange hessian that had probably been a fashionable colour last time Woolstock nick was done up, and he had dreamt of dreaming spires. One of his teachers said he could easily get to Oxford or Cambridge. Oxford was the one for Jason. He had seen Morse on the television and he meant to walk across the grass inside one of those quads. He meant to be a Fellow of Oxford University. In his mind the title appeared in capital letters.

He might have to change his name though; he couldn't imagine a Fellow called Jason. His middle name was William. He had never liked the name but it was more acceptable now what with Prince William being a bit of a heartthrob. Will Flint, Fellow of Oxford University. Yeah, that sounded about right.

Jason Flint would change his name as soon as he enrolled.

As of today he was going to disband his gang. He wasn't going to associate with them anymore.

He would need a lot of money to pay his way through university. His mother hadn't got any and heaven alone knew where he father would get any money from. He was in the Priest at Prayer usually, he had money but he couldn't be expected to put his hand in his pocket to pay for his only son's education. Flint senior measured all expenditure in pints. You've gotta be jokin' he would say, I can get thirty pints for that. If you want fancy trainers you can get yourself a job. So no, there was no help to be expected from that quarter.

There was also no chance that Jason Flint, sorry William Flint, was going to spend the rest of his life struggling to pay off a massive loan. Not when someone else could pay it for him before he even went to Oxford.

He wouldn't be greedy. He would check up on the internet how much a first class degree from Oxford would be likely to cost, then he would divide it between the blokes he saw coming out of Nook Cottage. With a skilful bit of investing, it would even be possible to make a bit in case any of the punters didn't pay up.

The idea of getting something for nothing was too deeply ingrained in Jason Flint for it to be erased immediately. No, he had seen an advert on telly that said 'don't work harder, work smarter' and he realised this could be applied to his own field of endeavour.

 He would steal smarter. No more risks, Avril's punters would be more than willing to trade their reputations for a little cash. Jason sniggered. Correction; a lot of cash.

By the time the red and yellow bus trundled into Camp Hill Jason had it all worked out. He might even give Summer Saunders the elbow. She wasn't going to follow him up to Oxford with her short skirts and swaying hips, snapping gum mid sentence like a tart.

No, girls like Summer Saunders would be behind any bar he visited in Oxford. Then, going out with her would be acceptable. Bringing a girl like that from home would not.

Yes, Summer Saunders would have to go. He would tell her tonight. Afterwards.

In his mind's eye, Jason Flint had an image of the type of young woman William Flint would eventually marry. She would be from Oxford too, of course. She would know how to dress and would be able to hold a conversation on something other than the latest gossip about some footballer's girlfriend.

After all, this woman may be, sorry – would be, called upon to be wife to the Master of one of the Oxford colleges.

William Flint was intending to go far.

***

Lottie's week had begun in a far happier way. One of her bedrooms was fitted out with all the things she needed to maintain and improve her figure and fitness. She had a flat screen television affixed to one wall so that she could watch the instructor dance through the exercise DVD whilst she joined in on a large mat that cushioned her moves and prevented damage to her knees and ankles. She wore small weights attached to her wrists to firm up her arms.

The only machinery she had was a very fancy treadmill. Lottie wasn't a fanatic.

After her workout she showered and forced her exhausted body to skip lightly down the stairs. She made tea and toast and picked up the parish magazine for something to read whilst she ate.

Ah, yes, she had intended going to Cassie Mellon for a massage last week but something must have cropped up. Since then Charles Pendleton had added his recommendation to Cassie's work. She had nothing else planned for today until she presented herself at Nook Cottage for her tarot reading. A massage would be the very thing. She had left a message on Avril's machine saying that she would be over at Nook Cottage at three o clock. Yes, she had plenty of time.

***

Atlantis Warbeck stood tall and straight, arms reaching out to the ceiling, hair cascading down her back. She was a tree bereft of leaves. She was 'Autumn'. Bill moved around her taking photographs, making encouraging comments like those he had heard famous photographers make during fashion shoots.

Atlantis lay on the floor, crumpled at the foot of Bill's faux Grecian column. She was a heap of leaves discarded by her parent tree. Her arms reached out before her as if she were drowning and clutching at an imaginary straw. Her head was held up, gazing at something unseen yet urgently desired. Her hair foamed around her shoulders like a titian wave crashing on a tempest-beaten shore.

***

The art critic of the Lyeminster Echo had taken his photographer to see 'Summer'. His was a jaded view. Bill Warbeck had never produced anything any good in the whole of his miserable career but the Echo was a local paper reliant on local people for its existence.

He had waxed lyrically over daubs produced by schoolchildren but they had the excuse that they were schoolchildren. Bill Warbeck had no such excuse.

He usually murmured 'make it look as good as you can' to his photographer as they parked the car and strolled down the street towards the gallery.

Today he didn't need to. Bill Warbeck had actually come up with something good and he wanted to see the impact it had on his colleague without forewarning him.

The gallery owner shook hands and led them proudly to the main exhibition area. He flung back the doors just as he had when he had shown 'Summer' to Bill. The art critic had almost fainted when he first viewed the picture. Now he watched as the photographer blinked hard before walking from one side of the room to the other, gazing in rapture at the unbelievably exquisite 'Summer'. For a moment he forgot that this was the work of Bill Warbeck whom he had been heard to say should never be allowed within a hundred yards of a paintbrush unless he was using it to emulsion a lavatory wall.

'The editor wants to make posters out of it as a Christmas gift to the readers.' The critic said.

'Yeah, he told me. To be honest I thought silly season had come early but this...this is a triumph. I don't know what its value is artwise, but I know it'll make a brilliant picture.'

The gallery owner gathered up these words and salted them away so that he could repeat them to Bill. Now that he was at last on track, he needed to keep the spurs to Bill's flanks. Bill Warbeck could make the gallery's name and fortune.

Bill must never get wind of this because he would immediately take his work elsewhere. He was a nasty little runt of a man; ungrateful and ungracious. The gallery owner had no illusions about Bill Warbeck.

***

Lottie lay face down on Cassie Mellon's treatment table. Her face poked through a hole in the couch and she inhaled the lavender scented vapours that arose in fragrant wisps from the oil burner on the floor.

'Lavender is very relaxing.' Cassie said as she smoothed oil over Lottie's back. 'It reaches the bloodstream in seconds and does untold good.'

Lottie didn't care. She felt relaxed and sleepy. Cassie Mellon had a sing-song way of talking whilst she worked. Her voice was as soothing as the massage. She talked about thoughts being the most powerful forces in the universe and Lottie decided she was crazy; well-intentioned, but crazy nonetheless.

This thought knocked up against something in her mind and she realised that this kind of thinking belonged to the old Lottie and the old Lottie was long gone. The new Lottie was open to all ideas and philosophies so she opened her mind and her ears and listened to what Cassie was telling her.

After a few minutes she was actually asking questions and beginning to accept some of the wisdom Cassie imparted.

Having descended from her high horse Lottie became fascinated by this whole new outlook on life that gave Cassie Mellon an enviably serene manner.

'If I wanted to follow up on this, how would I go about it?' Lottie asked. 'Do you give lessons?'

'No, I'm sorry.' Cassie said.

Cassie continued to speak but Lottie was no longer listening. She had always been able to undertake a course to learn anything she wanted to know.

'Then how can I learn more?' She could hear a note of hysteria in her voice and Cassie's soft chuckle as she insisted that she take deep breaths and centre herself.

'I told you; you can buy a book.'

'Oh good. Which one?'

'The one that speaks to you.'

Well, that was a stupid answer. The one that speaks to you? How was a book going to speak to her?

'I must go to the bookshop and look through a few.'

'There, you're finished.' Cassie said. 'Sit up slowly otherwise you may feel dizzy. I'll go and get you a drink of water.'

Lottie felt so different when she sat up that she did have to take a moment to balance herself. She drank the water Cassie offered her. The feeling of weakness had disturbed her. She was usually so strong.

'I love your picture.' She said to cover the moment.

'The Taj Mahal?' Cassie stood beside her, head tilted to one side, as she too drank in the beauty of the picture on the calendar. 'The universal symbol for love.'

Her voice had taken on a dreaminess that made Lottie cut a glance at her. 'There are only two emotions you know, Lottie; love and fear. Always choose love.' Cassie snapped out of her strange mood and smiled broadly.

Lottie left Hallelujah House feeling refreshed and made a mental note to make this a weekly arrangement. She checked her watch. She had plenty of time before she was due at Nook Cottage for her tarot reading and something Cassie had said was prickling at her memory. It was that thing about there being only two true emotions, love and fear. She had read that somewhere and she had no idea where.

The light was flashing on the phone when she opened the front door. She pressed the button and listened to her message as she hung up her coat. Avril Major was sorry but she was unable to keep their appointment today as she was feeling off colour but she would call later in the week to make further arrangements. She offered her apologies.

That was a blow but challenging Avril was not the first thing on her mind at the moment and she was relieved to have an excuse not to beard her in her lair.

This relief quickly turned to guilt. Jane Pendleton was relying on her to find out what she could about Avril Major and here was she eager to be presented with a way out of doing what she had promised to do. If she couldn't help one friend, she could certainly keep her word to another.

She had to order the bread for the Halloween party. Gwennie had relayed an edited version of Fanny Barstock's request and, on meeting that lady the previous day, Lottie had negotiated that she and

Susan would provide the bread rolls and sausages for the celebrations.

The walk down to ...And Circuses, Henry Ludlow's wonderful bakery, was just what Lottie needed. Her massage made her feel lithe and limber, and, stepping out in the chilly October air blew away any residual cobwebs. The delicate scent of wood smoke confirmed that autumn was really here at last. The season was so vivid in the countryside and Lottie looked forward to welcoming winter and spring.

Lottie spoke to a few casual acquaintances as she enjoyed her stroll. Slowly her determination to speak to Avril returned. Avril wasn't to know that she had returned home after her massage. She would present herself at Nook Cottage at the appointed time and see what happened.

***

Inside Nook Cottage Avril Major was pacing the floor.

The meeting with Ronnie had shaken her. So much so in fact that her proposed shopping trip was cancelled and, as soon as she had escorted him to the

Granby, she said her goodbyes and scurried back to the station as quickly as Aunt Minnie's broken down shoes would allow. She was eager to change out of Aunt Minnie's garb so that Ronnie wouldn't recognise her if he happened to see her again.

Even in her own clothes and with her cherry red hair backcombed up into a cloud of curls and an extra thick daub of scarlet lipstick, Avril felt vulnerable. She had stood in the disabled toilet at the station and squared her shoulders. She turned from side to side to examine herself from as many angles as possible. She looked fine. She looked attractive and confident. She looked like Avril Major of Nook Cottage.

But inside she was a quivering wreck.

***

She had waited in the station toilet until her neat gold wristwatch told her the bus to Lyeminster would be arriving outside very shortly. Then she picked up her bags and had to restrain herself from running.

A young mother with a baby in a buggy and a fractious toddler hanging from her hand was already at the stop and Avril, desperate for some sort of normal interaction, bent over to coo at the baby and tickle the cheek of the toddler who, seeing a stranger, clung more tightly to its mother's hand and stopped whining. The mother smiled at Avril. 'Thank you,' she said, 'he's overtired. We've been walking round town all morning.'

The bus slid into the bay with a swoosh of air brakes and Avril helped the woman with the buggy then went to the back of the bus where a step would, she hoped, deter the woman from following her.

Avril toyed with the idea of calling Sonny and asking why Ronnie was in Lyeminster. The thought was almost instantly rejected; Sonny would only tell her what he wanted to tell her. He had always been secretive and a good thing too. She hadn't wanted to know too much about Sonny's business.

Avril knew that she had no great psychic gifts. She was attentive and intuitive. She knew the way people ticked. She could recognise patterns of behaviour and she could read tiny flickers as they crossed faces. Her tarot readings had started out in London as a front for her other activities. And they had continued in the same vein since she had moved to Whittington Edge. But they had another purpose too.

A lot of the women in Avril's London circle had been none too bright. If they had two brain cells to rub together, Avril knew they would have chosen a different life. The ones married to members of Sonny's circle were cheap, common and loud. They flashed their husbands' money about on expensive jewellery that looked as if it came out of Christmas crackers and on tarty clothes and plastic surgery.

One year there had been some competition to see who could have the biggest boob implants. Sonny had even suggested that Avril might like to enhance her charms. Avril smiled, baked his favourite chocolate cake making the frosting with laxative chocolate, and demanded sex until he was begging for mercy. The boob job was not mentioned again.

Some of these women could cause Sonny trouble in his field of operations. This was where Avril's psychic 'gift' came into its own. She would offer to read the tarot. No one ever refused. With great stupidity came great superstition and Avril could implant ideas far more easily and cheaply than the plastic surgeon implanted boobs. Avril was Sonny's secret weapon for manipulating the men by manipulating their women. Sonny missed her. Avril was subtle. Sonny didn't even know what subtle meant. Which was another reason why Avril couldn't talk to Sonny about Ronnie.

***

She had reached Nook Cottage without running into anyone she knew. She still felt jittery. There was no way she could keep up her psychic facade whilst she felt this way so the first thing she did when she closed her front door was to phone Horse and Trumpet Cottage and cancel her appointment with Lottie Colenso. She could think of a reason later. A bilious attack perhaps.

After she made the phone call she leaned on the door, relieved to be home. She also shivered and it wasn't because of the cold. Every time she thought about Ronnie she felt sick. Somehow the face of the man had morphed into that much more dangerous face that she had seen staring out of newspapers every time they were short of a story and wanted to compare present day crimes with those of an earlier age.

It was the eyes. That was what did for her. Those eyes. She would have to ask Sonny about him.

First though she had business to deal with. Mr Monday had been postponed. He had wanted a morning appointment again as he had had last week but, because she was collecting Ronnie, he would have to be fitted in later.

Avril rang him and confirmed that she could see him that evening. Mr Monday was exultant about this and suggested a few variations which he would be more than happy to pay extra for.

Avril, ever the businesswoman, hesitated until he had offered a higher rate before she acquiesced.

Avril had barely put the phone down from talking to Mr Monday when it rang. Startled, she picked it up and was dismayed to hear the self satisfied drone of Mr. Saturday's voice. She loathed the man. Thinking about it, the only one of her clientele that she didn't loathe was Monty, but she couldn't think about him now because the superintendent was waffling on in the tone that said he was very pleased with himself.

'I'm sorry, lovey, I didn't catch that,' Avril said. She gave her head a small shake as if that would aid her concentration; Avril knew from past experience that it was as well to listen when a copper was spinning you a line.

'I said that you can rest easy. That little scrote, Jason Flint, has held his hands up to your break in, and, after I encouraged him a bit, to a lot of other offences too.'

'And I told you, Jason did not do it.' Avril was so angry she was almost shouting.

'He admitted it, love.' The tone had turned to patronising.

'He was bullied into it then.' She took a deep breath. She couldn't afford to alienate him. 'Shall I see you on Saturday?'

'I'll be there on the dot. I expect I'm due a little reward for solving your problem.'

Avril replaced the receiver and shuddered. She was so angry she needed to vent her feelings. Sonny.

She would call Sonny. He was the only person who would understand.

'How sure are you that it wasn't this Jason Flint?' Sonny asked when she had come to the end of her tirade.

'Absolutely. He's a nice lad. He would never do such a thing and now this conniving copper has got him a record. I can't tell you how angry I am.'

'You don't need to; I can tell.' Sonny chuckled. 'Oh well, the good thing is I've got Ronnie local so, if there's any more trouble I'll sort it out. You can forget about your copper.'

Avril's heart sank. She'd done it again. What was wrong with her? At this rate her whole life would disintegrate. She had managed to sound chirpier when she said her goodbyes to Sonny but now she dropped into a chair and had to fight back tears.

Ronnie.

If she had to suggest someone who may have broken into Nook Cottage, Ronnie would be her first choice.

But, of course, Ronnie had been in London at the time. Now Ronnie was in Lyeminster and, with one word from Sonny, he would off Mr Saturday. What had she done?

***

Lottie meanwhile had let herself into Horse and Trumpet Cottage from the Church Lane side the better to support her little white lie about not finding the voicemail message. She changed into a different coat and shoes and set off for Nook Cottage.

Avril Major knew she looked distracted when she opened the door to Lottie. She didn't bother saying that she had cancelled. There was no point. Lottie Colenso obviously hadn't picked up the message. Lottie looked cheerful. That was a bonus. Avril could do with cheering up. Her entire life felt as if it was teetering on a ledge and beginning to tip over.

She led her visitor into her living room and gave her the cards to shuffle and, as she did so, Lottie changed her mind. She couldn't go through with this when Avril was in such a state. She felt sorry for the woman.

'Avril,' she said, 'I think someone is watching your house.'

'Who?'

'I don't know his name. He's not local. He stands underneath the chestnut tree smoking cigarettes. He's been hanging around for about a week. I've only seen him late at night when I close my bedroom curtains. I've not seen him at any other time.'

'What does he look like?' Avril asked, but, before Lottie could answer, she said, 'short, ratty, mad eyes?'

'Certainly short,' Lottie conceded. 'And he has a really distinctive walk.'

'That'll be Ronnie.' Avril said. 'And I bet he was behind my break in too'

Her head fell back against the chair and she closed her eyes. More than anything, she wanted to ring Sonny and tear him off a strip but she daren't do that. She had to keep Sonny sweet.

'I... I think I'd better go.' Lottie knew that Avril's mind was miles away. She stood up slowly, silently and made her way to the door.

She took another look at Avril but there was no sign of movement. It was as if she had been turned to stone.

Not wanting to be alone herself at the moment, Lottie decided to visit the rectory and see if Jane was free for a chat. At least she could report that Avril did indeed have a London accent.

***

Arriving home, Jason Flint went straight to his football album and secreted the Superintendent's card behind a picture of David Beckham. Then he glanced around his room and realised that this was not a suitable environment for William Flint, future Fellow. Things were going to have to change. He would clear some of this old junk out and turn his room into a proper study. He would build bookcases and start buying some decent books.

His leather jacket was the first thing that had to go. He opened his wardrobe. There it was; the jacket that he had saved every penny for. Over a year it had taken him. Now it was redundant because William Flint wouldn't wear a thing like that. He unpinned the badge from the collar; the badge that had so nearly got him into trouble.

He looked at the enamelled wolf that had reflected the light from the surrounding shops and identified him on the CCTV pictures even more clearly than his face. He tossed it up and down a couple of times, feeling its weight as he caught it again. Then he sighed and pinned it back on the collar. It belonged there.

For a split second he considered handing the jacket on to his deputy leader. It could be like a crown handed on from gang leader to gang leader.

Something about that appealed to Jason. He liked the idea of continuity which began with him. But no, that was the sort of thing that could come back and embarrass him when he was famous. He couldn't afford to be connected with such things; it could cost him a knighthood.

He wouldn't throw the coat away though. He could envisage a time when Will Flint, darling of television discussion panels, the go-to guy for the witty sound bite or the erudite opinion, would be called upon to show a more fun side to his character. He could produce the leather jacket as a symbol of a wild youth; a time when he had approached a crossroads and taken the right turning; an example to others of what they could do should they choose to try. Jason Flint's leather jacket could even be featured on the cover of his autobiography. Yes, that image appealed to him. He would pack it up in one of those bags his mum used that had all the air sucked out of them so that stuff didn't go mouldy. Then he could hide it at the bottom of the airing cupboard. He didn't want it in his room any more. Not after he had gathered his information.

Gathering information was work for Jason. Once it was safely in his possession he would become William Flint. He would refuse to answer to any other name. This would tell his teachers and his parents in no uncertain terms that he was serious about his future.

He even knew when this transformation would take place. It would be in double English on Friday. By then his plot would be well underway and a public declaration of his future plans would only help to demonstrate his new good character should any such demonstration be required.

CHAPTER FIFTEEN

Whittington Edge had been deceptively quiet during the week but beneath the surface people and schemes were running riot.

Today was the day that Jason Flint had decided was the perfect time for him to show his new colours and for Will Flint to burst into life.

He had been busy up until this very moment. He had wrapped up in the gloves and scarf his mother often urged him to wear and had taken himself off to the charity shop in Woolstock where he had purchased a book. The book was of no interest to him but it was full of words and would serve his purpose.

Next he had visited the chemist and bought a pair of tweezers. The stationery shop was his last port of call and he equipped himself with glue, notepaper and envelopes.

He had drawn a blank with Avril's Wednesday caller, he had no idea who he could be, but he knew Bob Rogers and Arnold Pickard and he had decided that the rest could wait.

Wednesday evening was spent cutting and pasting words onto sheets of paper. Most blackmailers used too many words.

Remember Rich Lowe, he reminded himself. Keep it simple. So he composed his letters with care, long enough to make his demand, and banal enough to disguise his superior knowledge of English.

His mother and Summer Saunders' mother spent their weekends at car boot sales and his mother's share of the car boot booty yielded a broken down typewriter. On this he typed the envelopes whilst his parents were out. All these things he did without removing the gloves. It wasn't easy.

It was getting late when Jason slipped out of the house and walked back into Whittington Edge. Fortunately the buses ran late and he headed for Lyeminster with the letters neatly tucked inside a larger envelope inside his pocket; he couldn't afford to have any forensic evidence from his coat adhering to the letters. Jason Flint had thought of everything.

Almost.

The flaw in his plan was that he had no idea how to collect the money. Still, he had made his demand. His first two benefactors would soon know how much they had to find and now he had to work out a way for them to give it to him. His letters said that he would contact them later with instructions. He wondered whether blackmail techniques were available on Wikipedia.

The main post office in Lyeminster stood in a side street that was full of bars and nightclubs. Jason took the letters from his pocket and discarded the larger envelope in a bin two streets away. Then he allowed himself to be carried along by the throng past the post office where he dropped the letters casually into the collection box without missing a beat. If the cameras ever checked, Jason would not be spotted turning round to look at the box. No one would ever pick him out.

***

Dexter Hardman arrived early at Horse and Trumpet Cottage on Thursday morning. He was looking uncommonly dishevelled and Lottie invited him in.

'I need to talk to you, Lottie.' He said. He raked his hand through his thick corn coloured hair and followed her through to her sitting room.

'Whatever's wrong?' Lottie was so concerned by the lack of Dexter's usual panache that she forgot her duty as hostess and sat down on the sofa opposite him.

'I've been at Pennyman Cottage all night.' Dexter said. Lottie could well believe it; Dexter looked haggard. 'Is Beau unwell?'

'You could say that. I've come to you with his blessing. He doesn't want what I'm going to tell you to get around the village but he asked for your help and wants to keep you in the loop.'

A wash of cold certainty swept over her. 'It was Adelaide, wasn't it?' She whispered.

'I'm afraid so. Beau said he had asked you to approach the police on his behalf. They found a necklace around the... oh this is terrible.' Dexter wiped a hand over his face and cleared his throat. 'Beau had given Adelaide a gold locket. It was found underneath the... you know. It had fallen through but when they interviewed Beau he told them about it and they went back and found it. I was visiting him yesterday when they arrived.'

'Thank goodness for that. It would have been dreadful had he been alone.'

'Yes, he also gave Adelaide a ring and that hasn't been found. The police went back and looked but it wasn't there. Keep that to yourself, by the way, the police are hoping that the ring will turn up and identify the killer.'

'It must have been distinctive,' Lottie probed.

'Beau had it made to his own design so it's going to be hard to disguise.'

'Poor Beau. I hope he doesn't think that Adelaide was killed for the ring.'

'The man's in pieces.'

'And poor you. It must have been terrible.'

'He tells me he's doing some work for you.'

'He must put that right out of his head.' Lottie said quickly.

'No, I've told him to get onto it right away. I've known Beau for a number of years and keeping busy may be just what he needs to hold him together.'

'I do have something happier to report.' Lottie told him. 'I visited the rectory the other day. Charles is home and he wasn't attacked.'

'He wasn't? Then what happened to the poor man?'

'According to Jane, he had taken to hammering those little metal things into the heels of his shoes. She says he feels guilty that he can afford to have his shoes properly repaired when some of his parishioners are almost destitute. Anyway, he decided to try these little metal things and his heel slipped on the paving stones outside in Church Lane and he fell catching his head on my railings as he tried to save himself.'

'Poor fellow.' Dexter smiled. 'I really am tempted to laugh. I suppose it's his hair shirt mentality. He's a lovely man but he must know that depriving himself is hardly likely to help anyone else.'

'He certainly knows that now. Jane was not amused. She really went to town on him and our dear rector is feeling severely chastened. I don't think Jane has ever argued with anything he's done before this.'

'Good for her. We chaps need to be kept on our toes. You ladies let us get away with far too much. I'll nip round and see him later. I'll take him a book to read. That should cheer him up.'

Dexter was still chuckling about this when he left.

**

Lottie didn't usually have the radio on but, after Dexter left she ran the vacuum cleaner round preparatory for the Murder Club meeting and turned on the news whilst she gave the ground floor its weekly dusting.

Michael Garnet, husband of Rosa, had confessed to her murder. When the Murder Club were assembled, Lottie repeated this piece of information.

'Why did he do it,' Susan wanted to know.

'According to the news, they were both having affairs. They had enjoyed an open marriage for a number of years and it had worked out well for them. Then, Michael's lady friend broke it off.

He insisted that Rosa should dump her lover too. She refused so he lost control, killed her and left her in the alley.'

'I heard at the library that the woman you found on the roundabout was called Adelaide Barrett, Lottie,' Gwennie said as she took a sip of her tea.

All eyes swivelled to Gwennie. Lottie was thinking that it was amazing how quickly word got around. She knew Dexter wouldn't have said anything. Beau was unlikely to. So...

'Adelaide Barrett?' Susan frowned. 'I don't think I've ever heard of her'

'The name doesn't ring a bell for me either,' Lottie said.

No one looked to Lottie; they all knew she was a newcomer.

'I have heard of her, strangely enough,' Gwennie said. 'She lived here and mother said she had 'gone to the bad'. An illegitimate child, I believe. Mother said she should have been sent to one of those homes for girls who were out of control. They were run by nuns and, mother said, they got the punishment they deserved.' Gwennie took another sip of tea whilst horrified glances were exchanged over her head. 'Mother said she would send me to one, if I didn't behave.'

The more Lottie heard about 'mother', the more grateful she was never to have met her and the angrier she felt on Gwennie's behalf.

'So what happened to Adelaide Barrett?' Lottie asked at last.

'The baby was adopted, I think. They all were then. And I think Adelaide was sent away in disgrace.'

'Are her parents still in the village?'

'No,' Gwennie's face screwed up with concentration. 'I think...yes I'm almost sure...'

Gwennie bit her lip and everyone waited with bated breath. 'Yes, that's it. They moved away. They used to live on The Green but the shame was too much for them to face so they sold up and moved right along Main Street to where it becomes Woolstock road, way beyond the doctor's surgery. There's quite a pretty little house there. It's got carvings around the eaves. Looks a bit like the Hansel and Gretel house. I'm sure that's where they went. You have to look hard to see it though, it's surrounded by trees.'

Lottie wondered if she should go and take a look.

***

Friday was the day that Avril set aside to pamper herself. This was mostly because Friday was also the day that Mr Slippitt came to call and Mr Slippitt was the most unwelcome of all her visitors although Mr. Saturday may well have taken that position now.

But Mr Slippitt was destined to be her pension. He was a revolting little man with irritating requirements and a vast fortune; not that anyone would guess by looking at him.

Avril wondered if squandering his money would be worth the sacrifice involved in securing it.

At the moment she could see no way around it. If she could choose, she would throw in her lot with Monty but did Monty have the money she needed? How could she find out?

So on Fridays, she treated herself to a session with Cassie Mellon before Mr Slippitt arrived and went through the motions to keep the horrible man sweet.

She started her day with a leisurely breakfast in her beautiful conservatory.

Unlike the rest of the house the conservatory was full of Mediterranean colours; the blue, orange, vibrant red and green that she remembered from her days at the villa before Sonny went crazy and decided he had to return to the East End – and ruined her life.

***

She had bought a large golden bird cage and it was in the corner with a backdrop of greenery in the garden that would look like a fitting habitat for the bird she intended to buy. Avril wanted a parrot or a macaw or whatever it was that possessed rich plumage to echo the colours of its surroundings. She was still working out the logistics of the bird. She had to sound out Mr Friday and make sure that this wouldn't be a deal breaker. Perhaps she could do that tonight.

For the time being she was sitting at the mosaic table, enjoying her pot of really good coffee in the autumn sunshine. She picked up her croissant warm from the oven and bit into it. Flakes of delicious buttery pastry fell like snowflakes onto her plate. Then a loud hammering at the door made her fingers clench involuntarily and the whole pastry disintegrated all over the table, her lap and the floor.

Avril was not pleased. She took a sip of coffee and hoped that the intruder would go away. The hammering was repeated and now her name was being shouted through the letter box. Really this was beyond toleration.

'I've received a letter.' Bob Rogers said when she opened the door and he stormed in without waiting for an invitation. 'Look.' He thrust the piece of paper towards her but Avril was too old a hand at this sort of thing to take it from him. She leaned forward and quickly read the words. She could feel the blood draining from her face.

Mr Monday was not much of a man. He wasn't strong, brave or reliable. She had always despised him but now, at this very moment, she realised just how much she detested him too.

This was a sign. She had to pack in this depressing way of life and cash in Mr Slippitt. The thought held no appeal whatsoever and a rising tide of horror threatened. What did she have? How could she live for the next thirty odd years with nothing to look forward to at the end of the day but Mr Slippitt and his antimacassars, doilies and fairy cakes and endless games of scrabble? Panic threatened.

Her life stretched ahead perfumed with Mr Friday's carbolic soap and the lavender polish she sprayed on her radiators to please him, and the nosegays of flowers, and the constant stroking into place of his shirt, tie and hair. Avril felt doomed.

Mr Monday was almost dancing around the room shouting about his wife and his reputation. She had to drag him back to earth before she could consider her own future. If he went to the police or this dirty little blackmailer made what he knew public, Avril's life in Whittington Edge was over.

Something had to be done.

Avril stood and pushed Mr Monday into a chair with one well manicured finger. 'Sit!' She barked.

Mr Monday sat. He began to wave the bloody letter about again and any minute he would be yelling again too. At this rate someone would hear him and may even come to investigate.

'Quiet!' She snapped.

Mr Monday subsided. Used as he was to obeying orders he immediately calmed down and waited for her to tell him what to do but his eyes were still wildly looking in every direction. The letter in his hand rustled as he trembled. Avril lifted her chin and peered down at him, the dominatrix in full possession of herself and her subordinate.

'You will go straight home from here. You will burn that letter. You will take the ashes and divide them into two. You will put each half into a bag and find two separate dustbins or waste bins to put them into. You will do that now. You will telephone me within the next hour to tell me that you have obeyed my orders to the letter. Do you understand?' She wished that she was wearing her stilettos. Orders had more authority when issued from a greater height.

'Couldn't you burn it for me?' The letter quivered as he held it out. Yes, she could have burned it but self preservation wouldn't allow Avril to even touch the accursed thing. She despised this man so much that she couldn't contemplate touching him or anything he had touched.

He would never again be welcome at Nook Cottage and he would have to find some other way of dealing with his preferences.

But first he had to be removed.

'Do you understand?' She said more quietly, more threateningly, eyes narrowed.

'Yes, mistress.'

'Then go. I am setting my timer. If I don't hear from you by the appointed time you will no longer be welcome here.'

Bob Rogers scuttled away promising that he wouldn't let her down.

Avril watched him go, wondering whether he could be trusted to complete this mission and knowing she would have been safer taking care of it herself. She was still pondering on this when her second caller rapped at the door.

Arnold Pickard was as red as a turkey cock. Avril refused to allow her dismay to show. He too had a letter. She peered at it and shrugged. 'So,' she said, 'someone has noticed you calling round for our regular bible discussions. Does that bother you?'

The churchwarden's piggy eyes glittered. 'No, my dear, it doesn't. I thought that this coming week we could read a few verses of Leviticus.'

'We could do that.' Avril agreed. She took in his lascivious laughter and wondered what the passage of Leviticus was about. 'And that abomination belongs on the back of the fire.' She said opening the door of her stove and waiting for him to consign it to the flame. She wished she had done the same with Mr Monday but he needed the discipline of obeying her orders. The churchwarden may just be capable of finding a way to turn the letter against her if she allowed him to keep it.

***

In less than twenty four hours the identity of the woman on the roundabout had been released and was known to the whole of Whittington Edge, and Beau Derek was not the only person to be distressed.

Lottie was in her side garden tidying up a plant that had drooped outwards almost totally blocking the path to Church Lane when Atlantis Warbeck came into view. The woman was talking to herself. Her hair floated out behind her festooned today with bits of silver paper and feathers.

'Good morning.' Lottie called out a greeting. Atlantis stopped. She looked about distractedly. 'How are you this morning?' Lottie said.

Atlantis homed in on the direction of the voice and immediately hurried towards Lottie's gate.

'It was my mother.' Atlantis said. 'I'm on my way to see Beau. He knew her, you know.'

Mention of Beau had Lottie's antennae on red alert. She didn't want Atlantis bothering him whilst she was in this state.

Imagine the two of them together; the two most unstable residents of Whittington Edge working one another up into a frenzy until all Dexter's good work was undone and they both fell apart.

'Mrs Warbeck, Atlantis, do please come inside and have a warm drink. You look as if you need one.' She opened the gate and ushered Atlantis through into the house. Atlantis followed as docile as a lamb. Lottie found some fruit tea and made good strong coffee for herself.

'Now,' she said in her most soothing tones, 'tell me all about it.'

'The woman on the roundabout,' Atlantis said, 'she was my mother.'

Lottie blinked and waited. Could this be true? She didn't know Atlantis well enough to know if she was the sort of person to bolster herself by making up stories.

'When did you see her last?' was the best that Lottie could come up with.

'I've never seen her. Not really. She had to give me up when I was a baby. She was sent away and I was

470

handed over to an orphanage. It was the way they did it in those days. I was given some papers when I left so I know her name was Adelaide. They never gave me her surname but it has to be her, don't you see? It has to be her.'

Lottie thought it quite likely but didn't want to say so lest Atlantis immediately dash from the house and go pounding on the door of Pennyman Cottage.

'I understand. I really do. And I understand how upset you are. Beau is equally upset. He came here to meet Adelaide and he has searched for her for such a long time that he is now distraught. We have to give him time to recover before he meets you. I think then he will be delighted to have a genuine contact with the woman he loved so much. Do you think you can give him that time, Atlantis? I would hate it if your first meeting with Beau was spoiled.'

Atlantis became very calm. She looked at Lottie without seeing her. She sipped her fruit tea.

Then she took a deep breath. Her shoulders dropped. All the tension seemed to drain out of her and Lottie worried what was coming next.

'You're right, Lottie,' Atlantis smiled a weak watery smile. 'I will do that. I would like to get to know my mother through him but now is not the right time. I... I don't quite know what to do now.'

'I think it would be a good idea for you to go to Cassie Mellon for a relaxing session. Shall I call her for you and see what she recommends?' Lottie was halfway to the kitchen phone when Atlantis agreed.

Luckily, Cassie Mellon was at home and had enough time free to lavish some care and attention on Atlantis.

'I didn't mention your mother.' Lottie said when she replaced the receiver. 'You don't need anyone quizzing you about this any more than Beau does at the moment.' She hoped that Atlantis would take the hint but didn't feel she knew her well enough to say more.

***

Double English was grinding on in its usual way. Jason Flint's crowd at the back of the class were jeering and sniggering and Dr Harris in his academic gown stood before his desk attempting to cast bread upon the waters all the while knowing that he was casting pearls before swine.

He had been offered a position in a private school and was wishing he had taken it instead of squandering his genius on this bunch of ingrates.

His main disappointment was slumped in his chair, its front two legs off the ground as he leaned against the back wall of the classroom watching his idiot friends perform for him like seals at the circus. Jason Flint, as fine an intellect as Dr Harris had ever met; what was he doing wasting his time with all this fooling about when the world beckoned, full of promise and opportunities were Jason bright enough to see it?

Dr Harris turned to the whiteboard and picked up a marker pen. He had nothing to write. He just needed a second or two when he could escape into his own thoughts. The sound of a chair banging back onto all four feet made his blood run cold. One of these days his class was going to erupt into a riot and he didn't know what he would do.

'I apologise for this bunch of morons, Dr Harris.' Jason Flint's voice rose easily above the muffled din.

Dr Harris envied him. His own voice was now a dusty relic of its former richness. He turned to face whatever Jason Flint had planned. As he turned he glanced towards the door and tried to work out how long it would take for him to reach the corridor if he needed to escape. The teacher had once been a strong young man. Now he was scared stiff by a rabble of unruly youth. The knowledge shamed him.

'Right, you lot,' Jason stood and fixed every pupil with a threatening eye. 'Dr Harris is a clever man. He has a lot to teach us and I for one would like to hear it so I would appreciate it if you would all shut the fuck up and let me learn something here.' The class subsided into silence. The clever kids who occupied the front couple of rows of desks exchanged sideways glances, grimaces and shrugs. Whatever had happened to Jason Flint?

Dr Harris didn't know whether to smile or run. He wanted to thank Jason but knew that would be a mistake. He compromised by nodding in his direction. Jason Flint sat down, apologising to the teacher again for interrupting his lesson. Dr Harris glanced at his wristwatch, noted that the lesson had only run for a few minutes and began again from the start of his lesson plan.

When Jason Flint's hand shot up to ask a question, Dr Harris almost fainted and had to perch on the edge of his desk to steady himself but Jason wasn't about to deliver the expected punch line. Jason had a genuine, intelligent question that moved the lesson on.

Jason Flint stayed behind after class and approached the desk when the classroom emptied.

This is it, Dr Harris thought. Here it comes. But Jason wanted to talk about his plans for a scholarship to Oxford.

Not trusting his hands to hold a pen without shaking, Dr Harris promised to recommend some reading material for him. 'I'll leave it in the staff room for you, Flint.' He said. 'If I'm not there just tell whoever answers the door and they'll give it to you.' Jason Flint nodded, smiled and left the room. Dr Harris clutched the edge of the desk for a moment before gathering his books together. He wondered if the reading list would remain sealed in its envelope on the staff room table until the day he retired.

***

Mr Friday left just after tea and Avril scurried around removing every trace of him from her living room. This was the only room he entered in Nook Cottage and that was fortunate because she couldn't bear to have this clutter all over the house.

She wiped the lavender polish off the hall radiator with a damp cloth, removed all the antimacassars, stacked and returned the multitudinous tables in size order to their places around the room.

Someone was out to get her. Her whole life was being tipped upside down.

Avril allowed herself a few minutes to wallow in her misery but she had come up the hard way. No one had feelings and emotions where she came from. There life was hard and raw and a show of weakness was an invitation to the pack to descend and tear its frailest member to pieces.

She didn't fool herself that she had any friends in Whittington Edge; she had clients none of whom she would entrust with the care of her empty birdcage let alone her confidences.

476

It was alright for the likes of Lottie Colenso who moved into a big house and into the inner circle of Whittington Edge life. Avril wasn't that sort of person and, even if she had Lottie Colenso's money, she also had secrets that bound her to isolation.

There was only one person in the whole world that Avril trusted. There was only one person she could talk to at all.

And she rang him now.

'If it's that kid who broke into your house – 'Sonny exploded.

'Jason didn't break into my house.' Avril's weariness could be heard in her voice. She was a good judge of character. She had told the superintendent that it wasn't Jason but he wouldn't listen.

Now the kid had a criminal record and she felt guilty about that; she liked Jason Flint.

Sonny, who knew exactly who had broken into Nook Cottage backpedalled quickly. He didn't want his wife starting to think too hard.

'You win, Doll. You know best. Tell me about the letters.' Avril unloaded her misery onto him. She told him about Messrs Monday and Tuesday.

Sonny had always known how to make her laugh. This was his redeeming feature. He wasn't handsome; never had been. He wasn't faithful; he probably didn't know what the word meant. But he wasn't jealous either and her little peccadilloes he treated in the same way as he wanted her to treat his. The only difference being that her diversions from the straight road of matrimony were business and his had always been pleasure.

Soon Avril was laughing at Bob Rogers and Arnold Pickard and the world felt like a warmer place.

'Do you need help, Doll?' He said at last.

'No, she sighed. 'It's the Halloween party tomorrow. I shall go to bed now. I have a pumpkin to carve tomorrow morning.'

'Will these two men be at the Halloween party?'

'I should imagine so. Everyone in the village will be there. If they don't turn up they will draw attention to themselves. Bob Rogers will definitely be there.

He's running one of the games, 'pin the wart on the witch'. He's spent weeks painting a picture of a witch. He seems very proud of it. The churchwarden will be hovering around like a bad smell, looking down his nose at everyone, I suppose. Why do you ask?'

'The churchwarden's dealt with, you burnt his letter yourself but you need to talk to the witch man and make sure that he followed instructions. You'll be able to do that when you pin your wart on his witch.'

'Yes, I will, won't I?'

'Night, Doll, sleep well. Don't let it worry you.'

'I won't Sonny. Thanks for listening.'

'Why won't you come home, Doll? I miss you.'

'I miss you too, Sonny,' Avril sighed. She did miss Sonny but she had no desire to return to the life she had with him before. 'But, if I came back, it would be a matter of minutes before one of the filth fitted me up again.'

Sonny knew that the copper who fitted her up last time was currently doing a ten stretch with daily attention from associates of Sonny's who were making his life a constant torment. Word was that the bastard had aged forty years since he went down and he hadn't done half of his sentence yet. Still, he had friends who would like to even the score so his Doll was right, she couldn't come back.

'We could go back to Spain.' He offered.

'We would have had immunity if we'd stayed there.' Avril reminded him. 'Now we've been back that's all gone. No, Sonny, I think we've burnt our boats.'

Sonny had one more call to make before he could return to running his nightclub and he made it as soon as he put the phone down on his wife.

***

The massage with Cassie Mellon had soothed Atlantis Warbeck considerably which was just as well because tonight was the night of the gallery party.

'Summer' was a bigger hit than even Bill had expected. The art critic of the Lyeminster Echo had waxed lyrical.

The photographer had produced sharp and detailed pictures of the painting and, on seeing the results, the gallery owner decided that a proper launch was called for.

He had contacted colleagues within the art fraternity and invited them to come to the gallery for champagne and nibbles.

When Bill Warbeck heard about this he was suitably enthusiastic. He laughed and joked and promised that both he and Atlantis, his muse, would attend. Atlantis would allow herself to be photographed beside her glorious image, he said.

When he cut the connection he scowled. 'It'll be vinegar and mousetrap, I suppose,' he said, 'but we'll have to show our faces, old girl.'

So Atlantis Warbeck regaled herself in her floaty finery.

She wore autumn shades for the party to show people how the golds and crimsons of the season shone into her face and reflected off her titian hair. She removed the pieces of silver paper from her tresses and replaced them with strands of copper and scarlet foil and a headdress of tiny golden bells that tinkled faintly when she moved. Sea green, sparkly, shadow exactly matched her stunning eyes and even Bill couldn't find fault.

Atlantis was the star of the evening. This was both a good and a bad thing. Bill hated sharing the limelight with anyone, even his wife, and brooded in a corner imbibing more champagne than he really should. Bill Warbeck was a nasty drunk and the fact that the champagne was flowing freely meant that he would have ended up dangerously inebriated come what may.

His salvation came in the shape of an obviously gay young man who flattered and fawned over Bill and kept referring to him as a great artist and the next big thing in the art world.

This attention bolstered Bill's ego and he held forth to his wide eyed audience of one on the difficulties of painting without a strong north light, the short-sightedness of a planning department that would not allow him the window he needed simply because his house was on some confounded list or other, and the difficulty of matching the colour of Atlantis' fiery locks using just commercially produced tubes of colour.

The young man asked questions that allowed Bill to feel superior and he skilfully swerved away from anything that may stretch Bill's knowledge far enough to provoke the artist's wrath.

And so the evening was a great success. Atlantis posed demurely beside the more flamboyant 'Summer' and Bill leered up at his masterpiece. He wore an artist's beret that one of the photographers supplied and held aloft a paintbrush from the selection the gallery sold as a sideline. He smiled his snaggle-toothed smile and Atlantis gazed dreamily into space.

The Lyeminster Echo donated a stack of newspapers to the event this being the day when the picture was published for the first time. The editor graced the gallery with his presence as did the owner of the newspaper and several local worthies.

Bill Warbeck knew that he had arrived. He was so intoxicated with his own fame and the vindication that this celebration afforded him that he didn't notice that his champagne was liberally dosed with lemonade; the gallery owner knew Bill well. He had not only supplied the champagne, he had also produced the young man whose job it was to keep Bill reasonably sober.

At the time that the Warbecks arrived home, Summer Saunders was raging to her girlfriends on Facebook about the way she had been treated by Bill Warbeck. She was Summer in the painting they had all seen in the Echo. She should be the one being feted as the new great model.

Fortunately Summer Saunders was unaware of the big party that had been thrown to publicise 'Summer' to the art world and, fortunately for Bill Warbeck, Summer Saunders' friends on Facebook didn't believe a word of her story and said so.

CHAPTER SIXTEEN

Activity at the church hall had begun before Lottie rose on Saturday morning. In fact she had been woken earlier than usual by a persistent rhythmic bong, bong, bong, such as would be produced by a large, loud and faulty bell.

She slipped out of bed and saw a troupe of small boys struggling to carry an old tin bath across The Green. Most were running around the bath shouting and hammering its sides whilst a few of their fellows attempted to walk inside it burdened by both the weight of the bath and the ear-splitting din.

The noise suddenly stopped. The bath was carelessly dropped onto the grass, the caterpillar of boys beneath it scrambled out and was replaced by some of the others and the procession resumed.

The hiatus in the drumming allowed another sound to be heard. Lottie looked towards The Priest at Prayer and saw Mrs Bettinson waving her fist aloft and shouting. No one could hear what she was saying and the boys weren't even attempting to do so but Lottie gathered that she was the proud owner of the tin bath and was doing her best to preserve it from such treatment. Lottie silently wished her good luck with that one and went to shower and dress.

The reminder that it was the Halloween party tonight was also a reminder that she had to visit ...And Circuses at some point and collect the bread rolls she had ordered. The prospect of meeting Henry Ludlow again lent speed to her movements.

***

Avril Major wasn't awoken by the transfer of the Bettinsons' bath from back wall nail to church hall. She had passed a restless night full of snatches of dreams interspersed with periods of wakefulness where dark imaginings tormented her.

They should have stayed in Spain. Everything would have been fine if they had stayed in Spain. They had a lovely villa. The beach was near enough for them to walk on the sand though they didn't swim in the sea as the villa boasted a large swimming pool. The ex pat community was growing with each passing year diluting the concentration of former criminals living the high life so that many of the old firm could only be discerned by the size of their homes, cars and jewellery. For goodness sake there was a fish and chip shop a couple of streets away, a typical East End pub, and there was talk of a pie and mash shop opening up though Sonny had dismissed that as someone's idea of a joke.

Joke or not, the talk of pie and mash set Sonny off hankering for the green liquor that adorned the meal. She had tried to make a version of this to give him a taste of home. She had grown parsley on the kitchen window sill to provide the authentic green colour. It was all to no avail. If anything it made things worse and Sonny's hankerings led them back to the East End and her downfall.

She had felt safe in Whittington Edge for most of the time she had lived here. There had only been one small glitch and she had dealt with that. Now every day new ripples seemed to grow on the still waters of her calm existence.

She cursed herself for telling Sonny about the letters. She had been upset. She needed a friend. She needed someone she could talk to and she had no one.

This was hardly the sort of thing she could have phoned the Samaritans about though God knew she felt desperate enough.

She was pacing about not even able to think about the coffee and croissant that were waiting for her in the conservatory. She noticed them standing on the mosaic table and wondered how they had got there. She must have been working on automatic pilot.

The phone rang. It was Mr Monday calling to see if she could fit him in for an extra session this lunchtime after he had set up his witch board at the church hall. She agreed.

She had intended never to see him again but a girl had to make a living and it wasn't in Avril's nature to turn away good money.

She took a deep breath and told herself to get a grip. She forced herself into the conservatory, picked up her linen napkin and applied herself to the breakfast that at first tasted like chaff but improved enormously once she had worked herself back into her role.

***

Susan phoned just as Lottie was filling her cafetiere with boiling water.

'Shall we go to collect the food together?' She asked.

'That would be fun. And what do you say we pick up some witch stuff at the hardware store ready for tonight. I saw that they had pointy hats and all sorts of things when I walked past yesterday.'

'Oh yes, I haven't dressed up since I was a child.'

'We should get something for Gwennie too,' Lottie added.

'Great idea. Uh-oh, your handsome detective has just pulled into Church Lane so I'd better go. Give me a call when you're ready to leave.'

Lottie reached the Church Lane door just as Marco was stepping through the gate.

'Do you have radar?' He grinned at her.

'No, I have observant neighbours. Come in. I was going to ask you about the radar; the coffee is just brewing.'

Marco dropped into one of the kitchen chairs as if he hadn't sat down in years. He lined up his notebook and mobile phone and Lottie put the coffee, cream, milk and sugar on the table and pushed a mug towards him so that he could judge the moment the coffee was to his liking.

'I called in to tell you a couple of things you've probably heard already.' He depressed the plunger on the cafetiere and poured coffee into both mugs.

'The good rector wasn't assaulted as was originally thought. He slipped on the stones in Church Lane.'

'I know,' Lottie smiled, 'apparently he's got himself so worked up about the disparity between his income and that of his poorer parishioners that he started nailing those little metal studs to the heels of his shoes.'

Marco burst out laughing. 'And that's what made him slip? I can well believe it. My uncle Luigi was a keen fan of those. He used to nail them into our shoes when we were kids. We asked for more and more of the things. If you got your balance just right you could skate on them. No wonder he came a cropper.'

'We shouldn't laugh,' Lottie said sternly between suppressed giggles that made her eyes water.

'I know. The second thing is that the woman on the roundabout was Adelaide Barrett. Why on earth didn't your friend say something sooner? We could have spread our investigation further had we known.'

'He thinks that putting a name to your fear makes it more likely to come true.' Lottie said. A sudden thought swept through her brain. Something she hadn't thought of for a few days. She must try to remember it again when Marco had gone.

'Possible.' Marco shrugged. 'I'm used to the old country superstitions. I know how deep they go so I'm more than ready to accommodate any others that present themselves.' He sighed. 'Besides, I can almost see the logic in that one. It must have felt like tempting Providence.'

Lottie was glad that he realised that. She hadn't wanted Beau to get on the wrong side of the police. He was such a gentle soul that any criticism would cut him deeply.

Marco tasted his coffee and added sugar.

'One thing you don't know; it looks as if Adelaide was garrotted with the strap of her shoulder bag. Keep that to yourself.'

Lottie's hand instinctively went to her throat.

'How are you doing with your investigations?' Marco asked after a pause.

Lottie wavered. 'I'll get my notebook.'

Heads together they read the notes and discussed the people listed.

'You've not lost your touch.' He glanced at her. 'I'm impressed that you have even entered your best friends' names. Well done. That's always hard.'

This scrap of praise made Lottie feel much better. She had approached her task objectively and, although some people could be upset to be included at all, none could say she had been unfair.

'Where do you think Biddy is going to late at night?'

'I've no idea. I saw her husband pass her a note in the library and they were easily close enough to speak. She says they still go on dates so perhaps they play games to perk things up.'

'Mm...' Marco said. He turned a few pages. 'Arnold Pickard, who is he?'

'The churchwarden.'

'And he's reputed to have an eye for young girls, I see.'

'Yes, and I would prefer him to be our prime suspect rather than Biddy.'

'I'm sure you would,' he grinned. 'Luckily, we have to keep in mind the age of the suspects at the time of the murder. Biddy probably escapes on that detail alone.'

'I can't tell you how happy that makes me.' Lottie picked up her mug, added a good slug of cream and took a sip before continuing.

'I've talked to quite a few people.' She said. 'Most of them seem genuine. One is behaving in an odd way but may have a perfectly innocent reason for doing so, so I don't want to say too much about that yet.' She boiled the kettle and refilled the cafetiere. Marco had finished his drink whilst she had only taken a few sips of her own. 'There is something I've noticed though.'

'Go on.'

Lottie brought a plate of biscuits to the table and set it before him. 'Someone is standing outside under that big horse chestnut tree on The Green in the evenings. I don't know who he is but he makes the mistake of smoking whilst he is trying to hide. This man stands there until very late.' She didn't tell him that she had never noticed the watcher after Avril Major's callers left because she hadn't told him about Avril's callers. 'I've seen him leaving but I couldn't see his face.'

'When did you notice this?'

'Last week was the first time. Susan stayed for dinner one night. We were talking until quite late and I watched her from the front door until she was safely inside Matchbox Cottage. Then, just as I was about to close my door, I saw the red glow of the cigarette. When I went upstairs I left the lights off and watched from my bedroom window. He was still there.'

'Did you recognise him?'

'No. I've never seen him before. He seems to be watching Nook Cottage and Avril Major says he sounds like someone she knows called Ronnie. He's thin and ferrety and I'm tempted to say that he has mad eyes but that is my imagination. Plus, Avril said that Ronnie had mad eyes. He's been here every night since.'

Marco smiled. 'There must be a heap of cigarette ends under the tree.' He said.

'You'd think so but, no. That makes me suspicious too. If this were a courting couple seeking shelter and darkness for example, there would be a pile of cigarette ends as you say but I walked very slowly along that side of The Green when I went for my walk this morning and I couldn't see a single one.'

'Now that is interesting. It speaks of someone experienced in covering their tracks at the very least.'

Marco watched her for a moment. 'You're fidgeting,' he said, 'what's wrong?'

'I have no right to ask you this, but, would you hold off on quizzing Avril about Ronnie? She seems very fragile at the moment. I intend to try to talk to her again and I don't want her spooked. If she is the one you have doubts about obviously you should ignore me and talk to her. I don't want to stand in the way of your investigation.'

'You're not smoking me out like that,' he laughed. 'I don't need to see her immediately. Don't leave it too long.'

'Thanks, I won't.'

***

The hardware shop was doing brisk business. Small witches and wizards were running around Main Street whooping and cackling. Some wore black bin bags with a hole cut in the top for their heads to poke through.

Lottie and Susan dodged between the members of the minor coven to reach the shop door.

Soon they were emerging again with three witches' hats and three wigs made of sparkling strips of foil. Lottie had green, Susan had blue and they had bought pink for Gwennie. They had also bought greasepaint in luminous colours.

'Gwennie will love this,' Susan said, 'I don't think she's used to letting her hair down.'

They hurried back to Horse and Trumpet Cottage to offload their purchases then set off again splitting up outside the butcher's where Susan joined the queue to collect the sausages whilst Lottie continued up Main Street to ...And Circuses for the bread rolls.

'Would you like my lad to help you carry these?' Henry Ludlow offered. 'There's an awful lot.'

There was an awful lot. Bags and bags were ranked along the counter and more joined them by the second. But Lottie didn't want Henry Ludlow's 'lad' involved.

She wasn't sure if the lad was his son or his apprentice. He was old enough to have a number of sons. But this reminded Lottie of the possibility of a Mrs Ludlow labouring in the back of the shop. It also reminded Lottie of her age.

Lottie stood, her resolve weakening as Henry Ludlow looped bag handles over her fingers. She would never be able to walk at this rate.

Rescue came in the shape of Dexter Hardman who materialised at the shop door just as Lottie was about to change her mind.

'Lottie, my sweet, you're not intending to carry all those on your own, are you?' He came forward arms outstretched. 'Let me take them.' He said and without waiting for her reply, relieved her of the majority of the bags.

They met Susan on Main Street. Dexter managed to take a couple of her bags too and they walked back towards the church hall together.

The cacophony that greeted them didn't bode well for the party. The women of Whittington Edge had been asked to bring in towels for the apple bobbing.

The doctor's wife and Fanny Barstock insisted on opening each of the offerings out and examining it before folding it again. This, they said was in order to make sure all the towels were folded in a uniform manner but there were those who had other ideas on that score.

Tidymans had done a roaring trade in hand towels and the doctor's wife and Fanny Barstock looked askance at every new item. Lottie found herself standing beside one of the women whose linen was currently under their scrutiny. The woman was bristling and Lottie tried to engage her in conversation to prevent a riot breaking out.

Cassie Mellon saved the day at one point by arriving to 'cleanse' the building and put protection on the hall lest the powers of darkness descend on the ungodly; Cassie did not approve of Halloween parties.

She rang bells and walked around the hall clapping her hands and getting in everyone's way. She set up dishes with flowers and candles and incense sticks on the high window ledges. She sat cross legged right in front of the door so that people almost fell over her. And eventually she left.

The schoolchildren had made a frieze that encircled the walls. Twenty five witches flew on broomsticks. Dozens of moons both full and crescent rode high above dozens of church towers and steeples.

Bob Rogers had brought in his witch board but had disappeared. Lottie wanted to congratulate him on his brilliant artwork but no one knew where he was.

She found Susan and Dexter in the kitchen. They were laying out sausages on baking sheets.

'When we've done these and covered them with film, we can escape.' Susan grinned. 'Come and help us.'

'I think you could help out in the hall, Dexter,' Lottie said. 'War is about to break out.'

'Why?' Dexter frowned. 'What's wrong?'

'There is a lot of discussion over the towels provided for the apple bobbing.' She explained. 'Those who invested in new towels are deemed to be ashamed of their household linen. Need I say more?'

'Oh, good grief.' Dexter darted to the door. He swung it open with a flourish and stood in the aperture waiting to be noticed. It didn't take long. Dexter was difficult to miss.

'Ladies,' he boomed in his best baritone, 'how hard you are all working.'

Susan burst out laughing.

'He's the best.' Lottie said. She was pleased that she had revised her opinion of Dexter because Susan seemed quite attached to him.

***

Over at Nook Cottage Bob Rogers was taking his leave. 'I'll see you at the party, won't I?' He pleaded. 'Maybe,' Avril said. Her voice was stern. He swore that he had followed her instructions regarding the blackmail letter but she wasn't sure she believed him.

Lottie and Susan were almost at the front door of Horse and Trumpet Cottage when they saw him hurrying back to the hall.

'Mr Rogers,' Lottie called out, 'I've just seen your witch. You have great talent. Bill Warbeck had better watch out. It seems a pity to stick pins into her but I shall be there tonight to try my luck.'

'Thanks.' He said, barely able to meet her eyes. 'I copied the witch off a cereal packet. I'll see you then.'

Both women watched as he hurried away. They exchanged glances but said nothing.

***

'If we are going to the party from your house I'd better nip home and change.' Susan said.

'Fine. Bring your things over if you'd rather and change here later. Gwennie dropped her stuff off earlier. She knew she'd be busy right up until the start. I'll put the coffee machine on.'

Lottie filled the various compartments of her ultra smart coffee machine and then walked through to her study. She wanted to lock the drawer to her desk that held her notebook. Not for one minute did she think that Susan or Gwennie would snoop. It was more that the book called out to her like the guilty secret that it was.

When she opened the drawer she decided to move the book to her bedside table. When she lifted the notebook out she saw a neat brown paper bag that bore the name of the station bookseller.

She lifted it out and dropped onto her sofa. She peeled the sticky tape away and risked a glance inside. Please don't let it be something dreadfully embarrassing, she thought.

The pink cover almost made her groan as she slid the book out but the smell of print and paper always gave Lottie a thrill. She loved the moment when she opened the cover and turned the first page of a new book. It felt like embarking on a journey to new and fascinating places.

Saving the best – or worst – till last, she turned to the back cover. That would tell her what the book was about and also give her a clue as to whether the journey would be worthwhile. There are only two emotions: love and fear. She read.

Lottie blinked slowly and read the words again. She had surely bought this book before she had that conversation with Cassie Mellon. A shiver ran down her back. Cassie had said that a book would choose her, she wouldn't choose it.

Putting aside all thoughts of this book arriving in her hands by some sort of psychic prompting, Lottie decided to put it on her bedside table and read some of it before she went to sleep. Susan would be here soon and she didn't particularly want to be caught reading the book until she had made a decision about it and she couldn't do that without giving it a fair trial.

***

Across at The Crow's Nest Atlantis was singing as she drifted around the house. Bill, for the first time, was working in his studio with the door open and he wasn't making rude remarks about Atlantis' voice. Atlantis was feeling valued by her husband for the first time in ages and it felt good.

He had painted over an unsuccessful canvas and was using it to sketch out his ideas for 'Autumn'.

Should he go with the idea of the stark tree, branches bare of leaves stretching up into a gold and purple sky? No, too obvious. Or should Atlantis be the leaves heaped by the wind at the foot of the mother tree? Or was there another option?

He paced about. She could be the tree or she could be the leaves. What else. She could be both.

He could paint two images of Atlantis one fainter than the other. Could he do it?

Was he skilled enough? Of course he was. He picked up his brush and began with renewed vigour. He sketched in a tree and a Grecian column and hated both.

At this point Atlantis dared to venture into the studio.

She put a heavily ringed hand on his shoulder and perused his ideas. 'I could always be the wind.' She murmured.

'What?' Bill spun round, his face showing interest. 'How do you mean?'

Atlantis pointed to the tree. 'If the wind could blow the tree to one side, you know, I could be alongside bending it in the fury of a storm or something.'

Bill's automatic response to all and any of his wife's suggestions was to pour scorn and tell her that she had no idea what she was talking about. But, still warm from the glow of approval from last night's party and aware that he actually needed Atlantis now that she was his muse, he turned back to the canvas.

The strange thing was that, as Atlantis spoke, he could see the painting. He knew exactly what it would, what it should, look like; and it could be a *tour de force*

'You're brilliant, darling.' He said and turned to give her a bear hug. 'I'll get a new canvas and begin work right away. What colour do you think the autumn wind would be?'

'I think purple.' Atlantis said. 'You could make the whole of the picture red and autumn gold and then have the wind as a colder colour coming in to whip the leaves away and prepare the land for winter. Then your winter picture would be all purples and blues and the series will look as if it were planned out. I think it would add to the drama.'

Bill stared at her. Never before had Atlantis offered advice on his compositions and she wouldn't have done so now had he not asked her. And by asking her he had discovered that Atlantis had imagination; far more imagination than he had.

He could see it now; he would adopt the colour scheme she had suggested for autumn. The winter landscape of blue and purple would follow on and he could find a way of injecting a little green or something into it to suggest the approach of spring. Then spring would take care of itself. There were so many colours around in spring that there would be no problem though he would concentrate on yellow and purple, but he must ensure that the emerald green that was in 'Summer' had its place.

The Warbeck Season Cycle. That's what they would call it. It would be famous. Collectors would squabble to outbid one another to possess the whole set. Maybe he should stop the Echo from distributing copies of 'Summer' in case it devalued the masterpiece.

No, there was no need to do that. He remembered a time when every living room boasted a Haywain or Flatford Mill and it hadn't affected Constable's reputation. In fact the advance pictures handed out by the Echo would be free advertising for him.

Five would be a nice number. Was there any way that he could manufacture an additional season? He would have to think about that. He may even put Atlantis' mind to work on it.

'Yes,' he said at last, 'purple. Purple would make a strong contrast and signal that a shakeup was on the way.'

Bill Warbeck had no idea when he said those words that his own shakeup was on its way and that purple would be the colour of his ruin.

***

The party was in full flow when Lottie, Susan and Gwennie adorned with distorted putty noses, luminous face paint, glittery wigs and pointy hats swept into the church hall.

Any hopes of making an entrance were dashed by the mayhem within.

Children ran between the adults, whirling them around.

The adults took this in good part; they were enjoying a return to childhood themselves. Wearing a silly hat and a wig seemed to strip their inhibitions.

Cassie's candles had burned away and had been replaced by jack o lanterns which glowed ghoulishly from every ledge. The lighting had been dimmed to enhance the effect of flickering candles.

The three friends all queued to pin their warts on Bob Rogers' witch. They moved on to a game like a coconut shy where the coconuts had been replaced by tennis balls adorned with googly eyes and lopsided smiles which each wore a black cardboard witch's hat.

By the time they arrived at the stall, the hats were all dented out of shape and several of the witches had lost eyes.

They circulated and spoke to people they knew. Lottie made a point of admiring anything she could see anyone had worked hard to produce; it was the least she could do, she had produced nothing herself.

Gwennie wasn't allowed much time to enjoy the party; someone could always find work for Gwennie's willing hands.

Lottie and Susan continued on their way until a sudden hush fell over the hall. They turned and saw Dexter framed in the doorway.

He wore a black silk opera cloak with a bright blue lining. He too had a pointy hat so high that he must have been seven feet tall. His wig was long and blue like Susan's.

He described shapes in the air with a long magic wand and, when he had the attention of the goggle-eyed children, he paused before sweeping the wand round over all of them. Bright blue sparkles flew out of the end of the wand liberally dusting the small audience. Even the adults ooh...ed and aah...ed at the spectacle.

Dexter produced a few magic tricks for the children and a blessed silence fell on the hall as they clustered around him.

The effect Dexter had on the women of Whittington Edge was amazing. Lottie had seen it before when he had called in after Charles's accident but tonight with his height maximised by the hat, he devastated them. Lottie soon realised that he had no idea of his power.

She had been highly suspicious of Dexter Hardman when she first met him but now she stood beside Susan laughing at his antics and revised that opinion. Dexter really didn't know how gorgeous he appeared to the fair sex. She found that most attractive.

When the magic show was over Dexter came to talk to them. The games being moved to the sides of the hall as a local string quartet was setting up for the older villagers to dance. Later it would be the young people who were being treated to a disco.

When the dancing actually started Lottie excused herself. She wanted to take this opportunity to talk to some people she had never met before and she wanted to allow Dexter and Susan to get to know one another better without her playing gooseberry.

Dexter and Susan, both tricked out in blue, looked like a couple. Dexter swirled his magic wand and twirled Susan around inside a mini tornado of blue sparkles. Lottie smiled.

Dexter and Susan were swirling around the floor to the music before Lottie reached the front of the queue at the bar.

She ordered a large jug of Halloween punch and headed towards a table occupied by women of her own age or slightly older. She had selected her targets with care, taking the time she had waited in the queue to decide which group looked most likely to be welcoming and talkative.

'May I join you?' She raised her jug of punch and filled up empty glasses before taking a seat. 'I hope this is nice, I haven't tried it yet.

Conversation was general and she listened attentively and smiled when anyone looked at her. Soon she was included in the group. Lottie had always been good at this kind of thing.

'They look good together,' the woman sitting next to her nodded at Susan and Dexter. 'You're friends with those two, aren't you?'

'Yes, I'm Lottie Colenso. I live at Horse and Trumpet Cottage. I haven't been in Whittington Edge very long.'

'You found poor Adelaide, I hear.' the woman said.

Lottie nodded. 'It was a terrible shock.' She managed at last.

They sat in silence as the music demanded that they listen for the next few minutes as conversation was impossible.

'I love your house.' The woman said when a quieter tune began. 'I admire it every time I walk by.

I'm Rosemary Blundell. My husband Frank' she nodded towards a pleasant looking man, 'is trying to keep the peace between Fanny Barstock and the rest of the world. That woman has all the charm and grace of a rogue elephant.' She shook her head and Lottie laughed. 'We live at The Laburnums next door to Nook Cottage on the opposite side from your friend.'

'I'm very pleased to meet you, Rosemary.' Lottie said as she took the proffered hand. It seemed strange to be shaking hands in such a situation, but still. 'Have you lived in Whittington Edge very long?'

'All my life.' She sighed. 'I knew poor Adelaide,' she said. 'When we were children.'

Lottie's surprise must have shown because she added, 'I have very good bone structure but I'm really as old as Adelaide. We were at school together.'

'What was she like?'

'Lonely.' Rosemary said. 'She was too tall.'

'Too tall?' Lottie echoed.

'Children are very cruel, Lottie, Adelaide Barrett was a good four inches taller than anyone else in our class. She had outgrown her strength as they used to say then. She shot up and was as skinny as a string bean. She wanted friends and the more she tried the more she got pushed out. As I said, children can be very cruel.'

'Did she never have a friend?'

'Little Avril Major came over from somewhere out east. Her mother was ill or something. She was a misfit too. She was tiny and very brown. That may have been due to constant contact with the tropical sun but my mother said she may have had a 'touch of the tar brush'. That's not politically correct nowadays but it was the way they spoke then.'

'I see.' Lottie said. She was trying to find a way to keep Rosemary Blundell talking and hoped that her friends wouldn't butt in.

'My mother used to call them Mick and Montmorency. I don't really know who they were but one must have been tall and the other very short. They did look an odd couple.'

'And did they remain friends for life?' Lottie didn't let on that she knew Avril had left Whittington Edge again.

'No, Avril only stayed for a year. She was lovely. She had a strange way of talking; very precise, very...eastern.' Rosemary paused for a moment and Lottie waited. 'She left and Adelaide was alone again. When she was older she tried to make friends by being over-friendly with the boys if you know what I mean. She got pregnant as you may imagine. I believe the baby was put up for adoption and she was sent away.'

'Did you never see her again?'

'I saw her when she came back.' Lottie's ears pricked up at this. No one else she had spoken to had ever suggested that Adelaide had returned. 'I felt very guilty about the way she had been treated as a child. I talked to her and welcomed her back and she said she had heard that Avril Major was back in the village and was going to visit her.

'She was so excited. I think she was hoping to rekindle the friendship. I invited her to call on me at The Laburnums but she never did and I never saw her again. Now I know why.'

'I wonder if she saw Avril.' Lottie mused. She wanted to make Rosemary Blundell feel better. No one should be pillorying themselves over childhood failings – at least that was Lottie's opinion.

'Oh yes, she must have seen her. She was going up the path to Nook Cottage when I spoke to her. She must have thought that the Avril Major who lives there was the same one as she knew.'

'Isn't she?'

'Heavens above, no.' Rosemary gave a mirthless laugh. 'You could peel an apple with this Avril Major's tongue; she's sharper than Fanny Barstock and that's saying something. 'No, this woman's not the Avril Major that I knew.'

'How can you be sure?' Lottie was trying to do 'agog with curiosity' and hoped that she didn't alert her new friend to the depth of her interest.

'The Avril Major I knew was tiny. It wasn't a case of her not having grown yet. She had the tiny stature that you see in some Asian women. And I don't think her dark skin would have completely whitened out even after years away from the sun. This one's taller than Adelaide ever was. Her skin is as white as parchment and she has a London accent.' Rosemary Blundell laughed and Lottie joined in.

'What did the police say when you told them that Adelaide visited Avril?' Lottie would lay a bet that this nice woman hadn't said a word. She was right.

'I haven't told them. I didn't see her go into Nook Cottage. It was the day of Prince William's wedding and, although I invited Adelaide to come round, I was rather glad she didn't. I love the royals and I was glued to my television all day. So, no, I haven't told the police. I didn't think I had anything of value to offer. Do you think I should?'

***

Here at last was her first concrete clue. As Jane Pendleton had asked, how common a name was Avril Major? Not very, she wouldn't have thought. She really must try to get that tarot reading organised. If she could just get Avril alone, she may find something out.

The Halloween party, having moved along from things to interest the village children, to music for the older generation, now decided it was the young people's turn and the string quartet packed their instruments away to much cheering and applause for a job well done.

A disco pumped up its volume and the lights dimmed further allowing coloured lights to swoop dizzyingly around the dance floor and ceiling as they reflected from five glitterballs.

Lottie and Susan and decided to call it a day and jointly descended on Gwennie to remove her before Fanny Barstock and her cohorts drained every scrap of energy from her. Lottie and Susan had noticed that Fanny Barstock, did little but hand down orders to the willing workers and they both felt resentful on Gwennie's behalf.

They were in the lobby making sure that they each had their handbags and swathing their outdoor coats around themselves when the outer doors flew open and a blast of icy air reminded them to button up warmly.

Borne through the door on this whirlwind was what turned out to be the evening's main attraction. And, had the three friends known this, they would have delayed their departure.

As it was, they watched a tall, slender woman clad entirely in purple as she paused in the doorway and then sashayed into the room, the doors swinging shut behind her.

'She'll catch her death,' Gwennie said. 'Who with any sense would be out at this time of night in a strapless dress and how high was that hemline?'

'I wish I could walk in heels that high,' Susan said. 'They must have been five inches.'

'She looked as if she meant business,' Lottie added. 'I wonder if she's here to surprise someone. Like a singing telegram. '

'What a lovely idea,' Gwennie beamed. She'll make someone's night. What a surprise.'

It has to be said; she surprised a lot of people. And she made a lot of people's night. But the intended recipient of her attentions didn't enjoy those attentions for long.

***

The three friends strolled back to Horse and Trumpet Cottage in the cool, crisp evening.

'That was wonderful.' Gwennie sighed. 'My ears are ringing from the noise.'

'Mine too.' Susan stretched her neck backwards and almost lost her hat.

'Look at that wonderful moon.' Lottie watched a moon so large and low that it seemed to be skating across the roofs of the houses of The Green.

'Perfect.' Susan agreed.

'Of course we all start again on Monday.' Gwennie yawned.

'We do?' Lottie was suddenly alert.

'It's the bonfire party next Saturday.'

Lottie managed not to groan.

Susan pulled a face. 'I must be getting old,' she said.

'The thought of another late night fills me with dread.'

A glass of merlot apiece and the plate of sandwiches that Lottie had made earlier and left in the fridge covered with film soon revived them and they leaned back in Lottie's comfortable chairs eating, drinking but saying little.

Loud whooping outside drew Lottie to the window. She looked out. A line of witches snaked out of the church hall, down Church Lane and back again. They danced across The Green and circled the duck pond. Legs kicked out and the conga music could be heard pulsing out of the church hall.

Further along a sporty little car nosed out of The Glimpse and turned into Old Whittington Lane. Lottie frowned. Biddy was off on one of her nocturnal trips. The car lights came on just after it turned onto the lane.

On the far side of The Green, Atlantis dislodged herself from the line and tottered unsteadily towards The Crow's Nest. Bill Warbeck followed. He was shouting something but Lottie couldn't hear what.

'I think the Warbecks have had an argument.' She said. 'Atlantis has just slammed the door in Bill's face.'

⁂

It was as dark as a witch's heart on the night of Halloween. The streets of Lyeminster were thronged with children carrying orange plastic pumpkins in which to collect sweets from their neighbours. Ronnie had bought a long black robe and a pointy black hat so that he could blend in. One or two attendant fathers wished him a good evening and Ronnie tilted his hat to them and continued on his way.

Halloween was the perfect choice for Ronnie's business. With his long robes swirling around him, he had hidden many of the tools of his trade about his person with no trouble at all. On the other hand, the car he had selected was going to be difficult to steal.

It was parked on a long, straight road in one of the better areas of Lyeminster. The houses stood well back from the road behind high walls and looming trees. He had carried out many a recce on the car late at night after leaving Whittington Edge, and there was never anyone around. No one was walking home in this area. And after eleven, no one would be there to see him.

Ronnie's idea had been to take the car early so that he could be hiding near to Whittington Edge well before the time he needed to be there. Now, of course, with kids milling around all over the place, it wasn't going to work and a Plan B had to be devised.

He couldn't go towards the welcoming lights of the pub on the corner; he couldn't risk being that visible. So Plan B turned out to be walking miles away from his target and, when he saw groups of kids being bustled home by worn out parents, he began walking back.

There it stood, black and sleek and as silent as a panther once it was running. The initial roar of power was the only threat.

Ronnie had the door open and his own brand of magic performed in less than two minutes. And then he was away, accelerating slowly, keeping the roar of that powerful engine down to a soft, gentle purr.

Being a master of his craft, Ronnie had worked out his route too. He kept to the suburban streets, cutting through neighbourhoods until he reached the old road to Whittington Edge. He knew where Bob Rogers lived and intended to run his Land Rover off the road. Once shocked and at a disadvantage, Ronnie would finish him off.

Thus Ronnie waited far back from Millstone Farm and awaited his prey.

It was a long wait. He wished he had brought a sandwich with him. Then he saw movement. No lights but definitely movement. He fired the engine and prowled forward silently, stealthily. Then he turned his headlights on, selecting full beam and stamping on the accelerator.

Glowing eyes reflected back at him. It was a witch! On Halloween. Ronnie could see a witch! He had no time to think. No time to rationalise. He kicked the accelerator and ran straight at the creature that rose up, its eyes ablaze.

The impact wasn't as hard as it would have been had he hit a Land Rover. The witch flew over his head, screaming as she went. Ronnie forced his legs to carry him over to where she landed and found Bob Rogers, dead with his head cracked open by his own millstone. The witch was a shattered pile of wood. Fancy being scared by a painting. Ronnie hoped no one would ever know.

He ran back to the car, kicked the accelerator and found a lay-by to park the car. Then he walked the rest of the way. The witch had shaken him but Ronnie would not remain shaken for long.

Luck was with him. A conga of witches was whooping it up across The Green when he arrived at the church hall. Only one other person remained watching the fun with disapproving eyes. Arnold Pickard. Bingo!

'I've dressed up for this,' Ronnie told him. 'But I'm not sure I feel comfortable with it. I wish the church was open so I could go and pray for these lost souls.'

'Good man,' Arnold Pickard beamed. 'Wait while I lock up here, and I shall make your wish come true.'

In more ways than one, Ronnie thought. 'Thank you,' he said, and fell into step beside the churchwarden.

CHAPTER SEVENTEEN

The silence of the early morning bells that usually summoned the faithful to St Jude's reminded Jane Pendleton that this was the last day she would have her beloved husband all to herself.

Morning service this week was to take place in another of Charles's parishes and be led by his replacement for the last time. Charles was much better now. The blow to his head had not been serious and the wound had almost completely healed but the bishop had insisted that Charles take a good amount of time off to recover fully and had brought in a locum to cover his duties at St Jude's.

Charles and slid luxuriously down beneath the warm duvet.

A lie-in on a Sunday was a treat indeed.

Jane, sensing that he was awake, snuggled into his arms. 'Do you have anything planned for today?' she whispered.

'No, why, what do you want to do?'

Jane rolled onto her back and stared at the ceiling. 'I would like to go out into the country for the day. I would like to leave the mobile phones switched off and your clerical collar at home and go for a walk and a picnic or a pub lunch somewhere.' She turned to look at him. 'How does that sound to you?'

'Marvellous.' His cautious side broke through and he added, 'we must take the mobile phones with us in case we break down.'

'Of course.' Jane stifled a laugh. How like Charles that was. 'But it stays switched off unless we do break down.'

'Shall we set out straight after breakfast?'

Jane pouted. 'I thought we'd make breakfast the first treat of our day. I thought we could go to the greasy spoon cafe on the bypass and have a 'full English' with whatever lorry drivers are on the road today. We could sneak out of the back door and straight into the car.'

Charles laughed at his beautiful wife and kissed the end of her dainty nose.

The rectory fronted directly onto The Green but it had the advantage of a short drive that led to a garage at the back. Jane eased the car out of the garage and Charles, minus his canonicals, hurried to the passenger seat.

It was a guilty pleasure to be sneaking out of the rectory whilst his parishioners were at their devotions but Charles had started his day with prayers as he always did and was sure that the Lord would understand. He after all had provided this wonderful day and drawn this wonderful wife to Charles's side. Surely He intended that Charles should spend time with her and a walk in the country would in itself be a hymn of prayer to the Almighty.

So it was that the Pendletons were incommunicado and miles away from Whittington Edge when news of the death began to circulate.

***

Lottie heard the distant tinkling of china and was instantly awake. Someone tapped on her door and she remembered that Susan and Gwennie had stayed over last night after the three of them had polished off two bottles of wine between them.

They had talked late into the night until no one wanted to turn out into the frost that was beginning to silver the grass of The Green.

Horse and Trumpet Cottage had plenty of spare rooms and whilst Gwennie twittered about presuming on Lottie's kindness, Susan told her not to be silly. 'I'm not going home and I only live a hundred yards away.' She said. And Gwennie had subsided and agreed to stay too.

'Come in,' Lottie shuffled up the bed and finger-combed her hair, blinking with the effort of looking wide awake.

Gwennie opened the door and tip toed inside. 'I thought I'd bring you a nice cup of tea.' She whispered. 'Susan is fast asleep. I'll take her some in a minute.'

'Why are you up so early, Gwennie?'

'I have to go and help Mrs Fleet. She'll be expecting me. She doesn't always sleep well.'

Gwennie pulled a small table up to the bedside and hurried out onto the landing to collect the tray she had left there. 'I'll just pour you a cup then I'll nip off.' She said.

Lottie watched the amber liquid curl into a cup and remembered their visit to the Rose Bowl in Lyeminster. She smiled at Gwennie.

'When you've finished at Templar House will you come back and have breakfast with Susan and me?'

'I don't want to presume'

'It's Sunday. This should be a lazy day. Let's share it together. We could have lunch together too. It was such fun last night. I want it to go on and on.'

'Well, if you're sure.' Gwennie's worried face broke into a grin. 'You'll think it silly, I know, but I used to dream of sharing a flat or going away to college and spending nights talking with friends.' She sighed. 'Mother and dad didn't approve of girls leaving home so it never happened but last night was a taste of the fun I once wanted.'

She sat on the edge of Lottie's bed for a few seconds and made sure that the tea was to her liking then she was off again, downstairs to prepare a similar tray for Susan and then out the door and hurrying across The Green to Templar House and Mrs Fleet.

Lottie showered and dressed but abandoned her fitness routine in deference to having a house guest. Before she went downstairs she telephoned Marco and recounted her conversation with Rosemary Blundell. 'I suggested she let you know,' Lottie said. 'I don't know how you can encourage her to do so without dropping me in it but do your best, won't you?'

***

Susan was not an early riser these days either but the tea and the visit from Gwennie had woken her too and the friends met in the kitchen, neither completely awake and neither able to return to their blissful slumbers.

'How on earth does she maintain the pace?' Susan groaned. 'I suppose she has to.'

'I think it's more that 'mother' has indoctrinated her to believe that enjoying one's life is a cardinal sin.'

Lottie had enjoyed her tea but her day couldn't really begin in earnest without the assistance of good strong coffee and she was busy assembling its components when her peripheral vision picked up someone hurrying from St Jude's Open. Dexter.

'Keep your eye on the side door,' she called over her shoulder to Susan. 'Dexter is coming our way. He may be looking for you.'

Susan was up in a flash and hurrying to open the door and intercept him if he was on his way to Matchbox Cottage. She picked up a carrier bag of rubbish that Lottie had left next to the Church Lane door and carted it up the path to the bin as a decoy in case he wasn't looking for her at all.

'Susan, just the person I wanted to see. I'm glad you're with Lottie I can tell you both together.' And he was in the kitchen, eyes fever-bright with excitement, sitting at Lottie's big kitchen table, waiting for his audience to settle down.

Coffee distributed, Lottie sat at the table and smiled at him. 'So what happened after we left the party?' It was easy to see that Dexter had some momentous news and it couldn't be about anything else. There hadn't been time.

'What do you know?' Dexter leaned forward. 'What was happening when you left?'

'We went during the dancing.' Lottie said.

'Yes, the noise was dreadful.' Susan added, and then wished she hadn't; she didn't want Dexter to think her a stick in the mud.

'And a woman in purple passed us in the lobby,' Lottie added. 'We came back here and had a glass or two of wine. Then we saw the conga of witches. That was a sight to behold.'

'And we saw Atlantis Warbeck slam the door in Bill's face.' Susan said. 'Whatever had happened to those two?'

'That's what I've come to tell you about.' Dexter paused for dramatic effect. Lottie and Susan hardly dared breathe in case it put him off. 'Everyone was dancing. The Warbecks seemed more harmonious than I've ever seen them before. They were dancing and laughing together and the sight was so unusual that people were heard remarking on it.'

Lottie frowned. 'So what spoiled this magical moment?'

'Your lady in purple,' Dexter gave a slow nod to emphasise his words. 'The doors opened and this vision of purple stood there. She was unbelievably tall. This may have been because she was wearing six inch heels. She stood for a moment and the crowd on the dance floor stopped dancing and turned to look at her. Her dress was the shortest I've ever seen and that's going some, I can tell you.

Anyway she wiggled over to the dancers who parted to let her through. Then – oh you're not going to believe this, it really is too awful – then, she kissed Bill.' Dexter screwed up his face in distaste.

'She kissed Bill? Bill Warbeck? Why on earth would she want to do that?' Susan asked.

'You may well ask. But she did. She kissed the ugly little gnome right on his revolting mouth with its smashed up teeth. And, the worst of it is, he kissed her right back; right in front of Atlantis.

'Now I've always thought that Atlantis had to kiss him because she's his wife and everything, but I've never worked out how she could bring herself to do it. Then this woman, who should really have more taste, kisses him right in the middle of the dance floor. It was horrible.'

'What did Atlantis do?' Lottie asked. She felt sorry for Atlantis Warbeck. She thought the girl had a rotten life with a revolting man. Public humiliation was so unfair.

'She stood and watched. I'm sure she couldn't believe it any more than I could. Then the purple lady stepped away from Bill, slapped him hard across the face and swept out again.'

'Who was she?' Lottie wanted to know.

'I have no idea.'

'And Atlantis just carried on dancing?' Susan was wide-eyed.

'I suppose the poor thing was too humiliated to know what to do.' Lottie said quietly. 'She probably wanted to cause a scene but didn't really know how to do that either. And she wouldn't want to show herself up, I suppose.'

'I'm glad she slammed the door in his face.' Susan said. 'I hope he had to sleep on a bench on in the cold. I bet it was because of the picture.'

'What picture?' Lottie asked.

'Of course, you don't buy the Echo, do you?' Susan glanced at Dexter whose face showed that he had had a revelation.

'I saw it.' He said. 'It's being hailed as a masterpiece.'

'One of Bill Warbeck's paintings?' Lottie guessed.

'Yes,' Susan said, 'he's got a painting of Atlantis on display in a gallery in Lyeminster. It's almost a nude according to the grainy little picture in the Echo but it's supposed to be really brilliant and the Echo is going to reproduce it and distribute copies to all their readers.'

'Is it really that good?'

'Hard to tell,' Dexter grimaced. 'As Susan said, the picture in the paper is of very poor quality and who knows how good Bill's work actually is? I doubt if

Lyeminster is swamped with Royal Academicians vying with one another to display their wares. Have either of you seen any of his offerings before?'

'He did put something in at a local art show.' Susan recalled. 'It was for charity and mostly the work of keen local amateurs.

'Bill had insisted that his canvas had the most important position and he had been accommodated because the organisers were in awe of a real artist deigning to allow one of his works to share space with that of rank amateurs.'

'Was it any good?' Lottie asked.

'I'm one of those people who know what they like,' Susan grinned, 'and I didn't like it. But what do I know?'

'Was that an 'almost nude' too?'

'No it was some abstract thing. All vines with odd things growing from them. Most peculiar. Atlantis told me that he paints a lot of things along the same lines.'

'I think I may take a trip into Lyeminster to view the masterpiece.' Dexter said at last. 'Would you ladies like to accompany me?'

Lottie and Susan exchanged glances. 'Yes, please.' They said in unison.

'Then how about if we go tomorrow?'

***

Lottie, Susan and Dexter were on their second mugs of coffee and still speculating on the identity of the mysterious purple lady when there was an urgent knocking on the Church Lane door and Gwennie hurried in. Lottie took a cup and saucer down from the cabinet for her and poured coffee into it. Susan helped her off with her coat. Gwennie was in a state.

'What's wrong, Gwennie, my sweet?' Dexter ushered her into a chair.

'It's Bob Rogers,' Gwennie gasped. 'He's dead.'

Lottie was fazed for a moment. 'Bob Rogers?' She murmured.

'Yes. From Millstone Farm on the old Lyeminster road.' Gwennie said.

'The man with the Pin the Wart on the Witch game.' Susan explained.

'Oh, I know.' Lottie's face cleared for a second. 'What happened to him? He didn't have a heart attack, did he? I saw him carrying that huge board into the church hall. It was very cumbersome even if it wasn't heavy. I remember thinking at the time that he should have brought it in his Land Rover.'

'It was the witch.' Gwennie said. She picked up her cup and took a steadying sip. 'He was walking home carrying his witch board. He didn't want to bring his Land Rover in case he had a drink. Anyway, he was walking home and he got knocked down by a hit and run driver. They say that someone stole a fast car in Lyeminster and it caught poor Bob and flipped him head first onto the millstone at the end of his farm drive. He was killed outright.'

Not for the first time, Lottie wondered at the efficiency of Mrs Fleet's bush telegraph. She also remembered Biddy leaving at speed in her sporty little car.

***

Across The Green at The Crow's Nest the atmosphere could have been expected to be frosty. Surprisingly it wasn't. There was no atmosphere at all.

Atlantis had refrained from locking her husband out completely the previously night. She had left open a small window through which, with a lot of difficulty, he could reach his arm and open a larger window. This he squeezed through having torn the buttons from his shirt in the attempt.

Bill Warbeck was an insensitive pig of a man – everyone around The Green was agreed on this – but he had enough animal cunning to know that being allowed shelter under his own roof was more than he deserved and he hadn't pushed his luck by trying to share Atlantis's bed. Instead he spent a miserable night of self pity on the hard chaise longue in his studio.

By morning Bill had no idea why he had been denied the comforts of hearth and home. He was the wronged party here. He had twinges from the lumps and bumps of the chaise longue and could only feel resentment towards Atlantis who he saw as the architect of his sufferings.

The punishment fitting for this unfair treatment was the withdrawal of his company. He sneaked into the kitchen and collected supplies to sustain him for the day. Then he returned to his studio, locked the door and cranked up his music to full volume. That would teach her.

If Bill had also intended to curtail his wife's slumbers with his boorish behaviour he was doomed to disappointment. One of Atlantis's foster mothers had once said that Atlantis could sleep through an earthquake.

When she was a teenager a runaway lorry had crashed into the side of the house demolishing a large section of it and leaving Atlantis's bedroom dangling precariously in space when the supporting wall beneath it crumbled to dust.

Atlantis slept through the whole episode and was surprised to be awakened by a fireman some time later. So Meatloaf's 'Bat out of Hell' only inconvenienced Bill who professed to need silence in order to work.

**

Only one of the older contingent of Whittington Edge knew the identity of the lady in purple.

Beau Derek was a member of Facebook and he began every day by checking what was happening in and around his adopted village. He had originally signed up in case any news of Adelaide found its way onto the site. It never had of course, but he had discovered a page where everyone and anyone in Whittington Edge were invited to add pieces of news.

He could easily imagine the glee with which the youngsters had hurried home from the Halloween party to fire up their computers and discuss the events that had taken place.

He had noticed that young people lived twice nowadays: once in real time and once again in cyberspace – and that life on the internet was much more exciting and colourful than reality. The party had been debated and dissected until Beau could almost believe that he had attended it himself.

There had been a lot of discussion about the dress adopted by the partygoers, who wore the best fancy dress and who had been looking at whom. Dexter Hardman came in for comment. He was described as 'dreamy' and 'gorgeous' and speculation on whether he was really too old for this or that teenager was rife. Beau made a mental note to tell his old friend. Dexter would be highly amused.

This was followed by basic stuff of the sort that appeared every day. Beau was skating over it when the incident involving the lady in the purple dress was mentioned. This caught his eye and he began to read in earnest.

'Oh dear.' He murmured when Bill Warbeck's name first appeared. 'They really shouldn't name names.'

Bill Warbeck was not a popular man on the Whittington Edge Facebook page. He was said to be nosy and to take photographs of people when he thought they weren't looking. The observations of the local artist ramped up with each entry. He was called a 'perv' because he leered at the young girls.

Mention was made of 'Summer' and the thinly clad model was cited as yet more proof of the sick mind of Bill Warbeck.

'The man's an artist you silly girl.' Beau Derek muttered. He shook his head and continued to read.

He had seen the picture and thought it rather fine. In fact he had decided to drive into Lyeminster and take a proper look at it. He may buy it to hang on the walls of Pennyman Cottage if it lived up to the promise of the photograph in the Echo.

Another entry further down the screen suggested that the model for 'Summer' wasn't actually Atlantis Warbeck. 'Anyone with half an eye could see that it was Atlantis' was Beau's comment to his empty study.

The libelling of Bill Warbeck continued in more and more vivid exaggeration – at least Beau hoped it was exaggeration. He laughed at a few of the comments. No one would ever take them seriously and he supposed that the owners of the site would remove the most offensive of them.

Then his attention was rewarded when Summer Saunders entered the fray to tell the world of Whittington Edge that she was the lady in purple. Summer Saunders felt slighted, she said, because she had posed for the picture that bore her name but the artist had seen fit to paint over her face and replace it with that of his 'boring old wife'.

Scores of entries hit the website almost simultaneously.

Beau could almost hear them like jeers and catcalls deriding Summer Saunders for trying to 'big herself up' as one of the contributors accused her.

No one stepped up to defend Summer Saunders' position.

There were numerous demands to know why, if she was Bill Warbeck's model, she hadn't let on.

Another comment said that Summer Saunders would definitely have been bragging about it were it actually true.

Fourteen people immediately 'liked' this remark and some went on to endorse it with other examples of where Summer Saunders had made sure that everyone knew what was going on in her life.

Another contributor who had been present at the party asked how anyone could bring themselves to kiss Bill Warbeck and, if Summer Saunders had really done that then she was a slag.

The number of 'likes' that this remark attracted made Beau fear for the stability of the website; at this rate they would bring Facebook to a grinding halt.

Summer herself was surprisingly reticent and did not rise to their bait. It was this and this alone that made Beau Derek wonder if what she had said could possibly be true.

He decided to telephone Lottie and ask what she thought. Or should he ring Dexter instead? He needed to think about that before committing himself.

***

Charles and Jane reached the top of the Beacon. It was so windy that their words were snatched away from their mouths and swept off to the points of the compass that were inscribed on the brass disc they were currently viewing.

'Lincoln cathedral is that way.' Charles pointed and shouted but Jane laughed, pulled her hair away from the buffeting wind and shook her head to indicate that she couldn't hear a word. Charles took her hand and walked her away from the summit and into the lee of the rocks where she had left their blanket and flask of soup.

They sat down relieved to be away from the noise of the wind. Her face felt stiff with cold and her news was dangerously close to the surface. If she didn't tell him now whilst she had some control left, she would spill it all out in a rush and explain it badly.

'Charles,' she said, 'I have something I have to tell you.'

Charles beamed. 'Then tell me, my darling.' He waited. He knew what it was. He had noticed the unusual mood swings. He had seen the evidence of tears on a couple of occasions.

He had asked her if she was feeling well, obviously, and Jane had told him she was fine. But she wasn't. Jane was pregnant and worried about how he would react. How could she be? Surely she knew that a child of his own was the pinnacle of a man's life. Any child they produced would be beautiful like its mother in thought, word and deed, not to mention inheriting her adorable face.

'Tell me.' He prompted when he could see she was still fighting to find the words.

'I've not been entirely truthful with you.' She bit her lip.

Charles was still waiting. He had expected her to tell him sooner than this. This was their child after all; his and hers. And he knew she must be bursting to tell him and she must know that he was bursting to be told but he also allowed that a woman may need a few days to accustom herself to the reality of motherhood before letting anyone else into the secret. Even her husband.

'I think I know what it is.' He said, hoping to ease the moment for her.

'You know about Edna? Jane's voice was almost a squeak and she turned from him to bury her face in her hands. 'I was so worried about telling you. Prison was bad enough but the murder...well I thought you'd send me away.'

She looked back to him and her voice dropped to a whisper. 'That's what my father would have done in this situation.' She burst into tears.

Charles gathered his wife into his arms. Never before had he been glad to see his wife weep. Normally he would do all in his power to calm her and stem her tears. Now they were a Godsend because he suspected that there was no baby.

All his hopes and dreams had been dashed as surely as if they had taken them in their hands and thrown them from the peak of the beacon onto the rocks below.

No baby.

He forced a smile. A baby would come at the time of the Good Lord's choosing. He had faith that a baby would be sent to them. They would be good parents. In time. But before that he had to get to the bottom of what was troubling Jane, and he had to ensure that she didn't see his shock reflected in his face.

Jane's words began to percolate through his disappointment. Edna. That was the name of the woman who asked Jane to visit her in prison. Murder...murder? What could his lovely Jane have to do with murder?

'Tell me all about it.' He stroked her hair and hoped that she couldn't hear the rapid pounding of his heart. 'I'll never send you away. You know that. We are one in the Lord and shall stay so for as long as we both shall live.'

He felt her take a huge breath and knew that he had been given the words to calm her. He said a silent prayer of thanks and looked up at the sky where he was sure a cloud scudding past formed itself into the shape of the cross. This he saw as God's acknowledgement. All would be well. He was looking down and would hold His servants in the palm of His hand and protect them.

'Edna Derry.' Jane said. 'The woman who wrote to me and asked me to visit her in prison. She's my mother.'

Jane struggled to sit upright so that she could look her husband in the eyes. It was important that she see the moment, the exact moment when he realised the truth and distanced himself from her. Then she began to tell her story leaving nothing out.

'When Dolly was due to be discharged, she killed the woman who had been victimising my mother. This gave mother the promised single cell because she made sure mother was blamed for the murder. She went to the governor and told her that mother confessed to her. She even went to court to testify. Now nothing can be done.

***

Atlantis Warbeck was severely wounded by her husband's behaviour. She didn't blame the purple lady for sweeping down on Bill like a vampire ready to drain every drop of life out of him. After all, who could possibly resist Bill with his bushy beard and the short sighted eyes that grew large with the effort of seeing? No, she blamed Bill. He knew he had this devastating attraction for women and he should by now be able to keep it under control. Last night had been her night. Atlantis's night. Her image had been reproduced in the Lyeminster Echo – badly reproduced, it had to be admitted – and she was famous for the first time in her life. Then that woman had appeared, grabbed Bill and he, faithless creature, had succumbed.

When she released him and slid out of his arms, Bill's was slow to release her and Atlantis could still see, in her mind's eye how his hands clung. He looked as if he were trying to reach out to her.

And all the while, Atlantis stood watching. Humiliated. Unable to take in what had happened and what was still going on.

Who was she? This purple lady.

What could she do? She could slap Bill's face as the purple woman had done and then storm out of the church hall and return to The Crow's Nest to wipe away her tears of shame or she could laugh and pretend she didn't care.

This was the route Atlantis Warbeck had taken. She had laughed. She had clapped as the woman teetered out of the hall on her spike heels. She had looked around as if this was the best joke she had seen for a long time.

And inside she was dying.

How she had performed that conga with the other witches all the way across The Green she didn't know. She had broken free of the chain with whoops of joy and headed for the sanctuary of her home, slamming the door closed as soon as she got inside. The tears were already flowing by then and huge, painful, gulping sobs were tearing at her throat.

She had heard Bill hammering on the door but couldn't bear to let him see how he had hurt her. She had crawled into bed and wept herself to sleep.

She was still sobbing when she woke. Her eyes were swollen closed and she was thirsty. Probably every drop of moisture had left her body via her tears and she was a desiccated husk of a woman in every way possible. To add to her misery, the whole room was throbbing along with her head.

The pulsating pounding that moved the entire room around her formed itself into a regular beat and slowly Atlantis recognised Bill's 'misery music'. So he was upset too.

Good.

Atlantis was shocked. She had never before, despite all the ways he had hurt her, relished his unhappiness.

She did today. She stumbled out of bed and went to the bathroom to wash her face. The woman, who peered back at her through reddened slits that had once been sparkling emerald eyes, looked and felt a hundred years old.

She tiptoed back to the bedroom. She didn't know why she tiptoed; Bill was unlikely to hear her. But she didn't want to do anything that might provoke him into investigating her whereabouts. She didn't want him to see her like this.

Was there any point to any of it anymore? Were her dreams of taking the art world by storm beside her beloved Bill to be snatched away?

No, she told herself, they were not. She was overreacting. She had to find a way to put this behind her; behind her and behind Bill. The only question remaining was how she could possibly do that. Splashing icy water on her face Atlantis tried to work out how she could overcome the pain and seize whatever opportunities presented themselves whilst ignoring Bill's odd little ways.

She could go to Cassie Mellon for a massage and a pep talk. That was what she did before.

But she knew what Cassie would say. She would advise that she rise above it and tell her that the things we dislike in other people are those things that mirror our own faults.

Well that was a load of old hooey. Atlantis never went chasing after other men so how could this be any sort of reflection of her own personality.

Besides, if she went to Cassie, Cassie would try to pour oil on the troubled waters of their marriage and Atlantis would resent that and rebel and end up hating Bill even more than she did now.

No, she needed to talk to someone who would take her side and tell her that Bill was a rotten little ratbag and then, maybe then, Atlantis would find it in her heart to defend him.

Avril Major. She would go to Avril and have a reading. It was well known that Avril had little time for men.

***

'It's time I left.' Dexter stood and took his coffee mug to the sink.

Lottie looked at Susan to see if she was expected to invite him to join their girls only lunch. Susan was giving no such signals and Lottie was pleased. Any discomfort this may have caused was neutralised when Dexter turned to look through the doors to the living room.

'Atlantis is crossing The Green.' He moved into the living room so that he could get a better view. The others lined up beside him. 'Where can she be going?' Dexter murmured. 'My goodness, I think she's going to Nook Cottage.'

Three sets of feminine eyebrows rose at this thought but Dexter was right. Atlantis marched up to Avril's door and was admitted without hesitation.

'She was expected.' Susan said. And the four friends all shared a knowing glance. 'And it looks as if she's taking wine to Avril. If it's her homemade concoction I hope Avril has a strong head; she'll need it. It has the reputation of being lethal.'

'Now ladies,' Dexter said when the door to Nook Cottage closed behind Atlantis, 'I have to love you and leave you. I promised to call in on Beau this morning.'

***

Avril may not be psychic but she had heard Atlantis Warbeck's sadness seeping over the telephone line. She had glasses and a bottle of wine lined up ready. She took the bottles that Atlantis had brought with her and placed them on the coffee table in reserve. Nettle and dandelion. Interesting.

Having been otherwise engaged the night before – the superintendent had nipped in for a freebie – Avril had seen nothing and heard nothing of the incident of the purple lady. She heard all about it now. She heard about it and her blood began to boil.

This was the trouble with marrying the bastards, she thought. Sonny was the love of her life but look at the trouble he had caused her. The women who 'didn't mean anything', the snide cracks to his friends when he knew she was within earshot, the many, many humiliations she had suffered over the years. And finally, the prison sentence that had fallen on her because Sonny had upset the filth.

Yes, she was convinced that women should never marry. They should keep men in their place. They should keep the whip hand. Avril smiled at this thought. She now did that literally.

'Kick him out, love.' Avril advised. She poured wine into the large bowl of a stemmed glass and handed it to her visitor.

Atlantis knew it was a bad thing to start drinking this early in the day but she could hardly say anything when she had arrived on the doorstep carrying two bottles now could she? She took a long drink and decided she was safe; the stuff was like fruit juice so no harm could come of it and she drained the glass.

Surprisingly, Avril had also drained her glass and refilled the glasses, looking with astonishment at the bottle that now seemed to be empty. She placed it on the floor beside her chair and opened the first bottle of Atlantis's potion. She sniffed it warily. It smelled good and she topped up their glasses with it.

'I know you're not supposed to mix it,' she told Atlantis, 'but it'll mix when it lands so what the hell?'

Atlantis giggled. This was what she needed. Cassie Mellon always told her that the universe led you in the right direction if you allowed it to. Today she was prepared to believe her. She clinked glasses with Avril and drank deeply. Soon both women were laughing and Atlantis felt amazing.

'But I love him.' Atlantis said as soon as she remembered that Avril had already pronounced on her problem.

'I love mine too.' Avril said. 'But I can't live with the faithless swine.' Some warning bell clanged inside Avril's mind but she ignored it. Atlantis Warbeck wouldn't leave Nook Cottage until Avril was sure that her memory of the visit had been erased completely.

'I'll do you a reading.' Avril offered. She picked up her cards and carefully removed the black silk square that 'held in their energy'. 'Shuffle these, lovey.' She rattled out a cough and handed the cards over. She may as well take up smoking again.

Atlantis shuffled and sobbed and drank more wine. A stray tear forced its way through her resolve and trickled down her cheek.

'Don't waste tears on him.' Avril's tone was sharp. How many tears had she wasted on Sonny? And how much good had it done her? She took the cards from Atlantis and pushed the tissue box closer to her.

Atlantis took a tissue and dabbed at her eyes. 'You'll get wrinkles if you keep crying,' Avril warned, 'and believe me; no man is worth a line on your face.' Especially a misery like Bill Warbeck. But she didn't say this out loud.

Avril had been swotting up on her tarot by way of a book during the long evenings when she had no clients and certain cards were supposed to foretell of disasters such as broken marriages.

None of those appeared in Atlantis' spread. In fact, the future looked nice and rosy for the lady opposite her.

'Pick out a card for your husband.' Avril spread the cards out in a fan before her visitor and Atlantis's hand hovered over them. She closed her eyes and reached out to pick out the first one that her fingers touched. This she handed to Avril.

Ah, here was the answer. Bill Warbeck was in for a lonely time. 'And another.' Avril ordered. The second card didn't bring overwhelming destruction to Bill as she had expected. Rather, it spoke of upheavals and radical changes that would all turn out to be for his own good.

Avril still thought that Atlantis should leave him. He was a waste of space. She could do so much better.

Atlantis left Nook Cottage in the early evening. She and Avril had drunk both bottles of dandelion and nettle wine as well as the bottle Avril had opened ready for the visit. From there they had moved on to gin. Avril found some croissants which she served to 'soak it up' as she put it, but nothing more substantial was forthcoming and Atlantis wasn't bothered anyway. She was too upset to take solid food.

The cold fresh air was immediately stimulating but soon hit Atlantis like a hammer.

She reached The Green and heard the door of Nook Cottage close before she began winding her way back to The Crow's Nest.

She fell face first on the wet grass and strong hands came to pick her up. She had no idea who her rescuers were but she allowed them to guide her back to the door of her home.

***

Dexter and Beau had been taking a turn around The Green, whilst Beau had told Dexter about the purple lady and sworn him to secrecy. They had been Atlantis' rescuers.

They expressed concern when Bill Warbeck eventually opened the door. Caught on the back foot he didn't respond immediately and had to be asked again where he wanted his wife taken to before he led the way to the kitchen which boasted a huge armchair. The rescuers eased her into the chair and watched with dismay as she sank down into a crumpled heap.

'Maybe you should call the doctor.' Beau suggested. 'She'll be fine.' Bill said. He was already angry with Atlantis and now these two seemed to be under the impression that he should be pandering to her stupid moods.

She was the one rolling home drunk. If he behaved like this he would never hear the end of it. Let her sleep it off in the chair. He didn't care. 'She'll be fine once she's had a bit of a sleep.' He said, adding, 'she usually is' to convince these judgmental snobs that he was the injured party here and that Atlantis was only one step away from being a lush.

***

Susan, Gwennie, and Lottie witnessed this surreal interlude as Gwennie and Susan were saying goodbye. They paused longer on the doorstep of Horse and Trumpet Cottage than would usually be the case so that they could see things to their conclusion. This was when Gwennie remembered another piece of information that she had forgotten to pass along.

'Oh, Lottie, dear, I forgot to tell you, Mrs. Fleet was talking to me today. She said that Beau had told her of your interest in Whittington Edge and she said that she has a lot of photographs going back several years should you wish to see them.'

'That would be wonderful,' Lottie gave Gwennie an impromptu hug. She had been wondering how to approach the reclusive old lady and now an opening had presented itself. 'Thank you so much.'

Gwennie was pink with pleasure. 'She said to give her a call anytime. She's always in.'

The tableau at The Crow's Nest was over now and the front door closed with a slam that bounced the brass dolphin knocker resonantly against its metal plate.

The ladies sighed their disappointment at not seeing what happened next but all three knew that

Dexter would soon enlighten them; Dexter Hardman loved gossip.

**

Lottie had learned in her previous life to strike whilst the iron was hot. Therefore when she saw Atlantis stagger from Nook Cottage she recognised this as the ideal time to approach Avril Major.

Rosemary Blundell's words at the Halloween party were bubbling to the surface of her brain. Rosemary was convinced that Avril Major of Nook Cottage wasn't the real Avril Major.

Lottie paused for a moment. She never went into an interview unless she had a firm grasp of what she wanted to find out. She already knew that Avril Major wasn't the real Avril Major because the real Avril Major was Jane Pendleton's mother and she was rotting away in prison under the name of Edna Derry.

The injustice of her situation made Lottie's indignation rise.

This Avril Major was Edna Derry's old cellmate. Lottie didn't need her to confirm this; at a stretch she could ask Marco Romero to track down the old cellmate but what would that achieve?

If this Avril Major did turn out to be some London brothel keeper who needed to change her identity, there was no way Lottie could prove that she had killed the other inmate and put the blame on Jane's mother. As she had already been released from prison, she wasn't in Whittington Edge hiding from the law. Marco would laugh in her face.

No, all the stuff about Jane's mother was off the table now. She needed to probe about the visit that Adelaide Barrett made to Nook Cottage. Rosemary had seen her walking up Avril's path. She hadn't seen her actually enter the cottage so she couldn't bank on that as a way to make Avril open up.

What she could talk about to Avril hit her with stunning clarity.

Mr Rogers.

Lottie watched the The Crow's Nest's closed door. Dexter and Beau would be inside for a little while getting Atlantis settled. She didn't want anyone to see her going to Nook Cottage. She decided against ringing Avril; if she gave her the chance to change her mind doubtless she would.

She watched Susan and Gwennie part at Matchbox Cottage and Gwennie continue on to Welham Lane.

When Gwennie was out of sight, she pulled on her coat and was about to hurry across to Nook Cottage when common sense hit. She would go to see Bella first. Lottie rang Bella Fleet and was delighted when she said to come over in fifteen minutes.

Lottie, with these few minutes to spare, used them to go through her notebook and consider the facts of the case as she knew them.

Jane and Charles Pendleton she had discounted almost immediately. Both were good, genuine people.

Susan and Gwennie and Blanche, ditto.

Avril Major was her favourite for the villain of the piece but Lottie's innate fairness made her realise that she was judging her on what she had done to Jane's mother. And also her odd behaviour and loose morals. Lottie was not proud of this and therefore was prepared to give Avril a lot of leeway.

Beau could never harm a hair on Adelaide Barrett's head so he was not a contender.

Dexter hadn't even visited Whittington Edge prior to Adelaide's body being found.

Who else was there?

She quickly jotted down the name of Rosemary Blundell, noted the information she had given and promptly removed her from the list of suspects. Although there was no better way of deflecting suspicion from oneself than by casting it onto another. She returned Rosemary Blundell to the suspect list for the time being.

Atlantis and Bill Warbeck were hardly contenders. She wasn't sure how long they had lived at Whittington Edge but Atlantis was surely unlikely to lead an unsuspecting woman to an isolated spot and kill her, especially if it turned out that Adelaide Barrett had been her mother. And Bill Warbeck was reputedly unable to see any woman over the age of twenty. He was a nasty little man but not, Lottie thought, in that way.

Cassie Mellon was not on her list. Cassie was so full of New Age goodness it was impossible to place her on the list at all.

Fanny Barstock. Mm... she was a possibility. But maybe that was Lottie's prejudice too.

The Myers were next on Lottie's list but she didn't know Gerald and she had nothing against him. Biddy, on the other hand, was driving out of The Glimpse at dead of night showing no lights. That was odd behaviour that had been noted despite the fact that Biddy was one of her best friends. Lottie sighed. Could she have knocked Mr Rogers down in her haste? Lottie's mind didn't want to go there. She puffed out a breath and added Biddy to the list.

It was with a heavy heart that she put the book back into her desk drawer. This time she did lock it away.

Lottie felt frustrated at every turn. She wanted to go to Nook Cottage and pummel Avril Major with questions. But she had no idea what she wanted to ask her about. Her neighbour was in no state to parry what Lottie was sure would be sharp decisive questions. But questions about what? What could she ask? What could Avril be tricked into revealing?

***

'Come up to my eyrie, Lottie,' a robust voice called. Lottie looked up the curved staircase and the slatternly Rachel shrugged and slouched back from whence she came dragging her broken down shoes across the black and white tiles with every step.

Bella Fleet sat at a small table by a window overlooking The Green in a redundant stretch of the landing corridor that led nowhere. On the table stood a small box and a tray of tea. Mrs Fleet had been ready for her. She smiled a bright-eyed smile and began pouring tea.

'Gwennie tells me you're interested in the history of Whittington Edge,' she said, 'and I think I have something that may appeal to you.'

Lottie accepted the proffered cup and saucer and gave Mrs Fleet her 'attentive' look.

'My grandson, Josh, lovely boy. He would do anything for me. Well, he decided that I needed an interest when my mobility started to become a real problem.

His answer was to buy me a camera. I can't tell you how long I spend by this window. I always have the camera to hand,' she patted the small camera on the table beside her. Lottie hadn't noticed it before.

'I started taking pictures of The Green at a certain time each day so that I could compare it as the seasons changed.' She pulled a face. 'It wasn't a bad idea but, apart from that horse chestnut tree, nothing much does change. 'So my next idea was to photograph the people going about their business but, as you know, few people walk around The Green. I have a picture of you on one of your early morning constitutionals and another of the rector's wife, but one picture really is enough.

But, if you would like to peruse them, you really are most welcome.'

'That's very kind of you,' Lottie thought that a few pictures of The Green would go a very long way.

'Perhaps you have some pictures of Horse and Trumpet Cottage when it was the old coaching inn?'

'There may well be one or two. It was closed some years before you bought it but I'm almost sure it was an inn at the time I began taking pictures.' She reached over and picked up the box, opening it and spreading pictures out on the table.

Soon, despite herself, Lottie was deeply engrossed in the photos. Bella Fleet pointed out various residents and had zoomed in on some of them, showing their faces so clearly that it was possible to see the ravages of time. Not for the first time, Lottie considered how cruel an art photography could be.

'Who is this?' she asked, handing over a snap of a young woman looking over her shoulder.

Bella Fleet took the photo and fumbled for the spectacles that hung around her neck. She shook them open and perched them on her nose. Then she craned her neck to peer through the lower half of the lenses.

'No idea,' she said at last, 'I think she was delivering leaflets.' She handed the picture back. 'When I got fed up with not seeing anyone different, I began watching – I have binoculars here too – and taking pictures only of people I'd never seen before. Here,' she began rummaging through the pile she had emptied onto the table. 'This is the first time I saw Charles Pendleton. Lovely picture isn't it? I think his goodness shines out of his face.'

Lottie took the picture and had to agree. 'You have a very good eye,' she said. Surreptitiously she turned the photo over and saw it was annotated with the date and time it was taken. She remarked on this to her hostess.

'Oh yes,' Mrs Fleet said, 'there's little point taking them unless you know when they were taken. If I know the person, you'll find their names on the backs too.'

Lottie continued to look and admire and interject the odd compliment but, inside she was thinking that she had to find a way to borrow all these snapshots and scrutinise them at her leisure. There must surely be more than this and if she could see Adelaide Barrett approaching Avril Major's house, she would be a step closer to solving the case. Maybe.

'Do you take photographs every day, Mrs Fleet?'

'Oh yes, every day.'

'Even on special occasions when everyone else is watching TV, such as the royal wedding day?'

'Of course. Do you want to see what I took when Prince William married that lovely Kate girl?' She closed her eyes and thought. 'That would be 29 April 2011. There's nothing wrong with my memory.'

'So I can see. I couldn't have told you the date.' Lottie smiled and watched the elderly hands turn over picture after picture until she pulled one from the heap.

'I sat here with my portable television,' Bella Fleet said. 'This was the only picture I took that day. Well, there are three, actually, but they are all of the same person. I was only just learning how to zoom in on the faces so it took some practice.'

Lottie's hand was shaking when she took the pictures from her. A tall figure in a red hat. Lottie's blood ran cold. That must surely be the same red hat.

She turned to the next picture and saw a smiling Rosemary Blundell talking to the woman. Then the woman again, looking out across The Green waiting for Avril Major to open her front door.

'You seem very interested in my small hobby, Lottie, would you like to browse through the pictures at your leisure?' Bella Fleet asked. 'If so, I could sort a couple of boxes out for next week.'

'I would love that,' Lottie said. 'But first, if you don't mind my dashing away, I would like to catch Avril Major whilst she is still under the influence.'

Bella Fleet laughed uproariously. 'Yes, you do that, Lottie, that woman isn't at all as she seems. I have a photo somewhere that I think is of Adelaide Barrett. I'll search it out for you. After I've watched you leave Nook Cottage.

The old woman's words sent a chill through Lottie but she turned and smiled at her. 'It seems we think alike, Bella,' she said. 'Please keep these photos safe. I'm sure the police will want to see them.

'And I will keep everything I find of Adelaide Barrett safe.' Bella said

To Lottie the woman's words sounded like a solemn vow. She hoped they were.

***

Avril opened the door. She looked bleary eyed. Lottie was glad. This mean that Avril had shared whatever she had given Atlantis to drink.

'I wondered if you could do my reading this afternoon.' Lottie injected so much brightness into her voice it was a wonder that this alone didn't dazzle Avril. 'Something has happened and I really do need some help.' Lottie banked on Avril not bothering to ask what was wrong and she was not disappointed.

'Come in, Mrs Colenso,' Avril said. 'I'll open a bottle of wine.'

The cards were already on the small table between two chairs in the living room of Nook Cottage. It looked as if Atlantis had also had a reading. They were neatly encased in a black silk scarf that Avril removed with due reverence before handing them over.

'Shuffle them for as long as you want and then put them down on the table using your left hand.' She ordered, groaning as she fell back into the chair and placed a careful hand over her closed eyes.

Lottie shuffled the cards and kept a wary eye on Avril. Her hostess was more than half drunk. Now they each had a huge glass of wine and time for investigation was running out. Especially as Avril picked up her glass and drained it.

She put the cards down on the table. Avril fanned them out face down. 'Pick out three cards to represent yourself.' She slurred. 'Use your left hand.'

Lottie, whose right hand was already reaching out, complied quickly, handing the cards to Avril.

'I wondered if you could find out anything Adelaide Barrett.' She said, inspiration suddenly descending and pushing all other thoughts aside. 'She was a friend of yours when you were children and I'm looking for answers.

Avril put down the three cards, picked up her wine glass, refilled it, and took a long drink that half emptied the glass. Lottie worried that Avril would keel over before she found anything out. 'She was no friend of mine.' She slid the cards apart and stared at them and then looked up at Lottie. She blinked hard to adjust her focus. 'I thought she could be the best friend I ever had,' she laughed, 'but it was all a mistake. Coming here was all a mistake.'

Lottie tried to read the cards. She could see 'Justice' printed on one but that was all she saw before Avril stacked them up again.

Lottie shrugged. 'I was told she was. She came over from the Far East. You knew her for a year when you were both nearly teenagers. Try to remember.'

'I thought it would be a laugh' Avril had finished her glass of wine now and her eyes were rolling. 'I chose the wrong name.'

Lottie thought it was worth taking a risk. 'She was seen visiting you.'

Avril's mind was doing drunken cartwheels. It was over. Someone had seen them together. Her voice emerged as a hoarse whisper that cracked into a cough. 'She shouldn't have come... shouldn't have come. Avril's brain was incapable of coherent thought. 'I'm sorry,' she tried to stand but her legs refused to cooperate. 'I can't do a reading at the moment. The spirits are unwilling to present themselves. Perhaps I could call you later in the week.'

'Of course,' Lottie leapt to her feet. She had certainly disconcerted her hostess. 'Don't bother to get up. I can see myself out. Thank you for the wine.' She hadn't touched the wine but she doubted if Avril would realise.

Before she left the stuffy room she turned and stared at Avril. Avril sensed that she was waiting and opened her eyes.

'I know that Adelaide Barrett came to visit you, Avril,' she said, 'I know that that was the last time she was seen alive. I shall be reporting this to the police. I'm sure they will want to talk to you because I think you killed her.'

Avril heard the front door latch click as Lottie Colenso left.

She saw her walk down the path and turn towards her own house. She was gone. Thank God. Then Avril turned over the cards again. Justice, the Magician and the Hierophant; Lottie Colenso was a dangerous woman. She was a danger to Avril, to Dolly Gumbrill. She pulled another card. The Tower. Lottie Colenso had come as a portent of her doom.

Lottie was shaking like a leaf. She waved to Bella Fleet to let her know she was out of Nook Cottage.

Avril was half stupefied with drink and that was the only thing that made Lottie feel safe. She may not remember Lottie's words. But Lottie felt sure that she would.

Somewhere in her drink-addled lizard brain Lottie's words would have lodged and soon they would emerge and Avril would recall them and Lottie would be in danger.

How could she have been so stupid? She had to get away. But first she must tell Marco what she had found out.

***

Charles Pendleton was aware that his Lord moved in mysterious ways but he wasn't averse to giving out the odd hint or two to help the Almighty know in which direction he wanted Him to move.

That being the case, as soon as he was sure that Jane was in a deep sleep he rose from their bed and crept down to his study.

He consulted the fancy pen holder that Jane had given him for his last birthday. Amongst other things it displayed the time in various cities around the world.

Then he waited.

He did a little more work on his sermon for his first Sunday back at the helm of St Jude's and read a chapter of his library book.

Then he checked the time again, lifted the telephone and dialled the number that would connect him to the home of his father in law. That gentleman was about to find that his placid son in law was capable of great wrath.

CHAPTER EIGHTEEN

Avril Major was probably the last person around The Green to learn of the death of Mr Monday. She hadn't attended the Halloween party and, as Lottie was the only person who knew of her association with him, no one immediately thought of her when the news broke.

Atlantis, who visited on Sunday, hadn't known about it and, even if she had, there was too much on her mind for her to mention it and that was without factoring in the mother and father of all hangovers.

Mrs Bettinson, who prided herself on keeping herself to herself, had told four people between leaving her cottage and arriving at the rectory where she proceeded to regale Jane Pendleton with all the gory details of the accident whilst Jane made them both a cup of tea prior to Mrs Bettinson starting work.

Jane was shocked and knew that she had to tell Charles about it as soon as she could but didn't want to prevent the cleaning lady talking; she too would have been upset and talking about things would help her so Jane sat down and listened.

Thus it was that she also heard about Bill Warbeck and the purple lady. She also heard about the witches' conga although she had seen that for herself from her bedroom window. She had smiled when she saw the fun the villagers were having and wished she had tried harder to persuade Charles to attend the party. He had declined to go in case his presence put a damper on the jollifications.

She hadn't seen Atlantis slam the door of The Crow's Nest in her husband's face. And she was glad of that because if she had she would have felt obliged to rescue Bill Warbeck from a night freezing on a bench and the thought of him occupying the rectory's guest room wasn't an appealing one.

When Mrs Bettinson was all talked out, Jane ventured into Charles' study where he was working on his sermon for the next Sunday.

He liked to start early, getting the scaffolding of his piece in place, as he called it, so that he could spend the next couple of days letting it work quietly at the back of his mind ready for a final polishing on Friday.

He found that some new and interesting ideas would filter up through his consciousness in that way.

She knocked on the door warily; she knew that Charles had left their bed in the early hours and had not returned until a lot later and she was worried that his kindness when she told him about her mother may have soured now that he had had time to consider the implications.

'Come in, my darling.' Charles beamed at her when she tentatively poked her head round the door.

'I'm afraid I'm the bearer of bad news.' She said.

The smile dropped from her husband's face and he rose to his feet and hurried to her side. What now? What further torments could be visiting themselves on his lovely, young wife?

His conversation with her father had gone better than he expected but he sensed that his own anger had been instrumental in piercing the armour of Papa Montrose's stuffed shirt.   He and Charles had attended the same public school and had been good friends whilst they were there but Charles had never learned to assume the arrogance that was the birthright of the Montrose clan and which rubbed off on all the other pupils.

Peregrine, being a Montrose, was used to everyone, barring royalty, taking their lead from him and changing any independent views they may have to coincide with his own.

Charles had always fallen in with his plans even to the extent of accepting Jane as his ward when her continued presence in the Far East proved to be an embarrassment.

Her father had been outraged when Jane declared her intention of marrying his old school friend but there was little he could do about it without inconveniencing himself and so he had given his permission.

When Charles had telephoned and ruined his day by berating him for failing to take care of his wife, Peregrine Montrose had been stunned. His clever mind ran quickly through his options as Charles spoke and he realised that he had no choice but to put diplomatic wheels into operation.

Jane's mother was not actually a British citizen. He had kept this fact secret in order to gain family approval of their marriage. He was sure that her shoplifting would therefore have been covered by diplomatic immunity. What could be done about the other matter he didn't know, but he was certain that something would turn up; for a Montrose, something always turned up.

If anyone had connections it was the Montrose family and he had no doubt that with a judicious pulling of strings he could secure her release. He would have to take her straight from the prison back to his home where he could quietly divorce her and return her to her family. It was certain that the powers that would help him would also insist that she be removed from the country before the newspapers caught onto the story.

Yes, he would begin calling in favours right away.

By the time Charles Pendleton replaced the receiver his old friend and father in law had a plan of campaign mapped out.

Now Charles looked at Jane's troubled face and wondered what fresh hell had opened its jaws to them. His thoughts were racing and he saw her realise this.

'It's nothing to do with my problem.' She said, rushing towards him. 'It's parish business.'

Charles sighed with relief. Then he berated himself. How could he take comfort from the fact that someone else was in trouble? Yet, wasn't that a frailty inbuilt in man by the Lord?

Everything was so difficult.

'Poor Mr Rogers was killed in a hit and run accident on his way home on Saturday night.' She said.

And Charles, to his eternal shame, sighed with relief.

***

Lottie had slept well and awoke on Monday to a bright and chilly morning. She was startled to realise that she had accused Avril Major of murder. Where did the courage, or madness, come from for her to do so reckless a thing?

Surely Avril couldn't have remembered. Avril was so far in the bag that it would be a miracle if she could see daylight. But just to be sure, Lottie braced herself to dial Nook Cottage and sound her out.

Avril picked up on the first ring, seemingly unaffected by yesterday's excesses.

'Hello, Mrs Major. It's Lottie Colenso here. I wondered if you would be able to do a tarot reading for me this afternoon? Lottie bit her lips together and crossed her fingers.

'Let me consult my diary, Mrs Colenso... sorry, today's out.

I can fit you in later on tomorrow. Would five thirty suit you?'

'That would be perfect. I'll see you then.' Lottie cut the call and slumped against the wall. She was safe. Phew. What a crazy thing to do. And what luck to escape unscathed. This tarot reading had been cancelled so many times that Lottie was beginning to look forward to seeing what the cards foretold for her.

***

The cursory cleaning at the rectory was completed in record time and soon Mrs. Bettinson was on her way to Nook Cottage to disseminate the news further.

En route she ran into Rachel, that slatternly girl who did all the rough cleaning work that Mrs Bettinson no longer undertook. She also looked after Mrs Fleet, though what that poor lady had done to deserve Rachel was beyond Mrs. Bettinson's understanding.

The older woman passed the word to Rachel who carried it with her to her next job whilst entrusting Mrs Bettinson with the news that Arnold Pickard had failed to return home after the Halloween party and his wife was wondering whether to report him missing.

'She'd be putting the bunting out if he didn't come back.' Mrs Bettinson said and both women, in rare agreement, went their separate ways still laughing at this slight on the churchwarden's wife.

Unfortunately Mrs Bettinson encountered no other neighbours during her short walk and was disgruntled by the fact that Rachel would have the kudos of spreading gossip that by rights was hers. Stumping up the path to Nook Cottage Mrs Bettinson silently berated herself for telling the grisly news to a person so well positioned to steal her thunder. She should have kept it to herself.

Then she could have told people individually.

Now that Rachel knew, people would be parroting the message back at her the next time she went shopping.

Avril Major was therefore likely to be the only person the old cleaning woman would have the chance to tell and she intended to make the most of it. If there was any way she could cancel her visit to Avril, she would have done so. Then she could dash down to Main Street and start spreading the word.

***

Lottie arrived home after an early morning trip to Lyeminster with Dexter and Susan to view 'Summer'.

They had all been stunned by the beauty of the picture.

'Who would have thought that nasty little Bill Warbeck could paint like that?' Susan said.

This echoed the views of both her companions who gazed slack-jawed at the flame hair and the alabaster skin of Bill's model.

'Quite, quite beautiful.' Said another voice close behind them. They all turned to see Beau Derek staring at 'Summer' with rapt attention.

'Thinking of buying her, Beau?' Dexter grinned. 'Indeed I am, dear boy. Indeed I am.' Beau said without taking his eyes from the picture. 'She has a look of my dear Adelaide.'

Lottie had put in a call to Marco on the way home and she reached Horse and Trumpet Cottage just before him.

Avril saw the blue car drift slowly around into Church Lane and her heart flipped over. Not more about that dratted Adelaide Barrett, surely. Considering that the woman had barely made a ripple on the consciousness of anyone in Whittington Edge all the time she lived there, she was certainly making up for it now. Honestly, why couldn't they declare it a natural death and let the poor thing be buried decently? It wasn't as if they were going to solve a great crime; no one had even noticed that she had gone missing until Lottie Colenso found her body.

The minute she saw Lottie Colenso, Avril knew she was going to be trouble.

The car door opened and the tall, handsome detective who visited Lottie Colenso emerged. That was odd. Why was this gorgeous man constantly on Lottie Colenso's doorstep? Did they think that she had killed Adelaide Barrett? Possibly. The person to find the body was often the prime suspect. Avril gave a throaty laugh that turned into a cough. Wouldn't that be a turn up for the book?

Mrs high and mighty Lottie Colenso being led away in handcuffs? She sighed. Nice thought but not likely to happen; Lottie Colenso had the look of the boringly upright citizen.

Still, she had spent enough time and thought on Adelaide Barrett so Avril repaired to her kitchen to warm up her croissant and make coffee. She had been expecting a call from Mr Monday. He had taken to asking for extra sessions recently and she thought he may do so again today. Maybe his dreadful wife had returned home early. Why so henpecked a man would actually pay for...oh well there was no accounting for taste

***

'Bin another murder.' Mrs Bettinson grunted as Avril opened the door to her.

'I'm sorry?'

'There's bin another murder.' Mrs Bettinson crashed the vacuum cleaner into the cupboard door. 'First that poor lady on the roundabout, now silly old Bob Rogers, God rest his soul. I don't know what this village is coming to. Really, I don't.'

'Bob – Mr Rogers is dead?' Avril's pale face paled even further. Mr Monday was dead? No wonder she hadn't heard from him. 'How terrible. I had no idea. I didn't go out yesterday so no one told me about it.

'And the churchwarden's missin'. He never went home Sat'day night. His wife wasn't too worried cos he's been keeping some very peculiar hours. He's a very peculiar man if you ask me, but we mustn't speak ill just in case.'

As she spoke, Mrs Bettinson, eager to finish at Nook Cottage so that she could take up her rightful post as gossip-in-chief before Rachel spoiled the tasty morsel of news by blurting it out any old how, was pulling the vacuum cleaner into the middle of the room and Avril was thinking. Fast.

This had the fingerprints of Sonny Gumbrill all over it. He was working his way through her list of clients. Mr Monday was dead. The poor man. He was a fool but he was harmless enough. Ok, so he irritated her but Sonny had no right to have him killed.

She would take bets that Arnold Pickard was dead too. This thought brought her up short. Arnold Pickard was a loathsome individual but he didn't deserve to die for his pomposity and cunning. This reeked of Sonny. She also knew that with Mr Monday and Mr Tuesday dead, Mr Wednesday, Monty, was next.

'I'm sorry, Mrs Bettinson, this news has upset me. Do you think we could rearrange your visit for later in the week?'

Expecting some protest, Avril pulled out a couple of banknotes from one of her purses and held them out as compensation. Mrs Bettinson had already unplugged the vacuum cleaner, wound up its cable and stowed it back under the stairs and she was ready to go.

She decided that her first port of call would be The Priest at Prayer; there would be a small knot of villagers there ready for anything to enliven their drinking hours. Then she would hurry to the Butterfly Bush where amongst the scones and flapjacks she could hold court. With the Butterfly Bush, being a new business, Blanche Tallentire would be glad of her bringing in more custom. She may even provide a complimentary pot of tea.

In Camp Hill the blackmailer also heard of the death. Terror rose in him. Enough terror to make him forget all about blackmail.

He would apply for a student loan like everyone else. What if the police found his letter? Will Flint, master of an Oxford college, began to fade away before his eyes. Jason felt sick.

Avril all but pushed her elderly cleaning lady out of the door. Luckily the woman seemed keen to leave. Never one to face the day without full war paint, Avril had already made up her face and was wearing a very smart suit. She touched up her lipstick and left the house immediately. She was carrying her carpet bag. She had to stop this thing before Monty became the next victim.

***

'Are you going shopping this morning?' Charles asked when he and Jane had comforted one another and spent a few minutes in quiet prayer and reflection.

'Yes. Is there anything you particularly want me to pick up?'

'No. I was thinking I'd go down to the church and say a few words to our Lord about Mr Rogers and your mother. Also, I think, I shall pray for the Warbecks. I know their problems fade into insignificance in the light of a death in the village but they are still very real to them.'

'I could come with you if you like.' Jane offered. 'Isn't there a verse in the bible about two being gathered together?'

'There is, my dear, Matthew chapter 18 verse 20 "For where two or three are gathered together in my name, there am I in the midst of them." It would be lovely to have you there by my side.'

'Then we will go together.' Jane hugged her husband. He wasn't going to cast her off as she feared. She worried that he had undergone one of those dark nights of the soul, but, if he had, something good must have come out of it because, as far as she could see, darling Charles was still the same.

***

'Do you have time for coffee or are you urgently required elsewhere?'

'Coffee. Definitely coffee.' Marco dropped into a chair and set out his belongings in a neat row. 'We now have a statement from Rosemary Blundell, thanks to you. She did telephone as you asked her to so your cover hasn't been blown.'

'Does it help?'

'In as much as it points the finger at Avril Major, yes. As regards anything approaching evidence...' Marco blew out a loud breath.

'You need to visit Bella Fleet at Templar House. I saw her yesterday. She takes photos of The Green and has a set of three of a woman in a red hat standing at the door of Nook Cottage on the day of the royal wedding in 2011. I'm sure it's the same hat, Marco.'

'I'll go as soon as I've finished my coffee,' Marco said. 'I don't know why I bother investigating. All the leads are coming from you.'

'Tell me about Bob Rogers.' Lottie said. 'Gwennie told Susan and me about it. She said that someone stole a fast car from Lyeminster and mowed the poor man down on the lane outside his farm.'

'That's the idea so far.'

'She said that he couldn't get out of the way or he didn't see the car coming because he was carrying a board with a witch painted on it that he had made for the Halloween party in the church hall across the road here.

'Apparently the car hit him and sent him flying up into the air. He landed hitting his head on the millstone that marks the entrance to the farm.'

'Do you have a problem with that?'

'Yes. I don't understand why a car being stolen from Lyeminster would be driving down the lane for a start. Why not go on the bypass and get to the motorway as soon as possible?'

'Maybe the thief knows the area and wanted to keep off the major roads until he was clear of the immediate vicinity.'

'True. It's not connected to the other body, is it?'

'It would be hard to see how.' Marco looked up to thank her when the cafetiere was placed in front of him. He caught a movement going past the Church Lane door and craned his neck to see who it was when the passers-by walked in view of the kitchen window. 'The rector and his child bride are going to church together.' He said.

Lottie glanced round. 'They do look an incongruous pair, I'll give you that.' She said. 'But they are a truly devoted couple. It's lovely to see.' She turned to the window and watched as the Pendletons parted at the church door. Charles opened the huge old door and stepped inside and Jane stood beside the notice board in the porch rearranging the notices and presumably removing the ones that were out of date.

She folded a couple of sheets up and put them in her bag. Then her head snapped around and she darted into the church only to be thrust back out again by the rector.

'Something must be wrong.' Lottie said. 'Charles has just given Jane such a shove it's amazing she's still upright. She stumbled and only the settle in the porch saved her.'

Marco was on his feet in less than a second. He had worked the domestic violence unit in his time and had a deeply ingrained aversion to men who hurt women.

Lottie was hot on his heels she knew there would be a good explanation for Charles' behaviour and she didn't want him to fall foul of Marco.

When she reached the Church Lane path Marco was up at the church and Jane was running towards her. Lottie ushered Jane into Horse and Trumpet Cottage and went to see what was wrong with Charles.

Marco had shouted a warning as he ran but Charles had dropped onto the settle in the porch and gave no indication that he was about to resume the assault on his wife. The detective sat beside him. That was when he saw a streak of blood on his face.

'Want to tell me about it?' He kept one hand near enough to the rector to be able to grab and detain him should the need arise. He was scanning the man's face. He didn't appear to be on the verge of some terrible impulse.

'You seem to be bleeding.' He said as he looked for an injury. When Charles failed to respond he looked up at Lottie who was hurrying to join them.

'I caught my face on the door when I stumbled.' Charles whispered. 'Please look after my wife.'

'She's in my kitchen.' Lottie told him.

'Don't let her come back here.'

Lottie met Marco's eyes over Charles Pendleton's head. Marco shot a look at the smear of blood on the rector's face and Lottie stooped down in front of him.

'Charles, if you have hurt yourself you must come to my house and allow me to clean you up.'

'It's the churchwarden.' Charles looked at the oak door and shuddered. He had pulled the door closed behind him. He would have slammed it had he the strength.

Marco stood and rested a hand on the big black ring that was the handle.

'It's horrible.' Tears began to run down Charles' face. 'I know you're used to this sort of thing, officer, but it truly is horrible. I couldn't allow my poor Jane to see anything like that. Tell her I'm sorry I pushed her away. That was an unforgiveable thing to do. Please make sure my darling Jane is alright.'

A few minutes later Marco decided that pushing his wife away was the kindest thing Charles Pendleton could have done.

The churchwarden was lying on the altar steps. He had been decapitated by the massive cross that had apparently fallen from the chains that had held it in place for years and it had landed right across his neck. There was blood everywhere. And there was no point approaching the body to check for signs of life because his head was looking back down the aisle from where it lay sideways on the ground several inches away from its shoulders.

Marco Romero went to pull out his mobile phone but he had left it on Lottie's kitchen table. He went back to the porch and closed the door.

'Make sure no one goes inside.' He ordered Lottie drawing her out of earshot of the rector. 'I need to call up the troops. Crime scene. The rector said something about the churchwarden. I think that must be him inside. Whoever it is, they're dead. Very dead.' He grimaced and then he was gone.

Lottie was wishing that she had asked him to bring her mobile so that she could call up Susan and ask her to look after Jane but the phone was beside her bed and Marco Romero was in too much of a hurry to go looking for it.

The rapid tapping of heels on stone sounded familiar and Lottie saw that it was Susan coming from Main Street with her shopping basket over her arm.

Susan approached, saw the rector and looked enquiringly at her friend.

'Could you do me a favour?' Lottie asked. She kept her voice light and gave Susan a hard look that she hoped would be interpreted as a signal not to ask questions.

'Of course.' Susan's eyes flicked to the rector again. 'I'd just made coffee for Marco when we had to leave it. Jane is in my kitchen. Do you think you could go and look after her for a while? Something terrible has happened.'

'Of course,' Susan said again. She hurried away and Lottie watched with relief as she let herself into the Church Lane door to Horse and Trumpet Cottage.

Marco soon returned.

Lottie stayed at the church until a ribbon of police vehicles wound into Whittington Edge. They parked in Church Lane and on Main Street effectively blocking St Jude's off from the rest of the village. Blue and white tape was strung across the entrance to St Jude's Open at both ends and a uniformed constable came along to shoo Lottie away.

'I'm glad you're here constable.' Lottie said. She had recognised the man's mission and refused to be dismissed like a nosy neighbour. 'This is the reverend Charles Pendleton. He is our rector and has made an upsetting discovery in the church. Detective Sergeant Romero is in the church securing the scene and checking the building out.

'He asked me to take care of the rector until he returned but now you're here I'll leave you to it.' She turned and put a hand on Charles' shoulder. 'This officer will take care of things from here, Charles,' she said, 'I shall return to Horse and Trumpet Cottage and look after Jane.'

'Not so fast, madam.' The constable took out his notebook.

'Detective Sergeant Romero has all my details.' Lottie said. 'And he knows where to find me. I know I can trust you not to allow the rector to re-enter the church. And not to enter it yourself, of course, as it's a crime scene.' And with that she hurried back to her kitchen where Jane Pendleton sat drinking tea with Susan Holland.

Jane looked up. She was puzzled, that much was easy to see, and Lottie realised that Jane had no idea why Charles had acted so unexpectedly.

'How's Charles?' she asked when Lottie went to the kettle to make fresh tea. Jane was trembling with fear. Had the Lord suddenly told Charles to cast off his wife?

'He sends his apologies.' Lottie smiled. 'He'll probably be quite a while. He's with the police.' Lottie saw that Jane was about to protest as she would; after all the police intervention at the scene was due to Marco thinking she was at risk from Charles. 'He found a body in the church, Jane. That's why he was so determined that you shouldn't enter. That's why he pushed you out of the way. The poor man was in shock. Is in shock, I should say. I've told him that you can stay here with us until he is ready to go home.'

'A body?' Jane's face whitened. 'What on earth is happening in Whittington Edge? First you find the poor woman on the roundabout. Then Mr. Rogers...' her voice trailed away. She looked around the kitchen as if a sane reason could be found if only she looked hard enough. 'Who is it?' She asked at last. 'Do we know the person?'

'It's too early to say.' Lottie said, skilfully dodging the issue.

***

Sonny was surprised to be told that his Aunt Minnie was at the door and demanding admittance. Avril, for her part, was pleased that the burly doorman who had been in Sonny's employ since he was in short trousers, failed to recognise her.

He had sent word to his boss and given a jerk of the head in the direction of the club where young women would be lavishing attention on Sonny's clientele. It was all Avril could do not to laugh out loud.

Thus it was that when Avril was led through the club by the deferential doorman, gentle classical music wafted over the speakers and there were no young girls in view whatsoever.

Would that it were so when she reached Sonny's inner sanctum. Her escort tapped on the door and opened it. An overblown floozy was wrapped around her boss.

Avril's professional eye noted the excessive lipstick and the heavy foundation that was beginning to crack with the eager smiles that were being lavished on Sonny.

Less is more Avril muttered under her breath. She had told her own girls this a thousand times. Her own girls had always looked classy. This trollop looked cheap, common, nasty and...and old.

Still, it wasn't the fault of the girl. Sonny hired them and this one would soon be fired. Sonny didn't like old meat; it made him realise how old he was himself.

He pretended to be taken unawares when Aunt Minnie stepped over the threshold and he pushed his chair back, pulling his feet off his desk and sitting upright. The girl stroked Sonny but simpered at Avril. She was trying to show her importance to the big man. Avril almost laughed out loud.

'Off you go, darlin', ' Sonny slapped her playfully on the backside. 'I've got company.'

Avril saw the quiver of badly toned flesh and turned her head away. So the playacting wasn't only on the girl's side. This was another of Sonny's ploys to get her back. He thought he could make her jealous.

Avril fixed the girl with her basilisk gaze and watched her walk around the desk. The girl swayed her hips defiantly but, as soon as she passed the point where Avril was standing, she almost broke into a run. Avril allowed herself a smile and turned her attention to Sonny.

Sonny sat up even straighter.

'Good to see you, Doll.' He said. He cleared his throat and rearranged some papers on his desk. 'An unexpected pleasure. We don't often see you in the Smoke these days.'

Avril watched, waited until his hands stilled and then she glared at him.

'What do you think you're doing, Sonny?' she demanded.

'Don't know what you mean, Doll.'

She let that hang in the air until it became too uncomfortable to bear. Then she leaned forward, fists on his desk, getting right into his face.

'You stop it, Sonny Gumbrill, you hear me? I know exactly what you've done and it stops here.

'The farmer was harmless enough. All he had was his life and you deprived him of that, you bastard.

'And the churchwarden – ok he was a pain but even so...' Avril was surprised to feel the sting of tears prickling her eyes.

She had convinced herself that Arnold Pickard was dead and that could only be bad for Monty. And Sonny hadn't denied it, had he?

She turned away from Sonny and pretended interest in his CCTV monitors which gave views of the club now alive with 'lovelies' and the alleyway outside with its dumpsters and pot holes full of dirty water. This was Sonny's only early warning system should the police decide to descend on his place of business.

She concentrated on the view of the alley a moment too long; long enough to get her point across.

Sonny was no fool. He wasn't a clever man or he wouldn't have allowed her to be dragged into his trouble, but he was a crafty one.

'I gave up a lot for you, Sonny. And I've continued to help you and keep your secrets. This is my business and I'll thank you to keep out of it.

''Alright, Doll. You're right. I'll call Ronnie back to the Smoke.'

So it had been Ronnie. She should have known.

'And don't send anyone else.'

'No, love, no one else.'

Avril pulled on her gloves and prepared to leave. 'And tell him to stop spying on my house.'

'Consider it done.' Sonny was in conciliatory mode now. 'If you're not in a rush I could take you out to dinner.' Sonny gave her his best smile. Then his eyes ran over her Aunt Minnie outfit and he winced. 'Did you have to come dressed like that?'

'My other stuff's in the left luggage at the station.' She said. 'I can change. She was angry with Sonny but she couldn't afford to upset him too much; Sonny was a nasty man with a nasty line in retribution for anyone who upset him too much.

Now she had made her point she had to soothe him down and a meal at a nice restaurant would be just the thing to restore the status quo.

It was Monday. She was in no rush to return home now, not now that Mr Monday's regular appointment had been permanently cancelled.

Home. Whittington Edge was her home now. This was why she had been so angry with Sonny. She thought of Whittington Edge as home and she wanted nothing to upset her applecart.

But, no, she was in no rush to get back. It had been such a joy to step onto the train after so many times of visiting the station just to collect Sonny's waifs and strays. And she was here, back in the place that she had always thought of as home and it wasn't home any longer. She was a visitor.

It was early evening when Sonny put her on the train back to Lyeminster. He had tried hard to get her to agree to them living together again. She had been tempted; Sonny had always been a temptation. Not a good thing for her but a temptation nonetheless.

It would have been easy to give in; to go back to the lovely house they had in London. To familiarise herself again with the things that she had painstakingly selected and arranged only to lose it all when that cowardly little copper fitted her up.

They stood on the platform. Sonny tilted his head to one side and gave her a rueful smile.

'I can't get you to change your mind, can I?' he said.

'No, Sonny, you can't. You know it would be suicide for me to come back here. You've got that copper enjoying a stretch and that's good. But he'll have friends and one of them will come after me if he knows I've set foot on his turf.'

'You're right, Doll. You're right.' Sonny sighed. 'We should have stayed in Spain. I should have listened to you. You were right and I was wrong. What can I say?'

The train whistled. Avril stepped aboard carrying Aunt Minnie's carpet bag. The guard marched down the platform slamming doors then the train lurched and began to roll out of the station.

Sonny waved. Avril waved. The train took the curve out of the station and the evening sun caught the rails making dazzling curves leading back to Lyeminster. Then she was gone.

As the train disappeared from view, Sonny allowed his expression to change. He pulled out his mobile phone and punched in a number.

'Ok, Ronnie,' he said. 'You do the butcher and then you come home.'

Sonny had always been good at recognising and eliminating risks.

CHAPTER NINETEEN

Tuesday morning was enlivened by Jonas Milton's honeyed tones on the telephone; just what Lottie needed to get her head together. She hadn't slept well with thoughts of Avril Major running through her head. What if Avril remembered Lottie accusing her of murdering Adelaide Barrett and had agreed to read the tarot for her in order to do away with her too.

'Lottie, darling,' he said. 'I have to go to Aberystwyth to give a couple of lectures this week. I have a cottage not too far from there and I wondered if you would like to join me. I thought we could stretch it out to the weekend. I have an appointment back in Lyeminster on Saturday night but then we could go back for a further few days if you like.

Lottie thought it was a marvellous idea and told him so with more enthusiasm than he had expected. Jonas was pleased. Usually Lottie played things very cool and he was ready to move on from there.

She was busily sorting out which clothes she would take with her when she thought of Susan and picked up the phone beside her bed.

'Jonas has invited me to Wales for a few days.' She said. 'I shall still be able to go to Gwennie's firework party on Camp Hill because we will be back for Saturday night but then we may return to his cottage for a few days after that.

'Good for you.' Susan said. 'It will be good to get away from Whittington Edge before any more bodies start piling up. I hope Jonas intends staying at Horse and Trumpet Cottage on Saturday night?'

'I hope so too.' Lottie said, and she meant it.

This short conversation left Lottie feeling guilty. She was leaving Susan alone when there could be a maniac on the loose. She rang the old rectory and told Dexter of her decision to go away. She hoped he would take the hint and remove Susan from the carnage too. After all, he didn't seem to have any obligations.

When Susan called her back only a few minutes later to say that Dexter had called her out of the blue and invited her to join him on a city break to Barcelona, Lottie smiled and began packing in earnest. Susan had been talking about a book she had read recently about a man who lived in a tower in Barcelona. Dexter was obviously a man who listened, a rare creature indeed.

Marco arrived at her door during the morning to see if Charles or Jane Pendleton had said anything to her to after the discovery of the churchwarden's body.

'There is something I should tell you.' Lottie said after she had confirmed that the only conversation the Pendletons had been capable of was expressions of shock and fruitless speculation on who could possibly be laying waste to the men of Whittington Edge.

She knew she had to come clean about her other thoughts before she left for Wales. She gathered together the makings for the coffee and tried to find a way to broach the subject.

'What is it, Lottie?' Marco asked.

She allowed her shoulders to sag. Marco knew her so well.

There had never been any way of hiding anything from him.

'You asked me to look out for someone who wasn't what they seemed.' She began. 'Are you ready to tell me now who struck a discordant note with you?'

Marco looked wary for few seconds and she saw the precise moment when he decided to trust her.

'Jane Pendleton.' He said. 'Apart from the discrepancies in their ages, I felt that she was holding something back.'

'Jane Pendleton?' Lottie was stunned. 'But Jane is an absolute darling.'

A darling with a secret.

'I may be wrong.' He conceded. 'What about you?'
'My choice is Avril Major.' She said.

Marco frowned. 'The weird old bird at Nook Cottage?'

'She has gentleman callers.' Lottie raised her eyebrows and watched as the meaning of her words reached him.

'That's hardly a crime.' Marco said, 'even if it is a gruesome thought.'

'And two of them are now dead.' Lottie added.

Marco was pouring coffee into both their mugs and almost spilled it onto the table.

'Bob Rogers used to call on Mondays and Arnold Pickard on Tuesdays.' she said.

'Who is her Wednesday caller? I'm assuming she has a Wednesday caller?'

'He's a big florid man but I'm not sure who he is. I'm pretty sure that he isn't from the village. I wish I knew who he was, it's niggling at the back of my mind. I feel as if I've seen him but the view I get of Nook Cottage isn't all that good and he always arrives after dark. I may be confusing him with a butcher I've seen in Lyeminster, I can't be sure. Just in case, the butcher is Montague Flaxton. His shop is on The Approach between the market and Market Street.'

'I'll go and see her now.' Marco was on his feet. 'This man may well be the next victim. And it's possible that the man you've seen loitering under the tree is the killer.'

'Ronnie.' Lottie hurried after him towards the door. 'The man under the tree, I mean.'

'Oh yes, Ronnie. I'll ask her about him too.'

'I'm sorry I can't tell you more.'

'Don't worry. You've done well.'

'I have a confession to make before you leave,' she eyed Marco cautiously.

'Oh yes,' he waited.

'I accused Avril of murdering Adelaide Barrett.' She saw the alarm on his face and hurried on. 'She was drunk and may not remember.'

'And if she does?'

'If she does I could be in big trouble. Fortunately I've been invited to go away with a friend until Friday. I could kick myself for being so stupid.'

'Tell me where you're going and I'll tell you when you can return.' Marco was eager to go.

***

By the time Marco was knocking on her front door Avril was in Woolstock. She was on a mission and she had planned it like a military campaign.

Lottie Colenso had told her that Ronnie had been watching her. She knew from Sonny that Ronnie had killed two of her clients. She knew that Ronnie had visited Whittington Edge twice and was now sure that he broke into Nook Cottage whilst Sonny had her putting Arthur on the train. Sonny was a bastard. She hated him at this moment.

Her sleepless night had resulted in the decision that she had to cut all ties with Sonny even though it would be like cutting out her own heart. He would never allow her to live peacefully in Whittington Edge.

He would always be there, watching her, sending his goons to spy on her and report back, and, if she ever met anyone, Sonny would ruin it for her as she now saw he had ruined everything else in her life.

It was a hard decision but Sonny had to go.

She had rejected Mr Slippitt as her pension now too. The thought of antimacassars and doilies and that terrible smell of mothballs that enveloped him had made her realise that she couldn't spend the next twenty odd years in his company no matter how much money he was reputed to have.

Avril wanted Monty. He was bluff and ebullient and rather too loud. But he brought the fun Avril needed. She had visions of sitting with Monty either side of a blazing fire, enjoying a drink and laughing uproariously as they did every Wednesday night.

He may have a wife.

Avril chose not to allow that to get in the way of her plans.

They all had wives. She would find a way round it. Didn't she always find a way round everything? Hadn't she dispensed with Adelaide Barrett when she appeared out of the blue and threatened her new life? Standing there on her doorstep and denouncing her for not being the Avril Major she remembered.

It had been a joke to take silly Avril Major's name. Just a joke. It should never have backfired.

Why couldn't Adelaide Barrett just leave instead of making a fuss? It was so unnecessary. Stupid woman. Maybe she should do something similar with Sonny but no, she could never hurt Sonny even though he never stopped hurting her.

She sighed, cleared her mind of Sonny and looked Monty up in the telephone directory wondering why she had never before bothered to find out where he lived. Marina Gardens, Woolstock. Mm... Now where was that? She pulled a street map out of a drawer and failed to find it. Next stop, Google.

Marina Gardens proved to be a horseshoe of houses at least a mile away from Woolstock Marina. Google Streetview did not extend to Woolstock yet so she had no way of seeing what the houses were like but they were on very large plots so Avril's hopes began to rise.

She dressed in an expensive cream wool suit with an emerald green silk shirt. Her makeup was flawless as usual and, slipping her feet into black patent leather court shoes and her hands into black kid gloves, she knew that she wouldn't look out of place anywhere.

This was important because Avril had made her plan. She carried a large black bag. It had to be large because Avril was going prepared.

She caught the early bus from Whittington Edge and in Woolstock inspected the timetables that were displayed in frames on the bus station walls. It was important to her plan that she shouldn't do anything to make herself noticeable. She purposely waited at the wrong bus stand so that the CCTV wouldn't pick her up so easily.

When the bus for Marina Gardens pulled in, she darted across the road using the bus as cover and paid her fare in exact change.

Alighting a couple of stops past her destination, Avril continued walking in the same direction as the bus until it was out of sight. Then she turned and walked back towards her objective. So intent was she on her task that she failed to notice that she was being followed.

She heard a mobile phone ring and turned to see a boy, wearing a padded jacket and a woolly hat, cover one ear and turn away from the traffic the better to hear. Avril walked on.

***

The boy with the mobile phone was, in fact, Jane Pendleton. Driven to distraction by the plight of her mother, knowing she could do nothing to help her, yet having to do something, Jane had set out with murder in mind. She was following Avril Major and, come what may, regardless of the consequences; she was going to kill her. And then her phone had rung.

'Hello darling, good news.'

'Charles?'

'Yes, where are you?'

'Er...I'm out shopping. Why?'

'Your father's here and he wants to see you.'

'Where? Whittington Edge?'

'No. London. Hurry home my darling.'

***

'I'm sorry,' Lottie raised her voice and hurried around Horse and Trumpet Cottage seeking a better signal. 'You're where?'

'In Woolstock. Charles has just phoned me and I can't tell him where I am. Can you come and pick me up?'

624

'You don't have your car?'

'I came on the bus. It's a long story.'

Lottie realised she was wasting time and should be on her way, not quizzing Jane Pendleton at this particular moment. She noted Jane's location and promised that she would be there as soon as possible.

**

Marina Gardens was a sight to behold. The houses were huge; the gardens so large and long that the pillars and porches were often hidden behind trees. Yes, this would do very well indeed, if Monty really lived here.

The first house she passed was called Two Acres. How ostentatious.

The only sound in Marina Gardens was the steady tap-tap of her shoes on the pavement. Further along an electric gate clanged shut and a smart little car swept past her. She was glad she had dressed up. No one seeing her would think her out of place and remember her.

With each house she passed, Avril wondered if she had the right address. These really were very grand houses. Did a butcher make this sort of money? And, if so, why had she made do with gifts of meat instead of hard cash? Still, this wasn't the time to worry about that because she was about to rectify the situation.

Avril could see herself living in style in a house like these.

She and Monty would go to dinners held by the Chamber of Commerce in Lyeminster. Monty may even be a Mason and she would attend ladies' evening on his arm. She would look rather fine in a satin gown of midnight blue. Yes. That was what she would wear. She had it all worked out.

A red and white board was attached to the railings of Silverside. The name of the house told Avril she had the right place. The red and white board filled her with anger. Monty was selling up.

What was he doing? Where was he going? Why hadn't he told her anything about it? She deserved better than this.

Taking a deep breath, Avril pressed the intercom button beside the gate and a threadlike voice asked her what she wanted. This must be Monty's wife – at the moment. Avril's fury knew no bounds.

'I'm house hunting in the area,' she said in her snootiest voice. 'I have to leave on the lunchtime train and I saw your house as I was walking by. I wondered if you would allow me to view it.'

She could hear Monty's wife grumbling to herself but eventually she buzzed the electric gates open and Avril strolled up the drive relishing the first time she was approaching her new home.

A thin acidulated woman stood at the open door. Avril disliked her on sight but she smiled and lifted her chin and held out her hand. 'Avril Major,' she said.

'Oh, um, Margaret Flaxton.' The woman looked at Avril's hand as if expecting to catch something but managed to complete the formalities with a bad grace. Avril suspected that, had she not been wearing gloves, there was no way this woman would have touched her.

Avril really didn't like her. And she was glad. It would be so much more difficult to rid the world of a nice woman. This one would be a whole lot easier than Adelaide Barrett but not as easy as the woman in the prison.

Margaret Flaxton whisked Avril through the house at the speed of light. She managed to announce the purpose of some of the rooms but her heart wasn't in it. Avril's resentment began to dissolve with every step, every room. Her lovely Monty had been trapped in a sterile marriage with this frigid strip of nothing for many years.

Monty loved fun. He told dirty jokes and guffawed so loudly that the punch line was often lost in his merriment and his face became purple with laughter. He needed an outlet. He needed her.

And she needed him.

'Why don't you sit down and I'll complete the tour by myself?' Avril suggested. And, surprisingly Margaret Flaxton took her up on the offer.

'I'll be in the lounge.' She wafted a hand in the direction of a room to the left of the hall with leather club chairs and a huge, stone fireplace, and went to sink onto a sofa. She picked up the remote and zapped on the television, and Avril continued to spy out her new domain.

It was easy to pick out Monty's bedroom; it was large and scented with sandalwood, or was it cedar? She didn't know but whichever it was it smelled like the wood that pencils were made of when she was a girl. The wardrobes could even be made of the same wood. This was the smell that clung to Monty underneath the smell of meat. She slid a door open and saw Monty's clothes. Clothes she recognised. Clothes she had touched.

She touched a few now, running her scarlet tipped fingers along fabric so soft it made her shiver.

She opened more doors but failed to find anything belonging to Margaret Flaxton. Avril felt a lot better for that.

This feeling was reinforced when she found what could only be Margaret Flaxton's quarters. A bleak, white bedroom with no flourishes or furbelows except an ancient silver trophy. Avril bent over to read the inscription. It was lost under the tarnish of ages. A man adopting the pose of Robin Hood stood atop the black plastic base.

Avril shrugged and moved on. This miserable room was at the farthest corner of the house from where Monty slept. Margaret didn't expect him to be making midnight visits, then.

Good.

Satisfied with her findings, Avril returned to the lounge where Margaret Flaxton struggled to her feet with a bad grace.

'I presume you've seen all you want to see.' She said in tones that suggested that this had better be the case.

'Not quite.' Avril matched her frosty voice. 'I haven't seen the kitchen. And I assume there is a garden?'

Margaret Flaxton's face was a picture when Avril mentioned the kitchen; obviously Margaret never ventured into the realm of the cook.

'This way,' she led Avril into a beautiful kitchen fitted out with a range of top class cabinets. The worktops were black granite and the cabinet doors a soft pale green. Every modern piece of kitchen equipment was ranged behind glass doors. A wide window looked out over a rolling lawn surrounded by dense trees.

'And is there a shed?' Avril forced a bright smile onto her face. 'My husband must have his little workshop.'

***

'What are you doing out here, Jane?' Lottie asked as she waited for her passenger to climb into the car. She looked Jane Pendleton over carefully and didn't like what she saw. Anyone seeing her could mistake her friend for a youth. Where were the lovely stylish clothes? Where was the lovely, long, blonde, hair?'

'I, I was going to kill her, Lottie. I was going to kill her.' Jane burst into tears.

Lottie, in the process of reaching out to administer a soothing pat to Jane's hand, encountered something hard and icy cold. She glanced over and saw that Jane had pulled a gun out of her pocket.

'Put that on the floor,' Lottie commanded. She looked all around to check that no one had noticed. 'Where did you get that from? I'm going to pull over and you're going to tell me exactly what's going on.'

***

Thrusting open the back door, Margaret Flaxton led the way over paving stones that were dotted at intervals in a straight line into the trees. The shed, when Margaret found it, was difficult to get into. The door had swollen and was jammed.

'I must see inside,' Avril looked up at the sky. 'I think it's going to rain.' She opened her bag and pulled out a scarlet plastic raincoat. She put this on and took care to close all the poppers that held it in place. Her companion watched in disbelief.'

'If it rains at all, it will only be a light misting.' She protested.

'Nevertheless.' Avril smiled the smile that said she was not deflected from her purpose whether that be the donning of a raincoat or the opening of a shed door.

With a lot of pulling, the door burst open sending Monty's wife sprawling on the ground. Avril really wanted to put the boot in whilst the old bag was down. But she resisted the impulse and reached down a hand to haul her to her feet.

Margaret Flaxton was so skinny that her hefty tug almost propelled the woman through the air. Avril bit down on a laugh and she stood back to allow Margaret Flaxton to precede her into the shed. It was musty and not very exciting yet Avril pretended great interest in all it offered.

She told Monty's wife of the joinery that gave her fictitious husband so much pleasure. He specialised in marquetry tables, she said.

Margaret soon lost interest and turned away. Maybe she hoped that refusing to gratify her unwelcome caller by showing any interest in her ramblings would make her go away.

This was the opportunity Avril had been waiting for. She had spotted an old iron last just like the one her father had owned and upon which he had mended the family's shoes when money had been scarce.

It was the work of a moment to lift the last and heft it round in an arc that caught Monty's wife full on the back of the head.

Margaret landed on the dusty floor like a felled ox. Avril replaced the cobbler's last in the exact position it had occupied before and dusted her gloved hands.

It was amazing to Avril that the right implement always came to hand. In the prison she had liberally coated the shower floor with soap and dragged her victim by her hair, toppled her off balance and crashed her head against the wall. With Adelaide the long strap of her shoulder bag proved to be the perfect garrotte.

Now, she looked at the immobile Margaret and noticed that she wasn't bleeding. That was a good thing. It was the first sign of cooperation she had seen in Monty's wife and it would help with the cleaning up when she worked out what to do about the body.

She had some ideas already. She could bury Margaret Flaxton in the trees surrounding the property. It was doubtful that the back garden was overlooked but she must check. Avril removed herself from the shed and went to scope out the possibilities.

The solution presented itself within feet of the shed. Back amongst the trees she found a patch of periwinkles. The purple flowers were bravely blooming in a small clearing.

Avril had periwinkles in her garden at Nook Cottage. They were virulent little things that grew in carpets. It was an impossibility to try to stop them. They popped up all over the place and sent down suckers to form new plants.

She poked a shoe under the flowers. The whole plant lifted obligingly. It was growing densely and Avril knew that she wouldn't even have to bury Margaret as she had intended to do. She could just peel the vegetation back, haul her underneath and then replace it. The plant would grow as usual and absorb Margaret Flaxton back into the earth via its vigorous growth. The thought of Monty's dead wife being transformed into delicate purple flowers made Avril feel that she had done the woman a favour; she doubted she had ever given any joy to anyone during her lifetime. And Avril was sure that no one would ever find her. From the state of the undergrowth and the shed it was clear that Monty wouldn't come looking down here.

Avril closed the shed door and nudged it back into place.

She checked her red raincoat. She could see no signs of fallout from the demise of the ex lady of the house. She folded it neatly inside out. Then she rolled it into a tight ball and put it back in her bag.

She sauntered back up the path and let herself into the kitchen. Now she took a more leisurely tour of the house; her house. She tried out Monty's bed. She examined the books he had on his bedside table and switched on the television that he could see when his head rested on the pillows. The channel it was tuned to came as no surprise and Avril switched it off again.

Yes, she would like living here.

In Margaret Flaxton's room, Avril found and packed a suitcase. In it she put everything she thought would be precious to the dead woman. There was little jewellery but what she found went in there. There was no photograph album full of holiday snaps of her and Monty in their younger, happier days. So Avril put in all the clothes that looked to be her favourites.

During her tour of the house she had found several unused rooms. One had been set aside for storage and she carefully moved boxes so as not to disturb the dust of ages and slid the suitcase into a small space that disappeared again once the boxes were replaced.

The wonderful kitchen yielded little in the line of food. The massive, four door, American fridge held a carton of milk, an opened pack of filter coffee with a clothes peg holding its folded top in place and a wizened cube of cheese. There was less than a quarter of a loaf in the bread bin and that smelled stale. Monty must have a poor time of it here.

In the freezer, joints of meat bulged from the drawers but her predecessor obviously didn't roast many of them.

This would all stop right now. Avril removed her gloves and coat and pulled a huge joint of something from the freezer. She tugged at the plastic bag that was welded into the ice surrounding the meat. She found a roasting tin and wrangled the meat into it placing it in the oven. The plastic still clung to a fold in the meat so she would have to be on the ball and remove it as soon as the oven warmed up and before the plastic melted.

When Monty arrived home the house would smell like a home. Meat juices would be bubbling from the joint. She would search around and see if any vegetables were lurking in the freezer too. She had already found a bottle of wine and the wine glasses. Her dreams would come true. She and Monty would be sitting in Margaret Flaxton's lounge, one on either side of the fireplace, sipping wine and telling risqué stories. Then they would adjourn to his huge bedroom and his vast bed and watch a programme or two on that naughty channel he enjoyed.

Savouring the future she had engineered for herself, Avril made coffee and carried her cup and saucer through to what would now be the living room – Avril had never liked the word 'lounge' – and sat down in the chair she had chosen as her own. From here she would be able to look at Monty and see the television and, if she turned her head only slightly, she could look out of the window.

Yes, this was going to be wonderful. She would return to Nook Cottage tomorrow and collect what things she wanted but, truthfully, all she did want were her clothes. She would arrange for something to be done with the other stuff.

But that was all for tomorrow, or even next week. There was no rush now. Not now she and Monty were to be together for the rest of their lives.

It never occurred to Avril that Monty may have loved his dried up old hag of a wife and that he didn't want her dispatching so readily. She gave the thought consideration now and discounted the notion. What man in his right mind would be mourning Margaret Flaxton? Really, the idea was ludicrous.

***

'I'd had enough, Lottie. I couldn't stand it anymore. I know she's the one who sentenced my mother to a lifetime in prison for a crime she didn't commit.'

'Where did you get the gun from?' Lottie's voice rose in disbelief. She would ask about the crime later.

'In the Far East, women have to know how to take care of themselves. This is a gun my father gave me for the purpose. It always travelled with me in the diplomatic bag. I know how to use it.'

Lottie didn't doubt this for a minute. She thought Jane Pendleton was slightly mad.

'So you decided you were going to kill Avril Major today?'

'Yes. I thought...I think I thought that it would be taken as one of the series of murders that is ravaging our village.'

'And what made you change your mind?' Lottie's brain was doing cartwheels. Asking this was a risk. What if Jane decided that she did want to go ahead?

'I was going to do it at Nook Cottage,' Jane continued as if Lottie hadn't spoken. 'I dressed like this in the hope I wouldn't be recognised if anyone saw me.'

Lottie's blood ran cold. Marco could have been at Nook Cottage and been killed in the commission of this crime.

'Then I saw Avril leave the house. I waited in Church Lane. I hid behind your friend's car. Then I followed her. I got on the bus and she was behaving very oddly but I suppose I was too.'

'And then you came to your senses and called me? You haven't killed her, have you, Jane?'

'No. I was going to. I really was going to. I... I was following her and my mobile rang. It was Charles. He had heard from my father. Apparently he's arrived in London. Charles sent for him but he didn't tell me because he wasn't sure he'd come. But he has come and he wants to see me. Charles is taking me there as soon as I get home.'

'Where does he think you are?'

'Shopping.' Jane looked down at her padded jacket. 'He's not going to believe I went out like this, is he?'

'Take off your coat and hat and shake out your hair and I think you'll get away with it. Leave the coat and gun in my car. I don't know what I'm going to do with the gun.' With that, Lottie executed a neat turn and headed back to Whittington Edge her heart racing and her mind in turmoil.

All she could think was that Jane Pendleton and Avril Major had both had a lucky escape that morning.

CHAPTER TWENTY

Lottie drove the long way through Whittington Edge to Horse and Trumpet Cottage. She dropped Jane at the Main Street end of St Jude's Open and continued to the far end of the road and around in a circle that would take her home several minutes after Jane was safely out of sight in the rectory.

She had switched on the car radio to convince herself that everything was normal and began running through what she ought really to be doing instead of rescuing a friend hell bent on murder.

A strangled laugh escaped and filled the car with its scratchy sound and she forced herself to sing along with the music.

She needed to get away. To finish packing her case and let Jonas whisk her away to Wales. She should also let Avril know that she would not be attending Nook Cottage for the planned tarot reading. She told herself that this was not cowardice on her part. She wasn't scared of Avril Major.

She also knew this to be a lie.

Gwennie was waiting on her doorstep holding a carrier bag from the local supermarket. Lottie pasted on her best smile and leapt out of her car, slamming the door nonchalantly behind her and hurrying to open the front door. She had no desire to stand out in full sight of any of the houses overlooking The Green; she felt exposed.

'Come in, Gwennie. What can I do for you?' She led the way to the kitchen, unwinding her scarf and removing her gloves and giving Gwennie no chance to speak.

She put on the kettle and took Gwennie's cup and saucer down from the cabinet. Her own mug with its red poppies was already mocking her with its cheerfulness from the counter.

Lottie needed a cup of tea to convince her that life was as she knew it and that the rector's wife hadn't really been running around with a gun in her pocket and murder in her heart.

Gwennie put her burden down on the table.

'From Mrs Fleet,' she said. 'Some pictures she thought you might like to see.'

Lottie did want to see them. Very much. She made tea and, aware that she couldn't hustle Gwennie out of the house without appearing rude, she opened the bag and began going through them.

She passed them across to Gwennie one by one, identifying each subject. Gwennie laughed at the picture of herself and passed it back.

'I can't believe I still had that coat all those years ago,' she laughed.

Lottie could believe it. Mrs Furlong had kept her daughter so rigidly beneath her thumb that Gwennie

Furlong had never had the opportunity to cultivate the minor vanities that enhance the lives of young girls.

In short, she had turned her daughter into a dowdy middle aged spinster when she was still in her teens.

Dragging her mind away from this miscarriage of justice, Lottie told Gwennie of her plans for the weekend as she peered at the more hard to discern picture of Sadie Cartwright from one of the cottages near to Matchbox Cottage. Gwennie mentioned that she and Sadie had been in the same class at school. Lottie was horrified. Sadie looked years younger that Gwennie.

'I shouldn't keep you,' Gwennie began to rise to her feet.

'There's no need to go yet,' Lottie said. 'But what I do need to do, if you'll excuse me, is ring Avril Major and cancel our appointment.

She darted out into the hall, choosing to use that extension rather than the one in the kitchen. Avril wasn't back and the call went to the answering machine. Lottie was glad. She left her message and returned to the kitchen where Gwennie was turning a picture this way and that.

'Who is that, Gwennie?' she glanced at the picture over Gwennie's shoulder as she passed by.

'I really have no idea,' Gwennie mused. 'And I should really know. I've lived in Whittington Edge all my life. Do you recognise her?'

The snapshot was in colour and, although Lottie could make out Avril Major, the taller woman walking towards Horse and Trumpet Cottage by her side would have been a complete mystery, had she not been wearing a striking red hat.

This was Adelaide Barrett. Lottie's heart stuttered. She couldn't tell Gwennie this but she knew she was watching the unsuspecting Adelaide being led to her death. She glanced at the back of the photo. 29 April 2011.

Adelaide was smiling. Avril was wearing a calculating expression. Or maybe that was Lottie's imagination kicking in.

Either way, she froze. She had to get this picture to Marco. And quickly. Before Avril returned home. Before she had a chance to flee.

Gwennie noticed the time and said she really had to go because she was needed at the library.

'Shall I cancel the Murder Club for tomorrow, Lottie dear?'

Lottie absently agreed that she should.

As soon as she was alone, Lottie rang Woolstock police station. Sergeant Romero was out of the office, she was told, but she was put through to his mobile. Marco was engaged on another call so she left a message: 'I have a picture of what I think is Avril Major leading Adelaide Barrett to her death. Sorry to sound so dramatic but I really think this is what it is. I shall put it in an envelope for you and leave it at the desk in Woolstock on my way to Wales. I will be back for the bonfire party on Saturday.' She added her mobile number in case although she knew he already had it and rang off.

***

Time was marching on and Lottie, midway through her packing, really wanted to get back to it, so, a call from Jane telling her that Charles wasn't at home and she could come and collect her belongings was welcome.

'The car's open, Jane, help yourself,' Lottie said airily, hoping that she wouldn't come to call. In an attempt to dissuade her further, she added. 'I have to go down to the cellar to search for something I want to take on holiday with me. I hope all goes well with your father and I'll see you when I get back.'

Jane thanked her and cut the call. Lottie, who had remembered an ornament of a welsh woman in traditional dress, made her way down to the cellar to look through her boxes of china, propping up the trapdoor lid behind the old bar. Jonas would be sure to find it amusing.

Jane collected the gun and her coat and ran home with them. She felt guilty not calling into Horse and Trumpet Cottage as good manners demanded and looked back towards Lottie's house as she opened the rectory door.

That was when she saw a man creeping stealthily into the Church Lane door to Lottie Colenso's house. She dropped her belongings, picked up her phone and called the police as she ran back, following the man into Lottie's house.

Lottie was surrounded by pieces of pottery and other trinkets. She couldn't recall why she had ever thought she would want to see these again. Her back was beginning to set and she forced herself upright just as something shiny flew past her face missing her by a whisker. A knife! She looked up. Keith Kendall stood on the steps glaring down at her.

'Lucky move,' he said. Your next won't be quite as lucky.'

Lottie was frozen to the spot. Then she saw Jane's face peering down over his shoulder.

'Drop the lid,' she shouted. And Jane did.

Keith Kendall, caught by the heavy trapdoor, fell like a sack of stones. The trapdoor lifted again and Jane ran down to help Lottie who was sitting on Keith Kendall's back and holding him face down on the pile of china he had broken in his fall.

'The police are on their way,' Jane gasped. 'I rang when I saw him sneaking in. We have to tie him up. Do you have any rope?'

'Cable ties. On that shelf.' Lottie nodded towards the bundle she had bought to fix the wheel trim.

Soon Keith Kendall was neatly and securely immobilised and both women were in the kitchen drinking coffee when Marco burst in leading a reassuring number of his fellow officers.

They called an ambulance when they saw how Keith Kendall had landed. Someone retrieved the knife he had thrown at Lottie and bagged it as evidence and statements were taken.

When only Marco remained, Lottie gave him the photo of Avril Major and the woman she thought was Adelaide Barrett.

'Good work, Lottie, all round.' Marco said, collecting his phone and notebook and rising to leave. He dropped a kiss on the top of her head. 'Have a good holiday. You deserve it. I'll see you when you get back.'

***

Avril was lying on Monty's bed when she heard his key in the lock. She noted that he didn't call out a cheery greeting when he came in. That showed the level of intimacy in his marriage to Margaret. She had done the right thing.

She tiptoed to the top of the stairs and looked down at him. His bald pate shone in the afternoon sun. He was wheezing badly. She must make sure he changed his will before that wheezing got worse.

'Monty, darling,' she cooed from the landing.

Monty looked around to see where the voice was coming from. He finally saw her and, delight of delights, his face lit up. He wanted her. He really did. All trace of apprehension fled and Avril ran down the stairs and into his arms.

'Margaret said to tell you she was going away for a few days.' Avril told him between kisses. 'I think she may have said she wanted a break in Skegness.'

'I don't care where the old harridan's gone.' Monty said, picking Avril up and whirling her around. 'She's the reason I have to sell this place. I hope she never comes back.'

651

Better and better.

'Why is she making you sell the house?' Avril pouted to show her sympathies were entirely with Monty.

'She's my sister in law,' Monty released Avril and took off his coat.

Sister in law? Oops! That was a disappointment; Avril hated wasted effort.

'She came to live here when my brother killed himself to get away from her. Now she wants a share of the house.'

'Surely she has no right to this house?'

'Not really but my father loaned me the money for the deposit and he died before my brother married and before I paid him back so, morally, I suppose she is entitled to something.'

'Let's hope she meets a rich widower in Skegness and decides not to come back.' Avril had heard enough now about Margaret Flaxton.

Had she known before what she knew now, she would have rid Monty of the woman in a different way but there was no point crying over spilt blood.

'Can I smell roast beef?' Monty's piggy eyes were bright. 'Yes. I found it in the freezer.

'I'd better close the gates then. I left them open. I was intending to go to my club for the evening seeing as I wasn't going to visit you.' Monty's voice lowered to a growl and he moved in closer to take Avril in his arms again. 'I'd only nipped in to change.' He turned to a control panel hidden behind a picture and pressed a few buttons. 'That's it. The gates are secure now and we can settle down to a lovely evening of roast beef and...and other things.' He grinned at her. 'I hope you intend staying until the old witch comes back.'

'I'll need to nip back to Nook Cottage to collect a few things.' She tilted her head to one side and smiled up at him. Monty liked it when she did that. He said it made her look like a sexy schoolgirl.

The doorbell rang. 'I didn't lock it soon enough.' Monty laughed. He opened the door and was confronted by a short ratty looking man with a gun.

Ronnie.

Avril's hand went to her chest and she stepped round Monty intending to wrap herself in Sonny's authority and tell him to leave. She didn't move quickly enough. The gun flashed and Monty fell.

One glance was enough to tell Avril that he was dead. She fell on her knees beside him and looked up at Ronnie as she tried to cradle Monty's huge body in her arms.

She opened her mouth to yell at Monty's killer but the man was looking at her with dead eyes. He hadn't recognised her. Or, if he did, he didn't care. She had only a moment to identify herself. But then Ronnie frowned and looked over Avril's shoulder.

She followed his gaze and saw someone who shouldn't be there. She was holding what looked like a bow and arrow.

There was intense hatred on Margaret Flaxton's wizened old face as she took aim. She released the arrow and it hit Avril in the shoulder.

CHAPTER TWENTY ONE

Wales was wonderful. Jonas was wonderful. Lottie returned to Whittington Edge on a cloud of joy only to find Marco parked outside her house. Jonas greeted Marco and then made his excuses.

'I'll be back later.' He told Lottie. 'Enjoy your bonfire celebrations.'

'I will.' Lottie beamed at him and watched him drive away.

Marco collected her overnight bag from the kerb and headed to the Church Lane door of Horse and

Trumpet Cottage. 'You're travelling light, I see.' He nodded to the bag.

'Not really. All my other stuff is at Jonas's cottage in Wales. He has a lecture to give tonight and I'm promised at Camp Hill. He'll come back later then we're off to Wales again in the morning.'

'You make me feel very guilty because I think I'm going to cause you some upset.

'I'd better get the coffee going then.' Lottie threw her lightweight coat over the arm of the sofa and headed back to the kitchen. Nothing could spoil her mood today. At least, she hadn't thought it could.

'Ok, fire away.' Lottie said as she breathed in the aromatic steam from the coffee that was far too hot to drink.

'This is not good, my dear.' Marco said.

Lottie put her cup carefully on its coaster. The use of the endearment alarmed her. 'You're serious, aren't you?'

'Deadly.' He opened the folder that lay on the table beside him. 'I followed up your sighting of the Wednesday caller and it was Montague Flaxton.'

'Did you manage to warn him?'

'It was too late for that.' Marco took a long swig of coffee and held up a hand for her to listen. It's almost definite that Avril killed Adelaide Barrett. Or, I should say, Dolly Gumbrill killed Adelaide.' Thank you for the photo, by the way.

'Dolly Gumbrill?'

'Dolly Gumbrill was the wife of a nasty piece of work called Sonny Gumbrill; a well known crime boss in London. Sonny fell foul of a bent police officer who got his revenge by fitting Dolly Gumbrill up and sending her to jail. Sending Sonny to jail wouldn't have had the same impact; it's well known that Dolly is Sonny's weak spot.

'She had committed the crimes she was sent down for but there was an unspoken rule that should have protected her; the Met had a clear-up later and the officer is now serving a term himself.

'Anyway, I'm getting ahead of myself. I need you to identify a couple of people.' He pushed a grainy photo across the table to her. 'This has been cleaned up as best we can. It was taken from a CCTV film at

the bus station in Woolstock on the morning Avril
went missing.'

'That's Avril.'

'How sure are you?'

'Absolutely.'

He pushed another picture across. 'And this is
from the CCTV on the bus that she took. A lot of
people are unaware that we have CCTV on our buses.'

'That's Avril too. I'm sure of it.'

'How about this?' Another photo slid before her.

Lottie picked it up and peered at it. She turned it
to left and right and narrowed her eyes, looking
sideways at the image, silently offering up a prayer
that the image would not be that of Jane Pendleton.
Her brow wrinkled into a frown. 'No, I don't know
him.'

Marco released a long, steady breath. 'How sure
are you?

Here's another image; this time from the bus.'

'He was on the same bus as Avril?' Lottie squinted
as an image of the man leaving the bus was passed
across. 'Do you know, I think that may be the man

Avril called Ronnie. He was quite short for a man. Gave me the impression that he would have one of those mean, weaselly faces. But, as I told you, I didn't get a look at his face at all. What I told you about his mean weaselly face is pure guesswork on my part.'

'He followed her, but he got off the bus two stops after she alighted.' Marco retrieved his pictures, placed them back in the file and leaned back in his chair. 'Brace yourself. This is where it gets messy. This is also why I was sitting on your doorstep waiting for you; I didn't want anyone else telling you.'

'Go on.'

'As far as I can piece it together, Dolly Gumbrill was on the last few months of her sentence when a young woman was moved in as her cellmate. The new cellmate was in for shoplifting. Doubtless the poor girl thought she could do her six months or whatever and go back to her life.

'But fate in the form of Dolly Gumbrill was waiting for her.

'Dolly Gumbrill needed to escape her old life. She knew that, since the bent copper had been sent down, all his equally bent colleagues would be ready to swoop on her again.

'Dolly knew she couldn't return to her old life and therefore she needed to concoct a new one.

'It probably started out as a sort of game. It was easier to chisel this girl's history out of her than to make up a new identity. She probably was amused by the idea of an old, worn out hooker turning herself into a delicate, ladylike, little thing like the real Avril Major.

'The real Avril told her everything; she had neither the guile nor the common sense to keep quiet. She was an easy target for the likes of Dolly Gumbrill.

'The role suited Dolly Gumbrill's idea of a new life. She even decided to come to Whittington Edge where the real Avril Major had been so happy. But she had to keep the girl in prison for it all to work. So she killed another inmate and managed to foist the blame onto this young woman. The real Avril was now a lifer and gained certain kudos within the prison community and Dolly Gumbrill gained a new life.'

'How do you know all this?'

'Avril, the real Avril, made a full statement before she was released.'

'That's terrible.' Lottie realised what he had said a second later. 'She's been released?'

'Yes,' he fixed her with a piercing stare. 'She was the wife of a diplomat and could have walked as out now to most people's satisfaction.

'Especially with the rest of the tale I have to tell you.'

'So she's free,' Lottie sighed. 'That's good news.'

'Isn't it?' Marco took another deep breath. This was not a complete surprise to his friend. There were questions he would be asking Lottie at a later date.

'I'm guessing here but I think Dolly Gumbrill liked life as Avril Major and Sonny Gumbrill got annoyed. It's well known in Met circles that Sonny Gumbrill's weak point is his wife which is why she was targeted in the first place. If she hinted to Sonny that she was enjoying life in Whittington Edge too much, he would do whatever it took to tip up her applecart.'

'Like sending Ronnie to kill her friends?'

'Once I had the connection to Sonny Gumbrill it was easy to discover the identity of Ronnie. He is one of Sonny's fixers. He has a gun, a good aim, a sense of the dramatic and very little brain. If Sonny pointed him in the right direction and said 'shoot' he would do it. No questions asked.

'Ronnie likes fast cars. Someone answering his description stayed at a motel a few times, notably over the weekend of Halloween. We're sure he stole the car and ran the farmer down in the lane.

'The churchwarden was actually shot. The rest of the scenario was done for effect and is typical of the stunts this Ronnie is known to pull. He likes to add drama to his killings.'

'What about Montague Flaxton?'

'His staff reported him missing. We broke into his house in Woolstock. There we found three bodies: Mr Flaxton, the woman in the white suit who you have identified as the person you knew as Avril Major, and a second woman who, it would appear, was Mr Flaxton's sister in law.'

'Had they...I assume they had been murdered. Was it Ronnie?'

'Possibly. Though why he chose to do it at Flaxton's house is a mystery; the place is a fortress.' He poured himself a second coffee. 'Anyway, the forensics are not back yet so we don't know who did what to whom.

'We did find blood in the potting shed at the bottom of Flaxton's garden. Something happened there but that's all we know at the moment. The houses in the area are very large. All are protected by electric gates. No one knows their neighbours and the house to house pulled less information than any I've ever known.' Marco rose to leave.

'Keith Kendall will be sent for trial soon. You and Jane Pendleton will be needed as witnesses and someone will contact you. No need to hide anymore, Lottie.' He smiled. 'Anyway, I have to dash.' And he was gone.

Blood in the potting shed. If Gwennie had heard about that she would be having nightmares.

And Jane. What a lucky escape she had had. If Charles hadn't called her at that precise moment – it didn't bear thinking about. She could have killed Avril and ruined her own life. She could have killed Avril and been killed by Ronnie.

***

She sat alone in her kitchen now. Marco had gone. She had emptied the coffee pot and refilled it. Marco had pledged her to silence on the case and she would respect that pledge; keeping secrets was the one thing Lottie knew how to do well.

Everyone in Whittington Edge and Camp Hill would be hoping for details but they would get none from her. She drank coffee until she gave herself the jitters and poured the rest away.

***

Sonny Gumbrill sat alone in his office. He had sent away the young slag who was trying to curry favour with him. He could see her now, sliding onto a seat beside some greasy, old slime ball. He closed his eyes in disgust. He was so worried about Dolly that he couldn't stand having any of these women near him.

At another table in the club sat Ronnie. He had reported back. He had done the butcher. He had been paid – handsomely. Now he was enjoying all the club had to offer, free, gratis and for nothing.

This was what Sonny always did. A couple of his goons were beside Ronnie. Listening to his war stories, filling his glass with cheap champagne, inviting various girls to come and listen too. And they were listening on Sonny's behalf.

When the hit man was relaxed and half plastered, that was when the truth really came out. And the more times the story was repeated, the more details emerged hence the constant stream of girls.

One of the goons got to his feet and nodded towards the camera. Seconds later he was tapping on Sonny's door. Sonny was worried. He hadn't heard from Doll in days. She rang most days. It shouldn't have been this long.

'He killed a couple of women too. Says he wasn't expecting them to be at the house. Says he was expecting the butcher to be alone but they were there so he did them too. To keep it tidy.'

'Give it five minutes then bring him back in.' Sonny said. A nasty cold feeling was crawling through Sonny's guts. He opened his desk drawer and pulled out a framed photograph. This was his Dolly, all dressed up to go out for the night when they lived in Spain. He looked at it. 'Was it you, Doll? Did he shoot you?' A knock at the door made him take a stiffening breath. His face hardened. He put the picture face down on the desk. The goons ushered Ronnie into the room. He was so far gone he had no idea what sort of trouble he was in and they were careful not to give him a clue.

'You wanted to see me, Sonny?' He could barely stand. His face had that stupid grin common to drunks.

'Sit down, Ronnie,' Sonny lit a cigar and waved a pudgy hand towards his visitors' chair, 'tell me about the redhead.'

'Redhead, Sonny?'

'Yeah,' Sonny waved the cigar around and forced a smile, 'the one you told the boys about. That redhead.'

'She was just there, Sonny. You know how it is. She wasn't nothin'. She was just some old gal. I bet she was nice enough lookin' in her day but not the sort you or me would look twice at, Sonny, you know what I mean? She was there and I thought, Sonny wants it keepin' tidy so... I kept it tidy.'

'Right.' Sonny nodded. Then he brought up the picture of Dolly. 'This her, Ronnie?'

Ronnie leaned forward. 'Yeah, Sonny, that's her.' He gave a small snigger. 'Or that was her. Know what I mean? Didn't look like that after I did for her.' He laughed, exposing his ratty teeth.

Sonny realised that Ronnie hadn't been around long enough to remember Dolly but the two goons by the door remembered her well enough as twin sharp intakes of breath testified. Sonny stared at Ronnie. Ronnie stopped laughing. The smile fell from his face and all the colour followed it.

'What's wrong, boss?'

Boss. So he still had enough of his wits about him to know he was in deep shit. Good. What came next wouldn't be a surprise then. It wouldn't need explaining.

'Take him out of my sight and make sure I never see him again.' Sonny said. The goons stepped forward and pulled Ronnie out of the chair. Sonny swivelled his chair around and faced the wall.

'Wait a minute,' Ronnie screamed, 'listen!'

But Sonny wasn't going to listen. He couldn't even trust his voice to work anymore. He waved his hand and feet scuffled, a slap resounded in the small room, the door opened and closed and Ronnie's protests could be heard all the way down the corridor and through the door into the club.

Sonny turned back to his desk. This was his fault. He had asked Aunt Minnie to collect Ronnie from the station. Dolly had done what he asked. Ronnie wouldn't have recognised her when he saw her at the butcher's house. He would have had no idea who she was.

He picked up the photograph. He didn't want her to leave him for the butcher and now she had left him forever, entirely, always now to be alone.

Tears welled in Sonny's eyes. He hadn't known he was capable of tears. Dolly was gone. His Dolly. His life. And all she had been was collateral damage. The tears brimmed over and tracked down to his chin following the crevices and craters that time had etched in his ugly face.

He put the picture back in the drawer. He couldn't bear to look at her now. She would be accusing him from beyond the grave forever but he would bring her back and give her the biggest and best funeral the East End had seen in years.

Ronnie wasn't quick witted but it didn't take him long to realise he had made a mistake.

'I didn't kill her.' He tried to shout but his words were muffled by the massive arms of one of the henchmen who he knew were leading him to his doom. 'It was the old woman.' He spluttered. 'She came in through the back. I don't know where she came from. I just wasted the butcher like I was supposed to do. Then this old girl popped up from nowhere. She had a bow and arrow, of all things. It was wobbling all over the place. She would have shot me but suddenly she got it together. She shot the redhead. She could have been aiming at me. I don't know. I had to shoot her to protect myself. Go back. Tell Sonny it wasn't me.'

But the heavies weren't listening. Ronnie relaxed in their grip. It was no use. He had wanted the additional kudos that came with claiming the kill. Now it had all gone wrong. He had no one to blame but himself and no higher authority to appeal to. No one would listen to him. Not Sonny, not these goons. No one. And he couldn't blame them. How many times had he pointed and shot at Sonny's behest? Now he was on the receiving end. He knew it would come one day. It always did. One little mistake. That's all it took.

When he was bundled into the car with the blacked out windows, Ronnie's panic returned. He received a smack around the head for his trouble. The flying meat hook of a hand stunned and silenced him but not for long.

Ronnie was still protesting at the landfill. They had taken his gun from him when he entered the club; that was standing orders – no guns in the club. Now they gave it back to him just as he took the dive from the highest point whilst the supervisor took a tea break. He knew the way it worked. He knew it would hold one bullet only. Sonny Gumbrill's version of clemency.

He had a soft landing in the midst of the black bin bags full of rotting garbage but there was no way he could climb out. A lorry backed to the edge as he was trying to clamber to his feet. Its tailgate flapped open as the body of the lorry lifted. A consignment of restaurant waste cascaded down on him and Ronnie fell back. After the fifth lorry load he stopped trying to get up.

***

The party was warming up nicely when Lottie and Susan arrived at Camp Hill. Word of the murders at Monty Flaxton's house had yet to reach Whittington Edge and people were in the mood for fun.

'What's he doing here?' Susan frowned.

'Who?' Lottie looked around.

'Don't look. It's Chris and his wife and son. Keep walking.'

A pig roast had been set up undercover and the wafting scents of the meat made Lottie's mouth water. The bonfire was waiting to be lit. Lottie had seen some big bonfires in her life but never one like this. Men walked around the perimeter warning onlookers to remain outside the rope that had been pegged around a few feet from the pyre.

The wood had been stacked against a tall wooden stake that had been driven into the ground. The sound of the hammering as the support was secured had been heard all over Whittington Edge during the week apparently. Now the guy was hoisted aloft and fixed to the post. One of the gold shoes fell off during this procedure and was ceremoniously restored to its owner. Lottie was reminded of Cinderella and her glass slipper.

A chorus of oohs and aahs and admonitions to be careful accompanied the descent of the young man to the ground as the bonfire creaked, shifted and groaned beneath his weight but soon he was down and the happy children who had been awarded the honour of lighting the fire were led forward holding their torches carefully and touching them to wicks that protruded from the pyre.

Gwennie's face glowed in the firelight as the flames caught and whooshed into the air. Lottie took a step back. She rapidly revised her original view that the men holding the children behind the rope were being over dramatic.

Dexter Hardman came into view and headed towards Susan just as Chris noticed her and began to head their way.

'I'll slip away and take a look at the pig roast' Lottie told her. Susan smiled her thanks.

Lottie watched for a few minutes as Dexter registered with Chris and Chris's eyes narrowed when the handsome, blond giant wrapped an arm around Susan and bent to kiss her. That could do Susan's self esteem no end of good.

Over by the fire Atlantis Warbeck and Bill were walking arm in arm. Atlantis was wearing another of her long flowing dresses. Her titian hair cascaded almost to her waist. Tonight it was trimmed with seashells and what looked like toffee papers. It looked as if they had resolved their differences. Lottie was glad.

The tent with the pig roast gave off wonderful aromas and Lottie joined the queue, handed over her ticket and received the biggest pork roll she had ever seen. Trestle tables borrowed from the church hall lined the tent and she found a spot to sit whilst she ate.

Only two sides had been erected to the tent to shelter the cooker from the wind and the side facing the bonfire was open. So was the side facing the fallen tree and the small copse of saplings that had sprung from it. And it was at the edge of this copse that Bill Warbeck could be seen surrounded by a gaggle of girls with whom he flirted whilst they laughed at him.

Lottie's attention had been held by Chris who had returned to his wife looking most put out. Lottie smiled to herself and allowed her gaze to switch to Bill Warbeck's stupid antics.

Lottie's heart sank. The silly man. Couldn't he see that they were making fun of him? She had just wiped the last of the grease from her fingers when she noticed the look on Atlantis Warbeck's face. Even the warmth of the fire couldn't add any colour to her pallor. She was devastated. Lottie had been talking to the people sharing her table. Now she excused herself and hurried over to Atlantis's side. Atlantis didn't see her coming. She turned away from her faithless husband and walked deliberately towards the fire.

It took Lottie a second or two to see what Atlantis planned on doing. When she did realise, she broke into a run calling Atlantis's name and pushing people aside in order to reach her before the tendrils of her dress were sucked into the flames.

Atlantis was totally distracted. Lottie caught her arm through her own and steered her away talking to her quietly as she urged her away from the party and Bill.

'Shall we walk back down the hill together?' She said. Atlantis made no reply. Lottie looked around and caught Dexter Hardman's eye. He lifted his chin as if asking if she was alright.

Lottie nodded to him and he smiled. Dexter would take Susan home. She had been so wrong about Dexter. He was a good man and, if Susan settled down with him, Lottie would be delighted. All she had to do now was sort out what was to be done with Atlantis. A glance at Bill Warbeck told her that he hadn't even noticed.

Atlantis Warbeck walked silently beside Lottie who kept up a softly spoken commentary about the night sky and the fireworks that could be seen sparkling across the heavens. A lone plane stitched its way across the firmament and Lottie watched it, lights winking, and wondered if its passengers were looking down at the colourful displays in the sky below them.

Suddenly Atlantis broke free and began to run down the hill. Her hair flew out behind her. Her dress billowed out. Seashells clattered, bells jangled, the pieces of toffee wrappers rustled together. Arms outstretched, head thrown back, Atlantis gave out an eldritch screech and disappeared from view.

Hurrying to catch her up with little chance of doing so, Lottie's lungs were almost bursting. She rounded the corner in time to see the wraith that was Atlantis Warbeck plunge across The Green towards the duck pond. Oh no, out of the fire and into the water!

How many times in one evening could a person be called upon to save the same life? Lottie called out a warning. Atlantis didn't stop.

The fire in Lottie's lungs had become a constricting, painful lump in her throat when she reached The Green. She hadn't heard a splash. Would she have heard it? Could Atlantis have stopped on the edge of the pond and slowly walked in? Lottie visualised her lying down in the water with her hair and dress floating Ophelia-like all around her.

If this was the vision that awaited her, who could she call? She had her mobile in her bag; she could dial the nines and get help.

Barely able to draw in air, she stumbled the last few steps.

And the sight before her almost made her faint with relief. Beau Derek was seated on a bench by the duck pond. Atlantis was sitting beside him. He was holding her hand and murmuring quietly to her. He looked up and smiled at Lottie. He also shook his head to prevent her interrupting. Lottie was glad of this because speech was beyond her at the moment.

'Leave her with me,' Beau said, 'I'll make sure she's alright.'

Completely devoid of breath, Lottie nodded and made her way across The Green to Horse and Trumpet Cottage; she had no desire to return to the bonfire party. The lights of her home shone out in the darkness. Jonas was there waiting to welcome her home. Lottie was so relieved she could have wept.

EPILOGUE

It was several weeks before the truth came out. Ronnie had killed Dolly Gumbrill. But Margaret Flaxton had shot her first; with a bow and arrow. She had once won a trophy for archery. The Lyeminster Echo made a meal of that and published a photograph of an old and tarnished silver cup.

Apparently the scientists could work out the order in which things happened. Lottie had seen that on CSI but had never believed it was really possible.

Now, it was thought that she had been injured in the potting shed by someone who had hit her with a cobbler's last. How she survived that was subject to some debate.

But survive it she had. She had returned to the house, witnessed the shooting of Monty Flaxton and taken a shot at Avril with the old bow and arrow that had languished in the shed for years. No one knew if she meant to hit Avril.

Ronnie, they assumed, had been startled. He saw the old woman who had just shot the redhead and he shot her too. One bullet straight to the head. Execution style.

'He could have joined forces with her. There was no need to kill her at all.' Lottie had protested. But Marco explained that it wasn't clever to leave loose ends; that was Sonny's number one rule. That was why Sonny Gumbrill was so successful; he was a legend in London, Marco said. Avril would have seen it all.

The sister in law hadn't been able to go for the head. She probably didn't have the strength after being attacked and presumably knocked unconscious.

It was a miracle she had lived through that. But she was a feisty old thing, according to form, and anger could well have lent her sufficient strength to do what she did and Ronnie finished the job for her.

'But if Avril Major was really Dolly Gumbrill and Sonny Gumbrill's wife, surely Ronnie would have known her and known not to shoot her.' Lottie shook her head. None of this made sense.

'That's something no one will ever understand.' Marco said. 'And to be honest, now we know who did what, and now that they are all dead, there's little point it trying to find out much more.

'There are other cases to be solved. The budget has to be put where it can do most good.

Some of this was conjecture but Lottie was pretty sure that that was what happened. It was a sad day for Whittington Edge.

***

The truth would probably never come out. Even in these days of 'transparency' some discretion was allowed when nothing would be gained by full disclosure.

Charles Pendleton could have lost his wife had he not called her when he did; God did indeed move in mysterious ways and Lottie could be thankful for that. She hoped Jane was too. She also hoped that Jane would decide that discretion was better than telling her husband that she had been in Woolstock on the day of the murders.

Avril, the real Avril had been released from prison thanks to diplomatic sleight of hand and her husband had whisked his disgraced wife back from whence she came; what life would be like for her from now on they would never know.

Charles had held a service in which he had listed 'the fallen'. He listed them in alphabetical order. His wife was in the front pew as usual and his eyes strayed to her several times. Lottie wondered if he suspected something. Who could tell?

Whittington Edge had turned out in force for the memorial service.

Typically, Charles had found a positive note on which to end. He announced to the whole parish that Jason Flint had the opportunity of applying to an Oxbridge college next year.

'This is the sort of young person who gives the whole of Whittington Edge hope for the future'. Charles said, smiling broadly and holding out his arm to direct everyone's attention to the shamefaced young man who politely nodded in acknowledgement and who had unwittingly set the balls rolling in this bagatelle of tragedy.

Life in Whittington Edge returned to something approaching normal. Bill Warbeck who had disgraced himself at the bonfire party had left Whittington Edge for an indeterminate period. The art world had discovered him. His painting had taken the world by storm and he needed to distance himself not only from his wife but also from gossip in Whittington Edge. The darling of the art world, as he saw himself, couldn't be linked to any funny business. People had been known to gossip.

Bill was talking about renting The Crow's Nest out for a year or so since his wife didn't want to return home.

And Atlantis, distressed by her husband's behaviour, had found a new friend when she ran from the humiliation of the bonfire party.

Beau immediately took charge and Atlantis had moved into Pennyman Cottage with him as his friend and companion. Beau was now looking into the belief Atlantis held that Adelaide Barrett had been her mother. Atlantis had been fostered and, like so many such children, harboured a hope that her birth mother was a more romantic figure than the parents who raised her. Lottie wondered what she would do were she proved right and, in a way, she hoped that she was right; Beau and Atlantis needed each other and the link with Adelaide would help them both.

But tonight wasn't about Atlantis. Tonight was about Adelaide Barrett, Charles and Jane Pendleton, Avril Major – both Avril Majors, Bob Rogers, Arnold Pickard, Monty Flaxton and Margaret Flaxton, Monty's sister in law who had been attacked and left to die in the potting shed at the bottom of Silverside's garden, probably by Avril Major and who had fought against her fate long enough to try to kill her attacker. And, yes, Ronnie too. His body had been found in the landfill just outside London. His gun had been found close to him and matched to the bullets used in the Flaxton murders. The forensics people said that

Ronnie had saved his last bullet and killed himself. So, yes, Lottie said a word or two for Ronnie as well.

Sonny Gumbrill had made it known that his Dolly was to have a big East End funeral. Beau Derek was also planning a fitting funeral for his Adelaide. The Earl, his brother, had insisted that Adelaide be laid to rest in the family mausoleum at Berringer Hall. Beau was touched and the whole of Whittington Edge felt that this was a fitting tribute.

Lottie, unable to sleep, had sat up all night reading the Improving Tome, as she called the book that had chosen her at the station bookstall. It said that everyone chose their way of leaving this life before they were born. It said that the bad things that happened were also part of the plan and for bad things to happen, some other soul had to agree to play the opposing role and should therefore be thanked for doing so.

Lottie didn't want to think about this too much and certainly the idea of thanking Ronnie for these killings was a step too far for her, but it did make sense of some of the dreadful things that happened in the world.

When she was feeling more like it she would read some more of the book. It held a lot of sense between its covers. For now, it was hidden in the bottom drawer of her bedside table.

The doors of The Priest at Prayer stood open across The Green. Men in various stages of inebriation were spilling out onto the pavement. Whittington Edge was still old fashioned enough for most of the patrons of The Priest at Prayer to be male. A gang of youths were trying to steady a friend on a bicycle so that the rider could take his father home.

Life in Whittington Edge was carrying on as usual and doubtless, in some unfathomable way, all was well with the world.

Lottie sighed, drew the curtains across the window shutting out Whittington Edge for the night and went to bed. She had received an email advising her that Keith Kendal's trial date had been set and would she please contact the officer in charge of his case. She would do that tomorrow and then she would go to the garden centre and buy a red maple sapling. She would plant it in her back garden where it could be seen from her study window. It would be her secret memorial to all the people, both the good and the bad, who needed to be remembered.

THE END

THANK YOU!

For reading Long Shadows over Whittington Edge. This is the first book in a new series set in a small midland town. I hope you enjoyed spending time with the people who live there.

If you enjoyed the story, please leave a review of this book on the site where you purchased it. I read every review and you make a vast difference, believe me.

Catherine Cliffe

If you want to find out what has happened in Whittington Edge since the end of this story, **The Witches of Whittington Edge**, the second Tale of Whittington Edge is already available.

TALES OF WHITTINGTON EDGE

Long Shadows over Whittington Edge

The Witches of Whittington Edge

CONTACT ME catherinecliffe@yahoo.com

Printed in Great Britain
by Amazon

61927585R00409